THE broker

A NASHVILLE NEIGHBORHOOD BOOK

NIKKI SLOANE

Brokerage Edition

ISBN 978-1-949409-24-6

who made this book possible

ONE

Noah

I'd never struggled so much to close a deal, and it had nothing to do with negotiating terms or one party being difficult. In fact, the man standing in front of me was as eager as I was to get this thing done.

The issue was the naked guy on the other side of the room.

The man's wrists and ankles were shackled to the large St. Andrew's Cross that was anchored to the brick wall, but he didn't seem concerned about his restraints. No, his excited gaze was locked on to the woman approaching him, and when she reached out to run a hand across his bare chest, the man's hard dick jerked.

The woman was fully clothed in a strapless pleather corset and matching knee-length skirt. Everything was so tight, cinching her waist to be impossibly small, it was as if an invisible hand squeezed her body. It forced her curves up, making her breasts threaten to bulge out over the top of the corset.

Normally I wouldn't mind, but—

Goddamn, it was hard enough to focus right now. I didn't need to add a nice, big pair of bare tits to my distraction.

"This was one of my first custom pieces," Clay said. "It took me twenty hours, but I'm more efficient now. I shouldn't have an issue meeting your client's deadline."

My gaze snapped back to the man before me.

The first time I'd met Clay Crandall, I'd struggled to

believe him when he mentioned he made high-end BDSM furniture. The guy looked so reserved, so conservative, so . . . well—*nerdy*. Even down to the pair of glasses he wore.

He looked like the type of guy who was more likely to get off staring at spreadsheets than people in bondage.

But that was a rookie mistake on my part. I'd been in the lifestyle long enough to know better than to judge or make assumptions. There'd been all kinds of different people at the sex club I'd belonged to for years in New York. My first time here at Club Eros had shown me Nashville's scene was no different.

I ticked my head toward the St. Andrew's Cross, doing my best to ignore the couple playing there. "The pictures don't do your work justice."

Clay flashed me an appreciative smile.

I'd looked through the entire photo gallery he had available on his website. In a flat, two-dimension world, the sleek, tasteful furniture looked sexy, but in real life? It couldn't compare. The furniture was stunning.

Without it, this side room of Club Eros was what you'd expect from a sex club. Its walls were red and the floor black, and the space felt . . . borderline average. Maybe even a bit boring. But the rows of black folding chairs had an aisle down the center, and it led your eye straight back to the stage-like platform.

Perched on it, two large wooden beams crossed in an 'X' and stretched across the brick wall. Even when the St. Andrew's Cross wasn't in use, the piece had to be a showstopper. It elevated this clichéd room into something that oozed sex and whispered about power. It legitimized Club Eros.

And it was exactly what the club in New York was

looking for.

On stage, the woman was teasing her partner. She'd turned her back to him, rubbing her ass against his erection. When he moaned, she shimmied up the sides of her skirt over her hips, exposing her utterly bare lower body.

It was impossible not to let my gaze linger on the slit between her legs. I had come to the club to do the deal with Clay, not to play, but my dick throbbed with longing.

I hadn't fucked anyone since the move, and it'd been a month. No, wait—it'd been longer. More like *five* fucking weeks. My hand was getting quite the workout these days.

Clay eyed the couple but seemed . . . indifferent. Like this was something he'd seen enough times that it no longer held any interest for him. Or perhaps his disinterest wasn't with the act so much as it was with the people performing it.

The man and the woman on stage were only a little older than us. Both looked to be in their forties, and each was decent looking. But they couldn't compete with Clay's boyfriend and girlfriend, who sat in the back row of folding chairs, watching the impromptu show and politely waiting for us to finish our meeting.

My first time at Club Eros, it had been 'exhibitionist night,' and Travis and Lilith had taken the stage first. But before their scene began, a man, who I'd later learn was Clay, appeared with a piece of furniture that looked like a padded sawhorse. It had black legs, a black leather top that was trimmed with red accents, and silver rings dangled from multiple spots.

These rings gave Travis plenty of places to thread his rope through and tie his partner down. And while they performed, Clay stood to the side and watched like a boss supervising an employee.

The show had been straight fire, but more than once during it, my gaze had left Lilith's naked body and drifted down to the bench beneath her. I was friends with the owners of my club in New York, and knew they were planning to add a dungeon. A piece like that would be a great addition.

So, I'd sought Clay out to ask where he'd bought it. He gave me his card, I sent the website address to my owner friends and found myself brokering the deal for a small commission. Four custom pieces—the largest order Clay had ever received, he'd told me. But he was sure he could deliver them on time.

I barely knew him, but judging by his exacting personality, I felt confident he was telling the truth.

"Assuming your client wants to proceed," Clay's voice was professional, "I'll need fifty percent down so I can order materials."

I nodded. "What kind of updates will they get about the project?"

"Typically, I send photos when the piece is finished."

The woman on stage had finished teasing the guy. She reached a hand behind her, likely to steady his cock, and moved to lower herself on him. Her eyes hooded and his head tilted back, and they both let out a deep sigh of pleasure.

Fuck.

It was sexy as hell watching her take whatever she wanted from the man. The muscles in his arms flexed and corded as he tried to reach for her but was held back by his cuffs. But I knew it wasn't because he wanted to stop her. His hands probably ached to grasp her waist and control the tempo she fucked him with, but—no.

She was in charge.

When he lowered his head to look out at the few people watching the scene, it seemed like he loved being her plaything.

Focus.

"Would you be open to letting me inspect the pieces before shipping?" I asked.

Clay's eyebrows tugged together. He wasn't exactly frowning, but I could tell he didn't love the idea. "You'd have to do that at my workshop, and I don't typically let clients down there."

I sensed he wasn't concerned I might find his quality lacking; his discomfort was caused by something else. Maybe he viewed his workshop as a safe space and didn't want to sacrifice his privacy.

But as their broker, I had a duty to my clients.

"This isn't a typical order," I said. Meaning if he wanted to close, he needed to be flexible here.

"No, it's not," he reluctantly agreed. He pushed the side of his suit coat back so he could rest a hand on his hip. "If your clients want you to inspect the finished pieces, I'm fine with allowing that."

"Excellent. Then my clients accept your quote and," I thrust my hand forward, "I think we have a deal."

Clay had a decent poker face. His pleased smile was restrained, but his eyes gave him away. The guy was fucking pleased, and why shouldn't he be? He was going to make a decent chunk of change off this—but it wasn't just the money. His work was art to him, and it deserved to be seen.

After we shook hands, my gaze drifted back to the couple playing on the St. Andrew's Cross. The man stared at his partner with such hunger, I felt it deep inside. Not for the woman he was with though—my longing was more general and widespread.

I was envious of the connection they had.

In all the years I'd lived in New York, I hadn't found anything like that. But I'd been so stressed out and busy, I'd barely had time for myself. Certainly not time for anyone else.

Was there any chance things would be different here in Nashville?

I fucking hoped so.

The first thirty minutes after my realtor told me the offer on the house had been accepted, I'd felt both excitement and anxiety. I'd done the numbers a bunch of times and knew I could afford the mortgage. Plus, I had plenty of money in my 'rainy day' account. No matter what, I'd be fine.

And yet, no amount of convincing seemed to help with my unease.

I'd never owned a house before. And this one was *big*.

It was way too much for a thirty-six-year-old single guy, but I loved the house. Not just the space, but the neighborhood, the proximity to my new job, and best of all—I'd gotten it for a downright steal. It had sat on the market for months and gone through several price reductions. I didn't know the seller's situation, but it was clear she was motivated.

Thankfully, my anxiety evaporated by closing day.

My agent had told me everything was ready to go. I had the final walkthrough scheduled for nine a.m., and then we'd head to the bank where I'd sign and get the keys. I felt more like an adult than I ever had.

My agent's car was out front when I pulled up, but there was another car parked in the driveway as well. The seller of the house was waiting for us in the entryway.

"I'm Judy," the woman said.

She looked to be in her mid-fifties, and was so skinny, it seemed likely a strong breeze might blow her over. Her face was severe even as she attempted to smile at me.

"I hope you don't mind that I'm here," she continued, "but I wanted to show you how things work." She said it like she was doing me a huge favor and I should be grateful.

My agent Rob and I exchanged a look, but I pushed past it and strove for a friendly tone. "Hi there. I'm Noah."

She looked beyond me like she was waiting for somebody else to come through the door behind me. "Will your wife be joining us?"

What? "My wife?"

Judy grimaced. And then her expression went blank, like she realized she hadn't meant to make that face out loud. "I'm sorry. I guess I meant your *partner*."

"I don't have a partner."

She blinked as if she hadn't heard me right. "You're going to live in this big house . . . by yourself?"

"That's the plan." Not that it was any of her business.

"But you're so young." Her eyes filled with suspicion. "How can you afford it?"

Rob's eyes went impossibly wide. "Ms. Malinger, I don't think that's—"

I waved my hand, telling him it was all right. "I worked for a brokerage firm in Manhattan, and I invested my commissions wisely." I slathered on the fakest smile I possessed, showing her that while I wasn't thrilled by her question, I wasn't fazed by it either.

My agent cleared his throat, and his tone was pointed toward the woman. "I think my client might feel more comfortable if you'd step outside. If he has questions, we can discuss them after closing."

Judy laughed like Rob was being silly. "Oh, nonsense, it'll be fine. I promise I'll stay out of your way."

To prove her point, she stepped to the side, pulled out her phone, and stared at the screen, pretending we didn't exist. It made Rob glance in my direction, and the look on his face read loud and clear. *"You okay with this?"*

I nodded back. *"It's fine. Let's get on with it."*

At first, Judy stayed true to her word. She remained in the entryway and didn't bother us as we walked through the house, but I felt her presence anyway. Her gaze bore into my back as I strolled into the living room and scanned the empty, dusty space. I couldn't help but feel as if this were still her home and I was trespassing in it.

Technically, it was still her home—until I signed the closing documents.

She said nothing as we went left and explored the office and primary bedroom, where hair, dust, and crumbs littered the carpet in a perfect line where the headboard of a bed had once sat. She remained dutifully quiet when we walked past her and evaluated the kitchen, including the cabinets that looked like they hadn't ever been wiped out.

It was as if she'd moved everything out . . . except for all the dirt and grime that had accumulated over time.

I understood the house had been rented out for the last two years, but it seemed like the tenant had done a shitty job of cleaning, and Judy hadn't bothered to correct that.

Maybe she was bitter because I'd played hardball and offered well below asking. When she'd countered, I'd said no. I loved this house, but I was a risk taker and banking on the fact that if I lost out, another house I loved would come along. My New York dollars went a hell of a lot farther down here in Nashville.

I was by no means a clean freak, but I was annoyed with the state of the house. My moving pod with all my furniture inside was set to arrive tomorrow, and I didn't want to move my things in on top of existing dirt. It meant I'd need to call my folks and ask for help, when I really didn't want to bother them with this shit.

When we finished the walkthrough, Rob beat me to it. "Did you pack your vacuum first?"

Judy was confused. "What do you mean?"

He gave her a pointed look. "It doesn't look like anything has been cleaned."

"Moving's messy." She rolled her eyes. "Everyone knows the new homeowners' going to clean before moving in anyway."

My agent motioned for me to follow him out to the garage, where we'd be out of earshot. Once we were behind the door, he kept his voice low. "It's not the worst I've seen, but in my opinion, you'd be justified in asking for a cleaning credit if you wanted to. I'm sure she'll push back on it though, and it could slow down closing."

"I'm not thrilled about it, but it's fine," I said.

I was eager to get the deal done and start the next chapter of my life, and I certainly wasn't going to let a little mess stop that from happening.

TWO

Charlotte

While I waited for Preston to meet me outside the restaurant, I scrolled through Instagram, and when my focus landed on an image from Blooming Sage Lotions, it sent my heart plummeting into my stomach. The headline was bolded at the top of the graphic.

Statement, it read.

As I scanned the paragraph below, my heart sank further toward my knees. Two days ago, a customer had alleged the company, which had built its brand as being cruelty free, with no animal testing—was lying.

There had been a lot of evidence, including heartbreaking pictures of animals in cages. Even if it wasn't true, the pictures were damaging enough, but two former employees had come out since the post, confirming and expanding on the terrible things the company had done.

This statement Blooming Sage had posted?

It did absolutely *nothing* to help their case. It wasn't just defensive. It laid the blame on their supplier and these disgruntled ex-employees, rather than claim any responsibility. If any animal testing had happened, they'd been completely unaware.

They played the victim.

That shit wasn't going to fly with their customers, and a quick survey of the fiery comments proved it.

I sagged against the brick wall of the restaurant.

What the fuck was I going to do?

For the last two years I'd tried so hard to become a social media influencer. I'd spent countless hours building my platform, cultivating my network, and generating content. It had been such a struggle, and I'd had to claw my way to gain each new follower.

I loved the work, but shit—it was hard. Most of the time it was for very little return too. My father would argue my effort was wasted, but he didn't get it. He didn't seem to understand how important and powerful social media could be, which was ironic. He owned a multi-million-dollar talent agency, and his biggest client, Stella, was a darling of TikTok and Instagram.

This Blooming Sage fiasco was another problem I didn't need right now. They were the first brand to reach out to me, wanting to collaborate on three sponsored posts. I'd put up the first one already, with the next one scheduled to go up tomorrow.

God, getting this contract was the only proof I'd been able to show my father that my side business wasn't a total failure. That my dream could lead to something. A future where I wasn't totally dependent on him.

Now I was going to have to pull down the existing reel, return the money they'd paid me, and back out of the deal. I wasn't just appalled by the company's lies—I couldn't risk the blowback on my account.

The evening sun glared at me, and I started to sweat under my makeup. I'd spent the entire Uber ride getting here regretting agreeing to this date, and that was before I'd seen the Instagram post. But I'd been in town less than a month when the receptionist at Warbler Entertainment had called in sick, and my dad asked me—no, wait—demanded I fill in for her.

I hadn't worked at Warbler in years. But I'd done it when I was twenty, so I knew how, and now that I was broke and had no choice but to move back home, I couldn't exactly say no.

Preston Lowe was an event planner. He'd come in with his business partner and pitched Troy Osbourne's release party to Warbler, and after their meeting, he'd strolled right up to the front desk and asked me for my number.

He *was* cute, and his cockiness was kind of sexy.

I'd been caught off guard, so I wasn't thinking when I texted him my digits. He'd thrown a casual, *"Maybe we could grab dinner or a drink sometime,"* over his shoulder before leaving.

I knew I shouldn't have agreed to the date, but my life was such a dumpster fire right now, I figured one drink wouldn't hurt. It was flattering he was interested, and, unfortunately, I needed the ego boost.

He was a few minutes early, which was nice, but then we were told our table wasn't ready. *Table*? I'd thought we were just getting drinks. While we waited, he tried to make small talk, and honestly, I wasn't great about it. My mind was too focused on the Blooming Sage fallout.

"So, you still live at home?" I asked him, not paying attention to my tone, so it came out sounding unintentionally snotty. I didn't mean to judge him, and I certainly had no room to. The problem was now that I'd moved back home, it meant we *both* lived under our parents' roofs—while we were in our mid-twenties.

At least his business is doing well.

Once we'd been seated at our table, the date rapidly went downhill. Something was bothering him, and it was like he'd forgotten I existed. I'd been rude checking my phone when he first showed up, but now I was getting a taste of my own medicine.

It didn't take me long to figure out what he was so fixated on. Or, more correctly—who. The pretty girl sitting at the table next to us was obviously going through some shit with her mom and he was very, very invested in it.

Was he nosy, or did he know her? The way he stared at her made me think so.

I tried to get him to engage with me, asking him what drink he planned to order, but I couldn't compete with her. He was frozen in his seat, gazing at her like he was both pissed off and turned on.

When the server arrived, I placed the order for my drink. A lavender martini, which would look great with the color scheme I'd been consistent with on all my posts. But Preston didn't order.

When the girl at the table next to us launched to her feet and fled the restaurant, Preston rose out of his chair too.

"What are you doing?" I asked.

He looked at me like he'd never seen me before. Like he hadn't realized I'd been sitting across from him this whole time, and it came from him in a rush. "I need a minute."

And then he was gone, chasing after her.

My mouth hung open as I watched him go, and I blinked away my disbelief. Whatever was going on, I hoped he'd get it figured out quickly. But as the seconds ticked by, my heart rate began to climb with unease.

What if he wasn't coming back?

The longer I waited, the hotter my cheeks burned with both irritation and embarrassment. The girl's mom at the table next to me looked as confused and irritated as I was, but she recovered much faster. She went back to picking at her meal, her expression resigned like this had been an outcome she'd anticipated.

My phone had been resting face down on the table, so I turned it over, unlocked the screen, and began scrolling. I read down through the comments on Blooming Sage's post and then considered whether I'd need to make my own statement. Ultimately, I decided it would be better if I didn't.

No reason to call attention to my involvement.

I put my phone back down, and my gaze went to the entrance at the front of the restaurant. How much longer was Preston going to be?

My phone buzzed on the tabletop.

> **Preston:** Sorry, something came up and I need to bail.

I stared at the screen, waiting for more details, but no blinking gray dots appeared. He wasn't typing anything else. There'd be no further explanation, no real apology for the way he'd just straight up abandoned me.

"Seriously?" I groaned under my breath. "Asshole."

The woman at the next table looked momentarily offended at my language, but also . . . like she sort of understood?

It was at this moment the server arrived with my lavender martini and set it in front of me. I hadn't realized that when Preston had walked out, the server had put in my drink order anyway.

Maybe he knew you'd need it.

I stared at the pretty purple drink and the yellow flower

floating in it, then lifted my gaze to the server. "Hey, do you mind if I take this to the bar? My date just left me." Oh, shit. That sounded terrible. I pretended this wasn't a big deal and I wasn't wounded, and my voice came out probably too bright. "Something came up."

The server nodded. "Of course. I'll have the bartender open a tab for you."

I didn't tell him there was no need, that I'd only stay for one drink. Instead, I picked up my martini and weaved through the busy restaurant, finding an open seat at the U-shaped bar in the center of the space.

I'd come here for an ego boost, and instead I'd gotten the opposite. God, could my luck get any worse?

"Hey there, sweetheart."

I turned toward the man sitting next to me and sized him up in a microsecond. He was older than I was, but not by much. He had an attractive enough face, but eyes that looked like they were permanently bloodshot. And they rolled around wildly, as if he couldn't focus on any one thing for too long.

Was this guy wasted . . . or was he on something?

He'd called me *sweetheart*, which annoyed me. I pulled my lips back into something that could barely be considered a smile and turned away from him.

My gaze went through the bar and to the high-top table across the way. There were two men and a woman sitting there, with a round of drinks in front of them. The man who happened to be facing me appeared to be listening thoughtfully to whatever the woman was saying.

I swallowed thickly.

Holy shit, that guy was hot. And not the kind of hot that

only appealed to a certain kind of girl. He was, like, *objectively* hot.

My best guess was he was in his mid-thirties, so at least ten years older than I was. He had dark brown hair that was parted on the side and a short, neatly trimmed beard. I couldn't tell if he was tall or not, since he was seated, but he was in great shape. He filled out his gray t-shirt like he was modeling it, and its sleeves just barely fit around his toned biceps.

I studied the other people at the table, trying to figure out their relationship with one another. It was hard to see them because the bar was busy and the bartenders kept blocking my view, but eventually the woman raised a hand to run through her long red hair, and a wedding ring glinted on her finger.

The man I was interested in lifted his pint glass, showing his ring finger was bare. And the other man at the table wore a ring.

The longer I watched them, the more confident I was I had it figured out. Their body language made them look like a couple. And my guy? He was third-wheeling it tonight.

Did he sense I was watching him? His gaze lifted to mine, causing my breath to catch. Any other girl might have looked away, but not me. I held his gaze while a slight smile curled at the edge of my lips.

I didn't know why, but I wanted him to know I thought he was hot. The way Preston had ditched me had made me reckless and bold.

The man blinked away his surprise, and then a similar smile warmed his lips.

Oh, God. I was completely unprepared for how much

more intensely attractive he became when he smiled. Everything in my body tightened, and I—

"What're you drinking?" the guy next to me asked.

Nothing, I almost responded, because I hadn't even touched my drink yet. I kept my answer short, sending a message that I didn't want to be bothered. "Lavender martini."

He held up his cocktail glass, making the ice slosh around erratically. "Negroni."

"Cool," I deadpanned.

But the guy couldn't take a fucking hint. "It's good." He took a sip and set the glass down with a little too much force, so it banged against the bar. He didn't notice, though. "You want me to get you one?"

My gaze dipped down to my untouched martini, then back to him, and I delivered a flat look. "I'm good, thanks."

I angled my shoulders away from him, *really* hoping he would pick up on my signals. There was another man here I was interested in, and my gaze flitted to his table across the way. Their drinks were almost finished, and a server swung by, dropping off the check, which the hot guy snatched up. I watched the couple protest, but his credit card was thrown down with an easy smile.

If I was going to talk to this guy, my window was rapidly closing.

I picked up my drink and was just about to take a sip when I remembered the reason for ordering it. I snapped a few different shots, some where I was holding the drink and a few where it was resting on the bar. Then, I pocketed my phone and took my first sip. After all, I'd need some liquid courage before I made my approach on Hot Guy.

The martini was great, but I barely got to enjoy the taste.

"So, what's your name?" The guy who was under the influence of something leaned toward me, making the bar stool creak beneath him.

I didn't bother with a polite smile this time. Nothing else had seemed to work, so I pulled out the big guns. "Just so you know, I'm only having a drink while I wait for my boyfriend to get here."

The guy's expression clouded over like maybe he didn't believe me. "Okay." He arched an eyebrow, and his tone turned playful. "You could still tell me your name, though."

Jesus Christ. "Why?"

That, at least, seemed to have some effect. He looked confused. "Why?" he repeated.

"Yes, *why*? I want to know why you need to know my name."

He gave me an innocuous smile. "So we can chat until your boyfriend gets here."

Fine, I'd be direct. "Sorry, I'm not interested in talking to you. Have a nice night."

I picked up my drink and was about to move to the now-empty barstool beside me, when the man grabbed my wrist. He did it hard enough it made my drink spill over my fingers.

"What the fuck?" I said.

"Oops, sorry." His grin was so wide it turned my stomach. "Guess I'll have to buy you a new drink."

"Don't worry about it," I snapped.

But he didn't let go of my wrist, not even when I tried to tug it away, making my drink slosh on my hand again. My heart beat faster, and I hurried a glance across the way to the table.

No! Hot Guy and his friends were on the move, leaving.

"Get your goddamn hand off me." I yanked my arm back so hard it nearly sent him stumbling off his stool, but at least I was able to break free. I set down my glass and shook off the vodka dripping from my fingers.

He put his hands up as if telling me to calm down. "Relax. I'm just trying to be nice. Why can't we have a friendly conversation?"

Usually when I got scared or felt cornered, my instinct was to run, but tonight I was all fight. If he pushed me any harder, I was ready to push back.

"Because, asshole," I snarled, "I told you I don't want to talk to you." And I said it loud enough for the bartender's focus to snap in my direction. He abandoned the drink he'd been preparing and headed my way—

"Hey."

This deep voice hadn't come from the man sitting beside me; it had come from above. I turned and lifted my gaze, and my breath stuck in my lungs. Hot Guy stared back at me with questions in his eyes. *Are you all right?*

I was so surprised, I couldn't find any words.

The man sitting beside me didn't have that problem. He wasn't happy we'd been interrupted, and his tone was harsh and patronizing. "Oh, this must be the boyfriend you've been waiting for."

Hot Guy didn't miss a beat. "Yeah, that's me." He grabbed the empty stool, sat down beside me, and his voice was warm. Like he'd known me forever. "How was your day, sweetheart?"

THREE

Noah

I noticed the girl the moment she took a seat at the bar—long before I caught her staring at me. She was young and pretty, carrying a purple martini with a yellow flower floating in it. If I'd been ten years younger, I would have found an excuse to go talk to her. Hell, maybe even if I'd been just five years younger.

But the girl was too young for me now, plus I highly doubted she'd be into . . . the kind of things I was into.

It's been more than two months, a voice inside my head said. *Do you really want to be picky?*

No, I didn't, but women her age weren't usually cool with one-night stands. They were always looking for relationships, and that wasn't something I was willing to do right now.

Certainly not with a girl who looked just old enough to be sitting at that bar.

I'd come here tonight with a single goal, to meet Patrick and Shannon, and now that it had been accomplished, I knew I should head home. I liked taking risks, but something tugged inside me, warning me not to. This girl would be nothing but trouble.

For a brief moment, I thought she knew the guy sitting beside her, but I was less sure each time I glanced over. The way she leaned away from him, how she didn't seem to want to give him her attention, made me think he was hitting on her, and she wasn't receptive at all.

Except my resolve to steer clear faltered when we locked gazes with each other, and she'd flashed me a sexy little smirk. Her eyes held secrets, and they whispered about how much fun it would be to tease them out.

Fuck, my weakness was confident women.

It was why most of my recent relationships had been with older women. They'd grown out of their shyness, or inexperience, or politeness, and were less afraid to tell me *exactly* how they wanted it.

Sex had become more fun, and infinitely hotter.

Maybe this girl knew what she wanted, but chances were we wanted very different things. So I turned my attention back to Patrick and Shannon, finished the last swallow of my drink, and paid for the round.

I moved toward the exit, slower than I should have, like I was looking for a reason to stay.

"Because, asshole," the girl said forcefully, "I told you I don't want to talk to you."

That forced me into action. My feet carried me swiftly toward the girl, and the word burst from my lips. "Hey."

The bartender, like half the people in the restaurant, had picked up on the tension and was making his way toward the girl, but as soon as he laid eyes on me, he hesitated.

The girl turned in her seat, looked up at me, and seemed to stop breathing.

Maybe I did too.

Shit, she was even prettier up close. Her honey blonde hair was wavy with big curls, and her bright blue eyes popped against her fair skin. Her makeup was meticulous, and her sleeveless shirt was cut low enough to flaunt her appealing cleavage. The girl was slender, even her face, which accentuated her full lips.

Everything about her screamed high maintenance, yet I was still drawn in. She was so sexy, and I was so starved for attention I was willing to ignore every warning sign.

Her lips parted as if she were going to say something, but it never came. The silence stretched between us.

The expression on the guy's face sitting next to her filled with irritation. "Oh, this must be the boyfriend you've been waiting for."

"Yeah, that's me," I said instantly.

Boyfriend? What the fuck are you doing?

It was too late to take it back. I grabbed the stool beside her and plopped down at the bar, committing to the bit. I did my best to make it sound casual and familiar. "How was your day, sweetheart?"

A single blink was all it took to wipe the surprise from the girl's face. "It just got a lot better now that you're here."

I wanted to chuckle at her meaning, but I merely smiled. And then I motioned to her mostly empty martini and the puddle of vodka around it. "Do you need another drink?"

She angled her shoulders to face me, blocking the other guy out, and her tone went warm and soft. "Yeah, that would be great."

Shit, she was such a great actress that for a split second she had me convinced we were together.

I was about to ask her what type of drink, but she had me covered. "Lavender martini." She brushed a lock of hair back over her shoulder. "How was your day?"

"It was fine," I answered truthfully. "Busy."

The bartender had gone back to mixing the cocktail he'd

been working on, but he glanced in our direction. It wasn't to acknowledge my presence; it was probably more to check on the girl and make sure she was doing okay.

As soon as he placed the drink in front of the customer, I motioned to him. "When you have a minute, she'd like a—"

"Lavender martini," he replied, nodding. His focus slipped from us to the man seated beside her, and it was obvious he didn't like what he saw.

"You two don't look like a couple," the man grumbled, maybe more to himself than us. His gaze wheeled around and landed on me for a moment. "Isn't she kind of young for you, bro?"

The man's eyes were rimmed with red, and the way they bounced around . . . He was high on something. Coke? Molly? A fuck ton of Adderall? It didn't matter. I'd seen all sorts of shit during my stint in private wealth management at Hale Banking and Holding, and had a massive aversion to drugs these days.

So my pulse ratcheted up, right along with my desire to keep this girl from having to interact with him a moment longer.

Before I could open my mouth to say anything, the girl's head whipped around to face him. "I like that my man's older." Her voice filled with smoke as she glanced back at me. "Isn't that right, *Daddy*?"

Fucking hell.

If someone had asked me five minutes ago if this was one of my kinks, I would have said no, but now? Her eyes smoldered, and I worried I might sweat right through my shirt. The idea of being this little girl's 'daddy' was way more appealing than it should have been.

And it wasn't a stretch to say she looked the part of a spoiled brat, either.

I was happy to play my role and tried to match the heat she'd put in her voice. "That's right, baby girl."

Her grin was wide.

Less pleased was the guy beside her. The moment my statement registered, he looked like he'd swallowed his tongue. His head jerked back, and his upper lip lifted with disgust, so her gamble seemed to work. He swiped up his drink and guzzled the rest of it, choosing to ignore us.

"Can I get you anything, sir?" the bartender asked as he delivered her a fresh martini.

No, the voice in my head warned. *It'll make it harder to leave.*

My fake girlfriend was probably trying not to look too needy, but her expression pleaded with me to stay.

"Sure," I said. "I'll take a pint of Heineken." I didn't have any other plans tonight, and one drink wasn't going to be the end of the world.

Relief coasted through her expression, and she leaned an elbow on the bar. "Why was your day so busy?"

I considered how to answer in case the guy next to her was listening, wanting to keep up the game. "I had that big meeting with a potential client today, remember?"

She hid a smile behind the rim of her martini glass before taking a sip. "Oh, that's right. How'd it go?"

"Good. He signed."

"Oh, that's awesome." She sounded genuinely happy for me. Like I was a friend and not a total stranger. "Congrats."

"Thanks." I tried not to focus on her lips or think about what they'd taste like. *Probably lavender martini, dipshit.* I straightened in my seat. "Your day wasn't good?"

She gave a humorless laugh. "No, it wasn't." She hesitated, unsure of how to explain. "You know how I had that partnership deal with Blooming Sage?"

Um . . . "Sure," I lied.

A frown slid across her lips. "I'm going to have to pull out."

The bartender delivered my pint, and movement caught my eye. The guy sitting beside her held up his empty glass and proclaimed it loudly for everyone to hear. "I'll take another."

Rather than move, the bartender evaluated the man critically. "How about a water or a Coke instead?"

Confusion contorted his face, quickly followed by offense. "What?"

The bartender crossed his arms over his chest. "I'm not serving you another drink."

"Why the hell not?"

The bartender's eyebrow lifted into a sharp, upside-down V. "Come on, man. You *know* why."

The tension between them was thick, and I didn't want it to escalate any further. "Hey," I announced, "let me call you an Uber."

The man looked at me like I'd just offered to spit in his face. "What?"

Everyone except the man knew this was only going to end one way—which was with him leaving. I didn't care where he went after he left the bar, but I didn't want him driving. "Hey, it's no big deal." I tried to sound friendly, even though I felt none of it. "I'll even pay for it, if you'd like."

Yet the man continued to look offended. His gaze narrowed on me before turning toward the bartender, whose expression was steely. No amount of convincing was going to change the guy's mind and get the man another drink.

So he hopped down off his bar stool and wobbled on his unsteady feet as he pulled out his phone. "I can call my own damn Uber."

The girl said nothing as he shuffled his way toward the front of the restaurant, but as he disappeared out the front door, she let out a heavy breath. The bartender returned to his other customers, and she leaned close to me, lowering her voice. "What the fuck was his deal? Was he on something?"

"Oh, yeah," I said. "He was high as fuck."

Her shoulders relaxed. "Well, thanks for coming over and pretending to be my boyfriend."

"Don't you mean Daddy?" I teased.

She grinned, and I pretended not to see the heat in her eyes as she took another sip of her martini. "Right." Then she set her glass down and extended her hand. "I'm Charlotte."

"Noah." I took her offered hand. "And you're welcome."

We lapsed into silence, and I wracked my brain trying to come up with small talk, because I couldn't imagine we had much in common.

"What you said about signing a new client. True?" she asked.

I nodded. "It was." I left out that it was my first official client since starting my new role.

She picked up her martini and held it toward me. "In that case, cheers."

I obliged, clicking our glasses together.

We both took our customary sips, and she glanced across the way to the now empty table where I'd been seated. "Your . . . friends didn't want another round?"

She was fishing for information, and I held back my

smile. I couldn't blame her for being curious, but I wasn't going to tell her about my 'date.' "No, we just wanted to grab one drink together." I needed to shift the conversation away from that. "How about you?"

Her expression was suddenly guarded. "What about me?"

She obviously hadn't come to the bar for a drink. "When you showed up, you were already carrying a martini."

Charlotte made a face, and it looked like she was considering whether she should tell me. Once the decision had been made, her shoulders slumped. "Okay, so, I was on a date."

"Uh-oh." I hesitated. "That bad, huh?"

"Yeah," she said flatly. "I mean, he just got up and left."

Warning alarms triggered in my head. What on Earth had she said that sent the guy running? I hoped my expression looked blank and not judgmental. "He walked out in the middle of your date?"

She stared at her drink and traced the stem of the glass with a fingertip. "It wasn't during the middle, it was right at the beginning. We'd just sat down at the table, and I'd ordered my drink when he suddenly got up and hightailed it for the exit." Her tone was embarrassed. "He sent me a text message right after, saying that something came up and he was sorry." She tossed up a hand. "Whatever. The whole thing was super weird, and I shouldn't have said yes to that date in the first place. I didn't know the guy, and even before he bailed on me, I knew it wasn't going anywhere."

It just fell out of my mouth. "Then why did you say yes?"

"He was cute, and . . . " She glanced at me and licked her lips, nervous. "I've had a rough few months. It was nice to have someone interested in me for once." Her eyes abruptly went wide. "Oh, God, that makes me sound pathetic, doesn't it?"

"No, it doesn't," I said quickly. "To be honest, it's been the same for me recently."

Her eyebrows tugged together, shooting me a look like that couldn't possibly be right. "You?" She shook her head, making little waves ripple through her blonde hair. "No way."

"Afraid that's a true story."

"Well, that's not true anymore." The corner of her lips hinted at a smile. "I thought I made my interest pretty clear."

Shit, she had a point, and I found myself smiling back at her. "Yeah, well, I didn't like how that guy was bothering you," I admitted, "but I'm glad it gave me an excuse to come talk to you."

"Me too."

We were both quiet for a moment, and I glanced around at our surroundings. "This place is nice. Have you been here before?"

"No, I think it just opened."

"Oh, I didn't realize." It made sense. The place was trendy, clean, and filled with people. The newness of it was obvious now. "I just moved here."

Charlotte tilted her head. "Yeah? From where?"

"New York." I felt the need to elaborate. "Manhattan."

She peered at me dubiously. "What, are you, like, a finance bro?"

It had been a joking question, but she wasn't wrong, and I tried not to sound sheepish. "I was, yeah."

She seemed surprised and perhaps a bit impressed, which was a nice change of pace for me. Pretty much everyone held their nose while talking to me when I'd been at HBHC. Sure, they liked me when I was making them money, but otherwise

I was viewed as a pariah.

"Okay, wow," she said. "What brought you to Nashville?"

"A new job. But actually, I grew up around here. My parents still live in town."

I didn't tell her the truth, that it was my father's health that had brought me back home and not my career. I was the youngest of my siblings, and my dad was already in his late thirties when I was born. Now he was seventy-one, with a back shot to shit from years working as a roadie, and a recent pancreatic cancer diagnosis.

He was stubborn as fuck too, in complete denial of what his physical limitations were now. Even if he'd let my mother help him—which he wouldn't—she wasn't able to. As the baby of the family, unmarried and without kids, my older brothers had elected me as his new caregiver.

Telling her that wasn't sexy. Plus, how would this twenty-something girl relate to any of that?

"Yeah. My parents still live around here too." There was something off about her tone. She'd sounded . . . sad?

"Are you close?"

"To my parents?" Her reaction told me this was a touchy subject. "I guess. Not as close as I used to be."

Family was complicated and I didn't want to pry, so I shifted the conversation, asking what had happened with her brand partnership. She told me how hard she'd been working to build up her business, and the first company willing to work with her was now embroiled in a PR nightmare.

"You're an influencer?" Shit, I hoped she couldn't hear the disdain in my voice.

It shouldn't have been there, anyway. There was a lot of money in that industry, and she was running a small business.

I shouldn't judge or look down on her. Didn't I know exactly how that felt?

What a pair we made to the outside world. Me, a greedy stockbroker, and her, a vapid social media influencer. Maybe we had more in common than I thought.

I adjusted my tone and pushed out a smile. "That's cool."

She didn't look convinced but shrugged one shoulder. "It has its moments. Times when the work is fun and doesn't feel like work, you know?" Her lips skewed to one side. "And then there's days like today."

"I think most jobs are like that," I said.

"I guess I'm unlucky," she said, "because I've hated every job I've ever had."

I let out half a laugh. "When I started at my firm in Manhattan, I loved the work. I liked the," I searched for the right word, "challenge of it. But by the end? Yeah, I definitely didn't love it anymore."

There'd been times I'd come away hating myself. My only escape had been the club, and that wasn't a healthy way to deal with the stress. I was so burned out I could barely function.

"How about your new job? Do you like it?"

"So far, so good." It was drastically different than HBHC and seemed to be the reset I needed.

We made more small talk as we finished our drinks, and I got the impression we were both avoiding any kind of details. I took it as a good sign. Maybe I'd misjudged her, and Charlotte wasn't looking for anything serious. She told me she'd come out on a date tonight because she'd been looking for some 'interest,' and I was plenty willing to give her that.

She set her empty glass on the bar and then gave me a

playful look. "I finished my drink, Daddy." It was impossible to know if there was lust in her eyes—or if I just wished there were. Her head quirked to the side, and she asked it like it was rhetorical. "Should we head back to your place?"

"Sounds like a plan, sweetheart."

FOUR

Noah

We shared an Uber back to my place, and during the drive, Charlotte asked for my address. "I'm texting it to a friend," she said, "so they know where to start if I go missing."

Even though she'd been teasing, the guy driving locked eyes with me in the rearview mirror, wordlessly accusing me of plotting her murder.

"I get it." It was smart, because she didn't know much about me. I strove to match her joking tone. "Hope I haven't been giving off serial killer vibes."

She smiled and shook her head.

When we pulled up in front of my house, her mouth dropped open. "You live here?"

Pride swept through me. I shouldn't have cared that she was impressed, but I was anyway. "Yeah."

"It's really nice."

"Thanks."

We got out, and she followed me up the path and onto the front porch, waiting as I unlocked the door. I pushed it open—only to thrust a hand across the doorway and block her from entering. "So, uh . . . it's kind of a disaster in here. I wasn't expecting company."

Especially since Patrick and Shannon had told me they didn't play on the first date.

She laughed softly. "It's cool. I know you just moved

in." She ducked under my arm and stepped inside. "I'm not scared of some boxes or some—"

Charlotte pulled to a stop, and I didn't need to follow her gaze to figure out what she was looking at. I hadn't lied. My house was a fucking mess. There were open boxes and packing paper strewn about because I'd done a shitty job of labeling stuff, and nearly every day I'd had to cut one open and rummage through the contents, searching for something.

And there were large, empty boxes, and piles of plastic shipping bags stacked where a dining table was supposed to go, because I hadn't bought one yet.

"This place is a lot bigger than my last one," I said quickly. "I'm still working on putting together some of my new furniture."

Judy hadn't lied. It was stunning how fucking messy moving could be.

Charlotte was tense as she took in the chaos. I got the terrible feeling she was second guessing her decision to come home with me.

"This room is overwhelming," I announced. "Let's go into the kitchen. It's . . . better in there."

She followed me through the short hallway and let out a breath, like she hadn't been able to breathe in the entryway.

What I had said was true, that it was better in the kitchen, but it wasn't necessarily good. My mom had helped me one night this week, focusing all her effort on the kitchen, so most things were put away. There were still a few open boxes on my kitchen table, though, and some dirty dishes in the sink.

And of course, nothing was hung on the walls. The one painting I had that would work in here was leaning against the wall beside the pantry.

Charlotte scanned the room, and I didn't miss the way she eyed the dishes from my dinner last night. When she set her hands on the counter of the island, I got the weird feeling she'd done it to stop herself from going over the sink and starting to load the dishwasher.

Was she a clean freak and my place was a major turn-off?

She looked less uncomfortable here in the kitchen than she had in the entryway, at least.

"This is a big kitchen," she said, her voice echoing under the vaulted ceiling. "Do you like to cook?"

I shrugged. "I don't mind it." We fell quiet, giving time for awkwardness to creep in. "You want something to drink?"

As soon as the question was out of my mouth, I regretted it. Did I even have anything to offer her to drink? Thankfully, she shook her head. "How about a tour instead?"

"Sure." I gestured to the hallway.

For a moment, I was excited to show off my new place, but then reality hit me. The rest of the house was going to just be more of the same—boxes and packing paper strewn everywhere. Why hadn't I made more of an effort to unpack?

Probably because you just started a new job and it's fucking overwhelming.

I fumbled my way through the tour, showing off the office, the guest bedroom and the spare bedroom I planned to turn into a home gym. I didn't realize how much more work I needed to do until she peered into the nearly empty, undecorated rooms one by one.

At least I was strategic about it, saving the best for last. I turned the handle and pushed the door open. "This is the main bedroom."

It was the room that had sold me on the house. Two

thirds the size of my last place, the grand bedroom had a tray ceiling, a built-in bookcase, and a pair of tall windows that flanked the bed.

Which currently was unmade, but I hoped she could see past that and on to its potential.

This room could be sexy.

I just needed her to ignore the chair in the corner that was buried under a week's worth of dirty laundry.

Charlotte missed nothing. Her throat bobbed with a swallow, and she crossed the room, heading into the en-suite bathroom.

While she explored in there, I hurried to the chair, gathered up the clothes, and chucked them under the bed. It was ridiculous, but my options were limited. My laundry basket, the place where the clothes should have gone, was in my closet, which was through the bathroom.

She'd just finished her walkthrough when I met her in the doorway, struggling to act casual and not to look out of breath. It was wasted, though. She glanced over my shoulder, amused.

"What happen to the clothes that were on that chair?"

I feigned confusion. "I don't know what you're talking about."

Her smile widened. "Right. And if I went back in the bathroom, I'm sure the bed wouldn't suddenly get made either."

"We could test that theory." I meant it too, because if she wanted the bed made—I'd do it. But when I'd thought I had limited time to fix something, I'd decided the laundry was more urgent. Plus, if this evening went how I hoped it would, wouldn't we be messing the bed up anyway?

"That's okay," she said, brushing past me.

I hadn't started organizing the bookcase, so books were stacked randomly, along with the items I figured would end up there. An old award from winning my department's fantasy football league. A pint glass from my favorite bar at NYU. A framed family photo from a vacation we'd taken to Paris years ago.

"Is this your family?" She picked it up to study it, and a knot grew in my stomach. Even if it wasn't a major mood killer, which it was, I didn't want to talk about them right now.

It felt too personal.

"Yeah." I strode over, gently pulled the frame from her grasp, and set it back on the shelf. "Let's talk about something else."

I was standing close to her, too close for her not to notice. Her pretty eyes blinked rapidly as she peered up at me. "Okay. What do you want to talk about?"

"What's your stance on me kissing you?"

Her breath caught. "My . . . stance?"

"Yes. Are you for it or against it?"

"Oh." Heat flooded her expression, and her voice fell to a whisper. "I'm definitely for it."

"Okay, good."

And then I reached for her, setting one hand on her waist while sliding the other into her hair. I'd planned to lean down and set my lips on hers, but the girl was just as eager as I was and met me halfway.

Our lips crashed together. It wasn't the most skilled or seductive kiss I'd ever given, but it definitely seemed to be working for her. Fuck—it was working for me too. Her mouth was warm and soft, and our tongues tangled.

Heat spilled down my spine, and my heart kicked up a

notch. Charlotte kissed me back with a ferocity that matched my own, like she needed this as much as I did. I sank my hand further into her hair, and I didn't mean to, but I began to grip, dominating our kiss.

She let out a little sigh of satisfaction.

My dick jerked and began to harden inside my pants, but that wasn't surprising. I already had a hair trigger, plus kissing her only a few feet away from my bed was too much. Her fingertips bristled against my whiskers as she slid her hands up to cup my face.

I'd been worried we didn't have anything in common, but this? It was proving me wrong, because this girl knew *exactly* what she was doing. Exactly how to deepen our kiss so all I could think about was sinking down on the bed with her beneath me.

Our feet stumbled along as I shifted us closer to it, probably moving too fast for her, but she was able to keep up. Our kiss broke when I eased her onto her back on the bed and she sucked in a sharp breath. But then I was over her. My lips were on her again, and her surprise was forgotten.

The positioning was awkward with me bent over her and the unmade bed, and she must have sensed it. Charlotte crawled backward, getting me to chase her, and as I climbed on the bed between her parted legs, her greedy hands reached for me. They clutched at my shirt, stretching the cotton and urging me to take it off.

If I was starving, this girl was ravenous—and it was hot as fuck.

I rose, leaning back on my knees, and stretched the t-shirt over my head, flinging it away. She stared up with wide eyes and let out an appreciative sound at the sight of me, and I'd swear I could feel my ego swelling right along with my dick. To know this girl, who was at least a decade younger than I was, liked what she saw . . .

It was thrilling.

But it made the situation in my pants dire. Had I ever been so goddamn horny in my life?

Her hands wandered over my chest as I leaned down and kissed her again. I was glad to have my shirt gone because it seemed to be a thousand degrees inside this room. Was it the same for her?

Maybe she needs her shirt gone too.

I inched my fingers up under the hem, resting my palm on the warm skin of her stomach, testing the waters. I didn't want to move too fast, but that wasn't an issue for her. Charlotte placed a hand over mine and dragged it up until I could cup her breast.

I groaned my approval and squeezed, before tracing my fingertips at the edge of the lace of her bra. Her back arched into my touch, her tongue slicked against mine, and she ground her lower body against my erection.

All signs for me to keep going.

Thoughts were dim in my mind, clouded with need. I jerked the cup down and gripped her bare breast, pinching her nipple. Since her shirt wasn't off, I couldn't see exactly what I was doing, but in a way, it made it hotter. I enjoyed exploring her like this.

But Charlotte was too impatient.

When she went to sit up, she nearly knocked our teeth together, but I backed up just in time. Her arms crossed and her hands grabbed the sides of her shirt, and then she lifted it over her head so fast, it was practically a blur. The sweep of her hair fell around her bare shoulders, and she tossed the shirt aside.

I didn't get much time to view her black bra or the way her tits looked inside it because her hands threaded into my hair. She yanked my head down to her, and I obliged her with a thorough kiss.

The teasing words came from me, low and throaty. "So aggressive."

She drew in a deep breath. Shit. Had my comment accidentally caused her shame? God, I hoped not. That was the last thing I wanted.

"Fuck," I continued. "I'm so into it."

I moved to bury my mouth in the crook of her neck and sucked at the spot where her pulse was pounding, and I had to gnash my teeth when she ground herself against the fly of my jeans. *Jesus.* My dick was throbbing and straining against the denim, so the sensation of her rubbing on me was pleasurable agony.

The bed was quiet as I shifted, trailing my mouth down over her collarbone and inching toward the black lace. My short breath bounced off her bare skin as I worked my way lower, and I didn't miss the way goosebumps lifted on her forearms.

A smile burned across my lips.

She couldn't see it, though. I had my mouth nestled between her breasts, and a sound escaped from her that was so quiet, it was barely a moan. I hooked a finger in the cup of her bra, tugged it down, and closed my mouth around her extended nipple. I lost myself for a moment in her soft skin. Usually, when it came to sex, I was thoughtful. Or maybe calculating.

But tonight, I was mindless and reckless, and I had no idea if my dry spell was causing it . . . or the girl beneath me.

She gasped when my teeth clamped down on the sensitive bud. But the sound wasn't tinged with pain; it seemed to simply be surprise. Her grip on my head tightened, not to push me away, but to hold me close.

My tongue spun circles around her nipple, and I sucked, and I savored the quiet whimpers of satisfaction she made.

I gave the lace of her bra another tug and commanded her with a voice that was probably too strong, "Take this off."

If my order bothered Charlotte, she didn't let on. Maybe she liked that I'd matched her aggression. She complied instantly, wedging a hand underneath her, unhooked the clasp, and then the lace was pulled out of my way.

I had my mouth and hands on her tits before she'd finished pulling the straps down her arms. I teased with my lips and my tongue, nipping at her and following it up with gentle kisses. One breast, then the other . . . and back again.

Her breathy whine echoed through every inch of my body.

More, she'd wordlessly said.

Yes, I almost whispered back.

We reached for each other's pants at the same time, and when I chuckled, amusement lit her eyes. She pulled back her hand, using it to brush a strand of hair out of her face so she could better watch me work.

I popped the snap of her jeans and dropped her zipper, revealing the edge of more black lace. Had she worn the sexy matching bra and panties for her date, the guy who had foolishly abandoned her? I grinned to myself.

His loss was my gain, and I was very, *very* happy about it.

Her back arched off the mattress when I slipped a hand

inside her undone jeans, delving my fingertips beneath the waistband of her underwear. She was slick and warm, and it pumped more heat through my body.

She clamped a hand on my shoulder. "*Fuck*."

That was exactly what I planned to do. With my fingers, my mouth, my cock. Could I wring an orgasm out of her with each act? Shit, I couldn't wait to find out.

It was hard to figure out which was hotter—watching her squirm as the edges of my fingers rubbed against her clit, or listening to her short, labored breaths. But her jeans were tight and there wasn't a lot of room to maneuver inside them.

They had to go.

She lifted her hips to help me as I peeled the denim down her legs, but when I slipped my fingers under the waist of her black panties, she tensed.

"Those stay on," she said breathlessly.

FIVE

Noah

I blinked away my surprise and caressed my hands down Charlotte's legs instead. This was more than okay with me, anyway. The black lace wrapped around her hips was see-through and sexy as hell. If anything, I was grateful. She looked so good lying across the tangle of my sheets in nothing but that tiny scrap of black fabric.

I flashed her a wicked smile and slid down, positioning myself between her parted legs. I dropped kisses across her trembling stomach, giving her plenty of warning of what I intended to do. She didn't stop me, though. Her hands raked through my hair, encouraging me to do it.

So I settled in, nestling between her thighs, and hooked a finger in the crotch of her panties. As soon as I pulled the fabric out of my way, my mouth was on her.

The gasp that tore from Charlotte's mouth was epic.

She bucked as my tongue fluttered over her skin, and her fingers tightened in my hair. Shit, she was so warm and soft and wet . . . I closed my lips around her clit and sucked oh-so-gently, but she jolted like it sent an electric shock through her system.

"You like that, huh?" I whispered. She had her eyes closed, but I was sure she could hear the wicked grin on my face.

Her only answer was a quick, jerking nod, and her eyebrows pulled together as if she were trying to focus on the sensations.

I used the tip of my tongue to tease her. To draw needy moans from her lips, and trembling quivers from the legs wrapped around my head. She was so fucking responsive, my dick jerked, wanting to remind me of its presence.

Like I could fucking forget.

While one hand was busy holding her panties to the side, I shoved the other down between my body and the bed and massaged my erection. I varied the speed of my mouth between long, slow licks and fast, furious flutters, trying to gauge which she preferred, but it was impossible to tell.

It seemed like this girl was a fan of everything.

One of her hands vanished from my head so it could glide up the length of her body and came to a stop on her breast. She squeezed and rolled her palm in a circle, moving like a mindless, sexual creature.

Fucking hell. She was so goddamn sexy.

And I was kind of floored by it. With all my experience, I'd never seen a woman this young be so assertive. So confident. Charlotte wasn't timid or bashful or worried that I might judge her.

Plus, none of this seemed to be an act, or a performance for my benefit. It felt . . . genuine. It was such a turn-on, I felt a crushing need to bring her to orgasm, and to do it now. To show her just how sexy she was.

I abandoned my dick and slid my index finger as deep inside her as I could.

"God, *yes*," she breathed.

The muscles inside her clamped down when I began to pulse my finger, swiping my tongue across her clit in a matching rhythm. Her hips rocked, moving her pussy against my mouth to the exact angle she wanted.

"Noah," she whined.

I didn't lift my head, didn't pause my tempo. "Hmm?"

"You're going to make me come."

That's the plan.

She'd said it like a warning. Maybe she was enjoying herself and didn't want to come so soon, but I wasn't sure how much longer I could hold out. I *wanted* her. I wanted her almost as badly as I wanted to push her over the edge into ecstasy, and my body and mind were at war with each other.

Wait, no. This war was stupid. I knew what needed to happen.

I kept up my driving tempo, even as I pushed a second finger inside her, and swirled the tip of my tongue against her velvety soft skin. The pitch of her moans changed, as did her hurried breaths, swelling toward the big finish.

And when it happened, she left no doubt about it.

"Oh, my God, I'm gonna . . . " Her back bowed and every muscle in her seemed to tense, and she cried the word like I'd ripped it from her lungs. "*Fuck.*"

She writhed as the orgasm rolled through her, and I watched with both satisfaction and lust. Her pussy's rhythmic clenching on my fingers was echoed with the throb of my cock. And the sound of her moans filled the room and clouded my head, pushing all thoughts away but the girl quivering beneath me, splayed across my bed.

I'd always enjoyed making my partner come, but I didn't remember it being this . . . *pleasurable.*

When her gasps and gulps of air began to quiet, I could hear my pulse thundering in my ears. It turned out that making her climax had a powerful effect on both of us.

I crawled up the length of her body and collapsed onto my side next to her, planting a kiss on her bare shoulder. It was tame, but I figured she'd probably like a few more moments to recover. Her orgasm had sounded consuming.

Plus, I still had my pants on and needed to get to work rectifying that.

My hands damn near shook as I undid the button and jerked down my zipper. I moved with speed, but was clumsy with desire, and I only had my jeans and underwear pushed down around my knees when Charlotte's hand locked on my shoulder. She shoved me, forcing me to roll onto my back, and climbed on top of me.

I grinned up at her in pleasant surprise. There was that assertiveness I liked so much. But she was straddling me, and when she ground her body against mine, all thought evaporated.

Her sexy panties were the only barrier between us, and the fabric was whisper thin. It meant I could feel every move she made as she rocked her body over me. Every slide of her hot pussy along the length of my cock. Each rotation of her hips, which pressed the damp fabric against my sensitized skin.

Fuck, it made me wild. I was drunk with lust and filled my hands with the weight of her small, perfect tits. I didn't deserve a night like this. Didn't think it was even possible to still pull a girl this hot, and yet, here we were. Only a heartbeat away from sex—

Oh, shit.

Where the fuck had I packed my condoms?

Before the move, I'd emptied my nightstand drawers. They had to be in one of the boxes in the bathroom. But which one?

I've been so distracted with that thought, I hadn't realized Charlotte was slowly working her way down my body. As she mouthed kisses down my bare chest, her hand closed around my dick.

One firm tug from her wrung a groan of pleasure from me, and my vision hazed. The second pump of her fist felt even better, and I had to lock my teeth to prevent another moan from escaping.

The ends of her long hair trailed over my skin as she continued to move down, making her way toward my waist. Was she going to—?

"*Yes,*" I sighed.

Her mouth was like lava when it closed around me, and the power of it forced my eyes shut. She kept going, too, nearly to the base. It was instinctual, the way my hips thrust, trying to get her all the way down, but she seemed prepared for it and retreated.

Her tongue swirled and her cheeks hollowed out as she sucked. The heat of it moved through my legs like an electric current. My heart fell out of rhythm and sputtered along. And it was almost impossible to catch my breath.

Once again, my body and my mind went to war with each other. This blowjob felt so fucking amazing I didn't want it to end, but at the same time . . . I wanted to be buried deep inside her pussy, not just her mouth. It was more fun if we were both getting off.

I watched the mesmerizing bob of her head, and my fists clenched at the sensation. She was, like, way too good at this. If she wasn't careful, I was going to finish in her mouth.

Charlotte was focused, as if determined to make that

happen. I unclenched one hand and used a fingertip to trace a line on her forehead, sweeping back the hair out of her eyes. They fluttered open, and her gaze reeled around until it locked on mine.

The connection between us pulled taut as she stared up at me, her lips wrapped around the thick length of my cock, which was wet and glistening with her saliva. The image of it sent another surge of lust coursing through me.

It came out in a low, rushed voice. “Do you want me to grab a condom?”

She hesitated, considering something. Then, she backed off me, leaving her lips beside the tip of my dick. “Uh . . . that’s okay.”

Um, what?

Did she mean she wanted to have sex *without* a condom? Because that was a hard no for me, an absolute dealbreaker. I liked kids well enough—but I didn’t want them right now, and I definitely didn’t want them with a woman who was nearly a stranger.

Plus, while I liked taking risks in my life, gambling with my health wasn’t one of them.

Her lips parted and she slipped me in her mouth once more, but I was too distracted to completely enjoy it. I peered down at her over my heaving chest. “I guess I was asking,” I whispered, “if you were ready for me to fuck you.”

I’d meant for it to sound seductive, but maybe my tone had been off. Charlotte jerked back, letting my dick fall from her mouth and land with a *thump* on my stomach. Her expression was difficult to read, like a mixture of embarrassment and shame, and I didn’t understand at all.

Had I offended her? Because up until now, I’d thought her

signals had been clear and she wanted this as much as I did. Cold worry swept through my chest. Had I moved too fast? Made her uncomfortable, and she'd only gone down on me out of obligation, feeling like she needed to return the favor?

"I, um . . . " Unexpected color warmed her cheeks, and her gaze ran from mine. "I don't do that on the first date." Her throat bobbed with a heavy swallow. "Sorry."

It was weird to feel both disappointment and relief at the same time. Did I want to slide inside her and find out just how sexually compatible we were? Sure. But I liked doing all the other stuff a lot too, and it was hard to be disappointed about her just wanting to suck my cock.

I tilted my head and pushed out a smile. "There's no reason to be sorry."

"I should have told you sooner," she said, "but you're really fucking hot, and it's been a while for me, and I got impatient." She pressed her lips together for a moment, and then the truth spilled out. "I was worried if you found out you weren't going to get laid, you'd want to stop."

I let out a breath. Somewhere in her past, she'd probably had that experience.

God, I wanted to shake my head. I knew there were people out there who only did oral if they thought it was going to lead somewhere, or that it was all or nothing when it came to sex—

Those people were fucking idiots.

To me, sex encompassed a hell of a lot more than just putting a dick in a pussy, and I found all forms of sex and foreplay satisfying. So if she didn't want to go any farther tonight, that was no problem.

"I didn't mean to tease you," she continued. "I was going

to let you finish in my mouth."

Her earnest tone and eager expression punched a laugh from my chest. "Oh, were you?"

The corner of her mouth quirked into a sultry smile. "Yes, Daddy."

It was unclear if she was joking or half serious. But there it was again, this strange feeling of excitement running through me. Why was I kind of into it? I didn't get a chance to examine it further, because Charlotte lowered back down, taking me in her mouth.

This time, she kept her eyes open and focused on me.

The connection of our gazes while her cheeks hollowed out, and the deep pull of my dick into the back of her throat, was straight fire. Once again, my fists clenched the sheets beneath me. I was nearly naked, and the ceiling fan was on, but I began to sweat anyway.

"That feels," I said between two enormous breaths, "so fucking good."

She made a noise of approval, like a hum, and the vibration just kicked everything up another notch. I didn't make any attempt to leash my moans. I wanted her to hear how much I was enjoying it.

Not that there was any doubt in her mind, given the way I moved, subtly bucking my hips. The steady stroke of her mouth began to pick up the pace, while her luscious tongue flicked over my tip and the sensitive underside.

I didn't know how long she spent going down on me. Time seemed to suspend. At one point, she shifted on the bed, adjusting to a more comfortable position. Then her hand joined the mix. Her fingers wrapped around the base of my cock, gripping tightly, and the intense pressure squeezed a groan of pleasure from my body.

I loved how she wasn't delicate with me. Like she somehow knew if it was too much, I'd tell her. Her fist pumped in time with her mouth, making my slippery skin glide in and out of her grip.

She'd given me the heads up, so it only seemed fair to return the favor, and my words came out like gravel was lodged in my throat. "Fuck, you're going to make me come."

She gave another one of those sexy hums, and the orgasm that had seemed close was suddenly right on top of me.

Up until now, I'd been good. I'd avoided trying to take over, to take control. But my mind was no longer operating at one hundred percent, and my body took charge. My hands delved into her hair, holding her head still so I could pump from below.

I shouldn't have been surprised that she was into me fucking her mouth like this. Rough and mindless. But Charlotte held perfectly still, making it easy for me to move how I wanted to. When a sexy moan bubbled up from deep inside her, it pushed me past the point of no return.

Heat fired through my limbs.

It traveled along every scalding nerve ending until it reached my center, and I came in a long, loud rush. True to her word, she didn't retreat as my dick pulsed and filled her mouth with my cum. I shuddered with each wave, turned my head to the side, and groaned from the overwhelming pleasure.

When the pressure changed and she swallowed, the intense sensation made me flinch and contract. Charlotte sat up, swiped a finger across her lips, then collapsed beside me on the bed so we were both staring up at the spinning ceiling fan. The bare, warm skin of her arm pressed to mine, and maybe she was hoping to nestle in against me, but I wasn't ready for that.

My recovery was slow.

I pushed out a long breath and hung my forearm over my forehead, using the back of my wrist to wipe away the sweat that clung there. My heart was beating faster than the ringing bell at close of business, and the rest of me was heavy and unmovable.

And yet a lightweight feeling washed through me, like a fleeting moment of euphoria.

When it was over, I rolled onto my side to face her, not caring that my pants and underwear were still awkwardly bunched around my calves. Her gaze stayed fixed on the ceiling, and I watched the rapid rise and fall of her chest. Maybe she needed to recover too.

She could sense my gaze was on her, but she didn't turn her head when she spoke. "Thanks for tonight." Her voice fell to a hush. "I know it's weird to say, but I . . . needed it."

There was a tug in my chest, like a rope being pulled taut. The force of it was so intense, I struggled to reply. "Anytime." It had come out sounding playful, but I'd meant it. "I needed it too."

She finally turned to look at me, and her eyes were unfocused. Was she adrift in her thoughts? I reached over and trailed my fingers along her jaw line, urging her to come closer and meet me halfway for a kiss.

There was another pull in my chest when our mouths came together, and this time it was more powerful. Far too big to write off or ignore. I had the terrifying thought that my body longed for her, like a magnet when it came close to another, drawn together.

I didn't want a conventional relationship, and I wasn't interested in romance or finding a soul mate. It meant I didn't 'date,' at least not in the traditional sense.

And yet, at the end of our kiss, the question just popped out of my mouth. "So, when's our next date?"

Charlotte drew in a deep breath, and her gaze dropped from mine. She stared at the center of my chest like it was more interesting than her Instagram feed. Abruptly, she turned and flopped over onto her back. Her face skewed with an expression that looked a hell of a lot like distress.

"About that," she said.

But nothing followed it.

She paused for so long I wasn't sure anything else was coming, and the moment hung tense between us. Was she going to reveal she didn't want anything else from me? I should have been excited about her hesitation. I'd brought her home, hoping for that outcome.

So why the fuck was I worried she was going to say this was a one-time thing?

Finally, she pushed out what she'd been holding on to. "I know I said I don't have sex on the first date, and I don't, but . . . "

Oh. I let out a knowing laugh. "Not on the second date either, huh?"

She shook her head. "I don't sleep with a guy," she turned and set her nervous gaze on mine, "until I'm in love with him."

I froze, and a million thoughts darted through my brain in that moment, but only a single word could escape my lips. "Oh."

It was clear she was waiting for more from me, but what

the fuck was I supposed to say? I was willing to explore more with her, but *love*?

That wasn't going to happen.

Getting involved with her would be cruel—I'd just be leading her on.

"Well, full disclosure," I said, "I don't really do 'love.'"

She looked dubious. "What do you mean, you don't do 'love?'"

My post orgasm brain left me unfiltered. "I've got a lot going on right now. I don't have time for it."

It was like I told her I only wanted to invest in GameStop. "I'm sorry, you don't have time for it? Who doesn't have time for love?"

I didn't like how judgmental she was being, even if part of me worried she had a point. "Seriously, I don't have time for it." I mashed the pillow under my head and frowned. I needed to be truthful and set expectations. "Really, I don't have any interest in it. Maybe you think that makes me a dick, but I'm being honest here. I don't want or need romance."

Charlotte's mouth hung open as she processed my statement.

Then confusion narrowed her eyes. "Okay, why'd you ask me for a second date?" Disgust abruptly swept through her face. "Oh, I gotcha. You'll pretend you're interested until you close the deal, and then you'll ghost me."

Irritation heated me up, but it was partially self-directed. I understood that it sounded bad, but . . . "That wasn't what I was going to do."

She didn't believe a word of it, judging by the way she sat up, fished her bra from the tangled sheets, and hurried to put it on.

"Okay, just wait a minute. Let me explain."

Um, how are you going to do that? You don't even know why you asked her for a second date.

She turned to look at me over her shoulder, waiting impatiently for me to continue. I scratched the center of my forehead, willing the words to come.

"I don't date," I said. "Not in the traditional way, at least. I do better when my relationships are," I searched for the right word, "transactional."

"Transactional," she repeated, and her tone turned bitter. "*Nice*."

"It's better that way," I admitted. "The relationships in my past were complicated." How much detail was I supposed to give her? "When I was in New York, all I cared about was my job. I was too focused on that to do the things I needed to do, so every one of my relationships suffered. Not just the romantic ones, either."

She wasn't convinced. "But you're not in New York anymore."

I reached down and pulled up my pants. "It's not going to be any different here."

"You don't know that." She said it like a child trying to reason to get what they wanted.

I finished buttoning my pants and gave her the most direct look I possessed. "I don't *want* it to be any different here. It's better to not get attached to me, because ultimately, I'm just going to let you down."

She blinked, staring at me with disbelief. "Seriously? Do other girls buy that shit?"

"What?"

Charlotte climbed off the bed, snatched up her pants,

and shoved her foot into one of the legs. "The idea that you won't date someone 'for their own good.' That you're—what? Saving them from falling in love with you and getting their heart broken?"

I frowned and got off the bed on the side opposite her. It made me sound like an asshole, but I lifted a hand in surrender. "It's the truth."

"Sounds more like an excuse." She jerked her pants up and did up the fly, and her tone filled with sarcasm. "Why buy the cow when you can get the milk for free, am I right?"

I fucking hated that saying, and my frustration got the better of me. "Some people don't need love in a relationship to feel fulfilled. In fact, some people don't even need love to have sex."

Her shoulders tensed, and she drew in a sharp breath. I hadn't meant to be so cutting, and so my words sliced us both. And while the bed was a physical divide between us, it suddenly felt wider than a football field.

"Well," she said, yanking her shirt over her head, "I do."

"Why?"

Her movements slowed. "What do you mean, *why*?"

"We did a lot of things tonight, Charlotte. We got naked and we went down on each other. Wasn't that a kind of sex?" I realized how confrontational my posture had become and tried to relax, softening my voice. "I'm just curious as to why full-on sex is too much, but everything else is okay." The idea popped into my head and was out before I could think better of it. "Is it, like, a way to keep your body count low?"

Well, shit.

Shock wasn't a strong enough word for emotion that splashed across her face. She lifted her chin and glared at me.

"I don't have to explain myself to you."

"No, you don't. I'm sorry. Forget I said anything."

It wasn't fucking likely because she turned and strode for the door. *Fuck.* I picked up my shirt and tugged it on while chasing after her.

I caught up to her in the entryway, and the Uber app was open on the screen of her phone. I scrubbed a hand over my face while coming up with a way to repair the damage I'd done.

"I didn't answer your question," I said. "I didn't ask for a second date just so I could fuck you." Could she hear how genuine I was? I hoped my expression made it clear I was serious. "I asked because I want to see you again."

She lifted her distrustful gaze from the screen.

"You should say no," I told her. "I'm sure we're at different places in our lives, and we want different things, and it's probably a bad idea." A frustrated sigh escaped my lungs. "But if you give me your number, Charlotte, I'm going to call you."

There was a flickering spark of hope in her eyes, but it quickly died. "And then what? I don't want a 'transactional relationship,' whatever the fuck that is." She punched the icon on her screen, ordering her ride, and then leveled a pointed gaze at me. "You say you don't have time for love, but I don't have time to waste on a guy who's telling me that dating him is never going to lead to anywhere."

She was absolutely right, so why the hell did I feel this urge to push back, to try to encourage her to give me a chance? I should be smart and overrule the feeling.

She's too young for you anyway.

"Give me your number," I demanded.

She shook her head and reached for the door. "Have a nice life, Noah."

SIX

Charlotte

Tonight had been a rollercoaster of emotions, so I should have known there was another steep drop waiting for me when I got home.

My mom was in the kitchen, washing dishes when I came in, and she didn't even look up from her task as I toed off my shoes.

"Your father wants to talk to you. He's in the living room."

My stomach twisted into a tight ball, and for a split second, I considered running away. But I wasn't a little girl anymore, and running away had gotten me into this situation in the first place. I straightened my shoulders, tucked a lock of hair behind my ear, and tried to sound nonchalant. "Did he say what it was about?"

"You'd have to ask him." Her tone was a total mystery.

Either she knew and was purposefully being vague, or she hadn't a clue—and it was most likely the second one. My mother was born and raised in West Virginia, growing up in an ultra-traditional household, and like her mother, she was content to be the picture perfect little housewife.

My father made all the decisions and rules, and she was utterly submissive to him. She loved it, too—I'd swear she was never happier than when she was setting dinner on the table. I didn't quite get it, but who was I to complain? She was a great mom.

There was a set of pans beside the sink, waiting their turn to get scrubbed. "You want me to help you finish those?" I asked.

It wasn't just a stall tactic. All my life, my mother had been obsessed with keeping a clean house, and it had rubbed off on me. I felt the urge to wipe down the countertops, to dry the dishes in the drying rack and put them away.

It was why it had taken every fiber of my being not to start cleaning at Noah's house earlier. He was a bachelor, and I knew I shouldn't have expected much, but—damn. He was messy.

Fuck me, the whole evening had been *messy.*

"No, thanks," my mom said. "I've got it. Go see your father."

I swallowed a breath and made my way toward the living room.

There was some college football rerun playing on the TV, but my dad wasn't paying any attention to it. He sat on the couch, his laptop was set up on a TV tray in front of him, and he had his phone pressed to one ear.

My dad was a powerful guy. He ran one of the most successful talent agencies in Nashville, and right now he seemed so deep in his conversation that nothing else existed. I hesitated in the doorway. He looked busy, and I could come back—

Come here, he motioned as soon as his gaze landed on me. Then he flung that finger toward the empty spot beside him on the couch.

Without uttering a single word, I could tell he was upset with me, and I trudged my way toward him. Oh, no. What had I done? I sifted through the day's events, trying to figure out what the issue might be.

I'd been good, hadn't I?

Shit, I *hated* this new dynamic between us.

Growing up, I'd always been a daddy's girl, and my parents had showered me with love and praise. We never fought. I never got into trouble. And they never pushed back when I wanted something. If I made a mistake, they were willing to give me an endless number of second chances.

Everything had been so . . . easy.

Looking back now, I was well aware I'd taken it all for granted.

But I'd been young and dumb, leading to my idiotic decision to go back to school, even though I'd never been that strong of a student. My father had moved Heaven and Earth to make it possible, pulling strings and calling in favors to get me into Davidson University.

I'd probably never know what all he had to do, but I was fairly certain he'd needed to get Stella, his biggest client, involved. And because she was such a sweetheart, she'd done it for both of us.

My first year of school wasn't that bad or hard. But the second year? God, how I struggled. The classes were boring, and college wasn't at all what I'd thought it would be. Everyone was so serious and knew exactly what they wanted to do. I even tried switching my major from business to marketing before the spring semester, but it didn't help much.

Also not helping was that I met Zach in the spring at a March Madness watch party one of my friends hosted. He was older, alumni, and I think I was already halfway in love with him by the end of the night.

As time marched on, I realized trying to get a degree had been a terrible idea.

There was no way I could endure another two years of

it, and once I'd come to that conclusion, it was impossible to get motivated to go to class. So of course I didn't pass most of them.

When my parents checked my grades, it was the first time they truly looked disappointed in me. It was such a strange, uncomfortable feeling that I panicked. I swore to them it was a fluke. Next year would be better, I promised.

My parents reluctantly agreed but cautioned me against spending too much time with the new boyfriend. I agreed that when the summer was over, I'd buckle down and get my college career back on track.

I couldn't see it then, but the thing that attracted me the most to Zach—besides his looks—was how unserious he was. Sure, he had an okay job and a decent apartment, but I ignored all the red flags waving right in my face.

It wasn't right that a thirty-year-old guy wanted to spend every weekend hanging out at his old college. Or how he was so comfortable dating a girl who was eight years younger than him and was at a totally different stage of her life. I didn't see that I was just a way for him to relive his college glory days.

The love I had for him was blinding.

My parents weren't nearly as fooled. My dad tried to hide his unease with my much older boyfriend, and of course my mom deferred to whatever my dad did, but they knew how wrapped up in him I'd become. It was clear I hung on his every word, and they sensed my participation in school was suffering because of it.

Over the fall, my father's passive aggressive statements about the age difference grew louder and more direct, but I brushed him off.

The first fight we ever had came after my dad's stern

warning. If I failed out of school, I was told, there'd be no more chances. There'd also be no more campus apartment, no more car, and no more credit card.

Long overdue tough love, my dad had announced. He threatened I'd be on my own—but this felt hollow. A bluff.

I was certain he didn't mean it, not really.

At that point, I'd sunk so much into Zach, it was too late. I was spending nearly every night at his apartment anyway. In the mornings, he'd go to work, and I'd tidy up the apartment, run his errands for him, then spend the day making TikTok videos instead of going to class.

I'd been so fucking stupid thinking he loved me, it was embarrassing. I cringed now at the idea I'd been invaluable to him.

The truth was I'd become Zach's bang maid.

When I officially failed out of school, I put off telling my parents for as long as possible. I made up excuses, like my professors were slow to put my final scores in, or that the school's website kept erroring out when I tried to look up my grades. My panic and shame were so intense, I could barely breathe.

And when I couldn't avoid it any longer, I did something really, *really* stupid.

I used my credit card, the one my parents paid for and said was only for emergencies, to book me and Zach an expensive trip to Hawaii.

They didn't find out until we landed in Honolulu, and my father was so angry, he threatened to get on the next flight out and come get me. I dug in, refusing to tell him where we were, and I justified it to myself saying I needed the escape. More importantly, I needed the romantic trip to sweeten

Zach up, because at the end of it I'd have to ask if I could move in with him.

When we went to check out of the hotel, my credit card was declined, and Zach was so pissed he had to pay for it that he barely said two words to me during either of the long flights home.

My parents were waiting for me at my apartment.

I'd never had my father's harsh tone directed at me. "You have two choices, young lady," he'd said. "Leave him and come home, where we can work through this." He'd crossed his arms over his chest and glared at my boyfriend, like Zach was the cause of all this. "Or stay with him, and we're done financially supporting you."

"Come on, man," Zach scoffed. "She's an adult."

Which was ironic because my boyfriend never treated me like one.

But how could I choose anything other than him? He was my whole world, plus walking away meant I'd have to admit I'd made a mistake and face consequences. It was too scary to do anything but stay.

And it broke my father's fucking heart.

The guilt it caused was so crushing, my knees went weak and I'd struggled to stay upright as my parents left.

I moved in with Zach the following afternoon, but he made it clear that this was his space and not *ours*. He was doing me an enormous favor and reminded me of it every chance he got. There was nothing I could do. I had nowhere else to go because my father had paid to break the lease on my apartment.

Surely, he'd done it to force me to come home, but I told myself I didn't care. I was an adult and could make it on my own, I lied to myself. I refused to think about the damage I had caused because it was too shameful. Too painful.

By February, less than two months after moving in, the cracks in my relationship began to form. Once we hit March, they grew too big to ignore. Zach was frustrated all the time, upset that I didn't look harder for a job, especially because he didn't make enough to support us both.

He didn't care I was slipping into depression.

"Stop feeling sorry for yourself," he snapped one evening after he came home from work and discovered me watching Netflix. "You did this. You made this choice, and you forced it on me."

Our fairy tale romance became a nightmare. He spent every weekend at the college bars, and I grew tired of going with him. He typically ignored me the whole evening, and . . . God. Neither of us were college students anymore. Why did he even like this?

It wasn't exactly fair, but I began to resent him.

He bitched endlessly about not having any money, but he never had a problem buying overpriced beers and greasy food. Sometimes, he'd even splurge and buy drinks for people he'd just met. Kids, really. He craved their attention, wanting to be known as the 'big man on campus.' I didn't understand it at all.

When I started sleeping on the couch, that was the final straw, the end of our relationship.

"Pay rent or move out," Zach announced at the end of April, his tone cold and indifferent and like he'd never loved me at all.

"I don't have anywhere to go," I said.

He looked at me like I was an idiot. "Of course you do. Go

home, Charlotte."

As hard as our breakup had been, I also felt an enormous sense of relief when it was over. Like I'd been released from some kind of spell. As if I'd been given permission to finally make the right choice.

I dreaded calling my dad, but I also longed to hear his voice, and I cried so much during our conversation, he barely understood any of it. He stayed stoic, though, unmoved by my tears. Maybe he thought they were a ploy to soften him up, but they'd been one thousand percent genuine. At the end of it, he told me he'd clear his schedule and where I could meet him for lunch.

Our conversation in person lasted more than two hours, and I shook like a leaf the whole time. At least I came prepared—not just to face the consequences either. After several apologies and a hell of a lot more tears, I laid out a plan for me to come home.

I'd do whatever my parents asked—without question—and earn back their trust. I'd get a job and put myself on a repayment schedule for the trip to Hawaii. It might take years, but I was committed.

I was determined to show them I understood how badly I had fucked up.

He listened to me with the skepticism of a man who'd been burned before. Then he sighed heavily, said he'd talk it over with my mom and get back to me. I spent a sleepless night on the floor of my friend's dorm room, and in the morning my father called.

I was allowed to come home.

It would be probationary, he warned. They wouldn't be giving me back my car or my credit cards any time soon, and if I was caught lying or refused to do something they asked of me, the deal would be off.

I couldn't agree to it fast enough.

The first few days after I'd moved back into my old room were . . . awkward. I danced around my folks like the floor was made of eggshells, doing everything in my power to be helpful and perfect.

And now here it was, three weeks after I'd moved in, that we'd encountered our first issue. I sat with my back straight on the couch, dutifully waiting for him to finish his phone call. When it was over, he set his phone down and closed his laptop, giving me his full attention.

My breath stuck awkwardly in my lungs.

"How did your date with Preston go?" His tone was easy, but there was nothing casual about his question.

I pressed my lips together and swallowed hard. I hadn't told anyone about it, only that I was meeting a friend for a drink. "How did you know?"

"I didn't. It was a guess. Erika overheard him in the office when he asked for your number." He settled back into his seat and a slight frown crossed his expression. "Is there a reason you didn't tell me?"

My shoulders sagged. "I wasn't trying to keep it from you, I swear. I'm not interested in him like that. Honestly, I wish I hadn't said yes to him."

My dad softened a degree. "That bad, huh?"

"It wasn't great."

He nodded his understanding. "I'm sorry to hear that. He seems like a good enough kid and he's your age, but you can't have a relationship with him."

"Why's that?" My heart beat faster. Was this the moment

my parents told me I'd need their approval on who I dated?

"Because his company is handling Troy's release party and you're going to be working for Warbler. So you'll need to steer clear of anyone involved with the company."

I had my hands in my lap and tried not to fidget with my fingers. "Are you putting me back on the receptionist desk full time?"

God, please, no.

I'd done that job for a year after graduating from high school, and I despised it. I wasn't any good at it, and the one day I'd filled in this week had been torture.

"No, your mom made a suggestion, and I think it's a great idea. I was complaining about how messy the Warbler office has been getting recently, and she said you might like tidying it up." He plastered on a smile. "We'd knock two hundred off your debt for each visit, and I was thinking twice a week."

I held perfectly still, trying not to show my dismay. "You want me to be a . . . janitor?"

He laughed lightly. "I was thinking more like a cleaning lady, but if you want to call it that, that's fine." He gazed at me like this was a pretty sweet offer. "What do you say? I don't need another receptionist. Irene does a great job, plus, I didn't think you liked it all that much."

No, I didn't.

And I didn't *hate* cleaning either, but . . . shit. He'd posed it as a question, and there was only one answer I could give. I'd promised them I'd do whatever they wanted, even if that meant swallowing my pride.

"Okay." I mustered a weak smile and attempted to sound pleased, even though I hated the idea. "What days do you want me to come in?"

The silver lining to having my new 'job' was I got access to my car again. I parked on the street outside of Warbler Entertainment, turned off the ignition, and glanced at the bucket full of cleaning supplies sitting in my passenger seat.

Just how I wanted to spend my Friday evening.

I pushed the thought away. I'd earned this humble sandwich, and I was going to eat it. So I grabbed the bucket's handle, got out of the car, and made my way up the sidewalk toward the building.

It was a little after six p.m. and the sun was sinking in the sky, so it cast a warm glow on the historic house that had been converted into Warbler's office. The main floor was the only part I'd need to deep clean, and as I stared up at the building, I was grateful. The second floor was the recording studio and green room, and my only responsibility up there was to dust and sweep the floors.

There wasn't anybody at the front desk or in the main room. No one was working late except my father, which was to be expected. Most of the Warbler team barely came to the office, anyway. Their business was done at venues or over lunch or on the road.

I set my bucket on Irene's desk, pulled on a pair of bright yellow rubber gloves, and surveyed the area, planning the most efficient strategy. There were two more desks in the room, each with a swivel chair behind it and a pair of comfy chairs situated in front of them. They were spots for employees to use when meeting with clients or doing some work in the office, and since they didn't 'belong' to anyone, the surfaces were bare.

My mother had taught me to clean from the top down, and start with the left wall and work my way around the room. I'd dust, empty trash cans, and then vacuum, I decided. Even though the floors were carpeted, I realized I'd need a broom. I'd learned a handy trick of putting a microfiber cloth over the top of the broomstick and using that as a duster for places too high to reach.

The broom and the vacuum were in a utility closet off the kitchen, so I headed that way. When I came around the hallway corner and stepped onto the linoleum floor, I pulled to a stop. A surprised sound burst from my lips.

The kitchen was a mess.

I should have remembered from when I worked here that Fridays were always the worst. People were too busy gearing up for the weekend to be considerate of others. A large collection of used coffee mugs and dirty plates from past lunches were stacked precariously beside the sink. The pot on the coffee maker was half full but looked like it hadn't been used for days. Christ, there was no telling how old that coffee was.

But all of this wasn't what had startled me.

It was because the kitchen wasn't empty.

A man stood with his back to me, washing something in the sink. I was pretty sure I knew everyone on staff at Warbler, yet I'd never seen this guy before. My entrance surprised him too, and he turned to glance at me—

"What the fuck?" I blurted.

I had been so, so wrong. I'd seen this man before . . . because he was the one I'd gone home with last night.

The same shock I felt was reflected perfectly on Noah's handsome face. He stood frozen, simply staring at me while water continued to flow from the faucet behind him. His question came low and crowded with confusion. "Charlotte?"

I was going to ask what the hell was he doing here, but heavy footsteps approached.

"Oh, you're here," my father said, although it was unclear who he was talking to.

The doorway to the kitchen was narrow, and he had me boxed in. It left me with no choice but to step forward and move closer, which I really didn't want to do. The proximity to Noah felt . . . dangerous. Just seeing him again made me question if I'd made the right choice leaving him last night, even when I knew it'd been the right one. He kept his gaze fixed on me, even as he reached back to shut off the running water, but then his attention shifted to the man who strolled in to stand beside me.

My father didn't sense an ounce of tension in the room. He gave Noah a once-over, and his tone was horrifyingly familiar. "Didn't realize you were still here."

"I just had a Zoom meeting with Michelle at SoFi," Noah answered like he'd been accused of something. "It was the only time she had available in her schedule."

My dad nodded, then cast a hand in my direction. "This is my daughter Charlotte." He flashed his signature smile, the one that could diffuse almost any situation and turn strangers into instant friends. "Charlotte, this is Noah Robinson. He's our new VP of booking."

My dad wasn't studying Noah the way I was, so he didn't see the other man's reaction to this information. He didn't notice how Noah's shoulders straightened, or that his Adam's apple moved with a thick swallow.

Noah's voice was just slightly off-kilter as he thrust his

hand forward. "Hey. Nice to meet you."

My breath got stuck in my lungs. My cheeks flamed hot, and it grew more intense with each passing second when I didn't reach out to take his hand.

After I'd left his place last night, I'd been sure I'd never see him again, so this moment felt so fucking cruel.

He'd said he was a stockbroker, hadn't he? What the hell was this finance bro doing at Warbler as a vice president? And a VP of booking, no less. It meant he didn't just work for my father—he worked *closely* with him.

"What happened to Huston?" I demanded, angry that no one had mentioned this new hire when I'd filled in for Irene earlier this week.

"He wants to retire," my dad said, "but he agreed to stay on and help Noah with the transition." My father's concerned gaze bounced from me to Noah's extended hand, which I was still ignoring. He had to utter it under his breath. "Don't be rude."

I clamped my teeth together and went to reach for the offered handshake, only to draw back my hand at the last second. *Fuck.* I was wearing those terribly unsexy yellow rubber gloves, the ones that went all the way to my elbows, and I pulled one off in such a hurry, the rubber snapped painfully against my skin.

"Nice to meet you, too," I said, clasping Noah's hand.

It was just a basic handshake, but the contact of his skin pressed to mine sent sensations from last night flooding through my mind and body. Could he tell? His eyes widened, and he pulled in a short breath.

"She's going to be helping us out here for the next few months," my dad announced.

Noah dropped my hand like it was made of lead, but he kept his tone light and curious. "Yeah? With what?"

"She'll be responsible for cleaning the office twice a week."

I wasn't sure if there was a flicker of disdain in his eyes, or if I just expected it to be there, projecting my shame onto him.

"Oh." It looked like he hadn't a fucking clue what to say to that. "That's nice."

"He's paying me," I said instantly—although I didn't know why. It wasn't like that made it any better.

"Yeah?" He gave a polite smile. "Do you do houses too?"

I don't think his joking tone had meant to tease, but I couldn't help myself. "Yours certainly needs it."

"What?" my father asked.

Shit.

Shit! The alarm that ran through Noah's expression was perfectly mirrored in my body.

"Uh . . . I mean, I assume," I babbled. "Since you probably just moved in."

"Yeah, you're right. Moving is messy." Noah lifted an eyebrow. "That's why my place is such a disaster."

My father was completely unaware of the subtext. "Is it? Well, I'm sure Charlotte would be happy to help you with that."

"Oh, Dad, that's okay—"

He didn't seem to hear me, and his focus stayed with Noah. "I'll give you her number, and you two should work something out." He leaned into me, bumping his shoulder gently against mine. "I know this one could use the extra cash."

God, kill me now.

I couldn't argue with him.

Not in front of Noah, and also because I'd promised to agree to whatever my parents wanted. Plus, my dad wasn't wrong—I *did* need the money. But my heart did a little somersault when I peered up at Noah.

For a split second, he looked like he'd just won some kind of battle.

Hadn't he? He'd wanted my number last night, and I'd refused to give it to him. Now my father was going to hand it over . . . and I couldn't do a thing to stop him.

But then Noah's smug expression dropped away, like he'd just remembered I was his boss's daughter and having any kind of relationship with me—even if it was just to clean his house—was a terrible idea.

"You don't have to do that," he said.

My father waved his hand. "Nonsense. She'd love to help, and I'm sure she'd be great."

"Really, it's okay," Noah said. "My house isn't that bad."

"Didn't you just use the word 'disaster?'" As soon as the question was out of my mouth, I wished I could suck it back in. What the hell was wrong with me?

The pitch of my father's voice lowered into seriousness. "Really, you'd be doing both of us a favor. Charlotte's in debt, and she needs the work."

Oh, my God. I stared wide-eyed at my dad and had to choke back the protest I wanted to make. The humiliation sliced through me, hot and stinging.

And I wasn't the only one feeling it. Noah's gaze darted away from me, like he wanted to pretend he hadn't heard it, so he could avoid any secondhand embarrassment.

One thing was clear, though.

Noah didn't want this arrangement any more than I did. Maybe my father couldn't see the desperate plea in the other man's eyes, but if he did, he chose to ignore it. He was unaware he was forcing this on a new employee, and that Noah probably felt trapped. He wasn't going to say no to his boss.

"In that case," he did his best impression of a deer caught in headlights, "that sounds . . . good."

Shit.

"Great," I bit out.

I couldn't look at either of them a moment longer. Instead, I busied myself pulling the rubber glove back on and began to plot how I could get out of this arrangement.

Because I could not clean his house.

I could not be around him again because he wasn't interested in giving me the kind of relationship I wanted, and I feared if I spent any more time with him, I wouldn't just waver on my 'no sex until love' rule . . .

I'd break it to smithereens.

SEVEN

Noah

On Tuesday, I made sure to finish all my meetings early, so it gave me time to put some of my shit away. Really, it gave me time to clean—which was fucking ridiculous.

Charlotte would be here soon to clean my house.

Or, at least, she'd come over to discuss that, and I thought we were both hoping our one meeting would be enough to appease her father.

I wasn't happy with the way my boss had foisted this upon me, but I was majorly pissed she was Ardy's daughter. I should have been glad for it because it was yet another reason to steer clear of her. My first year at HBHC, when I was young and dumb, I had fucked around with a coworker, and I wasn't going to make that mistake again.

Sex and business needed to stay separate.

So why the hell was I looking forward to seeing her again? It'd only been three days. And why did I like that her number was now saved in my phone?

I wiped a paper towel over my bathroom counter, cleaning up the loose whiskers left from my morning shave. That was when I noticed there was a glob of toothpaste in the sink and water spots splattered on the mirror.

No way was I going to have time to clean everything before she got here. In fact, I'd been doing triage for the last half hour, focusing on the worst, most embarrassing spots, and I doubted anyone would be able to tell.

Shit, why did I have to be such a slob?

When the doorbell rang, I angrily gazed at my watch. Was she early? I was supposed to have more time—

Nope. We'd said five, and it was exactly that. *Fuck.*

I tossed the paper towel in the garbage can, checked my reflection in the mirror, and headed toward the entryway. I pulled open the door, and as I took in the sight of her, my grip tightened instinctively on the doorframe.

The last time I'd seen her, she hadn't been prepared. She'd had on minimal makeup, her hair was pulled up in a messy bun, and she'd been wearing shorts and an old t-shirt. Today, she came ready, like she'd made an effort to look as tempting as possible.

Charlotte wore a pair of tight leggings, a purple sports bra, and a gauzy white shirt over it. The fabric was paper thin, so I could see her sexy bare stomach beneath it. Plus, the shirt was so loose fitting, it hung off one shoulder and exposed the intricate crisscrossing straps of her bra. Her hair was up in a smooth, sleek knot, and her makeup, while muted, was sultry.

The desire to peel her out of her clothes was so strong, so instantaneous, I went dizzy for a moment.

Internally, I wanted to scowl. Yes, she was hot, but she was too young for me, not to mention she was the boss's daughter. His *only* kid. Which meant she was probably spoiled as hell.

Her gaze worked its way up my body, and when her eyes focused on mine, her shoulders lifted with a heavy, preparing breath. "Hi."

"Hey," I said, backing away from the door to allow her space. "Come on in."

She stepped into my entryway, toed off her shoes without me asking, and peered around like she half-expected an ambush was waiting for her. When she didn't find one, her attention went to the living room.

"You made some progress," she said quietly.

I massaged the back of my neck. "Yeah. My parents came over and helped me out. Well, it was mostly my mom—my dad has a bad back and he just sat on the couch."

Um, why are you telling her this?

I gestured toward the space that was no longer a labyrinth of boxes. "You want to have a seat?"

She shook her head. "I'm good."

Her body language screamed she was uncomfortable and just wanted to get this thing over with, and I understood. I didn't like seeing her like this, feeling so awkward and unconfident.

I jammed my hands in the pockets of my jeans and did my best to act casual. "You don't have to do anything," I said. "You can tell him I changed my mind. Throw me under the bus if you want to."

"It's fine." Her words were clipped. "I need the money, and you need the help, right?"

I was trying to be a nice guy here. "Sure."

"Okay, what were you thinking? I mean, obviously, the kitchen. What else?"

Now I was irritated. "Uh . . . the bathrooms too, I guess."

"I don't do laundry." It came from her so abruptly, it was like she'd just thought of it. "I mean, I don't want to do *yours*. Bedding and towels are okay, but not clothes."

"Fine by me." I could certainly handle doing my own laundry. Plus, the idea of her doing it felt wrong.

"And I don't do windows. Too time consuming."

I nodded.

Then, she ticked her chin up, trying to look strong, but her uneven voice gave her away. "Bedrooms?"

There wasn't a point in cleaning the guest or spare rooms, but my bedroom was where I spent the majority of my time. "Just mine."

I hadn't put any heat into my words, but it didn't matter. Now we were both picturing the last time we'd been in there, and the air between us snapped tight.

Her effect on me was unreal and frustrating. Desire trapped inside me bounced around, searching for a weakness. It needed to escape, to have freedom and take what it wanted.

No. It's not allowed.

The fuck if that didn't make me want her more.

"And my office," I added.

She nodded. "Anything else?"

"I don't think so."

Charlotte began to move, strolling toward the kitchen, causing me to follow. "All right, I'm going to walk around and take a look." She pulled to a stop so suddenly, I nearly ran into her. "I mean, if that's all right with you? I'm trying to figure out how many hours I think it'll take so I can give you a quote."

I gestured toward the hallway. "Go ahead."

We didn't speak as she went room by room. There were no comments about the drastic improvement of my kitchen, with its empty sink and clean countertops. Nor did she say anything about the artwork hanging on the walls.

But she hesitated at the threshold to my bedroom.

"Everything all right?" I asked.

It forced her to keep moving, and she stepped inside the room, taking in her surroundings. "You made your bed today."

I smiled sheepishly. "I knew I was going to have company."

She turned in place, giving me a full view of her flat expression. "Don't think of me like that."

"Like what? A person?"

"Like a friend." She put a hand on her hip. "Maybe think of me as your employee."

I raised my eyebrows. "If you're asking to keep things strictly professional between us, I couldn't agree more, and you'll have no issues from my end."

"Good. That's good."

Her gaze shifted away to linger on my bed, and her expression turned cryptic. What was she thinking about?

Her voice lost some of its power. "Will you want to be here while I'm doing it?"

"While you're cleaning? I don't have to be." It seemed unlikely she was going to make off with any of my stuff. "Is that what you'd prefer?"

She looked relieved. "Yeah, if you don't mind." She pulled the neckline up over her bare shoulder, only for it to immediately slide off. "I don't want us to get in each other's way."

I was pretty sure I understood what she really meant, that this whole thing would be easier for her if she didn't have to see me. And why was that? Was I too tempting?

Stop thinking like that.

"Okay," I said. "Next time you come, I'll make sure I'm not around, but I've got too much to do to leave tonight."

She nodded, and with that settled, she padded on her socked feet into my bathroom. Her gaze swept over the large glass shower, the double vanity sinks, and the freestanding bathtub I doubted I'd ever use. Something caught her attention, and I watched her through the mirror as she marched toward the sink that was clearly mine.

A slow smile crept over her lips as she peered at the bare granite. "Did you clean before I got here?"

How the fuck could she tell? I shrugged one shoulder, pretending I didn't care and that I hadn't done it for her. "Maybe."

Her gaze lifted to connect with mine through the glass. For a split second, I saw the girl she'd been the other night, but a heartbeat later, she vanished. Charlotte turned, crossed her arms over her chest, and leaned back against the counter.

"One visit a week?" she asked.

I was one person. "Yeah, that should be plenty."

"I think it'll take me three hours, and my rate is forty an hour."

A humorless laugh punched free from my chest. "You're dreaming."

She tilted her head and shot me a hard look. "You have a big house, Noah. I don't think I can do it any faster—"

"No, you're dreaming about your rate." Explaining to Ardy why this deal with his daughter fell through should be easy now. "I looked at rates in this area, and most places don't charge more than twenty-five bucks." I spoke with the same direct tone I used when executing trades. "I'm doing you a favor; I'm not donating to *charity*."

Her eyes narrowed. "I guess I could do it for thirty."

"Twenty-five," I reiterated.

She committed the cardinal sin of negotiations when she dropped her arms, and a look of desperation overtook her face. She was letting her emotions drive the conversation, which had no place in our business discussion.

"Those other companies won't do as good of a job as I will."

Maybe she was right, but she sounded pouty, and that was the moment I knew I had won.

"Twenty-five is as high as I'm willing to go," I said flatly.

She glanced at the door to my bedroom like she was thinking about walking away, but I could practically see the thoughts in her mind. She needed this. I had all the leverage here, and she knew it.

She sighed with reluctance, although it felt forced. Like a production. As if the number she'd hoped to land on was twenty-five all along. "All right." She pushed off the counter and walked forward. "You've got yourself a deal."

I'd thought she was going to stop when she reached me, but she blew right past and marched into my bedroom. It left me feeling weirdly off-balance. "Don't you want to shake on it?"

"No." Her voice faded as she left the bedroom. "I've got too much work to do."

I held up my end of the deal, staying tucked away in my office and out of Charlotte's way as she got to work on the kitchen. As I read up on the markets and scrolled through financial subreddits, I could hear her moving around on the other side of the house. There was faint music, water occasionally being run from the tap, and the hissing sprays from a squirt bottle.

After she'd left my bedroom, she'd gone back to her car and brought in all her supplies, and then come into my office to show me a checklist on her phone of what she planned to do. I appreciated how organized she was, especially since she'd never done this professionally before.

"I watched some videos on how to start a cleaning service." The corner of her mouth quirked to the side. "If I'm going to do something, I want to be good at it."

"I can relate to that." Her ability to disarm my filter struck again. "That's why this first month at Warbler has been kind of stressful." I made a face. "Stressful is probably too strong a word, but this has been quite the career shift."

She slid her phone into the pocket on the side of her leggings and peered at me with curiosity. "Yeah, I was wondering about that. I know my dad's big on collecting people from wherever, but how does a stockbroker end up as Warbler's VP of Booking?"

"A valid question." I chuckled. "I grew up around the music industry. Really, my whole family did, because my dad got his start as a roadie and dragged us all over the place when he could. He eventually worked himself all the way up to tour manager, and after high school, my brothers and I would work for him sometimes too."

I didn't tell her about the friction it caused with my family when I decided to go to college. It had nothing to do with me getting an education or choosing a different career path. My parents supported that completely and understood I wanted more than late nights, hauling heavy sound equipment around, and living on the road.

It had everything to do with me moving to New York, moving so far away from them.

My family was tight-knit and resistant to change.

"My dad's last job before he retired," I continued, "was

with Warbler. He told Ardy—your dad—I was planning to move back and maybe looking for work, so he reached out."

"*Maybe* looking for work?"

"I still trade, and I'm pretty heavily invested."

She nodded like she understood, but I got the feeling it was an act.

The truth was, at my current position, I had enough in my portfolio that I could retire in ten years—as long as the market didn't tank, and I didn't fuck up and take too big of a loss. I liked being aggressive and I liked winning, but I always did my research before making a risky buy.

And while I could possibly live off my investments, I knew things could change in the blink of an eye and nothing was guaranteed. Plus, I was thirty-six, so I wasn't mentally ready for retirement. I'd get bored, and that? It could become a *big* problem. With time on my hands, I'd want to chase the dragon, to find the perfect stock that would net me millions.

I had to stay busy.

"I like research," I said, "and negotiations and working with people. Maybe I'm not a perfect fit for the role, but your father was willing to give me a shot."

Charlotte's gaze trailed over the black, geometric bull figurine on the bookcase behind me. "I'm sure you'll be fine," she said. "He's usually pretty good at finding the right people."

She left me in my office and got to work, and I spent the next forty-five minutes trying to pretend she wasn't out there in my kitchen, close enough that I could call to her and she'd appear.

This infatuation with her was weird and unsettling.

It was a good idea she'd asked me not to be here next time she cleaned. She was far too distracting, and I'd had to read the same article multiple times to actually take in the information.

Eventually, I was able to force her from her mind, but it only lasted a few minutes.

I caught movement out of the corner of my eye and found Charlotte lingering at the edge of my doorway. She didn't say anything, and hesitation streaked her expression. The moment I locked eyes on her, she startled, turned, and her feet carried her swiftly away.

"Everything okay?" I asked.

She halted and turned to face me. "Yeah. Yes." Whatever she'd been thinking about, she made her decision and began her approach again. "Would it be all right if I used your house in some of my content?"

"What?"

She stopped a few feet in front of my desk. "I shot one of those Day in the Life videos a few days ago, when I was cleaning Warbler. It did really well, got a ton of engagement. I kept getting asked about my techniques or what products I was using." She rested a hand casually on her hip. "Basically, they want more of that content, so I was wondering if you would mind if I did some filming here." Her smile was warm and convincing. "I'd make sure nothing personal gets used in the shot, that it couldn't be tied to you. No one will know where I am."

The pleading look in her eyes punched right through any of my concerns. Was this the same look she used on her father when she wanted to get her way? Because, Christ, it worked on me.

"As long as everything stays private," I said, "I guess that's fine."

"Awesome, thanks." She grinned and practically bounced her way back to the kitchen. Her excitement caused me to smile.

But it froze when a new thought wormed its way into my mind. Was that the reason she looked so damn good today? Because she hoped to make some new content?

She didn't make that effort for you. It was for her followers.

I shouldn't have cared. So why the fuck was I disappointed?

EIGHT

Charlotte

The first week, it was incredibly weird to clean the house of a guy who'd had his dick in my mouth, but . . . hey. At least Noah was paying me.

Which was more than Zach had ever done.

I sighed as I mopped the kitchen tile and tried not to think about my ex—but I failed.

Fucking Zach.

Shortly after I'd moved back home, I'd noticed my iPad was missing. The last place I remembered having it was in his living room. I usually left it on his coffee table, stored in a decorative tray I'd bought because his place had the barest minimum of anything. Hardly any silverware or furniture or décor—unless you counted Davidson University posters taped to the walls.

Me: Is my iPad still on your coffee table?

Zach left my text message on read all day, which was infuriating. How hard was it to text me back a simple yes or no?

The second time I went to clean Noah's house, it had been a lot easier. Sure, the place was messier, but he wasn't there. I didn't have that whining voice in the back of my head urging me constantly to go flirt with him. I could clean in peace.

That was the thing that was the most surprising about my new job, that cleaning somebody else's place was sort of peaceful. I didn't hate my biweekly trips to Warbler either. I liked seeing how fast I could get a task done.

Plus, it was turning out to be a freaking gold mine for content.

I couldn't tell how many people cooked their lunches in the oven at Warbler, but it was obvious it hadn't been cleaned in a long time. So I spent Thursday afternoon watching different YouTube videos to plan my attack, and Friday night I shot a time lapse of me scrubbing it clean with my favorite Scrub Mommy sponge. I'd used a plastic putty knife on the years' worth of grease baked on to the window glass, scraping the gunk off in several satisfying passes.

On Saturday, I recorded the voiceover where I explained my technique, and then layered it over the time lapse video. On Sunday morning, I posted it to my newly created profile, *Hot Girl Cleans.*

The profile name wasn't self-appointed. It had come from a comment on one of the cleaning videos I'd posted to my regular profile. *I'd watch this hot girl clean all day,* the guy had said.

I genuinely hadn't meant to make a thirst trap.

But that post got more engagement than I'd ever gotten before, and so I decided to lean into it. And with the creation of a new profile, I needed more videos to start training the algorithm.

I did a deep clean of Noah's dishwasher next, and when I had the post prepared, I texted a link to him for approval.

Me: Is it cool if I post this?

I waited with strange flutters in my stomach. I wasn't typically nervous posting stuff, plus I was confident the video was good. The lighting and sound were spot-on, and I'd edited the clips to move at a great pace. Just long enough to get the information out with no extra fat. I wasn't worried Noah would object to the post either. You could only see his kitchen sink and the dishwasher nearby, and everything looked like your basic kitchen. It was so generic, there was no way anyone could figure out where it had been shot.

These anxious flutters while I waited for his response were because I wanted him to *like* the video. To like my work, to like me. Why did it feel like his approval mattered more than any other viewer?

> **Noah:** Fun fact. I didn't know dishwashers had filters.

I snorted.

> **Me:** Didn't look like the previous owner knew either.

The little screened cup at the bottom of his dishwasher had been clogged with hard water buildup, food, and a papery sludge like someone had washed jars without removing the labels. I'd had to soak the filter in vinegar and then scrub it with an old toothbrush to get the crust off.

> **Noah:** That shit looked nasty. Sorry.

> **Me:** It was good for the vid. I don't want to be cleaning things that look clean.

> **Noah:** Makes sense. It's fine with me to post.

There was a tightness inside me that didn't go away with his approval. A twinge of disappointment lingered as I reread his text.

It's fine.

That was all the feedback he'd given me. Not *great*, or

amazing, or *you looked hot*.

I pushed my phone into my pocket and grew annoyed at myself. What had I expected? The guy didn't even like cleaning. He wasn't going to be interested in what I'd—

My phone vibrated with a new text message.

Noah: Video was great BTW. So professional.

A smile burst through my lips.

Me: Thanks.

The twinge evaporated in an instant, and I felt lighter the rest of the day.

When I wasn't cleaning the Warbler office or Noah's place, I also used places around my parents' house for content. I needed to build a library of videos as quickly as possible, so people had other things to watch after finishing the post they'd found me through.

By the fourth week of working for him, we'd fallen into a comfortable rhythm. I texted him when I arrived and keyed myself in through the garage, cleaned, and then texted to let him know when I'd finished. He always Venmo-ed me the money right after.

The arrangement was perfect. I was working on my own, slowly chipping away at my debt with my parents, and had my car back. Plus, my *Hot Girl Cleans* channel was taking off. My previous profile had been lifestyle, but it'd been too broad, too unfocused. This new brand wasn't just easier to create for—it was fun too. I didn't have to struggle to find followers either.

"Everything always works out for you," my friend Sasha had teased me last night when we'd hung out at her apartment. But her tone had been slightly off, and there'd been a hint of irritation, like maybe she wasn't joking.

"It doesn't feel that way," I said.

She laughed and shook her head, not believing me. "Okay."

I didn't say anything else or bother trying to defend myself. From her perspective, it probably looked that way, and she'd seen my parents bail me out enough times to think they'd cave eventually. My dad would say all was forgiven and forget about the rest of the money I owed.

But it was different this time; I could sense it. Things were on track right now, but if I made another mistake? There would be no more second chances.

Sasha topped off her glass with a blush wine that was so sweet it made my teeth hurt and offered the bottle to me, but I shook my head. She folded a leg under herself as she turned to face me on her couch. "So, this guy's house you're cleaning . . . does he, like, watch you do it?"

I laughed. "No. He's not even there. Which is was what I'd asked for, but now I sort of regret it."

"Why?" She took a sip of her wine, and her eyes lit up with mischief. "Because you *want* him to watch you?"

"You know I'm not topless when I clean, right? It's not sexy. I mean, unless he's into seeing me in rubber gloves."

This time I could tell her tone was teasing. "Really? I thought you wore the French maid outfit with thigh-highs and used a little feather duster." Her expression shifted as a thought formed. "You could charge him more if you did."

"Maybe I could." I mimicked her joking voice. "You want to explain to my dad how I'm earning the extra cash?"

She looked at me like I was being an idiot. "You don't have to tell him, you know."

Keeping anything a secret from my parents right now

was too risky, plus . . . "I'm his boss's daughter. Noah would never go for it."

Also, he'd already seen me naked. Why would he want to pay to see me scantily clad?

Sasha's head tilted with agreement. "Right." She took another sip of her Kool-Aid flavored wine. "So, what's his deal? He's not there, so I'm sure you've done some 'investigating.'"

I mashed my lips, trying to squeeze away my guilt because I hadn't been perfect. "I try not to snoop."

Whatever expression I'd been making, it gave everything away. "Oh, bullshit," she said. "Tell me."

Would doing that be a second invasion of privacy? Noah had left one of the bedside table drawers open half an inch. Not enough for me to see inside, but it'd felt like an invitation for me to take a peek.

I'd tugged it open six more inches and found what I'd expected—a box of condoms, a bottle of lube. But there were other sexy things too, like a Fleshlight, a tiny vibrator . . . Silicone bands that were most likely cock rings. Plus, handcuffs and a blindfold.

Fuck me, I'd whispered to myself. Noah was hot enough already. He had to be kinky too? It was so unfair.

And judging by the contents of that drawer, he'd already found a partner.

I'd had no choice but to ball up my disappointment, put it in that drawer, and slam it shut with a definitive thud.

"Okay, I might have peeked a little bit," I admitted, "but I didn't find anything surprising."

At least this time I was more convincing because Sasha frowned. "Well, that's disappointing."

God, she had no idea.

I was in Noah's living room, in the middle of vacuuming the new rug he'd bought, when his doorbell rang. I slowed, unsure of what to do. Could I pretend I hadn't heard it over the sound of the vacuum? It wasn't my house, and I felt strange answering the door.

Since I had my back to the entryway, I couldn't see who it was. It was a Tuesday, and in the middle of the afternoon, so it was probably some door-to-door salesperson.

I decided to keep trucking along. I needed to, because I had my camera going. I was filming coverage for either filler content, or something I could use behind a voiceover down the road.

The person at the front door was impatient though.

I waited less than thirty seconds before the doorbell chimed again, and it somehow sounded more urgent this time. They must have been able to see me through the window because when I didn't react, there was the sharp sound of knuckles rapping against the glass.

Shit. What if it was an emergency?

I snapped the vacuum into its upright position, flipped it off, and turned to face the entryway.

The shadowy figure I could see through the side window was slender, and as I marched closer, the woman became clearer. She was older, pretty.

Oh, shit. Was this Noah's mother?

I swallowed thickly and straightened my posture. I'd always felt so awkward meeting the parents of the guy I was with.

Girl, please. You're not with him, remember?

NINE

Charlotte

After I'd paused my camera, I unlatched Noah's front door and pulled it open just enough to block the woman's entry to the house. She didn't look like she was related to him, or like she was trying to sell something, either. She stood on the porch holding a paper plate loaded with cookies that was wrapped in pink cling film.

Was she a neighbor?

It was a little late to be welcoming him to neighborhood—he'd moved in more than two months ago.

I pressed out a polite smile. "May I help you?"

It was abundantly clear I wasn't who she was expecting, and her face twisted into a frown. "Yes, hello." She tried to see around me and into the house. "Is Noah here?"

"No, sorry. He's not."

"Oh." This was not the answer she wanted to hear, and her gaze fell to the cookies she was holding, like she wasn't sure what to do now.

"Did you want me to give those to him?" I offered.

She clutched the plate tighter, like she worried I was going to wrench it from her hands, and she tried to peer around me once again. "Is there a package in there for me?"

Um, what?

"This is my house," she explained. "I mean, it *was*, and—silly me, I forgot to update my shipping address." Her smile was off, and her expression was sort of calculating, like maybe she hadn't forgotten. "I ordered a mattress last week. You know, one of those ones that comes in a box? Anyway, I didn't realize my mistake until I saw the delivery picture and it was this front porch." She batted her eyelashes at me. "So, is it in there?"

When I'd arrived this afternoon, I'd come in through the garage and had noticed the large box sitting off to the side. I'd assumed it was his and hadn't looked at the label.

"I think so," I said. "Let me text him real quick." I pulled my phone out and began to thumb out my message.

"Oh, no, you don't need to bother him," she said quickly. "I can come back later. Do you know when he'll be home?"

This woman baked him cookies and drove over here to retrieve her new mattress, but now was totally willing to walk away empty handed? I finished sending my text and studied her closer, noticing her makeup, her nice clothes, and her jewelry. She was quite put-together for just picking up a package.

Unless she wants to pick up more than just her mattress.

I couldn't blame her for being attracted to Noah, or her wanting to shoot her shot, but . . . would he be interested in her?

She was almost old enough to be my grandmother.

"No," I said. "I don't know when he'll be home."

This answer frustrated her, and her disapproving gaze washed over me. "I'm sorry, who are you? You look a little young to be his girlfriend."

She was kind of rude, but I was unfazed. "I'm his housekeeper."

The phone in my hand buzzed, and Noah's name flashed

across the screen. “Hello?”

“Hi,” he said. “I thought it would be faster if we talked.”

Since we typically did it via text, it was the first time I’d heard his voice in weeks, and I tried to ignore the thrill that burst through me.

He spoke fast, as if he were busy. “That box showed up last night and I stuck it in the garage. I let my real estate agent know about it this morning, but is Judy still there?” He didn’t wait for my answer. “Can you put me on speaker?”

“Sure, just a second.” I tapped the icon on my screen. “You’re on.”

“Hey, Judy,” he started. “I put your box in my garage.”

Like me, excitement seemed to rocket through her at hearing his voice, and she tugged at the hem of her shirt before smoothing it out. It was like she wanted to make sure she looked her best, even though this was a freaking phone call, and he couldn’t see her.

“Hi, Noah.” She sounded as warm as the July sun overhead. “I’m so sorry for the mistake. I don’t know what I was thinking. Habit, I guess. I made you some cookies for the trouble, but I’ll come back later when you’re home.”

“I’d be happy to help you now,” I offered.

Judy’s eyes narrowed. “That’s sweet of you, but I’m sure the box will be too heavy.”

“You should be fine,” he said. “It’s really not that heavy.”

Her laugh was overly bright and fake. “Oh, of course you’d say that. You’re a big strong man.”

Wow. She was laying it on awfully thick.

She stared at me and lifted an eyebrow. “*What?*” her expression asked, feigning innocence. *“I’m not doing anything.”*

Oh, Judy, I need you to be so for real right now.

I slathered on an over-the-top smile. "You're already here," I said to her. "Why don't we just try it, and see if we can save you from having to make another trip?"

She froze, looking like she'd been backed into a corner, and her face soured. She flung daggers at me with her eyes, before grumbling, "I guess we could do that."

"Great, let me know how it goes," Noah said. He tacked it on at the end, his voice dropping downward like it carried more meaning than a simple sendoff. "Good luck."

I doubted she heard it, but I picked up on it. Was he wishing me luck on dealing with Judy?

I ended the call, told her to meet me at the garage, and watched her sulk as she went down the path that led to the driveway. Once I walked through the house, I pulled on my shoes, went out into the garage, and opened the overhead door. As it rolled up, I glanced at the side of the box sitting on its side.

It was only a twin mattress.

Although the thing was kind of heavy, it wasn't bad at all. The oversized box was more awkward than anything because it didn't have any handles to grab onto.

As I dragged it out of the garage, Judy stood motionless to the side, holding her plate of cookies as she watched. She made no effort to help. It was irritating, but I wasn't going to be defeated, so I lugged the box to the back of her SUV by myself.

Apparently, she was only willing to supervise and pop the back hatch. When it was open, I peered inside and saw the back seats were down already, ready for the mattress.

I looked at her, and she stared back expectantly.

Oh, I see.

I'd ruined her plans, and now I was nothing more than the fucking help to her. I clenched my teeth behind my smile, bent, and hoisted the goddamn thing in. It would have been a lot easier with her help, but at least I had spite powering me.

I slid the box in as far as it would go and turned to deliver my victorious gaze at her.

She was unimpressed. The cookies were shoved at me, and her expression was bitter as she pulled the hatch closed with an aggressive *thump*.

"Thanks," she spat out, and then moved to the driver's side door and climbed in.

I didn't have to wait long for her to go, and afterward I carried the plate inside, set it on the kitchen island, and tapped out a message.

> **Me:** We were successful, but I'm betting that's not the last you'll see of Judy.

I peeled back the side of pink cling film to look at the chocolate chip cookies inside. I'd lifted that woman's mattress into her car—didn't I literally deserve a cookie?

Once again, my phone buzzed with an incoming call and Noah's name appeared on screen.

"Hi," I said.

"Hey," he answered back. "What did you mean?"

"That shipping mistake? I'm pretty sure the whole thing was a setup."

"What? Why?"

I chuckled. "Because she needs a 'big, strong man' to help her test out that new mattress."

He paused. "Yeah, pass."

"Dude, I'm telling you, she wants that D. You should have seen how disappointed she was when she found out you weren't there." Did he need more proof? "She wanted to wait for you, and she made you cookies—which by the way—taste fucking fantastic. They might be all gone by the time you get home."

He laughed, and the sound of it was so nice, it did things to me. There was a longing for him that was getting harder and harder to ignore.

"I'm calling it right now," I said. "She'll be back."

He was probably just humoring me, but his voice was warm. "Okay."

The conversation between us lapsed for a moment, but it wasn't uncomfortable. A new thought hit me then.

"Hey, since I have you on the phone," I said, "can we switch next week's cleaning to Wednesday? One of my friends is getting married, and we're supposed to go bridesmaid dress shopping on Tuesday afternoon. I don't know how long it will take."

"Sure, that's no problem. I'll make sure I'm out of the house on Wednesday."

"Okay, thanks." I said it in an overly cheerful way to mask my disappointment, and mentally kicked myself again for telling him I didn't want him around while I was at his home.

Because after hearing his voice, it was pathetic how desperate I was to see him again.

I pulled into Noah's driveway, put my car in park, and peered at his house. He typically parked in his garage, so there was no way for me to tell if he was home right now. I eyed the bucket of cleaning supplies sitting on my passenger seat as I considered my next step.

Driving over without texting first was a bold move on my part. I'd asked to change to Wednesday for this week, and it was Tuesday. My plans with the bride and the rest of the bridal party had fallen through. My friend Brianna had texted the group this morning, telling us she was too sick to go dress shopping, and needed to reschedule.

So even though I knew there was a chance Noah wouldn't want me to clean or that he might be home right now, I decided it was worth the risk.

In fact, I hoped he was. I wanted to see him again.

After I turned the car off, I scrolled through my recent messages until I found my conversation with him and my gaze scrolled over our last exchange.

> **Noah:** You were right. Guess who just showed up at my house.

I'd sent back the GIF of Pikachu making a surprised face to tell him just how unsurprised I was.

> **Me:** Another wrong delivery?

> **Noah:** Yeah, but it won't happen again. I made it clear I'm not interested.

> **Me:** Oh, poor Judy. Can't blame a girl for trying.

> **Me:** Question tho. Did she bring any more cookies?

> **Noah:** I saved some for you.

There was a bubble with a pink heart in the top corner of his text from where I'd liked his message, and I got flutters looking at it now. That stupid heart didn't mean anything, and I didn't want him to read into it, because he was supposed to be my employer and nothing more.

Yet our text messages felt so . . . friendly.

Keep it professional. I quickly thumbed out a message to him.

> **Me:** Hey, my plans fell through and I'm in your area. Is it okay if I clean now?

I stared at the screen, waiting for the 'delivered' notification to change to 'read' with breath held. Usually, he was so quick to respond—but not this time. The status of the message didn't change. As I sat in my car, I tried to peer through the windows, but I didn't see any movement or lights on.

Time marched on, and my heart sank. Something had him too busy to check his phone, which meant he most likely wasn't here.

"What the hell do I do now?" I said to the empty passenger seat of my car. I'd only prepared for a few scenarios, and all of them had hinged on him responding to my text message.

I checked my watch, telling myself I'd give him another five minutes to respond. It was mid-afternoon, so it was possible he was in the office or out at a meeting.

Seven long minutes ticked by before I sighed, reached over, and grabbed the handle of my bucket. He wasn't home, and I was already here. Might as well get the job done.

I punched in my code to the garage door, stepped inside, and immediately slipped off my shoes. The house was disappointingly quiet and dark. I tightened my grip on the bucket handle and walked to the kitchen—only to pull to a stop.

"Hello?" I called.

There was no answer. There weren't any traces that Noah was home, but something felt strange. Off. I got the sense I wasn't alone.

The bottles of cleaner inside my bucket rattled quietly as I padded on my bare feet onto the cold tile floor of his kitchen. It made no sense for me to move with stealth, but I did anyway. Maybe part of me hoped to catch him by surprise, to see Noah in the wild.

There were no dirty dishes stacked beside the sink like there had been last time. In fact, the kitchen seemed to be in decent shape. I smiled to myself. Was he picking up some good habits?

I set my cleaning supplies down on the island and scanned the room. My first sweep would be decluttering and then I'd—

A pleasure-soaked moan came from his bedroom.

The sound of it was unmistakable and it wrapped around my body, squeezing me so tightly, I forgot how to breathe. My heart stumbled and beat faster. Had he not answered my text because he'd pulled one of the toys from his sex drawer and was too busy getting himself off?

A smart, professional person would have made a quiet exit so her client would never have known she'd stopped by. I knew the appropriate thing to do, yet I couldn't stop myself. An invisible force propelled me forward, and I moved down the hallway on silent feet.

I ignored the way his deep moan was followed with a softer, feminine one. *He's watching porn,* I thought. My brain refused to recognize that he might not be alone in his bedroom, so I was completely unprepared for the sight waiting for me when I reached the edge of his open door and peered around the corner.

His bed was a mess.

The sheet was a twisted rope, spilling over the side, and

clothes were scattered across the floor. My gaze lifted to take in the tangled bodies on the mattress, and I went utterly still. It was an unnerving feeling to be suddenly icy cold and scorching hot at the same time, and it meant I couldn't move. My feet became concrete, anchored to the floor.

Sweat glistened on Noah's bare skin as he cradled the woman's hips and thrust into her from behind. They were both on their knees, but she was bent at the waist and face down on the mattress, her arms outstretched in front of her.

She wasn't completely naked like he was; she wore a garter belt, dark thigh-high stockings, and a black blindfold that pinned her red hair in place.

As he fucked her, the redhead's fingers clawed mindlessly at the sheet beneath them. She reached for and found the headboard, making the large wedding ring on her left hand sparkle in the light.

TEN

Charlotte

My brain emptied at the sight of Noah fucking a married woman, and my face heated to a million degrees. I'd seen this redhead before and envied her, but today? Oh, I *hated* her. Not just because she was clearly cheating on her husband, but because of the man she was doing it with.

He's supposed to be mine, a bratty voice whined in the back of my mind.

God, I shouldn't have wanted him anymore. I fucking hated cheaters, and this should have been an enormous bucket of water extinguishing any flame that burned for him.

But it had barely any effect.

Worse, I immediately began to justify what he was doing. *He* wasn't technically cheating—he wasn't even in a relationship with anybody.

As I stared at the writhing couple on the bed, a thousand good reasons to turn and walk away played through my mind. And yet I remained, completely transfixed. The power of them together had an inescapable grip on me.

I wasn't sure I wanted to escape either.

The sight of them, of *him* like this, was the sexiest thing I'd ever seen. The redhead was beautiful. She was probably twenty years older than I was, and had a body to die for, one far superior to mine. She was stretched out across the bed, her perfect ass up for him, and there was barely a hint of jiggle as Noah's hips crashed against her.

His hands were clenched on her so tightly, there were dents in her skin around his fingers, but he needed to hold on like that. It was because his tempo was punishing, unrelenting. The sharp slap of their bodies meeting punched through the air over and over again.

All my blood rushed to the apex of my thighs, and I squeezed against it, causing a deep ache of pleasure.

Shit, why couldn't I get enough of watching them? I didn't dare pull my gaze away.

"*Fuck*," she murmured into the mattress. With the blindfold on, she couldn't see anything, and it undoubtably forced her to focus on the sensations he caused. It made me so fucking *jealous*.

Noah was in profile to me, so I could only see one half of his expression, but it was enough that I could tell it was full of determination. The muscles in his toned chest and arms created dips and curves, and my lust swelled so abruptly, I grew lightheaded.

It left me with no choice but to reach out and grab the doorframe to steady myself.

I'd been quiet, but it didn't matter. The movement must have caught his attention, and his head swung to the doorway. The moment his gaze landed on me, he froze with his dick buried deep inside her. My heart and the rest of the world seemed to stop moving right along with him.

I hadn't a clue what I looked like in that moment. His expression was full of shock, but there was the faintest hint of something else too. Worry?

Shame?

His wide, unblinking eyes didn't waver from mine, so he

had to notice how I hadn't moved from my not-so-hidden spot just outside the door. I hadn't backed away, or turned to run, or even lowered my gaze. My feet were rooted to the ground, and my hand gripping the doorframe tightened until it was white-knuckled.

Without thinking about the consequences, I made it clear to him that I'd been watching.

Did he see the desire roaring through me?

The silent plea for him to show me *more*?

His shock faded with each of his slow blinks, and dark heat moved in to take its place. The same thought I had now was wordlessly echoed on his face.

This is fucked up.

But . . . I might be into it.

The woman in front of him rose onto her elbows as she struggled to catch her breath, and even though she wore a blindfold, she turned to face him over one shoulder. "Everything all right?"

Noah flinched at the sound of her voice, like he'd been so deep under my spell, he'd forgotten all about the woman he was currently fucking. His chest lifted as he drew in a heavy breath, but his intense focus remained locked on me. It was as if he couldn't tear it away.

Oh, my God.

Was he waiting for my permission?

I was reckless, out of control, and gave a small nod before I could think better of it.

"Yes," he said to both of us, and then began to move again, but his gaze remained locked on mine.

Every long, slow stroke he delivered, I'd swear I could feel inside me. My pulse raced and my knees weakened, and

I leaned against the doorframe for more support. I watched his thick cock, glossy from the condom he wore, as it slid inside her, and it created a throbbing ache between my legs.

The intensity of it worsened the longer I watched, the longer our gazes trapped each other's. It was hard to breathe. Impossible to think. All I could do was stand there, half-collapsed against the doorway, and drown in his lust-soaked eyes.

His body was sheened with sweat, and the flex of his ass as he pumped into her was erotic. His hips moved and rolled, and somehow, I experienced the same flashes of pleasure the woman did, even though he wasn't touching me.

We were connected, though.

The bratty version of me wanted to brag to her that my connection to Noah was stronger. Deeper. Better.

When he picked up speed, she dropped back down, resting her forehead on the mattress and clenched fistfuls of the sheet beneath her. It must have changed the angle because it threw off his rhythm for a moment. In response, he slipped a hand under the back of her garter belt and closed his fist around it. Then, he turned his hand over, rolling the fabric over the back of his palm and cinching the belt so tight on her, it dug into her skin.

She whimpered with pleasure. "You're so fucking deep."

I couldn't tell if he'd even heard her. He'd resumed his blistering pace without breaking our stare, and his carnal expression caused blood to rush loudly in my ears. He wore an expression like this moment we were sharing was the only thing he desired. Like I was all he wanted.

It was so fucking hot.

The fire of it all drove my feet forward. One after the other, until I was just inside the door and could lean with my back against the wall. It freed my hands to hang loosely at my sides, but one of them didn't stay there long. It drifted across my thigh, and I wedged it between my legs. I had on a pair of capri length leggings that were soft and thin and clung to me like a second skin, so I didn't bother wearing anything beneath them.

It meant I could feel every whisper of movement from my hand nestled between my thighs. The side of my thumb brushed against my clit, and I shuddered.

What I was doing was twisted and wrong, touching myself while watching them, but I couldn't help myself. I was desperate to relieve the ache. And when Noah's lips parted and his eyes hazed, it told me just how much he approved.

The room became an oven, and it took an enormous amount of effort to drag air in and out of my lungs. Watching what each other was doing took a toll on us. Sweat dampened his temples, and his chest heaved with short breaths.

But he didn't stop looking at me.

Not even when the woman's moans swelled, and her legs began to tremble. "That's it," she urged. "God, I want to come. Make me come."

The muscles in his powerful, sexy arm corded as he pulled back on her garter belt. It caused her to bow up off the bed and onto her hands. Her breasts swayed and bounced with each of his violent thrusts, and the image of him fucking her was so scorching, it seared into my mind where I was sure it'd stay forever.

The woman cried out, and her whole body began to quake, leaving no doubt that she'd gotten her wish. As she came, her strangled sounds of ecstasy permeated every inch of the room, filling my body. I ground the side of my hand harder against my clit, sending shocks of pleasure darting down my legs.

The effect of her orgasm was powerful, and he wasn't immune either. Maybe he'd already been close, or maybe it was a combination of pushing her over the edge while watching me tease myself that did it for him.

His face twisted with enjoyment, and his eyes fell shut.

Perhaps he'd closed them to sever our connection and try to stave off his orgasm, but it didn't work. Noah's eyes blinked open, his gaze returned to me, and then he was done for.

He released his hold on her garter belt, gave her a final thrust, and then both his hands clenched her ass. His shoulders contracted, but he held on to her undulating body, chasing her and keeping himself lodged inside. I watched his eyes haze with satisfaction as he stared back at me, and I hoped I hadn't become too blurry for him in that moment.

I wanted him to think only of me as he came.

His deep groan . . . it stroked over me like a brush painting pleasure from head to toe. The sensation wasn't quite enough to push me into orgasm. It was just enough to leave me hanging there on the edge.

The room quieted as their bodies stilled, and the only sound was their labored breathing as they recovered. I wasn't breathing at all—the hold of Noah's gaze gripped like a vise.

But then the woman collapsed onto her stomach on the bed and a smile twisted her lips. "Goddamn. I can't wait to tell my husband how hard you just fucked me."

Her shocking words tore his focus from me. It snapped to the very beautiful, very *married* woman in front of him. With his attention gone, I'd been released, and cold, harsh reality crashed into me so rapidly, my knees threatened to buckle.

Oh, God.

I couldn't stay in this room, not for another second, but the now unwanted desire in my body made me slow. I turned to flee at the same moment the woman hooked a finger beneath the blindfold and tugged it off.

I darted for the hallway, but I wasn't fast enough. There was no way she hadn't seen me go.

Noah's voice rang out behind me as I tore down the hallway. "*Fuck.*"

I stumbled recklessly into the kitchen, not stopping until I reached the sink. My hips slammed into the cabinet, and I braced myself against the porcelain basin as I stared out the window, seeing absolutely nothing.

If I'd been able to think, I would have grabbed my cleaning supplies and gotten the fuck out of his house—but I became a statue, too stunned to do anything. I heard him and the woman moving around in his room, while my pulse raced at a breakneck speed, and my face burned like it had caught fire.

Finally, my gaze fell to the faucet.

In the movies, sometimes people would splash cold water on their face to calm or recenter themselves. Should . . . should I do that now? It'd ruin my makeup, but did I care about that?

I slowly reached out and turned the water on. It poured into the sink and began filling the pan that had been discarded there, the one I hadn't noticed when I'd been in the kitchen earlier.

It was a familiar task, so I went on autopilot. I grabbed the dish soap and sponge resting beside the sink and got to work scrubbing. I'd just finished when footsteps approached from behind. I didn't have to see to know it was him.

"Charlotte." Noah's voice was quiet and unsure. "I thought we said Wednesday."

"We did. My plans fell through, and I was around, so I thought . . . " Rather than face him, I pulled a towel from the nearby drawer and used it to dry the newly clean pan. "I sent you a text about it. When you didn't respond, I thought that meant you weren't home."

"I was," he paused, searching for the right word, "busy."

It just popped out. "Yeah, I noticed."

The tension inside me was so taut, I worried I was going to snap, but instead I turned and finally faced him. He was dressed now, wearing a pair of shorts, a dark green t-shirt, and an unreadable expression.

I was suddenly irrationally angry at everything. With Brianna for canceling the dress fitting. Myself for not going home when he didn't answer my text. With Noah for what he'd just been doing and who he'd been doing it with.

And most of all, because despite everything, he still looked so damn sexy to me.

My tone was harsher than any chemical in my cleaning arsenal. "You think her husband likes that you're fucking his wife?"

"Yes." There was no hesitation and no guilt. "He's the one who asked me to."

A needle dragged across a record in my brain. "Wait. What?"

He rubbed a hand over his jaw, making his whiskers brush quietly against his fingertips. "You remember how I told you I don't do traditional relationships?"

I didn't get a chance to answer because the woman, who was now dressed, appeared. She strolled over to stand beside Noah and flashed a friendly, reassuring smile.

It made my face burn even hotter, only this time with embarrassment. My gaze dropped to the island countertop. "I'm sorry," I mumbled, "for walking in on you. I didn't think anyone was home."

Her laugh was light and warm. "Oh, honey, don't worry about it." Her casual tone drew my focus up, and when my gaze met hers, she pulled her lips into a provocative smile. "I don't mind being watched. In fact, I love it." She glanced over at him. "Maybe Patrick could watch next time."

Was that her husband? The one who'd asked Noah to sleep with his wife?

He didn't look like he knew what to say, so the only acknowledgement he gave was a tight nod.

With that settled, the woman glanced at the screen of her phone. "He's about to pull up out front." She put a hand on Noah's shoulder. "Thanks. You were great." And then she leaned in and dropped a chaste kiss on his cheek. "You'll definitely be hearing from us again."

I stood, dumbfounded. Was she going to climb into her husband's car and then rate her afternoon with Noah?

Performance was great! Five stars.

He continued to look at a loss for words and stood motionless, his gaze locked on me. When she turned to leave, he came back to life.

"I'll walk you out," he said.

While I was alone in the kitchen, I stared at my bucket of cleaning supplies and urged myself to move. This was my chance to escape this awkward situation, and yet, I didn't want to. I had so many questions I was dying to ask.

So I remained by the sink, waiting for his return. I heard the front door open and then close, and the slow footsteps that led him back to the kitchen. When he reappeared, he seemed unsettled and raked his hand through his already messy hair.

I did my best to keep my tone light and teasing. "For a guy who just got laid, you look really uncomfortable."

He set his hands wide on the island and leaned over it as he considered something. His expression abruptly shifted to one that loudly read *fuck it*. "Have you heard the term 'bull' before?"

Was this a stockbroker thing? "As in, a bull market?"

He shook his head. "As in, a single male swinger."

My breath caught.

"Swinger," I repeated.

"Do you know what that means?" He asked it earnestly.

"I think so." The tension inside me tightened like a screw get another full turn of a screwdriver. "It's, uh, couple swapping. And maybe group stuff."

The moment the words were out, it charged the air between us. Heat smoldered in his eyes. "Yes."

"But you don't have anyone to swap." I'd blurted it without thought, and it came out sounding like I was sad about that. As if I was about to volunteer myself.

He gave a faint smile. "I don't have to have a partner. Anyone who enjoys casual sex, with multiple people, can call themselves a swinger. And any of those people can be inside or outside of a relationship."

I straightened away from the sink, taking a step closer to him. "You mean, like an open marriage?"

"It could be, but more likely it's ENM." When I made a face, he added, "Ethical non-monogamy. It means everyone is consenting to the sex, even if they're not participating in it."

He studied me, gauging my reaction, and must have seen I still didn't get it.

"Patrick dropped Shannon off at my place," he said, "fully aware of what was going to happen. Hell, he wanted it to happen. Don't you think that means he consents to it?"

Like he'd done to me, I asked it earnestly. "Sure, but why?"

"Why'd he give his consent?"

I shook my head. I wasn't trying to judge; I was just too damn curious. "Why'd he want you to fuck his wife?"

He considered my question for a long moment. "I don't want to speak for him, but I'm guessing because it turns him on." Did Noah feel the urge to defend the guy? His expression was serious. "It's not because he's weak, or can't give his wife what she needs, if that's what you're thinking."

"I wasn't—"

"Believe me, he's not weak. If anything, this arrangement shows just how strong and confident he is. How rock-solid their marriage *is*. He doesn't need to flex ownership of his partner or their relationship. In fact, he's secure enough he doesn't even need to be involved."

I blinked and processed what he'd said. Maybe he couldn't interpret what I was thinking, or I'd looked skeptical to him, because Noah frowned.

"You don't agree?"

"No, no, I do." I took another step toward him, and I hoped I sounded as genuine as I felt. "I never would have thought about it like that, but you make a good point."

His frown evaporated and he shifted on his feet, subtly leaning closer to me. Like my answer had pleased him.

I gazed up at him through new eyes. I only had sex when I had enough trust or was in love with my partner, and he was the opposite. Our preferences weren't any less valid than the other's, so I didn't have any room to judge.

Plus, I'd be lying to myself if I said his lifestyle wasn't fascinating as fuck.

"How did you meet them? I mean, if it's okay to ask." I swallowed a breath. "You don't have to answer."

He didn't look offended. "There's a club here in Nashville."

Even though we were alone in his kitchen, I whispered it like it was a secret. "A club? Like, a sex club?"

He nodded. "I met them at the bar my first night there, and we got to talking about what they were looking for." He reached up to massage the back of his neck. "Actually, the night you and I met, that was my first date with them."

Surprise coursed through me. "You're dating both of them?"

"No. Well, not in the way you think of dating." He must have felt the urge to clarify. "I'm straight and he is too, so we don't play physically with each other. But I treat them as a unit. A partnership. I wouldn't do anything with Shannon that he hasn't fully signed off on, and I don't talk to her without him."

"But . . . you'll fuck her without him." I jolted. "God, I hope that didn't sound judgmental, because I didn't mean it to. I'm just . . . " I trailed off, unsure of what to say.

"Trying to wrap your head around it?"

Relief swelled inside me. "Yeah, exactly."

"I'm sure it goes without saying, but if we could keep this between us . . . "

"For sure." I nodded enthusiastically, trying to convey how much I understood this wasn't my secret to share.

His shoulders relaxed, and that same pleased look he'd

given before crossed his expression. Fuck, it did things to me.

Except I didn't want it to. I was already so uncomfortably turned on.

"Gotta tell you, Charlotte." His warm gaze was inescapable. "You're full of surprises."

Was he kidding? In comparison to him, I felt as plain and vanilla as they came. "Me?"

"Yeah, you." He had no idea how seductive his soft tone was—or maybe he did. "You're not acting like you think what I just told you or what happened back there in my room was wrong."

"I don't think it was wrong." The air in the room went thin, and I said it in a hush. "I thought it was hot."

"See? *Surprising*." He moved closer, like he was being drawn to me. "How long did you stand there, watching us?"

"I was mostly watching you," I admitted.

"Because you were jealous?"

"I'm not sure that's the right word. Envious, I guess. And a little bit angry."

He froze. "Angry?"

"At the situation." I set a hand on my hip and decided to lay everything out there. "I want you, Noah." My bitterness bubbled to the surface when I put it into words. "I want you, but I can't have you, and that pisses me off."

He exhaled loudly, and it was like he'd been holding that breath in for the last month. "Yeah?" His expression mirrored the way I felt. "You should know it pisses me off, too."

ELEVEN

Charlotte

Noah's admission filled the room, taking up all the air so there was none left.

It destroyed any filter I might have had and made me ramble. "I came over today, hoping you'd be here. I was going to try to get you to kiss me." I felt wildly out of control. "To ask you to do things to me."

His eyes widened.

I'd expected my words to make him retreat—but instead he closed the last of the space between us so he was only a breath away. Close enough it would be easy for me to curl my fingers in his hair and yank him down into my kiss.

I clenched my fists to stop myself.

"We can't." His voice was firm, but everything else was in total contradiction, from his proximity to his lidded eyes.

"No, we can't," I agreed, my words as hollow as his.

God, the way he looked at me, it sent a shiver of pleasure down my spine. He stared at my lips as if he were searching for all the reasons he shouldn't kiss me and was struggling to come up with a single one.

"Where the fuck does that leave us, then?"

I didn't know how to answer that. Noah wasn't just my father's employee—he was kind of my boss too. I needed his money, and I needed his place to generate content.

"Friends?" I offered, although it was completely

inadequate. How the fuck could we be friends?

His eyebrow arched and his expression turned dubious. It announced he had the same concern.

"I could be a friend," my pulse sent blood thundering through my veins, "who watches you fuck other people."

Shock caused him to suck in a sharp breath and his shoulders straightened. "Is that what you want?"

Part of me thought this would be a consolation prize. Since I couldn't have him, this would be the next best thing. But the other part of me wondered if I was settling at all . . . or if I was getting a better deal than I realized.

I'd had sex before, but watching someone else do it was new and exciting.

What if the next time I watched him it was even hotter?

Just the thought made the throb between my legs return.

He'd asked if I wanted that, and it came from me in a whisper. "I wouldn't mind seeing a little more."

He didn't blink as he considered my statement, but his chest rose and fell with a heavy breath. There was restraint in him, like he was trying his damnedest not to show how much he liked this idea.

"All right." His voice matched my low tone. "I could do that for you, *friend*."

Then, his gaze worked its way over me, evaluating every inch. He noticed my flushed cheeks and the hurried way my chest moved from my short breaths, and whatever he was thinking about, it didn't take him long to come to a decision.

The brown of his irises seemed to darken like a storm gathering strength, and I was so distracted by it, I didn't notice when his hands settled on my waist. It wasn't until we were moving, him urging me back toward the island, that I became aware.

"What are you doing?" I asked.

Noah's expression was cryptic. "Helping a friend."

He had me pinned then, and the edge of the countertop kissed the small of my back. The coolness of the stone seeped through my shirt, in stark contrast to his warm hands. It made it difficult to think. "What?"

One of his hands slid down, gliding over my hip and thigh. The caress was gentle but sexual, and my body hummed with excitement. It didn't give a fuck about who he was or the consequences of letting him touch me like this. I'd been on a knife's edge watching him with her, and the conversation afterward had done nothing to help.

Noah tilted his head down, bringing his lips so close to mine, it was a cruel tease. "If you're going to be the kind of friend who watches me fuck someone else," I could feel the warm brush of air against my skin as he spoke, "then I'm going to be the kind of friend who wouldn't leave you hanging after."

How the hell did he expect my brain to function when he had his hands on me? I uttered the only word I could remember. "What?"

"You got so worked up watching, you put your hand here, didn't you?" The hand he'd rested on my thigh moved, sliding over the thin fabric of my leggings until it was nestled between my legs and cupping me.

I let out an excited sound of surprise, one that was tinged with need.

Thank God his question was rhetorical because my voice abandoned me. He sensed it, because a wicked smile curled at the ends of his lips.

"It wasn't enough, though, was it?" he asked. "You didn't get to come."

I pressed my lips together and gave the slightest shake of my head. Why did it seem like my answer pleased him?

Because he wants to be the one to do it.

When his hand moved, grinding against my needy clit, it pulled a whiny moan from the depths of my body. My hands curled around the edge of the cold countertop, holding on against the onslaught of pleasure.

"I know I shouldn't be doing this," he said, although it sounded like a lie. His fingers dragged across the center seam of my leggings. "Do you want me to stop?"

Once again, I shook my head, and that pleased expression that made him look so damn sexy flashed across his face.

"Take off your pants," he commanded, "so I can give you what you need."

All the air swept out of my lungs.

He was so different from the last time we'd been together. He'd been putting on a front before, hiding his true self so his aggression didn't scare me away. But now I'd seen behind the curtain, and I was grateful. Because this dominant version of Noah?

It was incendiary.

I didn't know how I was able to move because the excitement radiating inside my core made me shake, but I kept my gaze fixed on him and slipped my hands beneath the tight waistband of my leggings. He stepped back, giving me space to bend at the waist and slowly peel the clinging fabric down.

Every new, bare inch of skin I exposed to him made my pulse climb higher.

He watched me with a discerning eye, like I was a student

demonstrating something newly learned for an instructor. I tugged the fabric free from one ankle and then the other, discarding my pants in a wad on the tile floor I'd planned to mop later.

When I straightened, I was naked from the waist down, and I bit my bottom lip as Noah's gaze focused on the bare cleft between my legs. I wasn't overly bashful about my body, but we were in his kitchen, where bright afternoon sunlight seemed to stream in from every window.

What if his neighbors saw?

Wouldn't you like it if they did?

Heat burned in his eyes as his gaze rose to meet mine, and the intensity of it was so hot, I licked my dry lips, feeling parched. He moved abruptly, sliding his hands under my arms, and lifted until he had me seated on the countertop.

I gasped at the cold stone against my bare skin, but it didn't slow him down. His hands snaked under my shirt and tugged it up. I had to raise my arms to let him pull it over my head, and I held in the sigh of satisfaction I wanted to make. There was something I loved about being undressed by a guy.

With my shirt gone, all that was left was my white bralette. It was simple, but skimpy, and I'd chosen it this afternoon hoping I'd get an opportunity to show it to him. He moved to stand between my parted legs, and when his hand gripped my breast through my bra, I arched into his touch.

My skin was hot everywhere except where it touched stone, and my vision hazed with lust. I was no longer in control of my body—maybe I'd handed command over to him. And he wanted complete control, because when I reached to pull him into a kiss, he stepped back to prevent it.

"Lie down," he ordered. "On your back."

I pushed out a shallow breath.

The island wasn't small, and the countertop was empty, so there was enough room for me to do it, but . . . holy shit. I'd never fooled around out in the open like this, and my pulse roared like a runaway train.

He stood beside the counter, waiting for me to comply, wearing all his clothes and an impatient look. It was as if my failure to move had put us behind his schedule. God, it was seriously hot, and I was eager to please, so I pulled my legs up and turned to the side, making it easy to lie back.

The cold countertop pressed against my bare skin, causing me to release a quiet hiss, but Noah didn't let it distract him from his mission. He loomed at the edge of the island, his gaze sweeping over me as if assessing where he'd like to start.

Lying like this, basically on a table for him, was strange, and I wasn't sure where to put my hands. Resting them folded across my stomach would be awkward. Should I try to touch him?

Would he even allow it?

I didn't get to find out.

He grabbed the bottom hem of my bra and began to drag the fabric up, forcing me once again to lift my arms, only he stopped once he'd reached my elbows. My arms, wrapped in the bunched bralette, were pressed over my head. The counter wasn't long enough, so my hands dangled over the end, but he pinned my elbows to the stone with his hand on the bra.

"Stay just like that."

His tone was so stern, so fucking sexy, I let out a tiny whimper of excitement in response. *That* sound did not go unnoticed by him, and his gaze heated to an inferno as it swept from left to right along the length of my nude body.

I could only imagine what I looked like to him with my hands and feet hanging over the sides of his kitchen island. I was on display for him, completely under his spell, and the idea of it only turned me on more. I was wet—*so fucking wet*—and he'd discover it the moment he touched me, if he didn't know already.

I trembled with anticipation when he placed his palm on my knee. He didn't move it for a long moment. He drew in a deep breath, perhaps needing to gather strength for what he was about to do. But it was just as likely he was simply teasing me.

The tension winding inside my center was delicious.

Up his hand inched, sliding along the inside of my thigh and subtly urging my legs to part. And then his other hand skimmed across my chest, caressing my hardened nipples.

"Fuck," I groaned under my breath when his fingertips brushed against my damp, sensitive skin at the center of my legs. His gentle touch was a jolt of electricity, jump starting the stalled orgasm that had lingered in my system, bringing it roaring back to life.

His hand stroking over my upper body wandered everywhere, but the one between my legs didn't stray. He used the pad of his index finger to brush lines over my clit, and the pleasure was so intense, it bolted down my legs like lightning. The sensation caused me to jerk my knees up and find footing at the edge of the counter.

"I'm going to come so fast," I blurted.

He loomed over me with a satisfied smile. "Because you liked watching me."

"Yes," I breathed.

His left hand pinched one of my nipples and gently

tugged, while his right hand ground a tight circle against my pussy. "Which part, exactly?"

The heat and the pleasure were too much to think over. "When she came all over your cock."

My words surprised him, and he rewarded me with a dazzling grin. But then he feigned disapproval. "You've got a filthy mouth, Charlotte."

His left hand glided up my neck so he could push two fingers past my lips, filling my mouth and silencing my tongue. It muffled my moan he had created when he eased the first two fingers of his right hand deep inside me. I jerked, and I almost reached for him, but I caught myself just in time.

I didn't want this to stop, and he'd told me to stay still. I was desperate to be good for him.

As I assumed he wanted, I closed my lips around the fingers in my mouth and sucked, simulating what I'd do if he wanted to put his cock there instead.

But he didn't.

He pulsed those fingers in time with the fingers between my legs, fucking my mouth and my pussy at a slow, steady pace.

I squirmed and panted through my nose at how good it felt, all the while studying the determined, focused look etched on his handsome face. My hands that dangled over the side of the counter clenched into fists and then splayed out, and I laced my fingers together so I had something to hold on to.

Noah had put the fingers in my mouth for a reason . . . and it wasn't to keep me quiet. He withdrew his hand, his fingers glistening with my saliva, and trailed them down to join his other hand.

His wet fingertips pressed to my clit, causing me to flinch and arch, and I gasped with satisfaction. He drove his fingers deep inside me, ramping up the tempo and changing angles with each thrust. I knew what he was doing, how he was searching for the spot I liked best, but it all felt so amazing, did it even matter?

God, I was going to lose my mind.

In and out he thrust his fingers, all the while manipulating my clit with his other hand. My propped-up knees shook. My breath came and went in heaving gulps. My heart pounded so furiously, it threatened to break free from my chest.

The whole thing was fucking intense.

Easily the most erotic thing I'd ever done, and for a single heartbeat, I was mad at him for hiding this version of him the last time we'd hooked up. But how could I be upset with him now?

The orgasm rushed at me, surging like an electric current. My moan swelled to a gasp as the pleasure built, and built, and *built* . . .

"Oh, fuck," I groaned. Heat burst inside my center, traveling through my body in waves of ecstasy as I came. This time when I bucked against the counter, I couldn't control myself. I pulled my arms down, stretching the bra between my elbows and letting the fabric cover my face.

Not that I could see, anyway. The power of the orgasm had my eyes screwed shut.

Noah's fingers halted, both the ones inside and out, but the connection remained. My body clenched down, squeezing against his fingers and giving me aftershocks of pleasure.

He pushed out a loud, heavy breath that was laced with satisfaction.

When my twitching body lowered back to the granite countertop, and the orgasm's grip on me receded, he finally withdrew. His hands rested gently against my heated skin, one on the flat of my stomach, and the other across my thigh.

As soon as the blood stopped rushing in my ears, I worked to free myself from the bra, letting it fall to the floor. I moved as fast as my post-orgasm body would let me, sitting up and swiveling to face him.

I'd caught him off guard and his eyes went wide, and this time when I reached for him, he wasn't fast enough to stop me. I threaded my hands through his soft hair and yanked his face to mine.

"Wait," he said, and turned at the last second so I missed my target, my lips crashing against his cheek.

I caught my breath and pulled back to look at him. "What's wrong?"

He grasped my wrists, freeing his head from my hold, and stepped back from the island. His breathing and voice were uneven. "Friends don't kiss each other."

Um . . . was he serious?

I narrowed my eyes. "They don't finger fuck each other either."

"That was a one-time thing." His expression was stricken, full of confusion and doubt. Even he didn't believe what he'd just said.

I struggled with the whiplash he'd given me and gaped up at him. "What the fuck are you talking about?"

"Fuck. I don't know." Once again, he combed a hand through his unruly hair, which only made him look more unsettled. "I wanted to help you."

His statement hung awkwardly, like he'd left off the part

he'd meant to say. *I wanted to help you, friend-to-friend.* Thirty seconds ago, he'd been confident and in control, and now he was acting like I'd shattered that by trying to kiss him.

Which was a normal response to what we'd just done. The warmth in my system disappeared in the blink of an eye, and I was painfully aware of the imbalance between us. He had all his clothes on, and I was stark fucking naked. The chill of it clung everywhere.

I slid down off the counter to stand on my shaky legs. "You didn't have a problem kissing me last time."

"I know," he said softly. "And it's not that I don't want to. Believe me, I do."

He'd said it before, but I still bristled, because saying that he wanted it and wouldn't do it made me feel worse.

He sighed. "But things are different now. I shouldn't have done that."

That was what this was? Guilt?

I rolled my eyes. "I'm not going to tell my dad about it, if that's what you're worried about."

He frowned, but I didn't want to see it.

Instead, I picked up my discarded clothes, dropped them on the counter, and then got to work pulling my pants back on. I hated this pattern emerging with him, how he'd give me a mind-numbing orgasm, which was quickly followed by me getting dressed in frustration.

He sighed again, only this one was louder and filled with surrender. "I'm not allowed to kiss Shannon."

My hands slowed as I tugged my bra down over my breasts, and anger grew a lump in my throat. "Why are you telling me this?"

"Because when Patrick said I couldn't kiss her, I didn't

care. I like kissing and all, but I wasn't bothered by this rule. I don't *need* to kiss her." His eyes turned stormy. "But when I found out you're Ardy's daughter and I can't kiss you anymore? I was fucking pissed, Charlotte."

I turned to stare at the spot where I'd just lain naked on the counter for him. "I . . . I don't understand."

"I don't either." He said it begrudgingly, annoyed with himself. "I can compartmentalize a lot of things and keep my feelings out of it, but if I kiss you again? I don't think we can stay friends."

An invisible fist tightened in my chest.

"That can't happen." His expression was resigned. "We both know it won't lead anywhere."

Because I worked for him. Because my father was his boss. And because Noah was thirteen years older than me and didn't have time for love. There was a mountain's worth of reasons why we wouldn't work.

But my stupid heart did not care.

It wanted him, regardless.

"We have to stay friends," he said as he delivered a sad smile. "Hell, since I moved back, you're one of the only friends I've got."

He'd probably meant for it to sound like a joke, but I heard the truth buried in his words. The connection to him lashed tighter around me. I still had a few friends around from high school, but we were on different paths. They were all in college, in serious relationships or engaged, and had moved on with their lives. They weren't stuck or floundering like I was.

Coming home had made him lonely, and no one understood that better than I did. The only time I hadn't felt that same loneliness was when I'd been here at his house.

"Tell me I didn't fuck this up," he said quietly. "Tell me we can still be friends."

My voice was unsteady. "Friends who watch each other fuck, but don't kiss."

His shoulders lifted with an enormous breath. Maybe he was thinking about what a terrible idea that'd be, but it was overruled because of how badly he wanted it. He peered at me with an intense look and slowly nodded.

My gaze dropped to the floor, and I stared at the tile, wanting to collapse on it and pout about how truly unfair this all was. But rather than throw a tantrum, I swallowed my disappointment and formed a plan.

I couldn't have him now, but I could bide my time and convince him. I wanted this—and things usually worked out for me.

"Fine," I announced, pressing out a tight smile. "I can do that."

TWELVE

Noah

I lost my goddamn mind when it came to Charlotte. The girl put me off balance. No, worse—she made my brain stop working.

My afternoon with Shannon had been enjoyable enough until I'd spied Charlotte lurking in the doorway. Her face was flushed and her mouth hung open, and it was shameful how quickly my focus shifted to her. I'd expected the girl to back away with disgust when our gazes had met, but no.

She'd *liked* what she saw.

It wasn't shock making her cheeks red or her lips part, it was desire.

Everything that followed was a hazy blur of lust. Exhibitionism usually didn't rank high on my kink list, but when she was watching? It was so fucking hot, I could barely keep it together.

And when she'd put her hand between her legs, I was done for.

I'd been in the lifestyle almost ten years, and I'd had lots of partners and a wide variety of experiences. So how the fuck had this experience with her blown everything else out of the water? How had it been the most erotic thing I'd ever participated in?

And then our conversation afterward—it was almost cruel how curious and interested she'd been. Shit, she was too good to be true.

I saw so much of myself in her when I'd been starting out. If she'd been anyone else, I would have loved getting to show her more. To watch her open her eyes and see all the new things out there.

It was fucking stupid of me to put her on the counter and give her an orgasm, but I'd lost all reason, and it was entirely her fault. I justified it to myself, saying she needed it. That I owed it to her.

When it was over, I couldn't even bring myself to feel regret. There was no undoing it, so all we could do was move forward.

Friends.

I knew it was a terrible, selfish idea, but I couldn't stop myself. I'd meant what I said about her being one of my only friends, and if I'd been stronger, I would have cut her off. Trying to be friends with her was going to be an exercise in torture.

To put a finer point on that, after she'd agreed we'd be friends with fucked-up benefits, Charlotte announced that since she was already here, she was going to clean. My unease with the arrangement increased tenfold. I liked power imbalance when I was in a scene, but only when our roles were defined, and consent was given.

This was . . . messy.

Like a coward, I hid in my office and tried to focus on my trades. I didn't reply to the group chat with Patrick and Shannon, where they wanted to set up our next date. My head was swimming with thoughts of the girl who was in my bedroom, tidying up like nothing had happened there.

Was she as good at compartmentalizing as I was?

Maybe she was even better, because when she was done, she strolled into my office with an easy smile.

"I'm finished and heading out." Her gaze swept over me just like it should. It was casual and friendly, and I hated it. I wanted to see her as affected as she made me. But she was immune. "You want to stick with Tuesday next week for your cleaning?"

I cleared the stickiness from my throat. "Yeah, that be great."

"Okay." Her smile was bright. "Talk to you later, friend."

I sat to one side of Ardy's office and took notes as Huston discussed the pitches he wanted to make to the Electralights team. The music festival would be setting next year's lineup soon, and Warbler hoped to get another act included besides Stella, who'd headline.

My phone vibrated with a text message, and I glanced at the preview on my smartwatch.

Charlotte: Are you free tonight? I need a favor.

I dismissed the notification and tried to focus on my work, but I struggled. Whenever I glanced at my boss, the reminder of who his daughter was would play on repeat in my head.

Charlotte: I need to do something difficult and could really use a friend.

Shit. I pulled in a tight breath. I didn't have plans tonight, but even if I had, how the hell could I say no to that? Whatever it was, it had to be rough, because I couldn't imagine I'd been her first choice to reach out to.

Ardy understood his people needed to be accessible and probably didn't think anything of it when I pulled out my phone and typed out my response.

> **Me:** Yes, I'm available tonight. Everything okay?

> **Charlotte:** Yeah, I'll explain later. Can I pick you up at 7?

I sent back a 'thumbs up' emoji, then put the screen to sleep and pocketed my phone. She'd said everything was okay, but for some reason, I continued to worry. It was impossible to know her tone through text, I reminded myself.

But my concern for her persisted the rest of the day, and it didn't let up until she appeared on my front porch.

"Hey," I said, stepping out to join her.

It was on the tip of my tongue to tell her she looked nice, but I bit it back. She did look good, though. She wore a blue sleeveless shirt, white skinny jeans, and a pair of heeled sandals that made her almost as tall as I was. She wore the same makeup as the first night we'd met, and I got the sense she'd put a lot of effort into her look tonight.

Oh, shit. Was this a date?

The logical side of my brain was annoyed. Hadn't we said we were just going to be friends?

"Hi." She looked more relieved to see me, rather than excited. "Thanks for coming with me tonight."

I pulled my front door closed and locked it. "Sure. Where are we going?"

She hesitated, and her voice filled with embarrassment. "To my ex's place."

"What?" Oh, shit. Was that why she looked nice?

"I know this is really freaking awkward, but I didn't know

who else to ask. None of my friends like Zach." Her gaze refused to meet mine, and she stared at the center of my chest. "When I moved out, I forgot to grab my iPad, and he's been giving me the runaround about it since."

Moved out? We hadn't talked about her past relationships, so I'd had no idea she'd had one so serious—or so recent. Hadn't she told me it had been a while for her the night we'd met?

"I need to get it back," she said, "before my parents find out. They don't need another reason to hate him." She lifted her chin and set her gaze on me, trying to look strong. "I don't know how this is going to go. He might be fine and hand it over no problem, but he also might be an asshole about it. I figure it'll help if you're there."

It was a lot to digest, and when I didn't move or say anything right away, desperation crept into her eyes.

"You can say no," she said. "I know it's a big ask."

Was it, though? This wasn't hard, and it was something I'd do for a friend. *Any* friend. Plus, maybe it'd help us get back onto solid footing, to lead us into the friend zone. That was why I was going to say yes. It had absolutely nothing to do with my curiosity about her ex-boyfriend.

I gestured toward her car in the driveway, which was barely more than a glorified golf cart. "Let's go."

Charlotte's Toyota Yaris was red and tiny, and at least five years old because they'd stopped making them a while back. I eyed the microscopic passenger seat, wondering if I'd fit, but I did and got in without complaint.

As soon as she started it up, Stella's voice rang from the speakers, and it was so loud, I couldn't hear myself think. I was grateful when she turned it down to a volume we could talk over, before backing out of my driveway.

As she drove, she filled me in on her day, talking about her cleaning channel and the brand she was trying to build. She didn't need to tell me it was going well, because I kept tabs on it and had been watching the growth. My interest was just a side effect from years of analyzing the markets, I told myself.

I didn't watch her videos because I wanted to see her, and I was indifferent to the tight, flattering clothes she wore during them. And I definitely hadn't considered coming home early one night to catch her when she was cleaning my place and see where the conversation would lead.

Because I wouldn't allow it.

Without prompting, she told me about her vision for her fledgling business. How she wanted to collaborate with other influencers, and to be sponsored by big brands, and maybe someday sell her own merchandise.

But she spoke like these were fantasies, with no hope of them being anything more than dreams.

"All the admin," she said, "and the business stuff? I'm just terrible at it. I don't have a clue what I'm doing."

"Really? It seems like you're doing great. Every video you post is better than the last, in my opinion."

The second the words left my mouth, I cringed internally. Did that make me sound like a creep?

Charlotte glanced at me with surprise. "You watch my videos?"

I gave her a lopsided smile. "Think of it as a testament to how good they are, because I *hate* cleaning."

She grinned, and I shouldn't have liked how cute that made her look.

So I found somewhere else for my thoughts to go. "What's

the stuff you're struggling with?"

For a moment, it seemed like she wasn't sure where to start. "Okay, so I've got this list of companies I want to reach out to, but . . . I don't know. I don't know how to ask stuff."

"You mean, cold calling?" My mouth ran away with itself. "I could help with that, if you wanted."

What the fuck, I yelled inside my head. I was already stretched thin between Warbler, my day trading, and helping my parents. When would I have time?

"Yeah?" There was so much hopefulness in her voice, I knew I was screwed. I couldn't walk the offer back. She adjusted her hands on the steering wheel and looked pleased. "Awesome. I could use all the help I can get."

Well, great.

With that settled, I turned my gaze out the window and watched the landscape whip by. She was driving fast, even for an interstate. I'd discovered most Nashville drivers seemed to have difficulty finding the accelerator—but not Charlotte.

She also drove like she was required to keep the front end of her Yaris only a foot behind the car in front of her. The proximity made my blood pressure climb, and when the BMW in front of us flashed its brake lights, I tried to push the invisible brake pedal on the passenger side.

Why hadn't I offered to drive?

I liked being the driver, so this was hard for me, and I aimed for a joking tone. "Question for you. Have you thought about not driving up this guy's ass? Could be fun. Maybe you should give it a try."

She laughed, amused. "So sorry, *Dad*."

Instantly, her father's image flashed in my mind. "Don't call me that."

"Okay . . . *Daddy*."

Fuck, there it was again, that strange, exciting thrill. The effect of it was so strong, it barely registered she'd done what I asked, and the BMW pulled ahead, giving us breathing room.

But there wasn't much air left inside the cramped confines of her Yaris. Her *daddy* comment had charged the space, filling it with a sexual tension that was as unwanted as it was hot.

The longer we sat in silence, the worse it became. I needed something to distract us both. "So does this 'Zach' know I'm tagging along?"

"Nope. He doesn't even know we're coming."

I pulled my shoulders back. "What?"

"He hasn't responded to any of my texts, and it's been weeks."

As she took the offramp, I strangled back my unease. "What if we get there and he's not home?"

"Oh, trust me," she said. "He's home. Thursday nights he goes to the bars with some of his friends from Sigma Phi Alpha, so he'll be at his place pregaming right now."

I was about to make a remark about college kids, when I remembered that she was the same age as college kids. Plus, I didn't know what kind of breakup they'd had. If he wasn't responding to her texts, it probably hadn't been good.

What if she still had feelings for him?

Charlotte came to the stop sign at the end of the ramp, didn't bother with a turn signal, and then turned left. It forced my gaze to her dashboard so I wouldn't see anything else. Fuck, I was such a control freak, and the worst part was . . .

If she'd let me, I'd love to have control over her.

Friends!

The warning fired through my brain, causing me to gnash my teeth.

We listened to Taylor Swift sing about the smallest man in the world while we drove, passing strip malls and gas stations. We were on the outskirts of Davidson University, where it'd be a hike to campus, but I understood that. Rent was surely a lot cheaper out here.

Abruptly, the car began to brake, and I glanced around with concern. What did she see that made her need to slow down? Cars were in the other lane, coming from the other direction without issue and—

She turned left into the parking lot of an apartment building, and a frustrated sound escaped from me.

"What?" she asked.

"I wouldn't have used a turn signal there either," I said dryly. "It's nobody's business where you're going."

"Oh, my God." She laughed lightly. "Get in the back seat."

"Excuse me?"

Her tone was playful. "You need to be back there if you're going to backseat drive." She drove down the aisle of the parking lot, searching for a space, and gestured to something. "That's Zach's car."

Once we'd parked and she shut off the engine, Charlotte turned in her seat to face me. "You sure you're okay doing this? He's not the nicest guy when he's been drinking."

My blood ran cold.

Was this the real reason she'd asked me to come along? For protection? I glared up at the apartment building, already hating this kid's guts. I answered her question with action, pushing open the door and climbing out.

She did the same and stood beside her car, looking at me over the hood with a nervous expression. "Don't judge me," she said quietly and rushed. "I wish I'd been smart enough not to fall for him."

Oh, man. Her words punched me like a slug to the chest. My voice matched her soft tone. "Hey, it's going to be okay. I got you, Charlotte."

She nodded her acceptance, and then I followed her up the path to the front door.

Calling it a lobby would be generous. It was mostly just a hallway with a few mailboxes on one side and a set of stairs on the other, all lit by an underpowered chandelier overhead. She'd lived here once, and that had probably sucked. The apartment building was depressing.

Again, I reminded myself that college kids couldn't afford to be picky. My place at NYU had been a lot worse.

We went up the steps, and when she reached the door at the end of the hallway, she took a deep breath, visually checked in with me, and then knocked.

Approaching footsteps could be heard behind the door, and it swung open, almost as if the occupant had been expecting someone. But it was immediately clear Charlotte was not who he'd hoped it would be. His gaze swept over me and then her, and somehow he missed seeing how good she looked, because his smile drained away.

"What the hell?" he demanded.

I bristled at the dark tone he'd directed at her. Who the fuck was this guy? Zach's older brother? An uncle? The man was probably my age, and I sized him up. He was taller and seemed to be in excellent shape, but I wasn't intimidated. Most of the time, the guys who came out of the gate with aggression were the first ones to back down when challenged.

Because the door was wide open, I could see into the shitty apartment. Dirty dishes seemed to decorate every flat surface, and a sweatshirt and two pairs of pants hung haphazardly on the couch in the living area. There wasn't anything on the walls except for a poster of Davidson University's basketball team from their Elite Eight appearance years ago.

Everything about the place screamed a college kid lived here.

So, where the fuck was he?

Charlotte stood at my side, not withering under the man's pissed off glare. "I'm here for my iPad, Zach."

Holy shit. *This* was her ex-boyfriend?

THIRTEEN

Noah

I stared at Zach with new eyes, and my chest tightened with apprehension. I hadn't felt intimidated by his build, but his looks? That was a different story. The man was attractive, and definitely better looking than me. He had one of those sculpted faces with perfect symmetry, the kind women usually lost their shit over.

His hair was short and messy, and he was blond like Charlotte, although his was darker. They matched perfectly in the looks department too. God, what a pair they must have made together.

A foreign sensation stole over me—something I hadn't ever experienced in all my years in the lifestyle.

Jealousy.

It was a burn that crawled up from my stomach and wanted to escape through my eyes. I hated the feeling almost as much as I hated him.

Charlotte didn't wait for an invitation. She pushed past him and charged into the apartment, so I followed suit. I didn't want her too far away, or too close to her ex. There was a collection of liquor bottles on the counter in the kitchen, and a half-empty glass of what looked like whiskey beside it.

The mess of the place made me uncomfortable, so I couldn't even imagine how bad it was for her. She didn't show it, though. She sidestepped a pizza box on the floor and moved with purpose into the living room.

Christ, had it looked like this when she'd lived here? No. There was no way. She'd been bothered by my cluttered house the first time she'd come over, but this place was on a whole other level. It wasn't messy—it was dirty.

"It's not here," Zach said. When she ignored him and began to move stuff off the ottoman, his tone turned patronizing. "But feel free to look around."

She grimaced at the plate of food that had begun to mold and pushed it to the side. "Where's the tray I had here?"

"What tray?"

He must not have been able to notice it because it was buried under all the junk. She let out a sigh of relief, plucking a purple case from beneath a stack of papers and mail. "Got it."

He'd claimed her iPad wasn't here, and he wasn't thrilled she'd proved him wrong. His eyes narrowed. "Wow. You sure didn't wait long."

Did he mean me? Charlotte wrapped her hands around the purple case and marched forward.

The lack of acknowledgement pissed Zach off further, and he stepped in between us. "Why'd you bring your boyfriend along? Trying to make me jealous? Because you know I don't care."

"He's not my—" she started.

But he wasn't finished. His focus swung my way, so he could scan me from top to bottom. "She's definitely got a type, huh, bro?"

My fists clenched. I didn't enjoy the idea that I was anything like this guy. He seemed to be a loser in every sense of the word, and my voice was frosty. "We just came to get her stuff. Now that it's done, we're leaving."

"Great." His eyes brightened with a thought, and an evil smile dawned on his face. "You been enjoying my sloppy seconds?"

My shoulders stiffened as anger raced through my muscles, and I stepped closer to him. "What the fuck did you just say?"

His expression filled with panic, and he shuffled backward on uneasy feet. How the hell was he legitimately surprised by my reaction? It was like he'd expected me to shrink away or stay quiet, not surge forward.

Just as I'd thought.

This guy was all bark and no bite. When I moved to take another step, Charlotte appeared between us and planted a hand on the center of my chest.

"Let's go," she said. "This place is so gross, I don't want to be here another second."

The connection of her touch disarmed and diffused me. And she was right; I didn't want to be here any longer either. I closed my hand on top of hers and led her to the front door.

"That's right, run away," he said, sounding like a smug fuck. "It's what you're good at."

His comment slammed into her, and since I had hold of her hand, I felt her jolt. But I laced our fingers together and kept us moving. I considered leading her out into the hallway first, and then shutting the door between us so she couldn't see me giving him a piece of my mind.

Because he'd hurt her, and I didn't like that one fucking bit.

Instead, when I reached the threshold of the door, I turned to deliver a cold, victorious smile. "She's not running away, she's leveling up."

Zach gaped at me, lost for words. Then, his tiny brain

fired back up and he sneered. "Bet her dad fucking loves you."

"He does," I lied.

He seemed like the kind of guy who always had to have the last word, but I moved too quickly. I pulled the door closed behind us and set off down the hallway at a fast clip. Charlotte's grip tightened in mine, and she kept up with me, step for step.

Maybe we were both running from the last comment he'd lobbed at us.

She let me lead her to the driver's side of her Yaris, and when we reached it, she turned and leaned against the door. Neither one of us relaxed our hands to let go.

I peered down into her eyes, seeing all the hurt and upset that pooled there. "Don't let him get under your skin."

"Too late," she whispered. "God, I'm a magnet for losers."

"Are you?" I tugged the corner of my mouth into a half smile. "Because I'm the one who hit on you at the bar." I wasn't any good at dealing with emotion, and my go-to move was to deflect. I flattened my free hand to my chest and pretended to be wounded. "You think *I'm* a loser?"

It was the wrong play. She needed me to be serious right now.

I cleared the discomfort from my throat. "Hey. I'm sorry he was such a dick. Are you okay?"

She pressed her lips together and nodded. "I'm glad you're here."

"Me too." And I truly meant it.

Her gaze dropped to the iPad she held, and then shifted to our clasped hands. It made my heartbeat fall out of rhythm.

"What did he mean about running away?"

The question came from me before I could think better of

it, and her expression shuttered. Her shields came up at the same time she tried to drop my hand, but I wouldn't let go.

Her tone was brusque. "I don't want to talk about it."

"Fair enough." My head bobbed in a short, understanding nod. I didn't know why I'd asked, anyway. It wasn't any of my business. When I released her hand and took a step back, she gave me a sharp, evaluating look.

Whatever she was thinking about, it made me nervous.

"I'll tell you," she said reluctantly, "if you'd be willing to do me another favor."

Even without knowing the specifics, excitement shot through me. She wanted to make a deal—and I lived for making good deals. "What is it?"

She pushed off the car to stand tall. "I want you to take me to the club."

I already knew the answer, but I asked it anyway. "Which club?"

"The one where you met Patrick and Shannon."

She was worried I was going to say no, and I had to bite back a smile. Because I was sure this would be the easiest *yes* I'd ever give. But I took my time anyway, drawing it out like I was weighing the pros and cons.

"All right," I answered. "On one condition."

She drew in an anxious breath. "What is it?"

"You give me your keys, and I get to drive us back to my place."

She blinked back her surprise, then dug a hand into her pocket and produced the keys. She held them up, jingling them, but when I reached out, she pulled back. "Promise me, Noah."

Like she worried I'd renege on our deal.

Fuck. Was she thinking I was like the man upstairs in the apartment we'd just left? He'd done a number on her, for sure.

I softened my voice. "I promise."

It must have been convincing enough, because she handed over the keys.

After I banged my knees against the steering wheel while climbing into the driver's seat, I slid the seat back, repositioned the mirrors, and started the engine. She got into the passenger seat and rested the iPad on her lap, keeping her gaze fixed forward.

I sensed the tension in her and stayed quiet, focusing on the drive. When she was ready, she'd talk, and if she didn't . . . that was okay too. I'd take her to Club Eros regardless of how much she wanted to reveal to me.

Eventually, Charlotte straightened in her seat and pulled in a deep, preparing breath.

"I'm a spoiled brat," she announced.

Um, what? I shot her a questioning glance. Her focus remained on the windshield, her expression not giving anything away.

"That's what I've been told my whole life," she continued, "but I didn't believe it until Zach." Her voice was quiet and sad. "The first time he said it, I'd thought he was teasing me. He would call me a spoiled brat like it was some cute little joke he was letting me in on. Like, we were sharing it together."

My hand tightened on the steering wheel.

"I don't know why I ate it up." Her fingers curled around the edge of the iPad, lifting and closing the case lid repeatedly. "But I did. I fell in love with him, and I fell *hard*, and I just stopped caring about anything else." The steady thumps of the case lid closing could barely be heard over the music playing through her car's speakers. "My parents had given me a million chances already, so when I failed out of Davidson, I panicked. I knew that was it."

She finally turned in her seat to look at me, and even though I kept my attention on the road, I felt her gaze locked on me.

"So," her voice lost any power, "I ran. I used the credit card my parents gave me and booked a trip to Hawaii. I told Zach it was an early Christmas present to us from my parents."

Oh, shit. The thought formed quickly. Was this why she needed money? Why she hadn't refused when Ardy had pushed for her to clean my place? She needed to pay back her parents.

"I was really fucking stupid, okay? I'd never disappointed my dad before, and I didn't know how to deal."

She said it like she wanted to get out in front of whatever judgmental thing she expected me to say, but it was unnecessary. I wasn't in a position to judge anyone.

Sure, she'd made a huge mistake, but it was impossible not to feel for her, at least a little. I'd worked with Ardy long enough to know he was good guy, who was probably a teddy bear of a man when it came to his daughter.

But I'd also seen him when things hadn't gone his way.

When he'd been let down or disappointed, he didn't shy away from letting people know. He could raise his voice and get heated, so I was aware the teddy bear had teeth, and he would flash them if needed.

Had she been terrified to be on the receiving end of that?

Charlotte swiped a hand over her cheek, and that was the only indication I had that tears had begun to roll down her face. She didn't sniffle, and her voice didn't quaver.

"When my parents realized what I'd done, they cut off my credit card, and were waiting for me when we got back. He thought Zach had talked me into it, like I was under his spell. My dad promised all could be forgiven, but only as long as I ended it with Zach and came home." Her tone filled with shame. "But I couldn't. I was too embarrassed to admit defeat or face what I'd done. I told myself I loved him, and that would be enough."

Her focus drifted from me and went to the horizon where the sunlight was fading, and the sky filled with orange and pink hues.

"Spoiler alert," she warned, "it wasn't. I was cut off, with nowhere to go, and he was forced to take me in. So the first few months we lived together, I did everything right. I tried really hard to be the perfect girlfriend, but it didn't seem to matter to him. He resented I was there, and every time he called me a spoiled brat, he got a little meaner about it."

"He's an asshole," I snapped.

"Yeah, but . . . was he wrong? He said I hadn't worked a day in my life. That I didn't know what hard work was, but I thought that was bullshit. I worked *so fucking hard* to keep us together. I should have left him, but it was too late. I was in too deep."

"Sunk cost fallacy," I said. "Where you don't cut your losses and give up on a bad strategy because you're too heavily invested."

"Yeah, I guess," she admitted. "Our relationship ended months before I moved out, and those last few weeks were hell. When I left, Zach just had to throw it in my face that I was running back home. That's why him saying I'm good at running away got to me."

I took a long moment to contemplate all of what she'd just told me, and since she'd been so vulnerable, I felt the urge to return the favor. To show her she wasn't alone in being young and making a mistake. "I ran away, too."

That got her attention. "You did? When?"

"After high school."

Her expression turned plain. "Going to college isn't running away."

"It is when you do it to get away from your family." I turned left into my subdivision and followed the road as it wove through the neighborhood. "I could have gone to Davidson, or Western Kentucky, or even UT, but instead I picked the school that's nine hundred miles away."

"Why?"

I frowned. "Because my family can be a lot. I love them, don't get me wrong, but I'm not like the rest of them. I'm more," I searched for the right word, "independent."

"Meaning?"

"Meaning I like my alone time. When I lived here, I felt like they were on top of me, always in my business." I turned into my driveway, parked in front of the garage, and shifted in my seat to give her my full attention. "My family is totally cool spending every moment together. But for me? I felt like I couldn't breathe, so I put as much distance between us as I could." I shut off the engine and handed her the keys. "That makes me sound like an asshole, doesn't it? Running away because my family likes being with me too much."

She looked at me like I was being silly. "I'm an only child, so trust me, I get it. My parents mean well, but yeah. Sometimes they can be smothering." Her gaze drifted away, only to snap back to me with a new thought. "What about now? How's it been with them since you moved back?"

"It's not bad. I think they're making a conscious effort not to come on too strong."

"That's good," she said. "But to be honest, I don't blame them for wanting to spend time with you." Her smile was surprisingly shy. "I'm going to let you in on a secret. I feel the same way."

My pulse jumped, and it came out before I could stop myself. "Yeah, same."

Her smile grew into a full-blown grin. "So, when are we going to the club?"

Right. I got out my phone and checked my schedule. The club was only open a few nights a week, but I had some space this weekend. "Saturday?"

She didn't even think about it. "That sounds great."

An alarm blared inside me, telling me to get out of the car before I did something stupid . . . like putting my lips on hers. "Okay, I'll figure out a time," I reached for the door handle, "and text you the details."

Charlotte nodded and followed my lead, climbing out of the passenger side. I stood beside her Yaris, holding the driver's door open for her, and watched her round the back of the car. She didn't get in though. Instead, she stood at the side, with the car door between us, and I was grateful. I needed the barrier to keep me in line.

"Hey, thanks again for coming with me tonight," she said softly.

"Of course." I almost added '*anything for a friend*,' but was wise enough to leave it off, because the thoughts swirling through me were not thoughts a friend should be having.

She hovered there long enough for me to realize she was

waiting for something. An invitation, perhaps? I wasn't going to do that because nothing good could come from it.

Orgasms could come from it.

Yeah, but it wouldn't be worth the fallout after. I liked my job. And I happened to like Charlotte even more, which was why I didn't want to hurt her.

If she was disappointed I didn't ask her to come in, she didn't show it. She sat in the seat and gazed up at me with a bright smile. "Saturday," she said. "I can't wait."

I nodded and closed the door, unable to say anything, because I worried what would come out of my mouth. She was looking forward to me taking her to the club, but me?

It was concerning how fucking thrilled I was about it.

FOURTEEN

Charlotte

Excitement buzzed in my system all day, but it ramped up significantly when it came time to get ready for my evening with Noah. I twirled my long, color-treated locks of blonde hair around the barrel of my curling iron, studying my reflection in the mirror. Shit, I'd need to go easy on the blush and contouring tonight. I was already flushed, and it had nothing to do with the heat the iron was putting out.

I was going to a sex club tonight.

The thought played in a constant loop in my brain.

Once I'd finished my hair and makeup, I pulled on a black leather mini skirt and paired it with a maroon top. The shirt was satin and cut low enough in the front that I considered taping it in place, but ultimately decided against it. I didn't mind if the edge of my bra showed occasionally. In fact, I kind of liked the idea.

It was like a sexy little hint.

My overnight bag was already packed, which had taken me a lot longer to finish than I'd expected. Noah had told me it'd be late when we left the club, so I could stay in his guest bedroom tonight.

I packed options with varying degrees of sexiness, just in case he changed his mind about which bed he wanted me to occupy. He probably wouldn't though. My no-sex rule was still in place, and we might find sharing a bed too tempting and torturous.

After I'd zipped up my high-heeled boots, I stood in front of the full-length mirror in my closet and snapped a selfie. I messed with the settings until I had the color grading where I wanted it, and then laughed at myself. The pic was cute enough, but I wasn't planning on posting it to my socials. I'd edited it simply out of habit.

Me: Is this outfit okay for tonight?

I followed my message up with the picture, then set my phone aside as I awaited Noah's response, although I was confident I'd get his approval. He'd said the club had a dress code, but also that it only applied to men. Women could wear whatever they wanted—and as *little* as they wanted.

This outfit was bringing my A game.

It pushed the line for me, and was the kind of look that'd make my dad frown—but he wouldn't dare say anything about it. I wasn't much younger than his client Stella, and this was exactly what she'd wear on a night out.

I knew, because I'd talked to her stylist last year and bought some of the same pieces.

By sending the selfie, I'd spoiled the reveal for Noah, but I figured this was a good trade-off. Now he had a picture of me in his phone. Sure, he could watch my YouTube channel or my TikTok videos anytime he wanted, but this was different. This image was *only* for him.

Noah: Yeah, looks good.

It wasn't the resounding answer I was looking for, but I could live with it.

Me: Thanks. I'm heading your way.

Noah: See you soon.

I grabbed my purse and my overnight bag and made my way downstairs.

My father didn't seem to be home, and I nearly escaped the house unnoticed, but my timing sucked. Just as I opened the door to the garage, my mom rounded the corner from the kitchen.

Her gaze swept over my outfit and noted the overnight bag, and her tone was curious. "Where are you heading off to?"

Shit. I'd promised not to lie, but there was no avoiding it. "Uh . . . Sasha's."

She looked dubious. "You're wearing that to Sasha's?"

"We're going out, and I'm going to crash at her place after."

Her doubt cleared. "Oh. Okay, stay safe and have fun."

"Will do." The words were sticky in my throat and came out garbled. "Love you."

"I love you, too."

During the drive over to Noah's house, I constantly had to remind myself not to speed. My anxiousness to see him and my curiosity about the club combined to give me a lead foot. When I finally reached his place, I parked to the side in his driveway, out of the way, clasped my bag, and scurried up the front walkway.

I didn't get a chance to ring the doorbell, because he must have seen me coming and was waiting for me just inside the open front door.

"Holy fuck," I blurted. "You're wearing a suit."

His pleasant smile froze. "Is that bad?"

He glanced down at his charcoal gray suit and maroon tie, searching for what was wrong. Oh, my God. When I'd texted him the picture of what I was wearing tonight, had he chosen his tie to match? We looked like we'd planned it.

Like we were a couple.

"No, it's not bad," I said, and pretended to be irritated. "I just wasn't expecting you to look so freaking hot."

He laughed and adopted the same annoyed tone I'd used. "It's only fair. I have to deal with," he gestured to my outfit, "all *this*."

His gaze filled with heat, telling me just how much he liked what he saw, and warmth swept through me. This was the reaction I'd hoped for earlier, but getting it in person was way better than through a text message.

When I climbed the two steps of his front porch, he reached out and took my bag from me like a gentleman and motioned for me to go inside. I did and lingered awkwardly in the entryway. I hadn't prepared myself for how strange it'd feel.

Tonight, he wasn't my client.

Instead, he'd be my guide.

"You want something to drink?" he asked as he moved through the entryway and headed toward the guest bedroom. He raised his voice so I could still hear him while he was out of sight. "You might have to drink it fast, though. I already called for a Lyft."

"No, thanks. I'm okay." It was surprising he'd booked a car, because it was just after nine and the sun hadn't set all that long ago. I figured this club would be like any other and didn't get busy until late. "Do we need to get there soon?"

He reappeared and glanced at his phone screen. "Kind of. I was hoping to have some time to show you around before the show starts."

My breath quickened. "There's a show?"

"Calling it a show might be the wrong word. It's more like . . . a demonstration."

I swallowed hard and my voice fell to a hush. "A sexy demonstration?"

"Yes."

The cavernous space of his entryway became cozy and intimate when he came closer, and even he seemed to notice. His irises darkened with something that looked a hell of a lot like lust.

"It's hard to be friends with you," I uttered, "when you look at me like that."

Noah drew in a deep breath and didn't look away. A war was going on inside him between what he should do and what he wanted to do, and it seemed like desire was winning out.

"Sorry," he said, although he didn't sound sorry at all.

But then he broke the gaze, turning his focus to the small purse that dangled from my elbow. The bag didn't hold anything more than my phone and a tube of lipstick, but I had nowhere else to put them.

His gaze rose back to my face. "I know this will probably be a challenge for you," a slight smile tilted his lips, "since you're a 'permanently online' person, but you're not allowed to use your phone inside Club Eros."

"I can't have my phone?" I tried not to screech it, because he'd sort of just asked me to amputate a part of my body.

"You can have it," he clarified, "you just can't *use* it. If they catch you with it out, they'll ask us to leave, and neither of us will be welcome back."

"Oh."

"It's a safety thing. They don't want people taking pictures or video."

I nodded. "That makes sense."

The weight of my handbag seemed to quadruple when I realized it was no longer needed. I must have made a face, because he shot me a questioning look.

"I'm trying to decide if I should even bother taking this, then." I raised my elbow, jostling the little purse. "All it does is hold my phone since I don't have any pockets."

"I have pockets," he said. "You want me to hang on to it for you?"

I dug out my phone, but hesitated. "You don't mind?"

"No." He chuckled and plucked it from my hand. "I think I can manage."

I watched as he opened his suit coat and slipped my phone into the interior pocket, and the idea of it was *exciting*. The small device was such a big part of my life. It was an extension of me, so to know it was nestled inside his jacket, next to his heart, was deeply satisfying.

When I set my no-longer-needed purse on his entryway table, movement drew my gaze out through the front window. A black sedan turned into the driveway.

"Is that—"

"Our ride?" he said. "Yeah. You ready?"

Shit, I was *more* than ready.

We didn't talk about the club in front of our driver, like it was some secret we needed to keep, which was sort of ridiculous. The guy knew where we were going—he had the address.

But . . . did he?

Because when we got there, I didn't see anything that

looked remotely like a club. We weren't in the best part of town, and the street was dark. All the buildings around here looked like they were commercial, and most of them had gone out of business during the pandemic.

I got out of the car when Noah did, but I stood on the sidewalk in disbelief. "You sure this is the right place?"

It was a stupid question, since he'd been here before, but he didn't make me feel dumb. His laugh was light and casual. "Yeah. I know it's not much to look at from the outside, but I think that's kind of the point."

He gestured to the concrete walkway that was off the sidewalk, leading up to . . .

Oh.

There was a house nestled between two large warehouses, complete with a covered front porch. In another neighborhood, it would have looked cute, but here it was so out of place. It looked old, too, like it had existed long before the industrial buildings that grew up around it.

The windows were dark, most likely blacked out, making the place look empty.

But there was a large chrome E that was backlit, glowing in the night beside the unremarkable front door.

My pulse hurried along as I traveled the pathway and up the two porch steps with Noah at my side. He reached the door first and pulled it open for me.

The entry room was small, only large enough to hold a few people. The walls and ceiling were painted black, and the lighting in the room was low, nearly matching the darkness outside. There was a security guard waiting beside the door that led deeper into the club, and along the side wall was an elegant, shaded lamp and a tall desk. A woman was seated behind it, and she gave us a once-over, followed by a friendly smile. "IDs, please."

"I need my phone," I said to Noah. "My license is in the case."

He handed it to me, and while I fished my driver's license out of the slot on my case, he extracted his from his wallet and passed it to the woman. Once she'd finished scanning our licenses, she gave me a clipboard and pen.

"Membership form is the first sheet, the waiver is beneath."

She didn't have one for him, though.

Because he's already a member.

While I filled the forms out, Noah paid, and then the woman gave us a quick rundown of the rules. No phones, no going in the bathrooms opposite of our gender identities, and no harassment of any kind. If there were problems, staff wore gold nametags and were always nearby.

When we were all set, she nodded to the security guard, gave us a smile, and pushed a button beneath the desk. "Have fun."

The door buzzed and the security guard pulled it open for us. I kind of expected it to be like the scene in *The Wizard of Oz* where Dorothy is in black and white and when she opens the front door, everything changes to vibrant color.

It wasn't like that at all.

The inside of Club Eros looked . . . like any other club. There was a bar and a dance floor, and the lighting was dark and moody. A DJ booth was in the far corner, playing music with heavy bass and spinning a disco ball that cast glittering reflections everywhere.

There were more people than I expected, but hardly any on the dance floor. Most of them sat at the bar or the low tables scattered around the room, sipping drinks and holding conversations over the loud music. There were only a few couches and zero beds.

I put a hand on Noah's shoulder and rose on my tiptoes to speak into his ear. "It's just a bar?"

I hadn't meant to sound disappointed, but he'd picked up on it. He looked sort of amused and devious. "This room is, yeah." He motioned toward the bartender. "You want something to drink?"

"Sure. I'll have a cosmo."

I stuck close by his side as we strolled to the bar, but my gaze wandered around the room while he ordered for us. The outfits people wore were . . . diverse. At one table it'd be nice dresses and suits, and at the next it'd be pleather and latex. And it was odd how the tables were exclusively couples or groups, yet the bar was only men.

I kept my voice as low as possible over the music. "Are dudes only allowed to sit at the bar?"

He nodded. "Single men have to be invited anywhere else inside the club."

Oh, wow. "So, if I wasn't here, you'd . . . "

"Be sitting on one of those bar stools? Yup." Our drinks arrived, he tossed down his credit card, and then passed the martini glass to me. A smirk teased his lips. "Turns out your favor is doing me a favor."

I returned his smug smile. "Happy to help you out."

After he settled up, he pointed to the door on the far side of the room. "Ready to see the rest of this place?"

I took a sip of my drink so it wasn't so full, and nodded. "Lead the way."

We weaved through the tables, passed by the dance floor,

and strode through the open doorway. It was quieter here and more elegant too. The first room was a nightclub, but this one was a swanky lounge. There were velvet couches and oversized leather chairs, with low tables between them.

I only made it a few steps past the threshold before jerking to a stop. My drink sloshed over the rim of the glass, and the icy liquid dripped down my fingers.

An older man sat in one of the chairs, with his pants down around his ankles and a fistful of hair of the woman who was on her knees, currently blowing him. She bobbed her head, coating his dick with her saliva.

I blinked rapidly, maybe trying to clear the vision from my eyes. It wasn't that I was turned off by what I saw—it was just so shocking. Blood rushed through me, heating my body, filling it with a sensation that felt oddly like second-hand shame. Because it was so *public*, and I'd spent a long time believing that sort of thing should only happen behind closed doors.

At first, I couldn't look away. I stood utterly still, locked on to the woman's every movement. It was almost mesmerizing how she surged up and down and let his hold on her hair guide her pace. I felt the man staring at me, and I held my breath tensely in my lungs.

Watching Noah when he'd been with Shannon had made me uncomfortable, but only because it'd been so insanely hot, I hadn't known how to handle it. This? Watching these strangers? It only had a fraction of that heat. I felt uncomfortable in a different way, as if I'd intruded.

I ripped my gaze away, wheeling it around to look anywhere else, until it landed on Noah. His expression was . . . curious. Like he wanted to know what I was thinking.

"I'm trying not to stare," I whispered.

"Why?" He asked it so casually. "They want people to watch. If they didn't, they'd be in one of the private rooms."

"Private rooms?"

It was only then I noticed the rest of the space, beyond the woman going down on the man who continued to stare at us. The wall opposite the doorway we'd come through was lined with black doors, which were decorated with brass numbers, and all were ajar.

He followed my gaze. "Looks like no one's using them right now." He took a sip of his Manhattan, and then used his glass to point to the archway on the right. "We're heading that way."

I peeked into one of the private rooms along the way, finding it kind of underwhelming. All that was inside was a full-size couch and a love seat that had been arranged like a sectional in the narrow space.

Beyond the archway, there was an old, ornate staircase that turned the corner as it traveled upward. It was stunning and must have been original to the house but looked like a bitch to clean with all the woodwork. Just off the base of the stairs, there was another black door that hung open—although this one didn't have a brass number on it.

That wasn't the only thing telling me this room was different. The walls were painted a deep red, and the hairs at the base of my neck tingled with awareness. The doorway was at the end of the room, so I couldn't see much of the inside, but when I started to go in, Noah's hand went out to stop me.

"Not yet," he said. "Let's go upstairs first."

It made me wonder if whatever was in that room was the grand finale.

The staircase creaked and groaned as we climbed it, and then we were on the second floor, which was a bit of a maze and totally deserted. These had once been the bedrooms of the house, but the doorways had been widened to make it easier to move around. The flow of it still wasn't great, but I kind of liked that.

There were more quiet corners and alcoves this way.

The lounge atmosphere continued up here, but this one was cozier, with exposed brick walls and a fireplace—although this one looked like it was no longer functional. The most dramatic difference was that the side tables up here weren't empty. They had large dishes on them, like the ones you'd see filled with candy, only these shiny wrappers didn't contain treats.

"Is that a giant bowl of condoms?" I hadn't meant to giggle, but I couldn't help myself. There were bottles of lube next to the dish too. "This shit is wild."

He chuckled. "They want their guests to stay safe and have a good time." He was quiet for a moment, letting me take it all in. "This floor is the only part of the club where men are allowed to get naked."

I scrunched my face with confusion. "What about women?"

"They can get naked anywhere." He must have realized he needed to amend it. "As long as they're inside the club."

"Isn't that—I don't know, sexist?"

He shrugged. "If it is, I'm okay with it. It's safer this way, and . . . men are pervs. I'm glad I'm not seeing dicks the second I walk through the door."

Oh, my God. A grin spread across my face. "You're not wrong." My grin stilled as I remembered what he'd said. "Wait a minute. The guy downstairs was getting a blowjob."

"He was." Noah took another sip of his drink. "Maybe he forgot, but I'm guessing he knows he's breaking the rules. Some people like getting caught."

"What'll happen to him?"

"He'll get thrown out, and his membership revoked." He ticked his head toward the stairs, indicating he wanted to head back down. "Places like this have zero tolerance for rule breakers."

I walked beside him, having to move at a faster pace than normal because his strides were longer. "Places," I repeated. "You've been to others?"

"Yeah. There was a club in New York I went to often enough I became friends with the owners."

"Friends like us?" I asked as we descended.

He found my question amusing. "No. Claire and Enrique are in their late sixties, and they're heavy into masochism. That's not one of my kinks."

My breath caught. Well, now I *needed* to know what all his kinks were. I was dying to find out because . . . what if his aligned with mine? What if he could show me things I didn't even know I was into?

I wanted to learn them with him.

But I didn't get a chance to ask any of that, because I followed him into the red room, and my brain short-circuited.

FIFTEEN

Charlotte

This was more like what I had expected to see tonight.

The paint on the walls was the color of sin, and most of the furniture was black. Rows of folding chairs had been lined up, with a narrow aisle cutting down the center, and several groups of people had already claimed their seats. They faced the short, raised platform at the other end of the room, and the brick wall behind it.

The 'stage' only had one thing on it—a large wooden X.

Even though I didn't know what it was called, I knew its purpose. There were silver rings in various places, which I imagined were used to clip handcuffs to, or to tie off rope.

I could barely take my eyes off it.

And the room had a seductive energy swirling in the air, whispering that wicked things had taken place in here.

Noah's deep voice snapped me out of my stupor. "Should we find some seats?"

I turned to gaze at him. God, he looked so good in his dark suit, so confident and at ease. And why shouldn't he? This was his world, after all.

I nodded and followed him to a pair of chairs one row back from the front, lowered into my seat, and took another sip of my cosmo to help with my dry mouth. Did I look as anxious as I felt on the inside? I vibrated with anticipation, eager to see the sexy 'demonstration' Noah had promised.

I leaned over, catching a hint of his enticing cologne, and pointed to the X. "Are they going to use that thing during the show?"

"The St. Andrew's Cross?" Was that what it was called? "Maybe. Her boyfriend was the one who built it."

It only took me a second to realize who he was talking about. A woman stood to the side, just off the platform, talking to a man who held a small black duffle bag. She appeared to be in her late twenties, and had long, dark hair, a gorgeous face, and a body to match. Plus, her red dress was short and sexy, and fitted perfectly to her curves.

I wasn't typically attracted to women, but fuck me.

She was unquestionably hot.

A pang of envy shot through me. She looked like the kind of girl who rolled out of bed and was effortlessly beautiful, whereas I had to work so hard to look decent. I'd gotten fast and efficient at my hair and makeup routine, but it still hovered at around forty minutes if I wanted to feel confident I looked all right.

And my envy spiked higher as my gaze shifted to the man she was speaking to. Her boyfriend was equally attractive. He was tall and muscular, and if he'd told me he'd just come from a photoshoot to sell men's suits, I would have believed him.

"That guy," I subtly motioned to him and then the St. Andrew's Cross, "built that?"

"No." Noah gave the room a quick scan. "I don't see him yet, but I'm sure he's around. Clay always watches."

What? My focus went back to the woman and man, who'd stepped onto the stage and began to prepare. The duffle was dropped to the floor and unzipped, and I only caught glimpses between the people seated in front of me of the items being pulled from the bag.

A coil of rope.

Leather cuffs.

A long, thin stick with a leather heart shaped tip.

Oh, shit. Was that a riding crop? It made my brain slow to process what he'd just said. "She isn't performing with her boyfriend?

For a moment, he looked like he didn't know how to answer that. "No, she is." He motioned to the man on stage. "That's Travis," he said. "He's Lilith's other boyfriend." I must have made a face that announced I didn't understand, so he explained. "They're poly."

"Oh."

I'd never met anyone in a polyamorous relationship before. The idea of it was foreign to me. Unfamiliar. It wasn't something I thought I'd be interested in, but then again, I never would have dreamed I'd get turned on watching the guy I liked fuck someone else.

It was impossible not to stare at the gorgeous couple conversing with each other on stage. "Have you ever . . . "

"Played with them? No." He sounded faintly amused. "I wouldn't say no if they asked." His warm tone turned serious. "But they haven't, and I don't think they're interested in playing with others."

I cast a glance at him, giving him a once-over and didn't try to hide my smirk. "Their loss."

My comment brought his amusement right back. But then something caught his attention, and I turned to follow his gaze.

A man was coming up the center aisle, carrying a large piece of furniture. It looked heavy and wasn't like anything I'd seen before. The closest comparison I could make was like the sawhorses my grandfather had in his woodworking shop, only this one was beautifully constructed. It was painted a glossy black, and the top of it was padded with a red leather-like cushion.

Noah leaned over me, so the man in the aisle could hear his question better. "Clay. You need help with that?"

The man set the furniture down for a moment, either to rest or to push up the glasses that had slid down the bridge of his nose, as his gaze went to Noah. He recognized him, gave a brief smile, followed by a shake of his head.

And then he was off again, carrying the sawhorse-looking thing up onto the platform, where it was set to the side.

Clay always watches, Noah had said. This was Lilith's other boyfriend? My gaze bounced between the two men, and it pumped fresh envy inside me. Clay wasn't quite as attractive as Travis, in my opinion, but it was fucking close. He was hot, too, just more in a nerdy way.

Her two boyfriends didn't speak to each other, at least not with words, but when they exchanged a look, I would have sworn they'd just had a full conversation. Travis nodded in acknowledgment and Clay stepped off the stage, moving to take his empty seat in the front row.

The volume of conversations in the narrow room rose as more people arrived, and it was stunning how quickly every seat was taken. More people came in, filing into the back where it was standing room only.

"You were right to get here early," I whispered to Noah. "Glad we got seats."

There wasn't an announcement that the show was about to start. There also wasn't an introduction of the performers. Travis and Lilith moved to stand center-stage, and the room must have sensed they were ready, because a hush fell over the crowd.

The order from Travis was quiet enough I wouldn't have heard it if I'd been sitting any farther back.

"Take off your dress."

She peered out at the audience as she did it, grasping the sides of her skirt and pulling it up. Red fabric gave way to icy blue lace and flawless skin. Her bare stomach was toned, and as the dress continued to travel upward, it exposed the matching blue bra she wore.

Shit, her boobs looked amazing. The pale blue bra was demi cut, and her breasts nearly spilled out the top of it in a wicked tease. The lingerie was sexy and probably insanely expensive, and I would be lying to myself if I said I didn't want to see what was hidden beneath.

Her dark hair splashed around her after she'd finished pulling the dress over her head, and she turned to look at him—or perhaps to make sure he was looking at her. She dropped the dress like it was a challenge, a signal she was ready for the next step.

Travis lifted an eyebrow. *Is that so,* his expression read. He strode forward to the edge of the platform, shrugged out of his suit coat, and handed it off to Clay. Next, his fingers worked to loosen the knot of his black tie and undo the buttons of his dress shirt.

There was something for everyone to enjoy once his shirt was off. They could look at the stunning woman in skimpy lingerie, or the shirtless man who looked like he'd been carved out of stone.

It was instinctive, the way I tensed when Travis unbuckled his belt, slid it free from the belt loops, and coiled the buckle end around his palm. It left the other end dangling free from his hand and when he stepped toward her, I sucked in a breath.

Was he planning to *use* that on her?

I didn't know how to feel about that, but Lilith did. She focused on the strap of leather swinging from his grip, and electricity sparked in her eyes. She looked at that belt like she wanted it badly.

His back was to the audience, but he must have noticed her hungry expression because he paused. Something like a chuckle rumbled out of him, and he kept his voice low. "Maybe later."

Her excitement fell at the same moment the belt was dropped to the stage with a loud *thunk*, but that excitement returned as he bent and scooped up one of the pairs of leather cuffs he'd pulled from the bag. She offered her hands to him eagerly and held still as he latched each of the black cuffs closed around her wrists.

And when it was done, she laced her fingers together and held her hands out in front of her as if in prayer. There were lights overhead, angled toward the platform to light the stage, and it made the silver clasps dangling from her cuffs gleam brightly.

Travis took a knee to retrieve the other pair of cuffs, and while he fastened them around her ankles, I stared at her impressive shoes. The stiletto heels were so tall and thin, it was like she was balancing on needles, and my calves ached just looking at them. But she had perfect balance.

When he was done, he rose and loomed over her, showing the powerful flat of his back to the audience, but my focus didn't stay there. It was because he placed his large hand on the base of her neck so his fingers could collar her throat.

It didn't seem like he was squeezing, or that she was the least bit uncomfortable with it, but the action left me breathless. It was so . . . possessive. I bit down on my bottom lip. God, what was wrong with me? Seeing his hand wrapped around her throat turned me on, but the thought of Noah doing the same to me?

That turned me on a hell of a lot more.

Lilith stared back at her boyfriend like she was under his spell. Utterly enthralled. So much so, that when he began to guide her backward toward the St. Andrew's Cross, I doubted she even realized she was moving.

She held his gaze, unblinking, as he used his free hand to grasp one of her wrists and raise it to match one of the outstretched arms of the cross. There was a slight click of metal against metal as she was clipped to the ring there.

I hadn't realized my breath had gone so shallow until Travis's hand dropped away from her neck. Had it been like that for the rest of the audience? As if he'd been collectively holding their throats too?

A muscle deep between my legs squeezed against the ache building inside me as he worked to clip the rest of her cuffs to the cross. Once she was completely restrained, he stood back and admired his work. We couldn't see the expression on his face, but I imagined he looked pleased.

And why shouldn't he feel that way? She was at his mercy. While everyone stared at her, watching the rapid rise and fall of her heaving chest, she stared at him like no one else existed.

Wait, no.

Her gaze finally broke from his and went to the only other person she saw in this crowded room. The longing in her eyes didn't change, though. She was just as enchanted by Clay as she was Travis, even when he hadn't touched her.

He had a part to play in this scene—one that was bigger than just adding the set piece off to the side before the show had begun. I had been so distracted by the strange sawhorse thing, I hadn't seen him pick up the riding crop on his way to his seat.

He'd done it so he could easily pass it to Travis now that their girlfriend was bound spreadeagle to the cross. I shifted in my chair, anxious to see better between the people seated in front of us. I liked everything about this, from the way Lilith gazed at her partners, to the tacit approval Clay gave by handing the other man the crop.

Travis strolled to stand beside the cross, tapping the heart-shaped end of the black riding crop absentmindedly against his palm, before placing the leather heart gently on the center of her chest. Her eyes hazed as the tip dragged across her bare skin just above the edge of her bra.

His movements were unhurried and sensual. The tip of the crop carved a lazy path, gliding over her stomach, the juncture of her legs, and down the outside of one of her shapely thighs.

Everything about this was erotic.

It wasn't just the scantily clad woman trussed up to the St. Andrew's Cross and her attractive partner teasing her. The room was quiet, so riveted with anticipation that the first soft smack of the leather against skin could probably be heard clearly at the back of the room.

Travis gave her short, seemingly harmless slaps with the crop that mimicked the ones he'd given his palm. He followed the same path he'd taken down her body, although this time in reverse, tapping his way back up to her chest.

Lilith's lips parted to release a soft sigh of pleasure when he increased the intensity of his strikes. The next round he dealt her was shorter. *Sharper.*

I swallowed a big gulp of my cosmo, needing the temporary distraction so I could get hold of myself because—Jesus Christ, this scene was so freaking hot, and it'd barely started.

The woman on stage sagged against her restraints, shifting on her ankle-breaking heels, and looked like she was halfway to heaven. The crop smacked against her breasts, her stomach, the insides of her thighs, making her jolt and moan.

And it painted little pink hearts across her skin, heating from the sharp slap of leather.

Lilith groaned and writhed, but there was no doubt she enjoyed it. Her little gasps and moans dripped with need, and I'd swear I could feel them reverberating through my body. Everything in me was tight, on edge, clamoring for some kind of release, although I hadn't a clue what kind.

The room was full of strangers, and it wasn't like I was close to orgasm.

But I felt a need just like she did, and it was worse for me because I wasn't pinned down or constrained. The desire to touch myself was nearly overwhelming, and the only thing stopping me was self-control.

With his shirt gone, I could see every subtle flex of the muscles in Travis's arm as he swung the crop. He landed a hit between her legs, probably directly against her clit, and Lilith recoiled sharply with pain.

"*Fuck*," she gasped.

His tone was wicked, almost patronizing. "That's not too much for you, is it?"

She pressed her lips together and swung her head quickly side to side.

"I didn't think so." He slapped the crop in the same spot, but this time he held back . . . just enough so her moan didn't contain a trace of discomfort.

No, the one she gave was pure pleasure.

I clenched my hand so tightly on the stem of my martini glass, I worried I might break it. It was hard not to lose myself watching the scene. I needed to stay aware of my reactions, because I didn't want Noah to think I was shocked . . . but mostly I didn't want him to know how impossibly turned on I'd become.

Because I was embarrassingly turned on.

As we watched the man on stage decorate her body with more pink hearts, my envy came roaring back. I longed to trade places with her—only in my fantasy, Noah would be the one wielding the riding crop.

Fuck.

That might be one of my kinks, but I had no idea if it was one of his.

I couldn't help myself. I was too impatient and needed to know now. I leaned in until my lips were only a breath away from his ear and whispered it as quietly as possible. "Have you ever done anything like this before?"

He turned in his seat and pushed the sweep of my hair out of his way so he could do the same. It made his warm breath roll over the spot in my neck where my pulse was racing. "Like, BDSM?"

I gave the tiniest nod, not wanting to move away or give him a reason to either.

His voice was deep and seductive. “Not as much as I’d like to.”

A full body shiver ran through me.

SIXTEEN

Noah

Charlotte's reaction to my admission didn't go unnoticed by me. The shake of her shoulders was subtle, and her lips parted to drag in a breath.

She *liked* what she'd heard.

Fucking hell. I didn't just want to explore BDSM more—I wanted to do it with her. She'd been teeming with interest since we'd stepped inside the club, and now it seemed every inch of her was aroused.

If I touched her, what would happen?

Don't.

I clenched my teeth against the warning firing through my mind because it was pointless. I already knew what was going to happen tonight, what I was going to do. It was inevitable that I'd give up on fighting this thing between us. I couldn't stop it any more than I could stop a stock from tumbling after a shitty Q4 announcement.

A bead of sweat rolled down the side of Travis's face as he continued to swing the crop, varying his hits between hard and soft. The stage lights, the exertion, and the needy moans from his partner made him sweat, but what was my excuse?

Sure, it was hot under my suit coat, making my shirt cling to my back, but I was smart enough to know being overdressed had little to do with it. The cause was the blonde girl beside me, the one who was trying so hard not to squirm in her seat.

Did she have the same ache inside her as I did?

I smoothed a hand along the top of my thigh to occupy myself, so I didn't reach for her.

The sharp slaps of leather meeting skin paused because Travis hooked a finger in the cup of Lilith's bra and jerked it down. It exposed her small, soft pink nipple to both him and the audience, but not for long. He pinched the bead of skin and pulled, lifting the weight of her breast up and away from her body.

She snagged her bottom lip between her teeth and tried to bring her knees together, but her ankle restraints prevented it. Watching her writhe against her bonds, while her expression announced she was drunk with lust, gave me dark satisfaction.

So far, I'd only waded into the shallow end of the BDSM waters. I'd been controlling and dominating. Used blindfolds and restraints. I could purchase toys and certainly had a hook-up if I wanted to invest in more serious equipment.

My issue had always been finding the right partner, because one of the strengths of the swinger lifestyle was also its biggest drawback. I had to maintain trust with multiple people, balance their desires with my own . . . and sometimes we didn't find boundaries until someone inadvertently crossed them.

In New York, I'd played with the same couple for months. They'd told me multiple times what their limits were and reassured me what they wanted and could handle. But one night when I'd sent the wife happily back to husband with my red handprint on her ass, he lost his shit and I never saw them again.

So I'd played it safe since then.

I knew I couldn't get to the level of trust I'd need with a partner if I held them at arms' length, so it was unlikely I'd experience anything close to what Travis and Lilith were doing right now. Although I'd accepted that—it didn't mean my curiosity for it had vanished.

Travis jerked down the other side of her bra so both tits were accessible to him, plumped up by the fabric stretched beneath them. The heart-shaped end of the riding crop caressed gently over her nipples, only to abruptly slap against them.

Each little flinch she gave as he struck her made my pulse jump. Blood pumped hotly through my veins, wanting to flow straight to my dick. The last time I'd seen these two perform, I'd thought it was hot, but bringing Charlotte with me had pushed the heat to another level.

Travis lifted the riding crop, bringing it level with Lilith's mouth and barked his order. "Open."

She licked her lips and then complied immediately, opening her mouth so he could set the center of the thin wand between her teeth.

"This stays here," he said.

Now that his right hand was free, he placed his palm on the center of her chest and coursed a line down her body. It stopped between her legs, and he rubbed her pussy in a stroke that was aggressive enough that she tried to lift onto her toes. But once again, her ankle cuffs prevented that, as did her 'fuck me' shoes.

Her groan of satisfaction was muffled by the riding crop gnashed between her teeth, and she stared at him with bottomless eyes.

My mouth went dry.

In all my years and dozens of partners, I'd only had one person look at me like that . . . and she was seated next to me. The image of Charlotte naked and lying on my kitchen island flashed through my mind, making more heat flare inside me.

But when Travis lowered onto his knees, Lilith's attention shifted to look at the audience. Like last time, she wasn't bothered that anyone was watching her. In fact, I sensed she enjoyed it—but not as much as she liked the man watching her in the front row.

In the short time I'd worked with him, it hadn't taken me long to learn Clay was a guarded, private person. I'd had to earn his trust at every step in the process, and I still wasn't convinced I'd done that. When I'd gotten the pickup address for the New York order my friends had commissioned, I'd discovered he lived just up the street from my new place.

"Small world," I'd commented to him.

It had triggered his suspicion-meter in a major way, and it had taken several patient conversations to ease his fears and explain it was just coincidence. I wasn't interested in him, or going to invade his life, or reveal anything about him to anyone. That wasn't how I operated.

And it hadn't been my intent to show him I was with someone else when I'd offered earlier to help him carry the bench in . . . but I was sure it hadn't hurt either. Single guys had a bad reputation here and were looked at as predators.

Charlotte gave me legitimacy.

As she watched the couple performing on stage, I watched her with my peripheral vision. When Travis put his mouth on the center of Lilith's lace panties, I heard Charlotte's breath stall.

Was she thinking about what that felt like when I'd done

it to her our first night together?

Well, fuck. Now I was, too.

More heat and pressure swelled in my slacks, and I finished my drink quickly, like that would somehow stop me from getting any harder.

Travis's head blocked the view of what exactly he was doing to his partner, but it didn't take a lot of imagination to figure it out when he pulled the crotch of her panties to the side. Once again, her moan was filtered through the crop clamped between her teeth, and her head lolled to rest against the side of her extended arm.

The crowd was restless as we watched Travis fuck her with his tongue. Chairs squeaked and groaned as people shifted in them. The man sitting beside me had a hand under his partner's skirt, and he moved it quicker now, matching her labored breath.

Too soon, part of me wanted to warn him. *She's going to come too fast.*

If it'd been me doing this to Charlotte, I'd have slowed it down. I'd want her balancing on edge throughout the show, not finishing before it was over.

Lilith stared out at the crowd as Travis nuzzled into her lap, but her eyes were vacant, and I doubted she saw anything but the pleasure he was giving her. Trembles climbed up her legs and she panted between moans, her fingers curling into fists above the cuffs. The sensation of his mouth on her made the muscles in her arms strain against the restraints.

Christ, the scene was so fucking sexy.

She was strapped spread-eagle to the St. Andrew's Cross, her tits out and her boyfriend sucking on her clit, and her whiny cries of pleasure were muted by the long, black stick she'd been ordered to hold in her mouth.

The orgasm was building in her body, and her focus abruptly snapped to Clay in the front row. Why was that? Did she need his permission? Or had she been instructed to look at him when she came?

But a frustrated sigh came from behind the crop, along with her garbled words. "God, don't stop."

It was because Travis sat back on his heels, letting her panties snap back in place.

His laugh was almost sinister as he rose to his feet. "Why? Because you want to come?"

She nodded eagerly, making the leather heart at the end of the crop flop around.

He shoved a hand down the front of her underwear, massaging her clit, and studied the way she bowed and contracted against the cross.

"But . . . " he dragged it out, "do you *deserve* it?"

Once more, her head bobbed in an enthusiastic nod.

He wasn't convinced. "Let's see what everyone else has to say." He turned to look at the audience, and his gaze zeroed in on someone on the other side of the aisle, a few rows behind us. "How about you?" he asked. "You think she deserves it?"

It'd been a guy Travis had been looking at, and the man's answer came in a voice that was full of gravel. "Yeah. She's been a good little slut."

The comment caught Travis off guard, but he recovered in an instant. A slow smile burned across his lips before his focus drifted away, traveling across the crowd, before landing on a new person. "And you? Do you think this *good little slut* deserves to come?"

Every cell inside me became a screw that had been turned a quarter inch too tight. He peered at Charlotte, awaiting her response. She didn't seem to be breathing, so her unsteady voice had barely any power to it—yet it still flooded the room.

"Yes."

He nodded in acknowledgement, and his gaze resumed its search for more feedback. However, there was really only one person whose opinion mattered to him, and he focused in on his partner who was seated in the front row.

Clay didn't wait for Travis to ask his question. His head tilted a degree, and his tone was firm. "Not yet."

Whatever expression Clay had on his face, it had to be the same as the one Travis wore now. The man on stage looked so fucking pleased. "I agree."

Behind him, Lilith's head tipped back in disappointment. She was impatient, eager to get off, and I sensed it was the same for most of the people in the audience. But I had the same thought as these men, that it'd be more rewarding if they made her wait.

Travis marched over to the bench his boyfriend had set to the side earlier, and he began to drag it across the stage until it was centered in front of Lilith. She watched him with anxious eyes, like she was unsure if she'd love what he planned to do next, but she was excited regardless.

He stalked toward her, pulled the riding crop from her mouth, and tossed it aside. His gaze raked over her body, as if he were savoring the image and perhaps reluctant to do anything else. I didn't understand that until he reached up and unclipped one of her arms.

Ah.

Like him, I had a twinge of disappointment that her time

being bound to the St. Andrew's Cross was coming to a close. He unhooked her other handcuff from the ring, and while he bent to undo her ankles, Lilith lowered her arms back into the same 'ready' position she'd used before, holding perfectly still for him.

Such a good, obedient girl.

A deep, secondhand admiration swept through me. It was sexy as fuck the way they partnered together, and I was goddamn envious.

When she was no longer tethered to the cross, he grabbed the clasps dangling from her wrists and tugged her along to the side of the bench. She stood there, staring at the long strip of padding before her, while he freed her from her bra and dropped the lacy scrap of fabric to the stage floor.

He wasn't mean or rough when he pushed her down onto the bench, flattening her chest and stomach to the pad, but he'd been firm, and her long hair spilled over her face. She wiped it out of her eyes and shifted her body subtly to find a more comfortable position.

Still, it probably wasn't great. There was a padded bar wedged in her cleavage and she was bent over, her legs running parallel to the A-frame legs of the bench.

While she settled, Travis took off his shoes, pulled off his socks, and hurried out of his pants. It left him dressed in only black boxers, and they hugged his toned form. The guy clearly worked out more than I did, and although I wasn't attracted to men, I appreciated his defined abs and obliques. It displayed all the hard work he'd invested in his body.

Chances were Charlotte appreciated them too, but when I glanced in her direction, she seemed to be more focused on Lilith. Not that I blamed her. The woman wasn't just hot—she was stunningly beautiful.

And yet, the girl beside me was the one who held my interest. There was an innocence she seemed eager to shed, and watching her open her eyes to these new experiences was intoxicating. Her enthusiasm reminded me so much of how I'd been when I was new.

Travis padded on his bare feet to the other end of the bench, so he stood beside her head, and loomed over her. "Hands behind your back."

Her arms had hung loosely down to the floor, so I had expected him to clip her to the rings at the bottom of the bench legs, but he had other plans, apparently. She did as instructed, tucking her arms behind her back, and the black cuffs looked like thick bracelets on her wrists.

There were rings on the clasps, and it took him no time to clip her wrists together. Maybe with a certain amount of twisting she'd be able to free herself, but it'd be difficult, and it had to give her a similar feeling to being bound in a regular pair of handcuffs.

He jammed a hand under the waistband of his underwear, tugging it down out of the way so his dick was free. The woman across the aisle from Charlotte legitimately gasped.

Well, shit.

That envious feeling from before was back.

"I want this good and hard," Travis stared down at Lilith and demanded it in a rough voice, "so I can give you the orgasm you're desperate for."

Two things happened.

She opened her greedy little mouth for him to shove his impressive dick inside, and the woman sitting two seats over from me came abruptly. Her cry was loud enough that several people near us turned to see what was going on, including Charlotte.

Her gaze landed on the guy next to me and his hand disappearing up his partner's skirt, and it only took a fraction of a second for her to deduce what had happened. Her focus rose so she could exchange a look with me.

Her eyebrows lifted, right along with the corner of her mouth, and she seemed to be saying the same thing I was thinking.

Good for her . . . but too soon.

My chest swelled as I filled my lungs with a deep breath. I'd thought we had nothing in common, but the more time I spent with her, the more I realized I might be wrong.

Fucking hell.

What if we were the same person, and the only difference was we were at different places in our lives?

SEVENTEEN

Noah

I didn't want to think about it.

Instead, I turned my attention back to the couple on stage. Travis had hold of Lilith's head, sawing his dick back and forth, and pumping deep into her mouth. Although her eyes were closed, she seemed to be enjoying it as much as he was.

But the blowjob was quick.

He'd been mostly hard before it had started, and a few strokes was all it took to get him the rest of the way there. Her eyes popped open with surprise when he abruptly retreated. His underwear was pulled back in place, although his dick tented the front, and his feet carried him swiftly to the other end of the bench.

She was bent over it, and, like him, wearing only a pair of underwear, but he looked at the lace now like it offended him. His strong hands clamped down on the pale blue fabric covering her ass, and then he jerked them in opposite directions.

In one swift move, he tore the fabric apart. Threads ripped, the lace shredded, but he continued to pull and stretch until the panties were utterly destroyed. The ruined lace fluttered down her legs.

It was an impressive display of aggression, and he was putting on a show, after all, but I got the feeling that wasn't his true motivation for doing it.

"Travis, fuck," she muttered under her breath, trying not

to sound annoyed.

This was why he'd done it. He responded to her irritation with a sharp crack of his palm against her newly bare ass. "Ssh." He spanked her other cheek, this one harder than the last, and then smoothed his palm over the skin. "They were in my way. We don't want that, do we?"

He spanked her again, and the clap of skin hitting skin echoed in the room. The force behind it was more punishing than I would have expected . . . as was her response. Her eyes lidded with desire and her lips parted to sip in air. All her irritation was forgotten.

"No," she murmured. "No, we don't."

Christ, she'd said it in the same tone I was sure she used when she begged for something.

He doled out the blows with the same precision he'd used with the crop. Fast, light swats, punctuated with sharp, biting slaps that made her skin flush red. I had to control my breathing so it didn't go ragged, because this wasn't supposed to be my first rodeo. I'd seen them perform before.

So why the fuck did it have such a strong effect on me?

I was already sweating inside my suit, and the heat in the room cranked up another fifty degrees when he jerked his underwear down across his thighs and buried himself balls-deep inside her. There'd been no warning, and she gasped with surprise, but a strangled moan came right on its heels when he began to move.

He gripped her hip with one hand, the clasps of her handcuffs in the other, and gave her a hard thrust. The force of it made her entire body jolt from the impact. Then, he fucked her like he couldn't care less if she enjoyed it.

But I knew the opposite was true, that every beat of this

scene had been scripted with her pleasure in mind.

Clay didn't share the stage with them, but that didn't mean he wasn't participating.

When he'd completed the pieces for my friends' dungeon in New York, I'd gone to his workshop in his house to evaluate the finished products. I'd taken photos before they were boxed up, so we'd know if any damage occurred during shipping.

There'd been a journal open on one of the side tables with sketches of different pieces and lists of materials, but in the margins, he'd scribbled *other* kinds of notes. I tried not to be nosy, but his shorthand wasn't hard to decipher. There were detailed plans for scenes, some even included timelines.

He'd been distracted when I'd caught a glance, and because he was so private, I pretended I hadn't seen a thing. But that journal had been fucking fascinating, and I wondered if he planned all aspects of his life, even his moments with Travis and Lilith.

It was entirely possible this evening's show was being performed under his direction.

The brutal way Travis moved took a toll on everyone—not just Lilith.

Was he aware when he'd edged her, he'd edged the audience? Our restlessness shifted and tension built, climbing toward release. People wanted to fuck, or wanted to get off, or wanted to make someone else do that. There was a pulse running through us, beating in time with his furious tempo, and then speeding ahead to match her desperate gasps and whimpers of satisfaction.

Charlotte's legs were crossed, and I noticed the way her thigh muscles tensed. Was she squeezing that muscle deep inside her to give her a hit of pleasure?

When I thought about touching her, the warning in my head stayed quiet this time. Perhaps it had been destroyed in the heat of this night, burned away. I leaned over until my shoulder touched hers and brought my mouth close.

"Would you like me," I whispered, "to do you another favor tonight?"

She didn't take her gaze off the couple on stage, but she didn't need to. I felt the shudder roll through her shoulders and heard the enormous breath she pulled in. She liked my offer *very much.*

She pressed her shoulder back against mine and lifted her chin, turning her head toward mine, while still keeping her gaze fixed on the bench like a diehard voyeur. "Only if I get to do you a favor too."

Warmth raced through me. "What a hard bargain you drive."

I showed her I agreed to her terms by placing my hand on her thigh. I didn't ask if she was okay with me touching her, because I'd gotten ahead of myself, but as I suspected, she was okay with it.

More than okay, because as soon as she registered what I'd done, she uncrossed her legs and pulled my hand up so it rested on her inner thigh just beneath her skirt. The action made my head cloud with smoke.

Shit, she was dangerously confident and sexy.

When she'd texted me the picture earlier tonight, I'd cursed her short skirt. It was so teasing and . . . tempting. Maybe I would have been better at keeping my hands to myself if she'd worn pants, but honestly? They probably wouldn't have been a deterrent. They'd only have slowed us down.

I didn't move my hand when it was nestled between her legs. Just the heat of it against her smooth, warm skin was enough. Plus, she didn't need the reminder—we were both well aware of its location.

The violent slaps of Travis's hips against Lilith's ass were staccato and relentless. When he let go of the wrists he'd been holding behind her back, he latched a hand in her hair, gripping close to the scalp at the top of her head. It was so he could pull her up off the bench, making her arch like a bow.

Her tits bounced with his rough thrusts, and her moans swelled, signaling to everyone that she was close. Maybe only seconds away from losing control. He used his hold on her hair to turn her face toward the audience.

Fucking her like this was a workout, and he asked it through his labored breaths. "Are you going to come?"

"*Yes*," she gasped.

"Yeah? *Show* us," he demanded.

It wasn't clear if he meant him and Clay . . . or the audience, but she showed everyone anyway. Her mouth dropped open, rounding with a silent '*oh*,' and a full body shudder washed through her. He kept pounding into her throughout her orgasm, and the sight of this explosion of pleasure snapped the last of the control in me.

I moved my fingers on the hand wedged between Charlotte's thighs, just a little, but it was more than enough to draw a reaction from her, even though I was still a few inches from her pussy. Her tiny gasp was nearly drowned out by the loud moans coming from Lilith, but I heard it.

A lick of heat jolted through me, and the swelling in my pants intensified. I was sporting a semi and had to shift uncomfortably in my seat to try to keep it from getting any worse.

On stage, Lilith was still in the throes of her orgasm when Travis's seemed to start. Both of his hands moved to latch on to her shoulders and hold her at that angle for his final few thrusts, and then quickly ease her back down onto the bench so she didn't slam into the pad.

He pulled out, dropping his wet, fat dick on her ass, sandwiching it between her cheeks, and used his hands to push her cheeks together. A single glide back and forth was all he needed to finish himself off.

As he came, the muscles in his chest and arms corded like steel. His cum splattered across her back and bound hands in ribbons, and she gasped appreciatively.

Like she enjoyed it.

Like he'd rewarded her.

The crowd had been buzzing, but as he slowed to a stop, a hush fell over the room. The only movement was the heavy rise and fall of his chest, while he worked to catch his breath.

He took a half step back, tugged his underwear back up, and wiped the sweat from his brow with the back of his hand. Before he'd finished collecting himself, there was movement in the front row.

It was Clay. He stepped up onto the stage carrying Travis's suit coat folded neatly over one arm and slipped his hand into the interior pocket. A handkerchief was retrieved and passed to Travis, who used it to wipe at the mess on Lilith's hands.

The scene was winding down and some of the audience stood, making their way to the door, and they seemed to be led by the couple who'd been sitting beside me. The woman had made a beeline for the exit, probably in a big hurry to get upstairs and get their clothes off.

Charlotte and I stayed.

Maybe it was because I wanted to see the full conclusion to the scene. Or maybe it was because I couldn't get my damn hand to move away from her.

So we remained watching as a lot of other people filed out. Travis finished cleaning Lilith up, undid the clasps of her cuffs, and helped her to stand. She turned to face Clay, who stepped between her and the audience's view, then draped Travis's coat over her shoulders. He worked to undo the buckles on her wrists while his partner focused on her ankles.

They were so tender and caring with each other, the sexual energy in the room faded. The atmosphere was too personal, too intimate. We'd watched them get naked, play, and fuck, but this quiet moment after?

It felt weirdly intrusive.

Charlotte must have sensed it too, because she glanced at me and looked like she was about to say something.

I beat her to it, though, and gestured to her now-empty drink. "C'mon," I said softly. "Let's get another round."

When she nodded, it disrupted the spell enough that I was finally able to pull my hand away from her. But as we moved for the door, I felt the touch of her lingering on my skin. There was a craving in me to get her back in my hands as soon as possible.

We weren't the only ones who'd decided to grab drinks after the show, which meant the bar was crowded and we had to stand close together while waiting our turn to order—but I wasn't complaining. With her heeled boots, she was almost as tall as I was, and we fit together nicely in the cramped space.

"What's the plan after we get our drinks?" Her voice turned sultry. "Are we going into one of the private rooms so you can do me that favor?"

I'd been trying to get the bartender's attention, but now she had mine and I turned to look at her. "You like watching," I said. "So I thought we could go upstairs," I ran my heated gaze over her for emphasis, "where clothing is optional for everyone."

Her smile started slowly and built. "Yeah. Definitely." She looked so excited about it, I half expected her to say she wanted to forget about the drinks and head up there right now.

But I needed to slow her down, and my expression turned serious. "There are some things we have to talk about first."

Worry flashed through her eyes at the same moment the bartender appeared. I put in our order, and she waited impatiently for him to leave and start making our drinks before she could ask it. "Talk about what?"

I went with the easiest question first. "How do you think you'd feel about being watched?"

This wasn't what she'd expected, and it took her a long moment to consider it. And then she blinked, and it looked like she was holding in a laugh. "I don't think that's going to be a problem. You haven't figured out that I'm kind of an attention whore?"

Shit, she was right. Charlotte had been the center of her parents' universe growing up, and the goal for her now was to build a channel that got as many eyeballs as possible.

She thrived on attention.

Could the same be said of me?

In certain settings, yeah. Not as much with my family, but with my career. When I'd executed a major trade or negotiated a big deal, I made sure my name was all over it. And in the bedroom, I fucking *loved* being watched. Even if the woman's partner didn't want to see or be in the room during,

I knew they'd be talking about me after the deed was done. That gave me a dark satisfaction.

Oh, man. Maybe I was an even bigger attention whore than Charlotte.

After I paid for our drinks and we'd collected them, I turned to survey the room.

"Was that all you wanted to talk about?" She asked it innocently, but there was an edge of impatience beneath it. She was eager to get upstairs.

"No." I found what I was looking for and pointed to the empty table near the dance floor. The music was loud here, but not too loud to talk over, and if we went anywhere quieter in the club, it was likely we'd both get too distracted.

She shuffled begrudgingly to the table, and I had to hide my chuckle behind a sip of my drink. Her pouty attitude shouldn't have been a turn-on, but it fucking was.

We set our drinks on the tabletop that was lit with a single flameless candle, but when she moved to take a seat, I stopped her.

"I don't want to be friends anymore," I announced.

She jolted with surprise and immediately looked distraught. "What? Why?"

My heart went out of rhythm because there was no turning back. I got the same rush I did when buying a risky stock. The unknown was exciting, full of promise and danger.

Goddamn, she was pretty. I reached out to trace a fingertip over her forehead and down the side of her face, brushing her hair out of my way. The action stunned her perfectly still, so I had to curl my fingers beneath her chin and pull her mouth toward mine.

She'd asked why we couldn't be friends anymore, and

the words tumbled freely from my lips. “Because I want to do this.”

And then I pressed my mouth to hers in a searing kiss.

EIGHTEEN

Noah

Charlotte let out a soft cry of surprise when our lips met. My kiss had startled her for sure, but as it went on, she softened into me. I wrapped my arms around her, and her hands went inside my suit coat, wandering over my chest.

Christ, could she feel my chaotic heartbeat?

Or how much I'd been sweating beneath my suit . . . and did she know she was the biggest reason for it?

I angled my head to deepen the kiss, and she responded in kind. Her lips parted and her tongue slicked over mine, and I fucking felt the caress of it *everywhere*. But I was grateful for it because our kiss had started too sweet. It had been filled with more passion and longing than I was comfortable with.

We'd kissed each other like we'd been starving for it.

I slid one hand down her backside, grabbed a handful of her ass, and squeezed like I wanted to claim ownership. I needed to remind her that this thing between us should be about lust and desire. About two people with similar interests who could help each other out.

It couldn't be about anything else. Not romance, and certainly not love.

A sound of satisfaction slipped out of her at my possessive grip, and her response was to nip gently at my bottom lip. Her kiss was so provocative and seductive, I got lost in it, and I knew if I wasn't careful—it'd escalate beyond my control.

And I knew I needed to stay in control.

When I ended the kiss, she looked as woozy as I felt. Were we drunk? Shit, no, we'd only had one drink. Her hands were still on my chest when she leaned back and gave me a dazzling smile.

"Well," she said, "that's a relief." Her expression was victorious, like we'd been playing a game that she'd just won. "Now I don't have to spend the rest of the night trying to convince you to kiss me."

I chuckled and gripped the back of the chair, pulling it out for her, because there was a lot of shit we had to talk about. She dropped into it and patiently waited for me to take the seat across from her.

"Whatever this is going to be," I gestured between us, "your father can't know about it."

She snorted like that was the understatement of the year and picked up her martini glass to take a sip. "Obviously."

I needed her to understand how serious I was. "Because if he finds out, it's bad for both of us."

Her cavalier attitude faded somewhat. "Noah, I get it."

"Do you?" I asked it earnestly. "It's kind of embarrassing to admit this . . . but you need to know I'm the kind of person whose entire identity is tied to their career."

One of my general education classes in college made me take a personality test, and I'd scored the highest marks in the 'achiever' category. At the time, I'd written it off, but years later I'd come to realize how painfully accurate it had been.

I was goal driven to a fault, and had no problem making sacrifices as long as they'd get me results. And when I strove for something and *didn't* accomplish it? That failure hit me like a sledgehammer.

Charlotte peered at me with a dubious look.

"I was a broker for so long," I continued, "that's all I was. That's *who* I was. Making this drastic career change, moving to Warbler, has me feeling," I searched for the right phrase, "off-balance."

It wasn't adequate, but I left it at that. She didn't need to know how I second-guessed my decision to come back to Nashville on a daily basis. But maybe the drinks had been laced with something because the honesty kept pouring out of me.

"What I'm trying to say is, if I lost my job," I swallowed thickly, "I'd really struggle." It came out in a quiet rush. "It might, like, destroy me."

Her expression softened and she was more serious than I'd ever heard her sound. "I understand." Her gaze fell to the tabletop and her fingers traced the circle at the base of her glass. "After Zach, I'm beyond my last chance with my parents . . . so you don't have to worry about me telling them anything about us." She attempted a smile, but it was sad and didn't reach into her eyes. "I kind of like not being homeless."

We both had good reasons to walk away, and the weight of them hung heavy between us. She was young and impulsive, and although she'd talked about the consequences we both faced, I was concerned she hadn't *really* given them much thought.

You don't spend the first twenty-two years of your life being spoiled and entitled, and grow out of it in a few short months.

I pretended I didn't see any red flags. And even if I did, I sensed it wasn't enough to make me stop.

"This means we need to stop our arrangement of you

cleaning my house."

Alarm had her straightening in her seat. "What? Why?"

"It's a weird situation, you working for me while we're . . . "

While we're what? Fucking? In a relationship?

I wasn't sure what to say since we hadn't defined anything yet.

"I get that, but I need the job, and," she lifted a shoulder, "I thought you knew how to compartmentalize."

This was a dig at what I'd told her when I'd said we weren't allowed to kiss, and although I deserved it, it was still irritating.

And she wasn't done either. "Plus, you need me." She laughed casually. "We both know what your house would look like if I wasn't coming once a week."

"We need each other," I corrected through clenched teeth.

I'd revealed a few things to her tonight, but I was still struggling to admit to myself what a difference she'd made in the last six weeks. Not living in clutter and mess had been one of the only things keeping me sane during my big transition.

She acted like she didn't agree and announced it with a fucking smirk. The attitude she pulled lit me up, and a dark heat took over, seizing control.

"*Say it*," I demanded in a voice so commanding it shocked us both.

Charlotte glanced around in disbelief, as if checking to see if anyone else had heard my order. "What?"

"Say that you need me too."

I'd used a tone that was non-negotiable, leaving her to consider how she wanted to play it. Her eyes narrowed, she lifted her chin in defiance, and she sighed dramatically. "Fine. I need you too," a devious look darted through her eyes, "*Daddy.*"

The word poured gasoline on the smoldering fire inside me, burning away all thought.

"I'm going to take you upstairs and fuck that bratty mouth of yours while everyone watches. Is that what you want?" I leaned forward over the table so I could demand her full attention, even though I already had it. "Would you like that, Charlotte?"

My attempt to shock her failed spectacularly. She picked up her cosmo and leaned in, balancing her elbow on the table. "I would." She made a production out of sipping her drink, while keeping her sultry gaze fixed on me. "I guess that means we're done talking?"

My impatience wanted to say yes, but we still had things to figure out. I shook my head. "I need to know what kind of relationship you want with me, because I don't want to hurt you, and if we—"

"You won't."

It felt like I was suddenly two steps behind. "What?"

"You don't have to worry about hurting me. It won't happen, because I've decided you can't." She said it with the certainty of an inarguable fact. As if it was that simple and avoidable. "You decided you don't have time for love, right? Well, no problem. I've decided I don't have time for heartache."

My mouth dropped open.

How the fuck was I supposed to argue with that?

"Here's how I see this going," she said. "Neither of us wants anything serious, so I say let's just have fun and see what happens." Her head tilted as she pondered something. "Friends with benefits, if you want to put a label on it."

I stared at her, feeling a mixture of excitement and

something vaguely like disappointment at the same time. This was exactly what I wanted, right? So why did it feel like it wasn't enough?

It was foolish to ask, but I did anyway, wanting to clarify. "Friends with benefits, who are exclusive?"

Her throat bobbed with a swallow. "Well, if we're exclusive, then how am I supposed to watch you fuck other people?"

Thoughts swam in my head. "You'd be okay with that? Being with other people while we're together?"

"I'm okay with it, but," hesitation forced her to lean back in her chair, "remember how I don't sleep with someone unless I'm in love?"

I did a perfect impression of a statue, not wanting to reveal any of the thoughts running through my mind. "So, friends with benefits, but . . . "

"Not full benefits, no."

She looked at me with trepidation, like she thought her 'no sex' rule was a defect she wasn't sure I'd be willing to put up with. I hated that I'd made her feel that way.

"I didn't handle it right the first time you explained it to me. I'm sorry," I said. "There's nothing wrong with having boundaries."

At that moment, a scary thought descended upon me.

Kissing her the first time we'd been together had been nice, but it didn't compare to the one we'd shared tonight. The big difference between then and now was that I hadn't really known her then. Hadn't cared about her the way I did now.

God, what if she was on to something?

Did sex without feelings pale in comparison to sex with someone I'd fallen for? I had no way to know. It'd been so long since I'd had romantic feelings, and even then—I'd never been totally sure I'd ever been in love.

"Can I ask why, though?" I said.

She hesitated and something like fear moved through her expression. "Why I won't have sex without love?"

"I could be way off, but is this a worthiness thing?" I tried not to grimace. "No sex until a guy has proven himself worthy of you?"

Whatever confidence she'd had before, completely abandoned her as she took a long sip of her drink, and I got the sense she'd only done it to stall and contemplate her response. Then, she plunked it down and delivered a look that was so anxious it made my stomach twist.

"I'm going to tell you something," her voice was unsure, "I've never told anyone else."

My chest tightened uncomfortably. "Okay."

It took her a long time to form the sentence. "When I was a senior in high school, I got pregnant."

I held perfectly still, not wanting to show any reaction and unintentionally hurt her, especially because she clearly had more to say.

"I can't take the pill." Her gaze lingered over the glass in my hand, rather than my eyes. "I mean, I tried, but it made me feel foggy and depressed. I didn't get an IUD until college, so until then, I *always* used condoms. My boyfriend at the time, he seemed understanding."

Anger flared at the word she'd chosen and its implied meaning. "*Understanding*?"

"When I told him I was pregnant, he swore the condom must have broken. But he was weird about it, and . . . "

I tensed. "You had your doubts."

Her focus returned to me. "I don't know. I didn't think he was the type of guy who'd take a condom off during sex, but I also didn't think he was the type of guy who'd fucking ghost me when he found out, leaving me to deal with it on my own."

Fire burned up my throat. "If he took the condom off without you knowing, that's assault."

She frowned. "I'm not sure that's what happened. And at this point, I'll never know. I miscarried a few weeks later. My parents never knew because I was too fucking terrified to tell them."

Jesus. I sat back in my seat, processing it. "Fuck, Charlotte. I'm so sorry you went through that."

"Thanks," she said softly.

And I hated that she'd gone through it alone. But she was stronger than she let on, and she drew in a breath, exhaling it slowly, as if cleansing the bad thoughts away.

"So, since then, I've been more careful." Her half-smile was empty. "A handjob is safe. A guy wants to go down on me? Safe. Blowjob? *Safe.* If something goes wrong, it isn't going to accidentally change the course of my life forever."

"I get it." Fuck, did I understand. "I'm sorry if I made you share something you didn't want to, or—"

"You didn't." She softened. "Is it weird to say it felt good to tell you?"

"Not at all." The tightness in my chest eased slightly. "I'm glad you felt comfortable enough to share it with me."

She seemed to relax a bit too and leaned both her elbows on the table. "My 'no sex until love' rule is really more like 'no sex until trust.' And I trust you, Noah, I do. I'm just . . . not ready yet. Is that cool?"

"Of course," I said instantly. "It's more than okay with me."

"Good." This time, her smile was real. "Because all that 'safe' stuff?" Her eyes went wide and serious. "I really fucking like it."

A smile wanted to break on my lips. "Yeah, I do too."

She motioned between us. "Friends with benefits, then. *Most* benefits," she clarified. "I figure we can do, like, ninety percent of stuff together," her eyes smoldered, "and you can do the other ten percent with someone else while I watch." Her voice filled with smoke. "How does that sound?"

How the fuck did she do that? The heaviness of our conversation lifted, and thick desire replaced it in a heartbeat. "That sounds really fucking good."

She already knew the answer but asked it anyway. "Does that mean we have a deal?"

I straightened in my seat, smoothed a hand down the maroon tie I'd worn for her, and drained half of my Manhattan in a single gulp. "Yeah, we have a fucking deal. Grab your drink. I'm taking you upstairs."

She happily did as told.

This time, when we climbed the staircase to the second floor, there was a bouncer sitting on a stool on the landing at the top of the stairs. From his perch, he could see most of the lounge and keep an eye on the guests.

And there were guests here now. It looked like most of the crowd who'd watched the show had come upstairs and were scattered about the space. Some sat on the large sectional couch in front of the decorative fireplace, while others stood near the tall counter that served as a place to set drinks.

Conversations and laughter filled the rooms, as did low, seductive music.

Activities had already started for some folks, because

people were in various stages of foreplay and undress. A topless woman was sprawled out on the oversized ottoman in front of the sectional, and her partner was bent over, sucking on her tits.

I glanced at Charlotte, curious to see her reaction.

Her gaze was locked on the couple, and she stood still at my side, holding her cosmo like it was prop. Maybe she didn't realize she still had it.

I'd only been upstairs a few times, but I'd seen enough to know what this main room would descend into as the night went on. It'd become a frenzy of sex, with the most action happening on the sectional, so when Charlotte took a step toward it, I gently grasped her elbow to stop her.

"Do you want to watch," I said, "or participate? Because sitting on that couch means you're up for anything, including other people joining in."

She turned to look up at me, and it took my breath away. Downstairs, she'd been confident about what she wanted. But now it looked like she was realizing how very *real* this all was.

She was on the cusp of total overload.

I gave her an easy smile and used my hold on her elbow to lead her beyond the couch. "Why don't we keep exploring? I bet there's more to see."

She nodded and followed me through the main lounge, past the bathrooms, and into the room at the back of the house. It was much brighter than the main lounge and it was smaller too. The space was so packed with furniture, it probably felt cramped even if there weren't people in it.

But it wasn't empty tonight.

When we stepped inside, we joined at least a dozen other people. Some sat on couches and chairs, while others stood in a group by the door. All the focus was on the foursome in the corner.

Two women and two men, who had already shed some of their clothes, and the rest of it was pulled down or pushed up out of the way. It looked like they'd been in a rush to get to the good stuff and hadn't bothered getting completely naked.

The man who stood in the back corner had lost his shirt, and his pants were puddled around his ankles. The woman in front of him was bent over so he could fuck her from behind, and he held on to the skirt bunched at her waist. She was busy sucking the cock of the guy in front of her, and her breasts swayed and swung as she was spit roasted.

And the guy getting a blowjob was also busy. He was kissing the woman who stood beside him, and had a hand shoved inside her undone pants.

It wasn't the first time I'd seen a foursome, so my gaze left them and drifted to the girl standing beside me. She'd seen a lot tonight, but this looked like the first thing to truly shock her.

These people weren't gorgeous like Travis and Lilith had been. All four of them were older and none were in as good physical shape as the performers had been. These were regular people . . . and that made it almost as hot as the show, only in a different kind of way.

We were seeing something *real*. Something taboo and forbidden.

I liked watching, but Charlotte? She was a true voyeur. Her lips were parted, her face flushed, and her breath went shallow. Even if I wasn't acutely attuned to her, I'd be able to tell she was turned on. Hell, I'd be able to see it from clear across the room.

There was a small loveseat in the opposite corner that was empty, and it looked just big enough to fit us both.

She let me guide us over to it and sat down so quickly I chuckled softly. She'd sat down in a hurry because she wanted to get her gaze back on the foursome happening just ten feet away. When I joined her on the small couch, my weight made her lean into me, and I wasn't mad about the way her body pressed against mine.

I rested my arm along the back of the loveseat, which she used as an invitation to snuggle even closer. I was on fire both mentally and physically, sweating beneath all the layers of my clothes, but I enjoyed her proximity anyway.

It was fucking unreal to sit here with her, sipping our cocktails and casually watching a group of strangers as they fucked.

Whenever I came to the club, I made a conscious effort not to judge. I tried to leave inhibitions and closedmindedness at the door. But no matter what I did, I could not silence the part of me that wanted to critique tonight.

The guy who was fucking the woman was just hammering away. It was too fast, too constant, and what I could see of her face made it look like her expression was strained. Was she already exhausted? It had to be hard work standing like that, bent over, plus she had to contend with the competing rhythm of the man fucking her mouth.

Her heavy breasts swayed with the back-and-forth rocking of her body. The woman who stood beside the blowjob guy had her hand around his cock, holding it steady for her friend.

The scene was so sexy, Charlotte squirmed in her seat, rubbing against me. It'd been innocent enough, but my body reacted like it had been more, and I groaned in my head. We'd need to go at whatever speed she was comfortable with tonight, meaning if she wanted to stay right here and watch all night, that was what we were going to do.

But if she climbed into my lap and got naked? Fuck, I didn't know how long I'd last. I barely kept myself in check when we were alone, and fooling around in public, with other people watching, heightened the experience.

Jackhammer guy was still going at it, but his focus wasn't on the woman he was slamming into. He scanned the room, taking in the crowd who'd gathered to watch the foursome, and a devious grin smeared across his face.

He was fucking thrilled at all the people watching him.

But when his gaze snagged on Charlotte, an unease settled in the pit of my stomach. He looked at her for so long, it developed into a stare. It was hard to fault him for it. She was the most beautiful woman in the room and could join in with anyone she wanted.

It was hard not to feel a twinge of possessiveness at the idea, which was selfish. We'd just discussed this, and she'd said we weren't exclusive.

As the man continued to stare at her, she squirmed against me again, but this time I sensed it wasn't with excitement. It was discomfort, because the guy wasn't staring at her—he was fucking leering.

I told myself it wasn't possessiveness coursing through me, it was a desire to protect. Her drink was empty, and I finished mine in a big gulp, and then I rose from the couch. I collected our glasses, deposited them on the tray nearby meant for used glassware, and offered my hand to her.

"Let's go somewhere else," I said.

Relief washed through her, and she quickly slipped her hand in mine. Neither of us glanced back at the man as we went, and I didn't let go of her hand as we strode through the hallway.

The main lounge was even busier than it had been when we'd walked through on our way to the back room. The sectional was full of half-naked people, and the topless woman we'd seen earlier was now fully naked, straddling her partner who was on his back on the ottoman.

There was a dramatic shift in the atmosphere in comparison to the other room. It wasn't just that it was darker and moodier here, there was also a totally different vibe. This space felt feverish. Hedonistic. And we only stood at the edge, near the exposed brick wall. How much stronger would it be if we waded farther inside?

She must have felt it, too, because her hand tightened instinctively around mine.

That tiny reaction snapped whatever restraint I'd been holding on to.

Charlotte gasped as I turned to face her, grasped her waist, and moved in so aggressively, it forced her to stumble backward. Her eyes went wide and her back hit the brick with a thud, but I silenced whatever other sound she wanted to make when I slammed my mouth over hers.

NINETEEN

Noah

Our kiss downstairs was tame compared to this one. I'd had more than a month's worth of lust for Charlotte pent up inside me, and it spilled out in an urgent rush. The good news was I seemed to have had a similar effect on her, because her greedy mouth answered my kiss with the same ferocity.

My hands had been locked on her waist, but they refused to stay still. They glided up the sides of her body until I could cup both of her breasts through the thin satin shirt she wore. She lifted into my touch and rubbed her body provocatively against mine.

I bit back a groan of satisfaction.

We were wild, and reckless, and acting like the only way to extinguish the fire raging between us was by using each other.

Our kiss broke and the words tumbled from me unfiltered. "I want to know how wet you got from watching."

She peered up at me through heavy lidded eyes and stepped her feet apart, making room between her thighs. "Why don't you find out?"

It was issued as a challenge, and dark satisfaction rolled through me. I would never have dreamed that this girl matched my sexual appetite, and yet, here she was, daring me to put my hand up her skirt.

I dragged my heavy hand slowly down her front to build her anticipation, and I veered to the side when I reached her skirt. Down I continued to move, until I reached bare skin below the hem of her skirt, and then I changed directions.

My fingertips trailed up the inside of her thigh, and as my hand crept up, I carried her skirt up with it. When I brushed my fingers against her panties, I wasn't surprised to find them wet. I ground my fingers against her, rubbing her clit through the damp fabric, and a pleased smile grew on my lips.

"You're fucking soaked, you know that?"

Her only answer was to tip her head back against the wall and arch with pleasure. She had her hands on my shoulders, and her fingers tightened, clenching fistfuls of my suit coat.

There was music all around us, and I didn't mean the song playing from the sound system. Moans, and kisses, and bodies crashed against each other, filling the room with a symphony of desire. It was intoxicating.

But for her? It looked like she was drowning in it and would die a happy woman.

I rubbed a tight circle on her clit, and then pressed my entire palm against her, stroking roughly. Back and forth, over and over again. It made her chest heave as she pulled in large gulps of air.

And her moan was goddamn sinful.

Jesus, she looked so good like this. Pressed up against the wall, her lips kiss-swollen and my hand between her legs. I was sure I wasn't the only one who recognized that. There were plenty of other people in this room, but they barely registered right now. I was too absorbed in her to look anywhere else.

One of her hands fell from my shoulder so she could cup me through my pants, and the corner of her mouth tilted in a smile. She was happy to find I was already hard, and growing harder under her touch. We moved our hands on each other's bodies like we were horny teenagers.

Hot and heavy and *fast*.

The stroke of her hand down the length of me sent heat ripping through my center. It made me want to escalate and see how much she'd enjoy taking the next step. I gripped the sides of her leather skirt and pulled upward until it was bunched at her waist and her black panties were exposed.

I dropped a kiss on her lips, and planted more on the side of her neck, giving her time to stop me if she wasn't comfortable being naked in front of others. But she didn't seem uncomfortable. If anything, she was impatient for me to do it.

I took a step back, hooked my fingers in the sides of her panties, and jerked them down so they were pulled taut between her parted knees, just above the top of her boots. As my focus coursed up over her bare lower half, I was so turned on at the sight, my knees went weak.

I'd thought she'd looked good up against the wall before, but now? I practically growled it at her. "You're so fucking hot."

Her gaze was locked with mine, and she swallowed an enormous breath. It looked like it was taking everything she had to stand there, as if her need to come was threatening to crush her.

Don't be cruel, a voice whispered in my head.

When I came back to her, she sighed with relief, and I got the sense she was eager to have her hands back on my body. I understood that. I was eager to touch her too.

I plunged my index finger deep inside her, all the way to the knuckle, and her moan was so sexy, my dick jerked. God, her body was fire. She was hot and wet, and so fucking *soft*.

Starting slow wasn't possible. We were a runaway freight train, whose brakes had melted from the heat and could no longer stop us. I pulsed my finger in and out, fucking her at a tempo that pulled more moans from her and had her fumbling for my zipper. My pulse vaulted forward and the air in the room went thin.

It was hard for her to get my pants open.

My forearm was in her way, so she had to work around it, plus what I was doing to her was distracting. My mouth sealed over the sensitive spot on the side of her neck and sucked. The sensation had to feel good, because the muscles inside her body clamped down on my finger.

I was going to press a second finger inside her, but she'd undone the button at the waistband of my slacks and dropped the zipper, giving her enough room to fit her hand inside. The caress of her palm through my thin boxers injected lava into my bloodstream.

The fire she caused burned even hotter when her hand dove inside my underwear. Her fist closed around my cock, gripped me firmly, and slid up and down in a pleasurable stroke.

The sensation was powerful enough to make my vision haze and cause me to shudder. I blew out an uneven breath against the side of her neck, where it was warm and damp from my kisses.

She tried to go up onto the balls of her feet when I eased a second finger inside her, but her heeled boots wouldn't let her. Her gasp of satisfaction flooded my ears, drowning out any other sound in the room. She was so slick, it was easy to pump my fingers, and the faster I moved, the faster her tight fist worked me over.

If anyone was watching us right now, it had to turn them on. I had her pressed against the brick wall, fucking her with my fingers, while her hand moved inside my undone pants, jerking me off.

Charlotte's hips moved, maybe to encourage me to go faster or to change the angle to one she liked better. The shift caused the panties at her knees to fall and slide down around her ankles, but she didn't make any effort to step out of them. Perhaps she didn't even know, too preoccupied with the orgasm she was hurtling toward.

I wasn't ready for that, though.

Her hand stroking me felt too good, and if she came right now? I didn't know if I'd be able to control myself. I didn't want to come in her hands, plus I needed to fulfill the promise I'd made downstairs.

The words came from me much darker than I'd expected. "Get on your knees."

My brutal order didn't scare her. She shivered with excitement and moved like she couldn't comply fast enough. As she dropped down, I turned us so our positions were flipped and my back was against the wall.

I'd told her I was going to fuck that bratty mouth of hers while everyone watched, and I wanted to make sure my body wasn't blocking anyone's view. As she got settled on her knees, I worked to get things out of her way.

My pants and underwear were shoved down to my knees. My tie was slung over a shoulder. I undid the bottom few buttons of my dress shirt and pulled it open, exposing me from the waist down.

Charlotte's gaze flicked from my hard cock up to my face. She stayed patiently like that, as if she were awaiting her next order, but I could see every inch of anticipation radiating from inside her.

She wanted to do this. She was fucking *eager* to wrap her lips around my cock in this room where anyone could watch her as she sucked me off.

Yeah? That makes two of us.

I didn't command her with words. I ringed myself around the base to hold my dick steady, and threaded my other hand into her hair, urging her head forward.

"Oh, fuck," I groaned as she took me into the soaking heat of her mouth.

Her first pass was painstakingly slow, like she wanted to leisurely explore the length of me. I sank back against the wall, the brick pressing against the wool of my suit. But I didn't give a fuck right now if doing that was going to mar the fabric. I couldn't focus on anything but the way her mouth was gliding over me.

Inside my chest, my heart hammered away, searching for a way to break free. Sweat beaded on my brow and trickled down my hairline. When her tongue swirled, I flexed in response and fought to keep my breathing steady.

At first, my hold on her head wasn't there to control.

I let her go at the pace she wanted, but her languid movements were exquisite agony. I pulsed and throbbed, while need spiraled inside me. It tightened the muscles in my legs until they strained and ached.

Her mouth was goddamn insane.

Every spin of her tongue, each drag of my cock between her pursed lips, pulled me closer to an orgasm. I didn't know where to look because everything only heightened the experience.

I liked the way her sexy black panties were still caught around her booted ankles as she knelt in front of me. How her skirt was bunched at her waist so everyone could see her bare ass. And I loved the way the people in the room would glance over and flash me an envious, sexy smirk.

They were enjoying the show.

Pride swelled in my chest, and my hips began to move. In the beginning, she'd been the one fucking me, but now the power shifted between us. I had both my hands on her head then, holding her still so I could saw my dick in and out of her mouth at a quicker pace.

"Everyone's watching you suck my cock," I told her.

She hummed her approval, and Jesus Christ, it felt good.

I lowered my voice so only she could hear. "I see a lot of jealous faces. Shit, I bet half the guys in here wish it was their dick in your mouth right now."

Her beautiful eyes blinked open to look up at me, questioning if I was telling the truth. How could she think I was lying? If anything, I was probably being conservative. I hadn't missed the way a lot of the women at the club had looked at her either. They would have jumped at the chance to be with her too.

But I had to focus. I needed to know if it was a fantasy for her like it was for me. "Would you like that? Putting some stranger's cock in your mouth?"

Her eyes were electric, and she retreated enough to whisper it, her lips brushing over my damp skin. "Maybe."

It sounded exactly like a *yes*, but I wasn't going to move forward with inviting someone to join us unless I had her resounding consent. Plus, I wasn't sure I even wanted that tonight. Everything was so new. We'd just agreed to this relationship, and I didn't want to share her our first night together.

My eyes fell closed as she welcomed me back into her mouth.

Pinpricks of pleasure crawled up my legs, and they intensified when she attempted to take me deeper. The head of my cock pushed all the way into the tightness at the back of her throat, and the sensation caused my toes to curl inside my shoes. My body took over, and my hips surged forward, trying to gain even more access, pushing past the point of what she could take—

Charlotte retreated so abruptly, she nearly fell back, and one of her hands flew to cover her mouth. It muffled the loud gagging sound she couldn't stop from escaping, and her face flooded with embarrassment.

Every muscle in me went painfully tense.

I'd just fucked up colossally, and I stumbled over words in my head, searching for the best way to apologize as she fought to recover.

But to my shock, she wasn't looking for an apology. She straightened on her knees, seized my cock in her warm hand, and her mouth descended on me once again.

"Holy shit," punched from my lips.

It was followed by a heavy moan because she kept going and *going*. My dick slipped deeper, to the back of her throat again and then beyond. When I reached the same place as before, she was able to hold me there for one long, blissful second.

Her gag reflex protested again, but this time when she pulled back, her gag was silent. I could only tell it happened because she pinched her eyes shut and her shoulders heaved.

In any other situation, I might have found her frustrated look amusing. Like she was annoyed she couldn't get what she wanted. But it wasn't amusing to me now. Her perseverance was fucking *endearing*.

She didn't want to be beaten, didn't want to give up.

When she started her third attempt, my legs shook and the pleasure verged on overwhelming. At first, I'd wondered if she were too much of a princess to like sucking cock. I definitely wouldn't have pegged her as being interested in deep throating, but damn.

This girl was full of surprises.

"Yes," I said. "Fucking *yes*." My breathing had become so labored, it was hard to speak between pants. "That's it. Take it deep."

She backed off me just long enough to utter it through glossy lips. "Yes, Daddy."

I had no idea if she'd said it to push my buttons and get a rise out of me, or if she meant it. Did she want me to be her daddy? And . . . did I want that?

Yeah, I really fucking did, since that was the thought that pushed me over the edge. My hands clamped down on her head to keep her still, and it was the only warning I could give her. The orgasm roared up from deep inside me like an inferno, swift and sweeping, and leaving everything charred in its wake.

"Oh, fuck," I said in a rush. "*Fuck*."

Every spurt was a new hit of ecstasy, and I thrust my hips erratically, pumping her mouth full of my cum. My vision narrowed in, so all I could see was her, and I slumped back against the wall.

Was it selfish to wish this moment would last forever?

It didn't, though.

Sound returned to my ears, bringing me back to reality. We weren't alone, and it felt like we were surrounded by the music of sex on all sides. My hands were on Charlotte's head and my cock was buried in her mouth, and she was on her knees, unable to move.

After the mind-numbing orgasm, my brain wasn't yet back to full strength, and the command escaped my lips without approval. "Swallow."

The tight suction of her throat as she did it caused an aftershock of pleasure, and I flinched in response.

Had she done as I'd asked because she was a good girl, or because I hadn't left her much choice? Goddamn, her *daddy* comment had sunk its hooks into me, deep enough I worried I might not ever be able to get them completely out. I'd been so sure I'd already determined all my kinks—

But she'd unlocked this new one in me.

I released my hold of her head, and scooped my hands under her arms, lifting her up onto her feet. She sucked in a sharp breath and wobbled unsteadily at the sudden move, but I spun us again, so she had the wall at her back for support.

The kiss I dropped on her lips was quick. It was a brief detour before I bent down, grabbed the sides of my pants, and tugged them back up. She leaned against the brick, watching me do up my zipper, and her lips parted so she could drag ragged air in through them.

One of the benefits of coming was now that my orgasm was out of the way, I could put all my focus on her. And now that I had my clothes sorted, I intended to do just that.

I leaned in and set a hand on her chest, right at the base of her throat, and kissed her just above the line of my fingers.

Beneath my palm, her heart was racing. Despite the heat of the room, when I coursed my hand down the front of her body, goosebumps rose on her arms.

It was a powerful feeling, knowing I had that kind of effect on her.

I followed my hand as it slid down over her bare skin, sinking to my knees in front of her. My hand didn't stop moving, though. I trailed my fingers down her thigh, over her boot, and didn't stop until I reached the pair of panties resting across the top of her foot.

She'd 'worn' this underwear long enough.

I freed her from it, one foot and then the other, and tucked the panties into a suit coat pocket. She watched me do it, staring down at me as I knelt in front of her sexy, naked lower body, and she didn't object to what I'd done. If anything, she looked excited about it. There was a sexy gleam in her eyes.

Her legs weren't trembling yet, and she'd seemed steady enough balancing on one leg as I'd pull off her panties, so I felt confident she could handle what I planned to do. I put a hand on one of her knees and urged her to lift. It was so I could hook it over my shoulder and press her open.

She was so fucking smooth and wet. Even in the low light of the room, I could see her pussy glistening. I was sure I didn't need her permission—she'd probably beg me if I waited much longer, but I glanced up to check with her anyway.

Her expression was desperate. It demanded to know what the hell I was waiting for, and when I didn't move fast enough, she raked a hand through my hair and jerked me forward.

Goddamn, her aggression was such a turn on.

The first contact of my mouth was just a gentle brush of

my lips, but she sighed with contentment and slid an inch down the wall. I used my tongue then, caressing her sensitive clit in short strokes. Her skin was so lush, so soft, I didn't mind that the hardwood floor was murder on my knees.

She had all her weight on one leg, and it began to shake as I increased the intensity of my tongue. Whenever I fluttered it, she rewarded me with an appreciative moan, and the hand in my hair tightened. It was probably hard for her to stand like that and hold her leg up, since she wasn't using my shoulder for any support.

I reached up and curled a hand around her thigh, encouraging her to use me. My opposite hand moved to pin her hip against the wall.

Did she like the way the rough brick felt against the bare skin of her ass? Or was she too focused on the sensation of my tongue fucking her to notice?

"Fuck me," came a loud cry from across the room, but I didn't stop my task to see who the woman was talking to. It clearly wasn't us. "Oh, God, that's it," she groaned. "Yes, fuck me."

Her babbling was a bit over the top. Was she doing it for attention? Maybe she'd gotten jealous that Charlotte had all of it, and was trying to pull focus in her direction.

Not for long.

I paused and flashed an evil smile up at Charlotte. "Take off your shirt. Show everyone your tits."

My words made her jolt and her eyes go wide, but I got the sense it was only surprise at the vulgarity and not my command. She affirmed it when she took in a preparing breath, crossed her arms to grab the sides of her shirt, and began to pull it up.

Her black bra matched the panties in my pocket, and the cups were a see-through mesh—which was fucking perfect. The bra revealed everything with her tight nipples being visible through the thin fabric.

I ran my tongue through her pussy and imagined how we'd look to anyone else in this lounge. She wasn't completely naked, but she might as well have been, as she rode my face. Her hips moved, grinding her lower body against my mouth, trying to get my tongue exactly where she wanted it.

I needed to know and mumbled it against her damp skin. "Are people looking at you?"

"Yes," she whispered.

"You like that?"

Her answer was drenched in desire. "Yes."

It wasn't going to take long to make her come. She'd been responsive the other times things had gotten hot and heavy, and she acted like she'd been on the edge for a while tonight.

Since Travis and Lilith's show—but maybe even before.

I applied more pressure, and varied the speed of my tongue, studying her to gauge what she liked best and bring her closer to the brink. The trembling in her legs intensified, making it difficult for her to stand, so I tightened my hold around her thigh.

If she wanted to sit on my shoulder when the orgasm took her, I wouldn't mind. I just wanted her to get there, to experience the same satisfaction she'd already given me—

Huh. She'd triggered my orgasm with a simple phrase. Could I do the same?

I loaded my voice with seduction and made sure to say it loud enough for her to hear over her moans. "Come for me, baby girl."

All the air whooshed loudly from Charlotte's lungs, and she hunched over, like the orgasm that abruptly ripped through her was going to make her supporting leg buckle. She contracted and flinched and latched a hand on my free shoulder for stability.

Or maybe she'd done it because she wanted another connection to me while she descended into ecstasy.

I stayed on my knees and watched in awe.

When I'd called her "baby girl," I hadn't been prepared for its effect on me.

It caused a deep, possessive satisfaction, and that left me off-kilter. I'd never, *ever* been possessive when it came to relationships. In fact, I'd swung so far the opposite direction, my last girlfriend had accused me of not caring.

But tonight with Charlotte, things were wildly different. I hadn't invited Patrick and Shannon to the club, or chatted with anyone else, because I selfishly wanted her all to myself. I wasn't going to hold her back as she explored this new world, but I didn't want her to go off on her own yet.

I wanted us to explore it together.

She hadn't fully recovered from her orgasm when I unhooked her leg from my shoulder and helped her get her feet under herself. I put my hands on her waist as I rose, and then I worked her skirt down over her hips, putting it back in place.

Her top was still on the floor beside us, but I'd get to that later. I was standing in front of her, so my back would block her from view—and we were likely the most dressed people in this room, anyway.

She'd liquified and my hands were the only thing holding her up, and fucking hell if it didn't feel good having her in my arms like that. It intensified a million times over when I captured her mouth with mine.

Our kiss was passionate, and scary. It doused me in foreign and unwanted feelings.

Distance, my mind instructed, trying to tell me what I needed . . .

But I ignored it.

I deepened the kiss until I was lost in it and could no longer hear the voice warning me that I was taking a terrible risk by being with her. The fire between us was scorching hot.

And she wasn't the only one who could get burned.

TWENTY

Charlotte

When I spent the night at Noah's, I didn't sleep in his room. It was surprising—and disappointing—given what we'd done at the club. But he'd asked for this boundary, and I'd begrudgingly respected it.

It'd taken everything in me not to sneak into his bed in the middle of the night. I told myself that in the morning we'd get up, have breakfast together, and then fool around some more.

But when I strolled out into his kitchen wearing my sexiest pajamas, I found him fully dressed, finishing his cup of coffee, and he looked weary.

"Morning," I said softly. "Everything okay?"

He jammed the heel of his palm into one eye. "Not really. My mom called at seven. My dad's been throwing up all night, and she thinks we should take him to the emergency room."

My gaze flew to the clock on the microwave. Shit, it was a quarter to nine. Panic seeped out into my voice. "Oh, God, Noah. Have you been waiting on me?"

"I didn't want to be gone before you were up. I didn't want you to think I'd just left you."

My heart hurt for him.

And now I felt extra shitty about the situation because I'd spent ten minutes making myself look cute in the bathroom before coming out of my room. I waved a hand, signaling for him to get moving because I didn't want him to waste another second on me. He'd wasted too many already. "Go, go. I'll be fine."

"You sure?" he asked, but he was already rising to his feet.

I nodded quickly, saying nothing as he strode away from the kitchen table, leaving behind his coffee mug and a plate full of crumbs from his breakfast. When he reached me, he looked . . . befuddled.

Like he had no idea what to do with me.

The words came from him were filled with regret. "I'm sorry."

"Don't be," I offered. "And don't let me slow you down any more than I already have."

But he didn't move. He lingered in front of me, unsure of how to say goodbye, and I could see the question in his eyes. Should we kiss?

No was the answer he came up with. "I don't know when I'll be back," he flung a hand toward his pantry, "so help yourself to whatever, and stay as long you like."

"Okay."

With that settled, he gave me a final look, turned, and strode quickly from the room.

I remained in the kitchen, my feet glued to the cold tile floor, and my gaze turned absentmindedly to the table. *Well, this morning was off to a disappointing start.* I swallowed a breath and marched forward, collecting the used mug and plate, and carried them to the dishwasher.

The top rack rumbled as I pulled it out and—

A hand closed around my hip and turned me so my back was against the sink, and I found myself staring up at Noah's deep brown eyes. I only got a glimpse, though, before he crushed his mouth to mine.

Had he intended it to be a quick goodbye kiss? Because it became a hell of a lot more. His mouth tasted of longing and promise, and if he hadn't already stolen my breath with his stunning action, this kiss would have done it.

I fell so deeply into it that when he ended the kiss, I was dizzy. Unsteady. I blinked up at him, heavy with desire and yearning, and discovered he looked just as off balance. He held my gaze for a one single heartbeat.

And then he turned to flee a second time.

Without thought, I pressed my fingertips to my lips, as if checking to see if that had really happened or if I'd just imagined it. But my body was warm and buzzing, and the disappointment over him needing to leave faded substantially.

He'd gotten his 'out.' He could have left, but he made the choice to come back and kiss me. It hadn't been a quick, perfunctory one, either. He'd told me so without using words, showing me how badly he'd wished he didn't have to go.

He'd all but said, *"Until next time, Charlotte."*

Eggplant colored tulle cascaded over the top of the dressing room door, and I stared at the poof of fabric in disbelief. Brianna was on the other side, and her hand holding the hanger jutted up, waiting for me to take it from her.

"Really?" I muttered under my breath.

"Just try it on," she ordered.

I grabbed the hanger and pulled the rest of the dress over the door, doing my best to sound chill. "You got it, boss."

Below the door, her feet disappeared from view as she

headed off to find more options, although there couldn't be that many left. Sasha, Cait, and I had tried on nearly every bridesmaid dress in the bridal store.

I slipped the purple fabric over my head and shimmied my way inside the shockingly heavy dress. I glanced in the mirror as I struggled to pull up the back zipper, and choked back a snort.

There was no way I was going to wear this abomination.

It looked like the designer had wanted it to be strapless, but decided it was too simple and had to make a last-minute addition. The single shoulder was full of chiffon flowers, beads, and sequins. On its own, it was a lot. But when it was paired with the skirt and its never-ending layers, the dress was comical.

This wasn't a bridesmaid's dress. It was fucking ballgown straight out of nineties.

Brianna was waiting by the mirrors, and when I came out, I discovered I was the last one to finish dressing. Cait and Sasha looked at me, wearing the same purple monster, and judging by their expressions, they felt the same as I did.

I gripped the layers of tulle, sashayed over to the group with a giant grin, and channeled the little girl from *Despicable Me* as I shook my skirt. "It's *so fluffy*!"

The girls thought it was funny, but the saleswoman nearby was not amused. She lifted an eyebrow and turned to the bride. "We can get this one in navy. What do you think?

Brianna was exceptionally polite. "Wow. It's, uh, something. Might be a bit much."

All of us bridesmaids were feeling a little punchy from trying on so many options, and Sasha flicked at the floral strap of my dress. "It looks like you have a third boob."

I flicked hers. "You do too."

Cait climbed up on the pedestal in front of the mirrors and twirled in the dress, making the layers fly around. Her tone was joking and sugary-sweet. "I feel like a princess."

The tag caught Sasha's eye, so she put a hand on Cait's back to stop her and did a double-take at the figure scribbled there.

"Jesus Christ, it's twelve hundred dollars."

Cait's fake smile froze. "Well, now I just feel sad."

"Me too." Brianna turned her attention back to the saleswoman. "Any other ideas?"

"I have few more pieces we can pull."

Brianna put on a fake scowl and pretended to be a strict drill sergeant. "You heard the woman." She flung a finger at the dressing rooms. "Get your asses back in there."

I'd left my phone face-up on the chair in the dressing room, and as soon as I'd closed myself in the room, its screen lit up with a notification. Someone had texted me while I'd been out by the mirrors, and I swiped to unlock the screen.

Noah: Hey. What are you up to right now?

It'd been four days since we'd gone to Club Eros, and although we'd texted every day since then, I always got a thrill when his name flashed on my phone. Most of our conversations were about business. I'd had a video go mega viral on Sunday, which was super exciting, but now my DMs were full of people wanting something.

Two of them, at least, seemed like legit requests, and Noah had offered to negotiate on my behalf. The best part of it wasn't that he was handling all the stuff I didn't like doing—although that was nice.

No, it was that after we were done talking about business,

we'd turned to talking about other things.

Personal things.

Music, and TV shows, and yesterday he'd talked a bit more about his family. I knew his dad was doing better after spending the weekend in the hospital with an infection, and everyone was relieved he was on the mend.

But his dad was sick, and in complete denial about it, and that was really hard on Noah's entire family.

I was glad he'd opened up to me. I wanted him to feel like he could talk to me about anything, the way I felt about him.

Today, I strove to lighten his mood.

A normal person would have responded with words to the text he'd just sent, but where was the fun in that? I posed in front of the small mirror in my dressing room, trying to get as much of the purple monstrosity into the frame as possible, and snapped a pic. The lighting was nearly as awful as the dress, but it was good enough to give him the idea.

I sent him the picture without any context.

A new dress was pitched over the door. "Don't freak out that it's a size larger," Brianna said. "She said they run small."

The fabric was a pretty cranberry color, with a halter top and a skirt made of chiffon, and was much lighter than the one I had on. As I wiggled out of the purple dress, I smiled to myself while picturing Noah on the other side of the text exchange. Was he looking at me and wondering what the hell I was wearing?

I pulled on the new dress and zipped up the side zipper, and the saleswoman was right. It was a snug fit. God, why were women's dress sizes so fucking arbitrary? When I evaluated myself in the mirror, it caught me off guard. I hadn't expected to like the dress so much because it was pretty simple, but it was flattering.

A new notification popped up on my phone.

> **Noah:** Hope you win first place!
>
> **Me:** ?

I pushed open my dressing room door and strode out into the waiting area, clutching my phone in one hand. This time I was the first one dressed, and when Brianna's gaze settled on me, her mouth fell open.

I couldn't read her expression at all, and it stayed that way as Cait and Sasha came out. Cait was curvier than I was, and she'd probably need to go up another size, but the fit wasn't that bad, and the cranberry color looked stunning with her skin tone.

Sasha looked great as well, but that wasn't surprising. That bitch looked good in everything.

My phone vibrated.

> **Noah:** I assume you are competing in a beauty pageant.

I snorted and typed out my response, telling him I was bridesmaid dress shopping and, unfortunately, the bride had decided the purple dress wasn't making the final cut.

Brianna stood beside the saleswoman, and as she glanced between us bridesmaids, she frowned.

"You don't like it?" I asked.

"No, I do." But her unhappy expression remained.

Sasha couldn't have looked more confused. "What's the problem, then?"

"I like it *too* much. That color looks fabulous on all of you." Brianna let out a sound of frustration. "Damn. Am I going to have to change my wedding colors again?"

Noah: You could still buy the dress and wear it when you clean. Spin off brand: Fancy Girl Cleans.

I chuckled and thumbed out my next message, which was a huge mistake because it drew everyone's attention.

Me: I'm not spending $1200 on a cleaning dress.

"Who are you texting?" Sasha asked.

Shit. I dropped my hand so my phone was hidden in the layers of my skirt. "Just a friend."

That was the wrong answer, because Sasha's eyes narrowed. "Tell me you're not texting Zach."

"Oh, fuck no." I flashed an apologetic smile for my profanity to the saleswoman, who didn't seem to care.

Sasha knew all my friends, and I was being secretive, which set her on alert—so I was going to have to give her something. She wasn't the type to let things go. I'd specifically agreed not to tell my parents about Noah, and it had seemed safest to keep our whole relationship under wraps.

How would I explain it, anyway?

"It's Noah," I said simply.

Cait exchanged a look with the other two girls, checking to see if she was out of the loop, but Brianna looked just as lost.

"Who?" they asked in unison.

Sasha wrinkled her nose. "The guy whose house you're cleaning?"

"Yeah." I forced casualness into my voice. "He's helping me with some business stuff too."

An evil, knowing grin spread across her face. "Is he? And what's he getting out of this arrangement?" She straightened like whatever thought had just hit her filled her with excitement. “Did you go with my idea of the French maid costume?”

“No,” I said quickly—*too* quickly.

“Oh, my God, you did!”

“No,” I was firmer this time, “I didn’t. I mean, I may have thought about it, but just for my videos.” I tacked it on for good measure. “Not for him.”

It wasn’t the least bit convincing, and Brianna chuckled. “Why am I not surprised you’re sleeping with the guy you work for?”

The saleswoman acted like she suddenly had somewhere else to be. She excused herself and disappeared into the rack of dresses.

I sighed loudly. “I am not sleeping with Noah.”

“But she wants to,” Sasha pointed out to the girls.

I didn’t say anything, because what was there to say? And when I didn’t deny it, they knew she was right.

I didn’t *just* want to sleep with him, but to be with him completely . . . but it could never happen. I wasn’t at a point in my life right now where I was allowed to fall in love with anyone.

Most of all him.

“It doesn’t matter if I want to—because I’m not going to.” I said it mostly to remind myself. “It’s the last thing I need right now.”

The girls nodded in understanding and turned their attention back to the dresses.

The irony wasn’t lost on me either. I was building a brand, claiming to be an expert on cleaning things up, and yet . . . my life was a huge fucking mess.

I had cleaned every area of Noah's house except for his bedroom because I'd been saving that for last. As usual, his bed wasn't made and there were clothes on the floor, so my first order of business was to grab a laundry basket and tidy up.

I didn't touch his bed, though.

With the camera placement I had planned, it wouldn't be in my shot anyway.

Once I'd finished clearing the floor and decluttering the space, I brought in my video supplies and set up my equipment. When that was done, I finally stole a glance at the tangle of sheets on his bed.

Until next time, Charlotte.

That was what his eyes had whispered the last time we'd seen each other. Shit, I was determined to make that happen today.

But first things first.

He wasn't here yet, anyway.

The video on the agenda for today was about dusting. How to do it properly and quickly. I set up my camera, angling it toward the dresser with the mirror hanging above it, and clipped on my microphone.

I reread the notes I'd made on my phone to make sure I'd hit all the points I wanted to, rehearsed a few times, and got the camera rolling. It didn't take me long to shoot the video. I was getting better, more efficient, and honestly, I was having fun.

"How the hell am I having fun while dusting?" I asked

aloud to the empty room. If I had to rank my favorite chores, dusting would be near the bottom. I shook my head, then moved my camera setup, changing the angle to shoot B roll footage.

I'd nearly finished when Noah's voice rang out from down the hall. "Charlotte?"

An evil smile burst on my lips as I turned off my equipment. "In here."

As he made his approach, I glanced in the mirror, giving myself a quick check to make sure everything looked right. He appeared in the doorway but took only a single step into the room before halting.

His eyes went wide, and he stood awkwardly, like he was trying very hard to hold perfectly still. "What . . . are you wearing?"

TWENTY-ONE

Charlotte

I set a hand on my hip by the white apron sash, posing for Noah so he could take it all in.

His gaze started at my black high heels and worked its way up over the thigh high stockings and the skirt that was so short, it barely covered my ass. The fluffy white petticoat underneath the black skirt wasn't comfortable, but that was to be expected.

I bought the cheapest, sluttiest French maid Halloween costume I could find online.

The top of the dress was cut low and decorated with white frills, and I'd pulled my hair up into bun, so a few loose tendrils fell around my face. It called his focus to the thick band of black fabric wrapped around my throat. I'd had to buy the choker necklace and the feather duster I held separately, but it had been worth it.

The accessories made the outfit.

"I was inspired by your idea," I said, "of buying a dress to clean in. What do you think?" I shifted my weight to the other foot, swaying my hips and making the skirt ruffle. "Do you like it?"

My question was entirely rhetorical because the expression on his face told me exactly how much he liked it. Heat filled his eyes, and he stared at me like I was the most tempting thing he'd ever seen.

Yet he lingered in the doorway, unsure what to do. His fists balled at his side, and his face changed until he looked almost angry. Like I'd turned him on when he hadn't wanted me to.

I'd prepared for this, though.

Because I'd spent enough time with him to know he wasn't great when he'd been caught off-guard. He'd just needed another minute to process, and then we'd be fine.

Then we could get down to business.

When I bought the costume two days ago, I'd decided that since I was his maid, I might as well lean into it.

His gaze was glued to me as I sauntered over to his bed, set the feather duster on his nightstand, and gestured to the messy bedding. "While you're in here, I thought I'd ask. Do you want me to wash these sheets?" I leaned over suggestively, smoothing a hand across them, knowing my ass cheeks were peeking out beneath my skirt. "Are they," I glanced at him over my shoulder and emphasized the word in a smoky voice, "*dirty*?"

My sultry question spurred him into action, and he took a few steps deeper into the room. His expression morphed into one that dripped with desire. If this was a game, he was now ready to play.

I straightened and turned to face him, setting a hand on the top of my thigh so my fingers could play with the lace band of my stocking. "I bet they are." My voice clouded with more smoke. "I bet you've done things on these sheets that were fucking *filthy*."

The gleam in Noah's eyes was so hot, my legs threatened to go boneless. He took another step toward me, halving the distance between us.

"I have," he said. "Does that turn you on?"

This question was also rhetorical. I had no doubt he knew it did.

His gaze wandered seductively over me, packaged in the costume that was barely more than lingerie. "Did you wear this for me?"

I sank my teeth into my bottom lip and shook my head slowly, feigning innocence. "I wore it for the video I was making."

He didn't believe a word of it. "Uh huh."

"Really," I lied. "How was I supposed to know you were going to come home early?"

He reached out to put his hands on my waist and pulled me up against him so forcefully I stumbled on my heels and crashed into his chest. His arms trapped me like he thought I'd run, when that was the last thing I wanted to do.

"I'm not early," he said. "If anything, I'm late."

"Oh, are you? I must have lost track of time."

Again, this was a lie. I'd spent a lot longer deep cleaning his kitchen than normal, hoping to have him catch me once I'd moved on to cleaning his bedroom. The plan had worked perfectly, down to the way his hand gripped my ass and urged me up into his kiss.

It was hot and dirty.

His tongue pushed past my lips and slicked against mine, basically fucking my mouth. It was urgent, and aggressive, and exactly how I wanted it.

A tiny sound of surprise punched from my lungs when he picked me up and sat me on the edge of his bed. I wrapped my legs around his waist and gripped his face, holding him into our feverish kiss.

Or maybe I was holding on to him because of the

onslaught of emotions rushing through me.

I may have been the first girl he'd brought home into this bed—but I certainly wasn't the last. How many other women had been in here? I was too afraid to ask. Not because I was turned off by that or jealous . . .

But because I didn't get to watch.

God, was there something wrong with me? Seeing him with someone else was supposed to be wrong. Taboo. But Noah never made me feel that way.

I tore my mouth from his and blurted it out before I lost my nerve. "I want to watch next time you fuck Shannon."

He glanced away and groaned like the idea was so sexy it was overwhelming, and he couldn't bear to hear it and look at me at the same time. Then he drew in a heavy breath and fixed his gaze back on me. "I floated the idea to her and Patrick already."

When he didn't immediately continue, my impatience got the best of me. "And?"

"They're definitely open to it, but they want to have dinner with us first to get to know you." He cupped my cheek, and his gaze wandered over my face, studying my reaction. "Plus, they want to discuss boundaries."

"Boundaries," I repeated.

"Yeah," he said. "I told them that we're not interested in full swap, but they're wondering if you're going to participate in any way, or just watch."

He'd said it casually, but I wasn't fooled. He wanted to know this too.

"Participate with Patrick?" My pulse skipped. "Or with Shannon?" Because I'd never done anything with another girl and wasn't sure how I'd feel about it. I couldn't tell if it turned me on, or if it was the whole idea of playing with others that was doing that.

His expression didn't change; it was perfectly schooled. "It's whatever you'd be comfortable with."

I set my hands behind me on the mattress and leaned back as I considered it. "I only saw him the one time, and it's been a while, so I don't remember if he's hot." I made a face, realizing how that sounded. "Sorry. Is it shallow to say that?"

He laughed lightly, and God, he looked so handsome. "Nope. Chemistry is important, and that's a big part of why they want to meet you."

His earlier kiss had been blistering, but when he leaned over to deliver his next one, it was slow and sweet.

Had he sensed the uncertainty in me? His voice was hushed and genuine. "Don't feel any pressure. You don't have to have an answer. And if you do . . . everyone knows nothing is set in stone. You can change your mind at any time, for any reason."

His soft kiss drifted across my cheekbone and down the side of my neck, hovering just above the choker I wore. His warm breath tickled the loose hairs from my bun and caused my shoulders to shake in a delicious shiver.

"Do you want that?" I murmured. "Would you be okay sharing me with another person?"

He drew back just enough to give me a view of his dazzling, incredulous smile. "Are you kidding, Charlotte? That would be so fucking hot."

I couldn't get my brain around it. I flashed back to the night after Thanksgiving when I'd been out at the bars, and Zach had caught some guy flirting with me. Because I was head over heels in love with my boyfriend, I hadn't reciprocated in the least, but it didn't matter.

Zach had been so pissed, he'd given me the silent treatment the rest of the weekend.

There must have been a dubious look on my face because Noah tilted his head, pondering. "Let me ask you something. Why do you want to watch me with Shannon?"

My face flushed hot, but not with shame. It was mostly the memory that caused it. "It's hard to explain."

There was zero judgment from him. "Try me."

I sucked in a breath as I tried to organize my thoughts. "When I'm not participating . . . when I get to stand back and be outside of it, then I get to see you experience pleasure without any distraction. I'm not worried about what I look like, or thinking about how it feels, or what I should do next."

Shit, I was doing a terrible job of explaining it. I lifted a hand and pushed away the tendril of hair that was making the side of my neck itch, but it was mostly a stall tactic. Noah knew I hadn't said what I wanted to, and he waited patiently for me to continue.

I lifted my chin and stared into his deep eyes. "I like how I don't have to do anything but focus on you." The corner of my mouth tugged up into a half-smile. "Plus, I get to see you in your element, get to see what you're good at." My voice faltered just the tiniest bit. "And Shannon can give you something I'm not quite ready for."

He scrubbed a hand over his mouth as he considered what I'd said, and then that hand fell away. "We're a lot alike. You know that?" I didn't, and it was clear I needed convincing. "The reasons you just gave . . . those are the same for me."

"What?"

He trailed a teasing fingertip at my neckline, playing with

the white ruffle trim. "I want to watch you experience pleasure too. Getting to see someone else play with you? Fuck me. I want to sit back and watch every twitch of your body, listen to every little moan you make. I want to see your face when you come and focus only on that." He reached between our bodies and adjusted himself through his pants. "Shit, I'm getting hard right now just thinking about it."

Oh, God, I wasn't immune either. A muscle deep in my core clenched in response.

The pad of his wicked fingertip continued to skate at the edge of my dress, sliding over my cleavage. "I think that's the biggest benefit of us holding off on sex." His eyes brimmed with desire and power. "Right now, I get to focus completely, entirely on you."

I shuddered from Noah's words and his touch, and a smile ghosted his lips. He liked my reaction very much. His fingertips took an unhurried path across my skin, working upward until they traced the edge of the choker I wore.

"This reminds me of a collar," he uttered in the silence of the tension-filled room, "and it looks so fucking good on you."

Holy shit.

Goosebumps lifted on my skin, and my mouth went completely dry. I didn't know much about BDSM, but this I understood. There had been at least two people at Club Eros wearing collars, and I knew what they represented.

Control.

Maybe even ownership.

"Do you like wearing it," he hesitated, preparing for something, "baby girl?"

Fuck.

I sucked it in a sharp breath because the subtext to his

question was so powerful, I couldn't stay quiet. And I didn't waste time to even consider it. The answer burst from me in a fiery rush. "Yes, Daddy."

His kiss was brutal. It was so forceful, it pushed me down onto my back on the bed, and his hands went everywhere. They roved over my arms, my breasts, my stomach. He moved in a frenzy, like a man possessed.

As if my answer had overwhelmed him.

My breath went ragged when he slipped his hands under my fluffy skirt, and then his fingers were peeling my panties down my stocking-covered legs, and he hurled them to the floor.

"Oh!" I gasped and reached out, grabbing his forearm when he speared two thick fingers inside me. It was so sudden, and my body wasn't quite ready for the intrusion, but the uncomfortable stretch of his fingers . . . it felt sinfully good.

As he pumped his fingers in and out, I clawed at the sheets beneath me. He was touching me *deeply*. Deeper than he'd ever done before. Blood roared loudly in my head, drowning out thought. He stood at the edge of the bed, leaning over me, and set his other hand low on my stomach.

It was as if he was holding me in place, pining me to the mattress.

Concentration etched his face as he increased his speed, moving his hand faster and faster. Oh, God. He was hitting my G spot, fucking me at furious tempo and my body was purring in response.

My vision blanked out and everything went white, so I slammed my eyelids shut. It allowed me to focus on the sensations and the intensity building in me that was unlike anything I'd felt before. I was a slingshot being stretched back in preparation for release.

The force of it was so powerful, it was almost scary.

"Open your eyes," he ordered. "You look at me when you come."

All I could do was obey, and when my eyes blinked open, the sight of him stole the last ounce of my breath. He looked so fucking amazing, all determined and focused while his fingers plunged inside me endlessly.

My whole body trembled, and he was moving so fast I wondered how it was even possible. He was a blur. Or maybe it just seemed that way because I was out of my mind with pleasure. I was no longer in control of anything, especially the urgent moans that poured from me.

Everything was building, and building, and . . .

I came so hard, I cried out through my locked teeth. Bliss erupted and flooded through my limbs, and there was a gush of warmth between my legs. It was shocking how much wetter I'd become because I could hear the slippery glide of his fingers.

It was impossible to think about.

All I could do was endure the ecstasy as it continued to roll through me. I flailed and thrashed on the bed, gasping for air as the orgasm tore me apart. It wasn't until it began to recede that I had an inkling of what had just happened.

Holy.

Fucking.

Shit.

My face burned a million degrees. Had he just made me . . . *squirt*?

The mattress beneath me was wet.

Oh, my God. I couldn't catch my breath and scrambled

backward on the bed.

Noah wore a victorious smile. "Oh, baby girl, look at the mess you made on my sheets."

The heat on my face burned even hotter and I tore my gaze away from him, turning to look at the door because I didn't want to die of embarrassment in his bed.

But Noah climbed onto the bed and hurried across his knees until I was in his arms, and he had my face cradled in one of his strong hands. There was nowhere else to look but into his brown eyes that were full of anxiety.

"No, please don't be embarrassed," he said in a rush. "There's no reason because, goddamn it, that was so fucking hot." His face was just as handsome even when it was full of regret. "I made you do that, and I should have asked if you'd be okay with it. I won't do it again."

I had to pull air in and out of my lungs in small, measured sips because I was still buzzing. "Are you kidding? I fucking loved it, it just," I sucked in another breath, "surprised me."

Relief flooded through his expression, but I didn't get to see it for long because he delivered a kiss that turned up the volume on the buzzing in my body. "Okay, good. Because I wouldn't mind doing that again sometime." His gaze slid over my face and down my neck. "But right now, I want to take off your dress so I can see you in that choker . . . and nothing else."

I was fully on board with this plan.

TWENTY-TWO

Noah

Traffic wasn't too bad as I drove into the city, although Charlotte had us listening to Taylor Swift the whole way.

"The navigator gets to pick the music," she said.

I lifted an eyebrow. "I think Google Maps is doing the navigating."

Her response was to simply grin and turn the volume up another click, letting Taylor's voice drown out any other protests I might make.

I allowed it until the song was over and then turned the volume down so we could talk. "I got called into a last-minute meeting today." She pivoted in her seat to look at me. "I was in such a rush, I grabbed the first suit in my closet, which happened to be the one that needs to go out for dry cleaning."

"Uh oh." She chuckled.

"It was the one I wore to Club Eros."

Her amusement dried up. She didn't understand the danger, but my serious tone sobered her.

"I was sitting there at lunch next to your dad when I needed a pen. So I reach into my pocket, pull it out, and your pair of panties fell on the floor."

I hadn't given them back to her that night, and she hadn't asked, and perhaps we both liked how I'd hung on to them. But that had been more than a week ago, and I'd temporarily forgotten they were still tucked in that pocket.

Her pretty face filled with alarm. "Oh, shit. Did my dad see?"

I shook my head. "No, thank fuck." I flashed back to that moment when my heart lodged itself in my throat. "It was dumb luck he was facing the other way. I picked them up as fast as I could and shoved them back in my pocket, but Christ. It was awkward as hell."

The rest of the lunch, her underwear had been burning a hole in my pocket. The hit of panic it had given me made it hard not to question what the fuck I was doing with her. But it was too late, and I was in too deep, wasn't I?

We were on our way to our date with Patrick and Shannon, and she was just as excited about it as I was.

I turned into the parking garage and grabbed a ticket from the machine while Charlotte checked her phone. Her gasp was so sudden, I tapped the brakes and looked at the parked cars, searching for whatever I'd missed. "What? What is it?"

"It's an email from HomeHappy."

I relaxed my tense grip on the steering wheel and continued up the ramp, searching for a parking spot. "Yeah? What's it say?"

HomeHappy was a small business that sold cleaning towels for glass, because as Charlotte had explained to me, what you used to clean mirrors and windows made a big difference. I'd been in talks with them on her behalf for the last week.

"They want to do a giveaway post on Instagram, and they're offering me five hundred dollars for it."

"Nice," I said. "I'm about to be fifty bucks richer."

We'd settled on a ten percent broker fee for me, since I was handling her admin work. I'd tried to talk her out of it though. She needed the money a lot more than I did, but she'd insisted. The plan was to keep our business relationship separate from our personal one, and that went for her cleaning services and my business management.

This was the first deal I'd facilitated for her, but I had others in the works . . . and plans of what to do with my cut.

I found an available parking spot, parked, and shut off the engine. Charlotte didn't move, though. She made no effort to get out of the car, and I shot her a questioning look.

"Thanks for all your help." She said it like I'd had to move mountains to make the deal happen.

I laughed softly. "You're welcome, but it was nothing. All I did was send a few emails. You're the one doing the work."

"You don't know what a big deal this is for me." Her gaze shifted away, and she stared through the windshield at the bland concrete wall of the parking garage. "Usually, when I get emails or messages like this, I'm terrible about answering them. Sometimes I flag the email to handle later, when I'll have more time to come up with the perfect reply." She spoke like she was revealing an awful secret. "I don't think I'm subconsciously avoiding it, but I get nervous about what to say. And then time passes, and now I'm embarrassed about how long it's been without a response. Which, of course, makes it even harder to write back. So a lot of times I . . . don't."

I tugged my eyebrows together. "You're missing a lot of opportunities doing that."

Had that sounded lecture-y? That wasn't my intent. Her head tilted down so she could stare at her knees. "I know. I just get scared sometimes."

On some level, I understood this. She had a paralyzing fear of failure, and it was safer to not even try. But without risk, there usually wasn't a reward.

"You know, this is basically what your father does for a living. Kind of surprised it didn't rub off on you."

The second the statement was out, I cringed internally, but she didn't seem bothered by it.

"He tried to teach me," she shrugged, "but, honestly? It was easier to let him take care of it."

I tried not to make a face at how entitled that sounded, but must not have been successful, because when she looked at me, a sad smile crept across her lips. She knew exactly what I was thinking.

"Spoiled brat, remember?" Her voice went low and serious. "I'm working on it, I swear."

"I believe you." And I meant that genuinely. "But you should know," I shifted my tone to a playful one and reached for the door handle, "I kind of like it when you're being a brat."

She let out a laugh.

When we got to the crowded restaurant, Patrick and Shannon were already at the table, and he lifted a hand to wave us over.

I strolled at a snail's pace to give Charlotte plenty of time to evaluate his looks. "Thoughts?" I whispered.

She matched my hushed voice. "I can work with that."

I chuckled. When she'd asked about Patrick's looks, I'd tried to evaluate him through her eyes. He was in his early forties and twenty years older than her, but the age gap didn't seem to bother her. He had an attractive enough face and kept himself in good shape, which meant he was pleasant looking.

Thankfully, I looked better.

At least, I was confident I did in Charlotte's eyes.

Dates like this were always awkward in the beginning,

but conversation began to flow between the four of us after we'd ordered dinner and been served our drinks. It helped that I had a lot in common with them besides the lifestyle, and Charlotte was so outgoing. Plus, we didn't talk about anything sexy right off the bat.

This was a double date, and everyone treated it that way.

I shouldn't have been surprised at how quickly Charlotte seemed at ease. If anything, she was more relaxed than I was. It left me a little envious of her adaptability.

But right after we'd ordered dessert, she abruptly straightened in her seat. Something was wrong.

I leaned in close. "What is it?"

"It's nothing," she said automatically and set her dinner napkin on the tabletop. "I'm going to the restroom. I'll be right back."

She pushed back from the table, stood, and glanced hesitantly at the front of the restaurant. I followed her gaze, but I couldn't figure out what she'd seen that had her worried. The place was busy with guests finishing their meals or being seated at their tables, and servers darted around to deliver drinks and food.

Everything seemed . . . ordinary.

But she hurried away like she couldn't be gone fast enough.

"She's young." Patrick said it like an offhanded comment, but there was an accusatory tone buried beneath that I didn't care for.

"She is," I said. "Is that a problem?"

"No, not necessarily." He exchanged a look with his wife, perhaps seeking validation. "But young people don't always know what they want. She could be confusing your desires with her own."

He was worried I was pressuring Charlotte into this.

"Patrick and I just want to make sure she's interested." Shannon gave a pragmatic smile. "We don't want to take advantage."

"You wouldn't be." My expression had to be one of amusement. "Trust me, she's interested. She's the one who asked for it, after all." They were skeptical, and I shrugged, keeping my tone light. "You don't have to take my word for it. You can ask her when she gets back."

I wasn't upset about their skepticism either. I got that it came from a good place. I was her client and thirteen years older, and I was fully aware of that large power imbalance. A lesser person might take advantage of that.

I hoped my expression was as sincere as I felt. "I appreciate that you're looking out for her."

"Of course." Shannon relaxed into her seat and sipped her gin and tonic because my response had gone a long way to ease their concern. Now, her eyes lit with mischief. "She's so stinking beautiful, I'm a little jealous."

Her back had been to the hallway, so she didn't know Charlotte had made her return and overheard the compliment.

"*You're* jealous?" She grabbed her seat and dropped down into it, and she looked like herself again. "Because I feel like I'm the one who should be jealous." She put her napkin back in her lap and then gestured to Patrick. "He knows I saw you and Noah together, right?"

Patrick nodded. "Yes."

"Well, I wasn't just watching Noah." She tossed a lock of her blonde hair over her shoulder and picked up her martini. "I was looking at both of you, because how could I not? You're hot."

Shannon let out a pleased, surprised laugh. "Why, thank you."

The women held each other's gaze as the chemistry sparked between them. It distracted everyone at the table, so none of us noticed the man approaching until he was abruptly tableside.

"Charlotte?"

All the color drained from her face as she peered up at him, but the man didn't notice her discomfort. He was older—perhaps the same age as her father—and his curious gaze bounced from person to person around the table, before returning to her.

"Mr. Carson?" she asked with dread.

"I thought that was you. Small world, huh?"

She clearly had no idea what to say. "Yup."

"I just finished having dinner with Angela and had to come back because, like an idiot, I left my credit card." He smiled and put a hand on his hip, like he was settling in for a chat. "How's your dad? It's been a while since I've seen him."

She looked like the cat who'd swallowed the canary. "He's good."

Oh.

Earlier, she'd clocked him and had darted to the restroom so he wouldn't spot her. What if he told her father he saw her out on what looked like a double date . . . and she'd been much younger than everyone else?

There was no avoiding him now, and once more, he glanced at the table, perhaps waiting for her to introduce him.

But she didn't.

"Right," he said, trying to disguise his awkwardness, and raised his hands in faux surrender. "Anyway, I didn't mean to interrupt y'all. It was nice seeing you, Charlotte. Say hi to your folks for me."

"Sure," she lied.

As he shuffled off toward the exit, she turned to me, and although she didn't say anything with words, the look she gave spoke volumes. *Well, that wasn't great.*

No, it wasn't, but there was nothing we could do about it now.

"He used to work with my dad," she offered to the group.

Shannon and Patrick nodded politely but didn't ask any questions. Most people who lived this lifestyle liked their anonymity and assumed the same of everyone else. You didn't ask personal questions and understood people shared only what they were comfortable with.

Most of the time, this was a protective measure. Even if you were careful, there was still risk involved, and no one wanted a disgruntled partner, looking for revenge, to 'out' them and blow up their lives.

I cleared my throat and strove to change the topic. "Do you want to talk about boundaries? You already know ours."

Because I'd already told them Charlotte and I weren't having sex, so that was off the table for her. They'd probably found it odd but had no comments about it. Maybe they'd assumed it was a safety thing, and I wasn't allowed to be with her while active with other sexual partners.

"Sure," Patrick's focus slid from me to Charlotte. "We don't have many. As long as it's approved, we can be with other people, and it's fine to do that behind closed doors." He got a wicked glimmer in his eye. "Sometimes that's hotter."

Shannon chuckled softly. "Really the only rule we have is no kissing other people on the mouth. Typically, that's just for us. But—"

"We've talked about it, and we'd be willing to waive that rule for you, Charlotte, if you wanted to kiss Shannon." He leaned forward, setting his elbows on the table. "She's never played with another woman before."

My brain buzzed, but it wasn't steam at the idea of Charlotte being with another woman that caused my disorientation. It was a loud disapproval echoing in my head. "No."

Everyone turned to look at me in surprise.

Well, I was just as surprised myself. "No to Charlotte kissing other people," I clarified, "not the other thing." Fuck, I was all out of sorts. "That's my boundary, for uh, the same reason y'all have it."

Charlotte's stunned voice was breathy. "Kissing is only for us?"

"Yeah." I tried to play it casually, but it was so fucking weird to me I was willing to share her in any other way—

But not this.

Her expression softened, her eyes melting, and beneath the table her hand came to rest on my leg. It was like she wanted a connection to me, and I was happy to oblige, encasing her hand in mine.

Shit, the idea of us remaining simply friends—even with benefits—became hazier every time we were together. How much longer could I keep lying to myself that I didn't want more?

The couple across the table from us must have sensed the moment between us because they fell silent. They sipped their drinks and patiently waited for it to pass. And when our attention finally returned to them, Shannon wore a faint smile.

It was like she knew something I didn't.

"I've never been with another woman either," Charlotte said. "But I don't know if I want to. I mean, maybe?" She frowned and peered at Shannon like she was worried she'd offended her. "You're really hot, so don't think it's you. I just don't know if I'm ready for that."

Shannon grinned and shook her head. "No, no. You're new to this, and I'm sure it's a bit overwhelming, and we got ahead of ourselves because it's one of our fantasies. Forget we mentioned it."

"And since we're talking about fantasies, we have something we'd like to ask," Patrick chimed in. "We fully expect you to say no, but I'm bringing it up just in case you're interested." He glanced around, checking to see if anyone nearby was listening. "We have a date with a friend next week. He's a guy we've played with several times before, although he's been too busy the past few months. We finally got our schedules to align."

Shannon bit down on her bottom lip before speaking. "As long as he's okay with it, would you want to join us?"

I heard Charlotte's breath catch and my heart skipped a beat. "As in, all of us together?"

"You could just watch. You don't have to participate. But," she glanced at her husband, "we were hoping you might want to, because a group thing . . . that's another one of my fantasies."

My mouth went dry, and my hand tensed around Charlotte's.

"We're pretty sure our friend's going to be up for it," Patrick said. "Eli has a 'the more, the merrier' attitude. If y'all want to join, we could get together on Zoom. We'll introduce you and then we can share our thoughts about how we see the evening going."

Shannon drew in a breath and pressed out a persuasive smile. "What do you think? Would you be . . . interested?"

The answer burst from Charlotte with no hesitation. "Yes."

Her statement hung in the air, and she turned to me abruptly, her face red. She hadn't checked with me first, and now she was horribly embarrassed. Goddamn, it was the sexiest thing ever.

Shannon grinned and glanced at her husband. "Noah was right. I think she's into it."

I laughed and, beneath the table, I squeezed Charlotte's hand. "I think it's safe to say we're both interested."

TWENTY-THREE

Charlotte

The sun was so low in the sky, it was hidden behind the trees that lined the edges of Old Hickory Lake. It cast a warm glow on the dock and the trio of people standing at the end of it, who were waiting for Noah and me.

My pulse had been humming the entire forty-five-minute drive out here, and now it raced even faster.

The boards of the dock creaked underfoot as we walked toward the boat tied off at the end of it. When Patrick had invited everyone on a sunset cruise around the lake, I'd pictured a smallish boat. Maybe something sporty, or a little pontoon boat.

But this thing was large, sleek, and looked like a tiny yacht. There was a large awning over the top, covering the wheel, the lounge couches, and the entrance to go below deck.

"Hi." Shannon's gaze swept over me, taking in my emerald green top, white shorts, and gold sandals. "How was the drive?"

"It was good." Noah ticked his head toward the boat, and he sounded as surprised as I'd been. "This is your boat?"

"Yep, this is Nauti-By-Nature," Patrick said. "Would you believe me if I told you we didn't name her? We bought her used, and the original name was a good fit for us. Plus, it's bad luck to change it." He gestured to the cooler Noah was carrying. "Here, I can stow that for you."

While that was handed over, my gaze flicked to the other guy who stood beside Shannon on the dock.

As they'd expected, Eli had no problem with us joining in on their date, and Noah and I met him over Zoom.

He was similar to Noah in several ways besides the lifestyle. They were both in their thirties, in great shape, and attractive, which made it seem like Shannon had a type. Eli's brown hair was clipped so close to his head it was nearly buzzed, but it looked great on him. He had an angular face, and a smile with honest-to-God dimples.

He'd been cute in the video on Noah's laptop, and he was even cuter in person, wearing a designer shirt and shorts. If I'd seen him that night at the bar with Patrick and Shannon instead of Noah, I probably would have been interested in him.

But I was grateful it hadn't been Eli, because he paled in comparison to the man I'd arrived with.

There was a magnetic pull to Noah that was undeniable.

Shannon handled the introductions today, and when Noah shook Eli's hand, a spark traveled through my body. If everything went according to plan, these men would be with her tonight.

This shit was wild.

In fact, it was wild enough Noah had never done it before.

A gangbang. Or was it an orgy? Was there a minimum number of people for it to classify as an orgy? I filed it away to ask him about it later.

When it was time to get on the boat, I pulled off my sandals and accepted Patrick's hand. I didn't really need him to help me aboard since the lake was smooth, and the boat was right beside the dock, but it felt weird to decline his offer.

I got the sense he'd done it because it was habit and he

was a gentleman, and not because he wanted to touch me.

My overall feeling about Patrick was pleasant indifference. He was decent looking, and nice, and he certainly didn't give me 'the ick,' but he was far more interested in his wife than anyone else. Which was sweet. Maybe he was a little like me and his biggest kink was watching. Did he feel the same way about me as I did him?

Maybe. But I was just guessing, because Patrick was kind of hard to read.

Eli, on the other hand, was not.

Within thirty seconds of meeting him, I knew he was the kind of guy who said whatever thought crossed his mind.

When it was explained to him on the Zoom call I was new to all this and my participation was likely going to be minimal, his disappointment was clear. He said he hoped I'd be willing to join in on the fun.

This had nearly blown up the whole thing up, with Noah threatening to cancel because he was sure Eli would be too high-pressure.

But Eli's apology had been swift and seemingly genuine. And after we'd ended the call, I'd assured Noah I'd be all right. I didn't expect Eli to be aggressive, but if he was, I'd encountered those kinds of guys before and could handle myself. Plus, I knew Noah had my back.

Patrick had said their boat was older, but I couldn't tell. Everything about it seemed new and high tech, and it was in excellent shape, making me even more excited for our cruise.

Once we were ready, I took a seat beside Noah on one of the benches near the back, and Shannon and Eli sat opposite us, while Patrick finished casting off and started the motors.

It didn't take us long to reach the center of the lake, where long shadows stretched across the mirrored surface, and the incessant buzz of the cicadas hummed from the trees. With the engine off, it was peaceful, and I relaxed into Noah, enjoying the moment.

Drinks were passed around, and conversation flowed easily. It was clear that Patrick and Shannon were private. I didn't know their last name or what they did for a living or if they had any kids, but Eli was more forthcoming. He'd joined the Marines straight out of high school, and after an eight-year enlistment, he'd left and become a security guard and firefighter.

He'd lived a wild lifestyle while he was in the military, and it had carried over into his civilian life. I was surprised to learn he'd been in the lifestyle longer than anyone else on the boat, and that Shannon and Patrick had only been swinging for a few years.

"Her sex drive is higher than mine," Patrick said as he squeezed onto the bench beside his wife, "and I like watching, so that works out pretty great for us." He gave her a sexy, knowing smile. "I like seeing her happy when she goes out on dates, and I love hearing all about them when she comes back to me."

She had an almost dreamy look as she gazed at him, but then remembered there were other people around. "But we don't *need* it," she said. "Playing with others is just a fun bonus."

I liked hearing everyone talk so freely about it, because it was fucking fascinating to me.

The sun slipped further down, and the stars slowly became visible in the inky black sky. The mood on the boat was chill, but I wondered if they were all secretly pretending, as I did, that they didn't feel the undercurrent of electricity. The anticipation hummed in me, making it hard to focus.

The lighting on the deck was minimal, and Shannon was so discreet about it, I hadn't noticed her hand moving between Eli's legs until Patrick glanced down and let out a sound of approval. She was sandwiched between the men on the small bench, fitted perfectly up against her husband, while massaging the erection that was tenting the front of the other man's shorts.

It was no longer news to me I was into voyeurism, but what was surprising? How much I liked watching *someone else* watch.

It was sexy in a taboo, forbidden way how Patrick studied his wife. How he watched the hand decorated with her wedding rings slide back and forth and caused pleasure to twist on the younger man's face.

He brought his lips right to the shell of his wife's ear. "Should we head below?"

She nodded enthusiastically.

The lake was relatively quiet with hardly any boats passing, but we weren't alone, and it was clear they wanted privacy for our group.

Tonight's show would be closed to the public, invitation only.

I took Noah's hand when he offered to help me from my seat.

Once we were below deck, Shannon gave us a brief tour, and the interior of the boat reminded me a bit of a tour bus. It was compact, with a low ceiling and tight layout, made worse because there were five of us. But it was elegantly finished. The floor was hardwood, and the furniture was covered in leather, making it feel luxurious and upscale.

From the steps leading back up, the galley kitchen was to our left. On our right, white leather cushioned seating wrapped around a table, creating a U-shaped booth. The head, complete with a shower, was a small room past the galley, and the sliding door beyond that was open. It revealed a decent-sized bed tucked against the bow, surrounded by storage cabinets.

Shannon motioned to the booth for us to take a seat. There wasn't room to do much else, so I set my drink down on the table and went first. I slid around the cushioned bench, leaving space for people to sit on either side of me. Noah followed, as did Eli on the other side, but since the table was narrow, it didn't leave much room. My knees rested against their knees, and although it was an innocent touch, my breath went shallow.

I snatched up my White Claw and took a big gulp, trying to quench a thirst that I suspected my drink couldn't help.

Patrick pressed a few buttons on a panel on the galley wall, and music began to play through the sound system. It was a smoky, sexy mix of electronic beats and bass.

Was this playlist called '*Music to fuck to*?' Because it was perfect.

As Shannon finished her drink, she swayed her hips to the beat, and when her husband gripped her hips from behind, she rubbed provocatively against him. All the while, her gaze was locked on us, her captive audience at the table.

His hands wandered over her curves, caressing her, and she turned over her shoulder to kiss him. It was slow and sensual, and I strangely found the way she kissed him much hotter than the way he touched her.

"I think you need to lose this dress," he said, sounding full of seduction.

She agreed, and her vibrant red hair shimmered in the warm light of the cabin when she nodded. She held still as her husband stood behind her, grabbed fistfuls of the skirt of her dress, and dragged the fabric up.

The stretchy knit gave way, revealing sexy, purple lace panties, and as her dress continued up, her matching bra. The eggplant color looked good against her fair, lightly freckled skin, and once again, I was envious of her body.

Her dress was tossed aside, and the tension in the room wound tighter as everyone stared at her skimpy lingerie. I liked attention, but I didn't mind one bit that she had all of it right now.

Her husband wrapped his arms around her, and she leaned back into him, but his focus turned to Eli. "I want to watch," he said, "you make my wife come."

Holy shit.

Eli didn't need to be told twice. He was up out of his seat in a flash, and a huge smile broke out on Shannon's face at his enthusiasm. Patrick stepped out of the way, and it was like the changing of the guard when he moved and took Eli's now vacant seat at the table.

I finished my drink as quickly as possible, not wanting to miss a second of the show. Eli sauntered around Shannon and surveyed her like he was figuring out the best place to start.

Patrick had been deliberate and sensual, but Eli 's style was fast and aggressive. He stepped up behind her, smoothed a palm over her stomach, and shoved that hand beneath the lace of her panties.

My breath came and went in short bursts.

As he touched her, she bowed and arched, and her face twisted like he was wringing pleasure from her. The hand moving beneath the purple fabric wasn't gentle either. His fingers were insistent, demanding.

Her lips parted to draw in air in ragged gulps, and between them, she made little whimpers of need. It was clear he liked hearing it, and an almost evil smile burned across his face. He liked teasing her, but now it wasn't enough for him.

When he urged her forward, she stumbled until she had her palms flattened to the table, leaning over it.

I was much more interested in men than I was in women, but it was undeniable how hot she looked like this. Her full breasts were barely contained in her bra, and leaning over the table? It made her cleavage even better.

Eli didn't have to use words to order her to stay like that. Everyone knew, and she complied while he stepped back and shed his shirt. I'd noticed the dark artwork crawling up his forearm when I'd first seen him at the dock, but now that he was shirtless, the full tattoo sleeve was on display.

It looked good on him, but his chiseled muscles and defined abdominals? Yeah, those looked even better. There was no arguing he was physically attractive. Maybe if Shannon were to rate these two bulls on looks alone, she might say Eli held the edge over Noah.

But, God, she'd be wrong.

Noah was superior in every way to me.

The thought disappeared when Eli grabbed the sides of her panties and jerked them down her thighs, revealing the whisper thin landing strip of hair she'd trimmed there.

Excitement crackled over my skin, flowing toward the center of my legs.

He ground a hand against her, making her moan and writhe, and she stared at everyone at the table, her eyes heavily lidded with pleasure.

His voice was full of gravel. "Clear the table."

I wasn't sure who he was talking to, but Patrick was the first to act. He grabbed the mostly empty drinks from the tabletop, stood, and walked to the galley, setting them on the small counter. As soon as he returned to his seat, a pleased look flashed through his eyes.

Since Shannon's back was to him, she didn't have any warning, and she gasped as he spun her around, picked her up, and lay her down on her back on the table. She barely fit, and the locks of her long red hair spilled into my lap, tickling the tops of my thighs where my shorts ended.

She peered up at me with wide eyes, but they hooded again as he took a knee and spread her thighs wide, curling his hands around each one.

"*Oh*," she sighed as his mouth brushed over her.

I caught flashes of his tongue as it toyed with her clit, and I swallowed back my delight. He was eating her out right in front of us, and blood ran hotly through my veins. I wasn't the only one enjoying the scene, either.

Patrick's hands moved to unzip his pants and get his dick out. I couldn't see all of him, just the tip since the table partially obscured my view, but I could tell from his slow, almost lazy movements he was stroking himself.

Lust smoldered in his eyes as he gazed at his wife, watching as another man had his mouth buried in her pussy.

At Club Eros, the scene with Travis and Lilith had been up on a stage, and I'd watched from among a sea of people. Now, this private show was nearly in my lap, and it felt . . . special.

Exclusive.

Desire weighed me down, and I had to drag my focus over to Noah. I wondered what he thought about this, and when my gaze found his, my breath caught.

As I'd been watching the show, he'd been watching *me*.

There was no doubt he could see how turned on I was. That he knew the flush warming my cheeks had little to do with the temperature in this cramped space, and everything to do with the sex that clung to the air, invading my lungs.

Noah's expression was wicked as he leaned in and began to drop kisses on the side of my neck. I shivered with pleasure from the sensation. Had he kissed me there instead of my lips so he wouldn't block my view?

When his hand dipped between my legs, I groaned with satisfaction and parted my knees as much as I could to give him room. As he rubbed me through my clothes, the seam of my shorts ground pleasurably against my clit.

Fuck, it felt good.

Beneath us, the boat gently rocked. It was muggy inside the cabin, but maybe Noah's hot breath against my kiss-dampened neck made it feel that way. I gripped the sides of my shorts, enjoying all of his attention while watching the couple in front of us.

Eli's arms were beneath Shannon's thighs, and her skin dented around his fingertips as he held her open and feasted. Sexy moans and sighs poured from her mouth, and I quieted my own so I could hear hers better.

Her piercing eyes had a gravity as she stared up at me, wearing an expression that dripped with desire. It made steam fill my head, and a muscle low in my stomach clenched.

"Touch me," she rasped to everyone, and no one in

particular.

The kisses at the pulse point on my neck ceased, as if Noah were considering something. He pulled back, glanced at her, and pushed his other hand beneath one of the cups of her bra. As he squeezed a handful of her breast, he seemed to study my reaction. Like he wanted to make sure I was okay with this.

Um, yeah.

I totally was.

I zeroed in on the way his hand moved, how she arched into his touch, and I had to push out a heavy breath because the sight of it was so fucking hot.

Out of the corner of my eye, I noted Patrick as he continued to stroke himself, doing it at a measured pace and with the loose grip of a few fingers. It was like he was only interested in maintaining his erection, while savoring the experience.

When we'd come below deck, he'd closed the door behind us and turned on the air conditioner, but the small unit couldn't compete with what was happening now. Sweat blossomed on my skin, dampening the hair at the back of my neck.

I decided to take the initiative.

My hands closed on the bottom of my shirt and began to pull up, and as soon as Noah realized what I was doing, he was there, helping me along. He took the top from me and dropped it on the floor beside the booth. Cool air wafted over my newly exposed skin and pale pink bra.

I didn't get a chance to see how anyone felt about what I'd done, because he scooped my face up in his hands and kissed me aggressively.

It tasted like . . . *possession.*

As if he were claiming me and flaunting what only he was

allowed to do.

But the kiss broke when Shannon let out a gasp. The sharp intake of breath pulled our focus to her, and the tremble that worked its way up her body.

"I'm going to come," she whined.

Her deep eyes silently pleaded with me. I wasn't sure exactly what she was begging me for, but I reached out, trailing the pads of my fingertips down over her chest, and closed a hand around her breast. My touch excited everyone else in the room, which encouraged me to *really* go for it.

I inched my fingers beneath the cup of her bra, and Noah followed my lead, doing the same on her other breast.

Her skin was smooth and velvet soft, and I teased the hardened bud of her nipple while staring at Noah. God, I loved how we were both touching her, how we were *sharing* her. She seemed to like it too. Her back bowed up off the table and one of her hands fisted the front of her husband's shirt.

Was it our mutual touch that sent her over the edge, or was it the way Eli nuzzled between her thighs and fluttered his tongue?

She came hard, and fast, and loudly. Her cry of pleasure cracked the air, rippling through the rest of us. But she'd barely finished her orgasm before Eli was yanking her off the table and urging her down onto her knees. His hands ripped at his zipper and shoved his shorts and boxer briefs down so quickly, his dick bounced free.

He was *big*. His cock was so thick, long, and hard, it was almost scary.

But Shannon wasn't afraid. She grinned, wrapped her fingers around him, and gave him a single pump of her fist. Then she opened her mouth, fit it over his tip, and took him as deep as she could.

A smirk twisted his lips as he peered at Patrick. "You like watching your slut wife suck my cock?"

My mouth dropped open.

I'd expected Patrick to be pissed off by what the other man said, but—no. Patrick's expression was all heat, drunk with desire. He was *into* it. So much so, his light grip on his dick tightened and his fist stopped moving altogether, like he'd gotten unexpectedly close.

His smile echoed through his voice. "Fucking yes."

I was mesmerized by the way Shannon's mouth glided across Eli's impressive length. His cock disappeared between her rosy lips, and then reappeared, growing glossier with her saliva from each pass. Her tempo was steady and hypnotic, and it made his chest rise and fall with hurried breaths.

When he'd pulled her off the table, I'd left my hand resting there, and my fingers curled. Whenever I watched porn, I usually skipped over most of the blowjob scenes. They always ran a little long for me, and the guy wasn't as vocal as I wanted him to be.

But this? Holy fuck, it was hot. Watching her deliver this blowjob was so arousing, I grew impossibly wet and hot between my legs. Had I ever been this turned on before? The fog of it was disorienting, like I was tipsy.

Eli's heated gaze worked its way over my body, and while he was fucking another woman's mouth, his focus zeroed in on me. It traced over the mesh of my pink bra, and his expression was pure sin.

It wasn't the same as the guy who'd stared at me at Club Eros. Eli's unabashed lust wasn't completely unwelcomed, and his attention didn't cause discomfort. If anything, a tiny thrill shot through me. It was nice to be wanted.

But it still felt kind of . . . wrong.

There was only one person's attention I truly wanted. Even as I watched Shannon's cheeks hollow out as she sucked on Eli, I was acutely aware of Noah. I glanced at him as he shed his shirt, bringing his toned chest into view, and lifted my gaze to meet his eyes.

God, the way he looked at me. It was as if I were the only one here. Was it stupid to think he felt the same way as I did?

"Get in my lap," he said, his voice low. "I want my fingers inside you."

My heart sprinted faster at his command. Was this in response to the way Eli had been lusting at me?

It was awkward, scrambling over Noah in the tight booth, but somehow I made it work. As soon as I was seated in his lap, his hard-on pressing up against my thigh, and the table digging into my ribs on the other side, his fingers found the button of my shorts.

My hands shook with desire as I helped him undo it, drop my zipper, and wiggled out of them.

It was freeing being in only my bra and panties. I sat across his legs, my feet dangling over the end of the booth, and draped an arm around the back of his shoulders. Our mouths collided at the same time he pushed my panties aside and touched me—

Only for him to break the kiss and unleash a sexy groan. "Fucking hell, Charlotte. You're *soaking* wet."

Oh, my God.

Fire blazed across my face, but not with embarrassment. It turned me on even more to hear him say it, especially since it sounded like he'd done it to announce it to the group.

As his fingers rubbed deliciously against my swollen clit, I worked a hand between us and on to the bulge in his pants. It wasn't easy to do, but I enjoyed how the lightest stroke caused him to grit his teeth. My action made him escalate, and my mouth rounded into a silent '*oh*' as he pushed his middle two fingers deep inside me.

The stretch of it was so pleasurable, I shuddered and groaned with satisfaction.

He pulsed his fingers in and out in an unhurried, methodical tempo. My toes curled in enjoyment, and the distraction of it made it a challenge to get his pants undone.

But I managed by sliding back, just out of his lap, to create space.

When I curled my fingers around his cock, it was his turn to shudder. Shit, it was intoxicating having this effect on him. His dick was hard and jerked against my fist as I pushed my tight grip down, sliding from his tip to the base.

The movement caused my bra strap to tumble off my shoulder. The cup didn't fall completely—the edge of it caught on my nipple and barely hung on. The sensation felt good, teasing me nearly the same way it teased everyone else.

It clung on like an erotic threat.

As his fingers pumped in and out of me, he moved to match the pace of Eli, who had his hands buried in Shannon's hair and ruthlessly fucked her mouth. It was a demonstration of power, but one that Patrick fully endorsed.

He watched them as if captivated. Enthralled.

Waves of heat moved through me like a slow burning fire, and I fought to catch my breath. The slick slide of Noah's fingers injected me with pleasure, each deliberate thrust sending satisfaction ricocheting through my body. I was hardly moving my hand on him now, barely able to return a fraction of the pleasure he was giving me because my head was full of smoke—

And wicked thoughts.

The cabin was a million fucking degrees, and this room in the middle of a lake became otherworldly. It was a place that existed outside of norms or rules, and I struggled to think through the thick cloud of sex surrounding us.

A need pounded endlessly, drowning everything else out.

"I want you," I rasped, "to fuck me."

TWENTY-FOUR

Charlotte

Noah froze, his fingers lodged inside my pussy. His expression didn't make any sense. Why did he look so conflicted?

His hand retreated to my knee and his shoulders straightened, and cold worry hit me like I'd been doused with a bucket of water. I thought he wanted me as badly as I did him—and yet he was acting like this was a bad idea.

Like I'd asked for something I shouldn't have.

His arms tightened, pulling me back into his lap, and his eyes went bottomless. "Fuck. I really, *really* want to."

I swallowed thickly. "But?"

"Your inhibitions are way down right now. I'd be taking advantage of you."

Maybe part of me knew he was right. I was in a heady fog, not thinking clearly, but the spoiled part of me didn't care. It wanted what it wanted, and I'd worry about consequences later.

"You wouldn't be," I tried to persuade.

He didn't believe me. "I don't want you to wake up tomorrow and regret any of this. I don't want you to regret," he clarified, "being with me."

I exhaled as understanding began to roll through me. He studied my expression as if searching for something, and when he didn't find it, he leaned in. His voice was hushed, so only I'd hear his question.

"Do you love me?"

My heart stopped and I jolted, unable to do anything but blink at him with disbelief.

"Uh . . . " I started.

He chuckled. He already knew the answer and had only asked me to prove a point.

"I care about you, though," I said. "Like, a lot."

"I do too," he admitted. His hand resting on my knee began to move, sliding back and forth in a comforting, intimate gesture. "I care about you so much, Charlotte, it's kind of scary, and that's why we should wait. I don't want our first time to be like this."

He subtly ticked his head toward the woman on her knees and the man looming over her, wordlessly reminding me we weren't alone.

His voice filled with gravel. "I want you all to myself."

Oh. Well, now I wanted that very much too.

My heart restarted, sending warmth flooding through my chest. It silenced the hint of disappointment I'd had, because I'd never been great with patience or delaying gratification.

I pressed my lips together and nodded my acceptance. My gaze drifted from him to the people who were too busy playing to pay much attention to us. If they'd heard any of our conversation, they didn't let on.

A thought struck me then, and my focus snapped back to Noah. "Wait. You're still going to play with her, though, right?"

Because that had been the plan for the evening . . . but he'd made it clear multiple times that minds could change at any time. Had he decided against being with Shannon?

He must have heard the worry in my voice, because his smile was sinful. This was another question he knew the answer to. "You want me to?"

"I want to watch."

He set his teeth on my shoulder in something too gentle to be considered a bite and let out a muffled groan. The idea was so hot, it was nearly overwhelming. His not-quite-bite turned into a kiss, and he marched a line of them across the top of my shoulder, moving to the crook of my neck.

The hairs of his beard tickled my skin. "Are you going to play with him?"

Meaning Eli.

I had no idea how Noah felt about it because his tone and expression were emotionless. We'd talked about it before, and he'd seemed excited, but tonight he hadn't liked how much interest Eli was showing toward me.

Did Noah feel threatened by this other man?

"Do you want me to?" I asked.

"I want you to do whatever *you* want to do." He sucked on a spot just below my ear, and it caused an intense ache between my legs. "I wouldn't mind watching, but only if that's what you want. If you're into it. Don't do it for me."

Maybe it wasn't insecurity at all. His guarded state was an attempt not to pressure or sway me either direction, which I fucking appreciated.

My focus drifted to the tattooed man. Eli had been pretending not to listen in, but the space was small, and it had to be hard not to overhear us. He peered back at me with a dark hunger, eager to hear my answer. His hips thrust and flexed as he stroked his dick in and out of Shannon's mouth, and he was obviously enjoying it, and yet . . . it didn't seem to be enough.

He craved more, like he was the type of person who wasn't

satisfied until he had every little thing he wanted.

"I still haven't decided yet," I admitted.

Noah seemed pleased with this answer, but disappointment crashed through Eli's eyes. It was short lived, though. It flitted away as he stepped back, out of her mouth and the shorts waded at his ankles. He was completely naked as he bent at the waist, scooped up his shorts, and fished inside one of the pockets for something.

A gold foil packet was retrieved, and he cast everything else aside, setting his attention on the woman who was still on her knees in front of him. "You want me to fuck you?"

She nodded.

"Up," he commanded as he tore open the condom wrapper. "Bend over the table so everyone can watch you taking this dick."

Shannon practically leapt to her feet and moved to plant her elbows on the table. As soon as she was in position, she wiggled her hips at him and glanced over her shoulder to watch as he rolled the latex down over his thick erection.

Once that was done to her satisfaction, her attention swung to her husband.

I couldn't see her expression, but it had to be the same as Patrick's, which was full of love. He lifted a hand, set it on her cheek, and kissed her, like he needed that connection to her. To make sure they were bonded together while Eli grasped one of her hips and prepared to push inside her body.

He used his free hand to line himself up, and when he began to inch forward, a muted groan rumbled out of him.

"Yes," she gasped. "Fill me up with all that cock."

"That's it," Patrick urged. His posture shifted, reminding me of a kid who was too excited to sit still as he watched Eli's dick disappear inside his wife.

"It's so fucking big," she whined, although it sounded as if she loved it.

"Yes," her husband agreed. "Take it." The other man kept going until he was buried to the hilt, and a smile lit up Patrick's face. His tone went heavy with pride. "*Oh*, that's my girl."

Fuck.

It was so sexy, I had to sip air in slowly through clenched teeth.

As Eli began to fuck her, a fresh wave of steam filled my body. Once again, I was up close and personal with this private sex show, and there were so many exciting things to look at, I wasn't sure where to start.

His tempo ramped up quickly, and each slap of their bodies together sent waves rippling across her ass cheeks. I liked how his tattoo looked, the dark ink seeming to move as the muscles beneath it flexed.

I sighed with satisfaction and squirmed in Noah's lap when his fingers speared back into me. It felt so impossibly good, like he knew *exactly* how and where to touch me. I couldn't help the way my hips shifted, trying to get him to fuck me faster, and this subtle movement was all it took for the cup of my bra, the one that had barely stayed up, to fall.

Heat flared in his eyes as he stared down at my exposed breast, and—holy shit. He fucking *licked his lips*.

The idea he wanted his mouth on me, and wanted it badly, was so hot.

But he wasn't the only one who'd noticed my bra had fallen. Shannon was no longer looking at her husband. She was flat on the table, her face turned to me and her cheek flattened to the tabletop while enduring Eli's punishing rhythm.

"Can I," she breathed, "touch you?"

I sank my teeth into my bottom lip and nodded.

Her hand on my breast didn't physically feel any different from when Noah touched me, but my brain didn't accept it.

New, it told me. *Different*.

And that was exciting.

As her fingertips trailed across my sensitive skin, everyone else seemed riveted, fixated on her delicate touch. Even Noah, because the pace of his fingers slowed, no longer driving into me. When she oh-so-gently pinched my nipple, I let out a sigh of enjoyment, and it broke the spell over the men.

Patrick rose out of his seat, leaned over, and unclasped his wife's bra. The fabric and elastic sprang free, and it meant she momentarily had to stop what she was doing. She lifted off the table, leaving the bra behind, and her husband cleared it out of the way.

The sight of her topless was just as stunning as it'd been last time. Her breasts were full and beautiful, and I was sort of envious of her husband as his hands wandered across them. But then he took his seat and resumed jerking himself off, satisfied just to watch.

A deep moan came from her as Eli shifted his feet and adjusted the angle of his thrusts. He wasn't quiet either. His little groans and labored breaths were seriously sexy.

Shannon's touch returned to my chest, and this time it was less tentative. Her fingers bit a little harder on my nipple, and a moan escaped my lips, sandwiched between two ragged breaths.

And Noah's fingers. Fuck me, they were skilled, hitting just the right spot, and sent electricity zipping all along my spine.

"Do you want her to suck on your tits?"

The question had come from him, but it had sounded like it was inside my head, and the moment the idea was planted, there was no other answer. "*Yes.*"

"Ask her."

Oh, God. His command was so fucking sexy, I could hardly stand it. I stared into Shannon's eyes. We both knew what I was about to say, but she looked at me with desperation. Like if I didn't ask her right this moment, she was going to die.

"Will you," I panted, "suck on my tits?"

I only got a glimpse of her smile before her head dipped down and her mouth made contact. Her soft, damp lips drew a path across my breast, and when she reached my nipple, her tongue flicked the bud of flesh.

My vision blurred, not from the sensation, but from the heat of it all.

Noah had one hand between my legs and the other on my back supporting me, and when I arched into her needy mouth, he moved with me. He leaned me back, giving her more access and room to maneuver.

She needed it too.

Eli's tempo had accelerated to a furious pace. Was it uncomfortable for her, getting pounded into the table like that? Maybe, but she didn't seem to mind, and fucking hell—it was erotic.

I couldn't help but imagine what it must look like for Patrick.

Did he notice the bead of sweat as it rolled down Eli's washboard abs? Or was he focused on Eli's hands that clenched his wife's waist while she was getting railed?

Did his gaze include me, and how I was practically draped over Noah, naked except for a pulled-down bra, with his wife's mouth latched onto my breast?

Tension coiled inside me, building toward a big finish. I'd wanted to give Noah a handjob, but it was impossible now with everything happening both physically and mentally. There wasn't any space to work with, since his arm would be in my way, and I'd come faster if I wasn't distracted.

It wasn't going to take long at this rate. Shannon's greedy mouth felt good, but not as good as the fingers surging inside me. And those didn't feel as good as the connection of his mouth against mine, drinking up my moans.

My orgasm barreled down abruptly, hurtling me toward the edge . . .

And then it flung me right over.

I broke our kiss and cried out as I was crushed under a wave of ecstasy, shivering in his arms.

My recovery was slow.

I came back to reality, breath by ragged breath, letting some of the fog clear from my mind, before sliding out of his lap. I melted down the side of the booth and onto my knees and twisted my hands behind my back to undo my bra.

He didn't understand what I was doing until I reached for the undone sides of his pants. Then, his hands were there, easing me out of the way so he could take over. I let him, because that would be faster, and I was eager for what came next.

I sat back, impatiently waiting as he pushed his pants and underwear down his legs, lifted the wad of clothes over me, and cast them aside. They landed on the floor with a soft thump, and then he was as naked as I was.

His dick was hard, resting against his stomach, and I clamped a hand around it. His lips parted to exhale a deep, appreciative sigh, which gave me secondhand satisfaction. I delivered a few pumps, and although I wanted to continue watching the show, I also wanted to give him as much pleasure as I could.

So I bent, opened my mouth, and slid his cock inside.

As my lips closed around him and I inched down, he issued a groan. It sounded like pleasure and pain mixed together, as if I were both pleasing and torturing him. Shit, it was hot as fuck. I opened my jaw wider, allowing him to slip further inside, all the way to the back of my throat.

When I sucked hard and swiped my tongue against the sensitive underside of his tip, the muscles in his thighs corded with tension. Oh, he *really* liked that, so I did it again.

But my hair was in my way. I had to pause and push it back over my shoulder, but as soon as I began to pump my mouth over him, it fell again, It was annoying how it wouldn't stay, and just as I reached to hold it back, a hand was there, collecting the strands.

It wasn't Noah's—it was Shannon's.

"That's it," she cooed. "Get him ready for me."

Her dirty words caused a hit of pleasure, an aftershock from my orgasm. As she held my hair out of my way, my tongue spun cartwheels over the head of Noah's cock. It caused him to pulse and flex, which was hard on my jaw, but was totally worth it.

Eventually, I had to come up for air.

It wasn't the easiest blowjob I'd ever given. I was mindful of the table just beside my head and did my best not to bang my head on it. When I sat back on my heels, Shannon saw her window of opportunity and went for it. She seized Noah's cock, wet with my saliva, and gave it a long, thorough stroke.

On some level, I knew I was supposed to dislike this. Her action should have caused jealousy to roar through me, but all it did was make me burn hotter. Maybe something was wrong with me because I loved the way it looked.

Her gaze went from the dick in her hands, up to Noah's face, and her tone was pleading. "I want your cock in my mouth."

He considered her request for a single beat, and then he moved. His hands scooped under my arms and helped me onto my feet as he stood. The kiss he delivered was quick and almost chaste, even though we were both naked and his hands had moved to settle on my ass.

When it ended, he peered at me, and I understood the question that lurked in his eyes.

Are you sure you're okay with this?

TWENTY-FIVE

Charlotte

Was he kidding? I was one thousand percent sure I wanted this. A grin widened across my lips and I nodded.

Sure, this was all new to me, but—God. I felt so lucky to be invited into this world. This night was like an initiation. A turning point.

An awakening.

And I was so glad I got to do it with Noah.

With my approval settled, he turned his attention to the writhing couple, probably trying to figure out the best way to make her wish happen.

"Let me lean against the table," he said.

Eli reacted right away. He used his grasp to back Shannon up and made room for the other man to move in. When Noah did, he put an arm around me and pulled me along with him. He sat on the edge of the table, one hand curling around the end of it, and tucked me in at his side. I stood at the end of the booth, placed a bent knee on the seat cushion, and left the other foot flat on the floor.

We knew what the goal was, so I reached down and ringed my fingers around the base of his dick, and we peered down the slope of his body, watching as Shannon leaned in.

His cock slipped between her pink lips, and dear God, it was straight fire. One that burned a million degrees and was too hot to allow even a trace of jealousy or shame to exist.

It was stunningly erotic to hold him steady for her as she fucked him with her mouth, while she was getting fucked by someone else, and her husband sat to the side, watching it all happen.

Goosebumps prickled across my skin, and my heart beat more than a hundred miles an hour. The ache was back inside me, a need pulsing and begging for release.

"I might come just watching this," I whispered.

Noah's eyes went heavy, but I couldn't tell if it was simply lust, the meaning of what I'd said, or a combination of both.

Eli found his tempo again, and Shannon matched it, rocking back and forth between the men. It was downright pornographic, and I stood at Noah's side, utterly transfixed.

Her moans and whines filled the room, but they were garbled from the cock in her mouth. Noah held still, letting her work him over, even as Eli's thrusts increased in intensity, turning almost violent. But it threw off her rhythm, causing the dick to fall from her lips as she gasped for breath.

"Oh, I know," Eli teased. "It's hard to keep that dick in your mouth when I'm fucking you so good, isn't it?"

She issued another moan, latched a hand on the edge of the table for stability, and got back to work. Her copper hair hung down as she was bent over, and her eyes slammed shut. Was she getting close?

Pleasure painted Eli's expression because he seemed to be struggling. Not with maintaining his tempo, though. He was fighting to hold himself back from beating her to the finish line.

Beside me, Noah's chest heaved as he endured the blowjob . . . but his gaze was glued to me. Once again, he liked watching how *I* was watching. He enjoyed studying my reaction, every time I swallowed a gasp or blinked quickly to hide my wide eyes. His arm was banded around me, his hand low on my back, and when our gazes caught, he pressed me tighter into his side.

Without any warning, Shannon let out a cry that was pure ecstasy.

As she came, her legs shook so hard, Eli had to haul her upright. He grabbed one of her shoulders and pulled, and when she was standing, their bodies still connected, he grasped her elbows and dragged them back toward his chest. It forced her to arch her back, and it gave him space to thread his arms through hers.

This new position, with her arms held behind her back, was erotic. She could escape his hold if she wanted, but she wouldn't dare. She was too deep in the throes of her orgasm to care right now—plus, I suspected she loved his domination.

He fucked her while they were standing like that, grinding his body against hers and making her tits bounce. After this evening ended, it would be hard to pick which image was the hottest . . . but this scene was a strong contender.

Because he'd gotten her to come, the restriction Eli had put on himself was gone, and he didn't last long after that. When he came, he let out a loud wave of grunts and groans and jerked to a stop. Shannon's head was tipped up, her face to the ceiling, and she groaned right along with him, enjoying it.

I knew what that felt like, how much I liked the sensation when a guy's release pulsed inside me. I hoped soon I'd know what that felt like with the man standing beside me.

Eli's eyes were closed like Shannon's were, and their bodies remained still for a long moment. Then he released her arms, she slid off him, and she stumbled forward on unsteady legs. She collided with us both, but Noah's arm went around her, keeping her on her feet as she tried to catch her breath.

Without a word, Eli turned and disappeared into the bathroom, probably to get rid of the condom and clean up. The cabin lulled into silence for a tense moment.

What happens now?

I sensed Noah's gaze on me, and when I turned to look, I found his face full of intensity. His voice was deep and wicked and hushed. "You want me to fuck her?"

Again, there was no other answer I could give. "Yes."

"Tell me," he demanded. "Say it."

It was like he'd punched the air clean out of my lungs. His order wasn't just hot—it was incendiary. Shit, I wanted it so bad, my voice trembled with need. "I want you to fuck her, Daddy."

The beautiful brown of his irises deepened.

Then he straightened, and his arm fell away from me. Once he was sure Shannon was okay without his support, he padded on his bare feet a few steps and reached for his pants.

"Get on the table," he said, "like how I was."

It was clear this order was for me, and I followed it. I sat on the lacquered wood and found it warm in the spot he'd just left, and cold elsewhere against my heated skin. While I took my seat, he pulled out a condom, tore the wrapper, and put it on.

His intense gaze was almost reluctant to leave mine, but it did, and it swung to the other woman. They exchanged a look, him asking his silent question, and Shannon gave him a sexy smirk of approval.

My heart was beating in my throat when he led her to

the edge of the table and urged her to stand between my parted knees.

"Lean back on your elbows," he said.

Again, this command was meant for me. I dropped back, supporting myself on my bent elbows, and once I was how he wanted, he guided her to lean over and place her hands on the tabletop on either side of my body.

"*Oh*," I breathed.

The position caused her breasts to kiss mine, and the brush of her soft skin and nipples against mine was so much sexier than I'd expected.

I was only vaguely aware when Eli returned and slipped into the booth. I was more focused on the other woman, and the handsome man moving behind her, preparing.

My lungs squeezed as I watched Noah's eyes haze and heard Shannon's whimper of pleasure. I couldn't see exactly what happened, but I didn't need to. He'd eased himself inside.

"Fuck," I whispered.

This hadn't meant to be a command from me, but he seemed to take it as one.

Once he started moving, there weren't adequate words to describe how much I enjoyed it. God, I adored being beneath them, loved how he stared at me like he was fucking *me* and not the woman between us. He had one hand on her hip, but the other was gripping my thigh, and the connection between us felt powerfully intimate.

Like it was just him and me.

Once he established his pace, everything began to blur and fade, lost to the blaze of desire and pleasure. Shannon's mouth was on my neck, my breasts. I glanced to my left and saw Patrick was fucking his fist in earnest now. I looked to my right and found Eli leaned back in his seat, his arm flung casually across the back of the booth.

But he was staring at me with dark desire.

"Can I touch you?" he asked.

The answers came quickly when Noah asked them, but with Eli it was more complicated. I didn't feel much desire for him—it was more curiosity. But it was intense.

"Yes," I said.

He looked fucking thrilled, sat forward, and immediately glided a hand across my chest, palming my breasts.

I went into freefall with all the attention, but the wildest thing was . . . none of it mattered as much as Noah's. Could he tell how much I was loving this? How incredible it was to be sharing this with *him*?

Moans swelled from Shannon, and because of the way we were positioned, I could feel every one of his thrusts as they reverberated through her body. Eli had been satisfied when he'd started to caress my breasts, but soon it hadn't been enough. His fingertips skated across my stomach, trailing downward so he could fit his fingers between my legs and touch my clit.

I gasped. His simple touch, with everything else happening around me, was pure bliss.

A second orgasm for me loomed on the horizon, and it sounded like it might be the same for Shannon. Our group became a mass of sweaty bodies, moving, touching, *fucking* . . . held together by pleasure.

I was adrift in it, with my gaze fixed on Noah like he was my only anchor.

And eventually, a wave of ecstasy crashed over us, each

cresting at a different time. Shannon was the first to succumb, and when her orgasm's hold faded, she grabbed her husband's head and pulled him into a feverish kiss.

His fist pumped, his grip so tight it had to be hard for him to slide the head of his cock through it, but he did it. All the while, his shoulders rose and fell with his enormous, labored breaths. Then he shuddered, clamping tighter around the tip, and moaned through each pulse.

Cum leaked out between his fingers, streaking down his shaft.

It was dirty, and sexy as fuck.

"You going to come for me?" an unfamiliar voice asked.

I turned my head, finding Eli staring at me as his fingers rubbed faster on my clit. Sparks of pleasure radiated from his touch, but it was Noah's hand on me, the one that gently squeezed my thigh, that felt the best.

Had he done it to remind me of his presence? If so, it was unnecessary. He dominated my thoughts, and my focus never strayed far.

No, I almost said out loud to Eli. *I'm going to come for him.*

I stared into Noah's stunning eyes for as long as I could, until the pleasure became too much.

This orgasm? It tore through me.

The power of it shook me to my core, my elbows gave out, and I collapsed to the tabletop with a loud bang. As the bliss rolled through me, it grew more intense. Sharper. It verged on pain and deactivated my brain. So it took me a long moment to realize Eli's fingers were still pressed to me, and I had to squirm and put my hand on top of his to signal he needed to stop.

My clit was way too sensitive, but, thankfully, his sinful

fingers moved away.

As I lay across the table, my chest working overtime to drag air in and out of my body, I peered up at Noah and sensed his orgasm wouldn't be far behind mine.

I was right.

By the sound of it, his climax was powerfully strong. He groaned like he'd finished some Herculean effort, and his face, sheened with sweat, contorted. It filled with dark satisfaction, and his gaze pierced into me, like I'd been the one to give him all this pleasure.

It was so fucking hot, it stole my breath.

We were still melded together, unmoving, and as our bodies began to cool, awareness and tension crept in.

Shannon broke it with a laugh and attempted to straighten. "Okay. My legs are shot. I think I need to sit."

Noah acted quickly. He kept one hand on her as he stepped back and then offered her the other hand to help her sit beside her husband. She lowered gingerly into her seat, and as soon as she was done, Patrick was there, cradling her face and delivering a passionate kiss.

It was romantic. Sweet. A smile spread slowly across my face as I watched. Maybe it was intruding, but they didn't seem to mind. I didn't watch long, anyway. Noah slipped a hand under my arm and drew me up until I was sitting and then eased me off the table and onto my feet in front of him.

His kiss burned, but just as I opened my mouth to slide my tongue over his, he ended the kiss and lifted his head.

"I'll be right back," he murmured.

I tilted my head, watching him go, and enjoyed his sexy ass as he strode to the closet-sized bathroom.

The leather squealed against bare skin as Eli scooted over

in the booth, making room for me—but not much. He wanted me to sit right beside him. While I did want to sit because my legs were still trembling, post-orgasm, I wasn't going to.

Doing that felt weird, especially without Noah around.

I pressed out a polite smile and put a hand on the back of the booth for stability. "I'm good," I lied.

With Noah gone, the atmosphere in the cabin was awkward.

The fog of sex had lifted, and Patrick and Shannon were too busy making out to pay attention to anyone else. Eli stared up at me expectantly, like he was waiting for me to make small talk. Instead, I swiped a finger under each of my eyes, because I'd been sweating and was worried my makeup had started to run.

When I didn't say anything, he leaned toward me like he wanted to share a secret. Anxiety made my heart stumble, especially when his voice was playful and hushed. "He said no, but if you need someone to fuck you," his smile was lopsided, "just give me a few more minutes and I can do it."

My mouth dropped open.

In my surprise, I hadn't heard his approach, so when Noah's warm arm was abruptly around me, I flinched. I turned to him and caught only a glimpse of the anger in his eyes before his mouth crashed down on mine.

He'd obviously overheard what Eli had said, and he hadn't liked it one bit.

This kiss started like his others, but it quickly morphed into something else. It was intense and demanding, and since I had a hand pressed to his bare chest, I could feel just how fast his heart was beating.

This kiss was a statement. Not just for Eli, but for me. He was staking his claim, making sure everyone knew I was his and he was mine . . .

God, I fucking *loved* the idea.

When our kiss ended, I turned my head in my dreamy state and glanced down at Eli, finding his expression frozen in place.

"No, thanks," I said from the safety of Noah's embrace, and I weighed my words with all the meaning. "I'm perfectly happy like this."

TWENTY-SIX

Charlotte

When Noah asked me if I wanted to do dinner and a movie with him, he didn't clarify if it was a date. But it had certainly felt that way at the restaurant and now that we were sitting here in the dark theatre, sharing a bucket of popcorn—I couldn't see it as anything else.

I was so excited about it, I didn't give a shit about the movie and let him pick which one. He was buying the tickets, anyway. The movie was loud and violent, with beautiful people and minimal plot, so it didn't require a lot of attention.

Which was good.

It meant I could spend most of the movie being close to him and wondering if he was my boyfriend. If that was true, I knew what my friends would say. *Too soon. Just a rebound.* Or worst of all, *can't you date someone our age?*

It was exactly what my parents would say . . . if they survived the aneurism it would give them.

We were less than an hour into the movie when Noah pulled his phone out of his pocket and discreetly checked the screen. Someone had sent him a text message, and whatever it said, he wasn't happy about it. He sent back a short response and leaned over to whisper in my ear.

"I'm sorry, but I have to go. My dad fell, and my mom needs my help."

I turned to look at him with a face full of concern.

"Is he okay?"

"I'm not sure. All she says is she not able to help him get back up." He glanced at the gun battle raging on the screen, and then back to me. "You can stay and Uber home if you want to finish—"

I shook my head and grabbed my purse off the empty seat beside me. "Let's go."

He hesitated for a moment but must have realized we didn't have time to waste, rose from his seat into a crouch, and hurried down the aisle toward the exit.

Noah was tense on the drive over to his parents' house, but I couldn't tell if it was caused by the emergency . . . or the way I had invited myself along. We didn't talk, and the longer the silence stretched between us, the worse I felt. I was going to meet his parents, and during a crisis, when I wasn't likely to leave a good impression. God, I shouldn't have forced this on him—or his family.

But when I opened my mouth to tell him I was second-guessing my decision and he should drop me off somewhere, he turned into a subdivision. The houses here weren't as large or sprawling as the ones in his neighborhood, but they were nice and had cute landscaping.

My anxiety spiked when he pulled into one of the driveways, put his car in park, and shut off the engine.

"Do you want me to stay here?" I blurted.

He tilted his head in confusion. "What?"

"I didn't ask you if it was okay for me to tag along. I can wait here for you."

He stared at the steering wheel in front of him, and it looked like he was struggling to process. But he shook his head, pushed open his door, and began to get out. "It's fine. C'mon."

His tone was distracted, like he'd settled for the path of least resistance, and that made me feel even worse, but I'd done this to myself. I got out of his car and followed him up the path.

Noah's mother must have been watching for him, because she opened the front door before we'd reached the porch steps. She looked immensely relieved at his arrival, but as her gaze shifted to me at his side, her expression changed to one of confusion.

Or maybe distrust.

He'd told me his parents were in their early seventies, but his mom didn't look it. She had short, dark hair, great skin, and sharp eyes. I immediately got the sense those eyes didn't miss much.

"This is Charlotte," he said. "We were out when you called." His mother backed out of the way as we came in. "Charlotte, this is my mom, Theresa."

"Hi," I said automatically, "it's nice to—"

"Hello." Her focus turned back to Noah, and it was as if I ceased to exist. "He fell in the shower."

"The shower?" Noah's concern was thick. "Is he okay?"

"He thinks so, but we can't really tell until we get him up. I tried, but with my bad shoulder . . . "

He nodded and began to move down the hallway, with his mother following quickly. "Why was he in the shower at eight-thirty?"

"He wanted to take one after he finished mowing the yard."

Noah pulled to a stop and turned to show her his frown. "Why the hell is he still mowing the yard? You need to pay someone to do that for you."

She put a hand on her hip and looked annoyed. “I agree, but you know how your father is.”

I’d remained in the entryway, and he glanced back over his shoulder at me, delivering a quick look. *Stay*, it said. *I’ll be back in a bit.*

Which, of course I’d stay. I wasn’t about to be introduced to his dad while he was incapacitated and naked.

While they were gone, I stood awkwardly and struggled with what to do. It seemed rude to get on my phone, so I glanced around, curious about his parents’ place. It didn’t look like this was the house Noah had grown up in.

The entryway was open, there was a dining area to the right and the living room straight back, and a gallery wall of pictures hung over one of the sofas. My eye went instantly to the ones of Noah growing up.

I didn’t consider if it was rude. I let my feet carry me forward as my gaze traveled over the images of him and his family. It was mostly vacation pictures throughout the years, the family in front of the Washington Monument, the Grand Canyon, at Disney World.

There were a few where the kids were helping their dad with a tour. One of his older brothers’ weddings. Noah’s college graduation.

Damn, he’d always been hot. Like he’d skipped right over the awkward teenage years. I was envious.

When I finished looking at the pictures, I made the mistake of turning to my right and peered into the kitchen. I sucked in a breath and held it tightly in my lungs.

Used pans were stacked beside the sink. A dish towel that hung on the oven had brown stains from where hands had been dried on it repeatedly. The floor looked like it hadn’t been swept in a month.

But that wasn't the worst of it.

There was a kitchen table that had a collection of dirty plates, silverware, and wadded up paper napkins. It didn't seem like his parents' meal had been interrupted, since his father had gone to take a shower.

No, these plates had been abandoned here.

My mother would put up with almost anything. Her only absolute, unbreakable rule was when you were finished eating, you took your plate to the sink. I could not tolerate food and dirty dishes left sitting out, and before I knew it, I was stacking the plates.

They have so much to deal with. Might as well be useful.

I made quick work of loading the dishwasher, tossing the used napkins away, and wiping down the tabletop with a damp paper towel. And when that was done, I tackled the pans by the sink. If I hurried and got them done, I might have time to wipe down the kitchen counters and look for a broom.

The pans clanked together as I stacked one clean one on top of the next.

"What are you doing?"

I startled at the sound of Noah's voice and dropped the pan in the sink, making the sudsy water slosh around. Thankfully, he sounded surprised and not angry, and when I turned to face him, he only looked confused. I'd found a clean dishtowel under the sink earlier and used it to dry my hands.

"I'm keeping busy," I said, channeling my mother. "How's your dad?"

He sighed and walked toward me, stopping only a foot away, so I could peer up into his worried eyes. "He's all right," he lowered his voice, "but he's stubborn as shit." His gaze went to the stack of pans that were drying on the counter and flicked to the doorway leading to the living room. "You should stop cleaning. If my mom comes in here and sees what you're doing, she'll be embarrassed."

I'd been so compelled to clean, I hadn't thought about my actions or if they'd come off as offensive. They hadn't known I was coming, nor had I been invited into their home, and if the roles were reversed, I would have been mortified.

Shit.

"It's why I was nervous on the drive over here," he added. Why did he look so sheepish? "I knew it would be bad. Maybe even overwhelming for you."

My heart beat a little quicker. He'd been concerned for his father, sure, but he'd also been thinking about me during the drive. He got that mess bothered me, and fuck if he didn't know me better in a few short months than nearly anyone else.

Certainly better than your last boyfriend.

I motioned to the sink and gave him an embarrassed smile. "I'm sorry. I couldn't help myself." My expression turned serious. "With everything your parents are going through, it's totally understandable if stuff like this falls to the wayside. I'm happy to help. And wouldn't it be nice for them to have one less thing to deal with right now?"

His shoulders straightened and he tilted his head. He was acting like my question was so unexpected, he didn't know how to deal with it. As if consideration wasn't something he was sure I was capable of. He scrubbed a hand over his jaw, and it bristled against the whiskers of his beard, and then his eyes lit with warmth.

"Yes," he said quietly.

I thrust the dish towel at him and cast my other hand

toward the stack of drip-drying pans. "Then help me. Dry these and put them away, so we can finish before your mom catches us."

A tight laugh came from him, and he took the towel from me.

It was nice, standing side-by-side with him at the sink, working together. We made a great team. I finished scrubbing the last pot, unplugged the drain, and water gurgled down the pipe as I watched him finish his task.

God. Noah doing dishes was way sexier than it had any right to be. The muscles in his forearm flexed as he wiped the white towel over the stainless steel, and then he tucked the pot in a cabinet beside the stove, before returning to me at the sink.

Did he realize how powerful an effect he had on me? One simple look from him and my body heated.

"I'm sorry the movie got ruined." But he gazed at me like he wasn't sorry we'd ended up right here in this moment together.

"It's okay." I tried to sound sexy and seductive. "I'm sure you'll find a way to make it up to me."

His smile was wicked, and he placed a hand on my cheek, holding me still so he could seal his lips over mine. His kiss was deep and thorough, and so intoxicating, I forgot where we were. The longer it went on, the more serious my concern became that I might liquify into a puddle on the floor at his feet.

Noah ended the kiss right as my need for him became dire, and he hovered only a few inches away, teasing another kiss. "Any suggestions?"

All I could think about, all I could see was him. "You have

such a beautiful face," I said. "I just want to sit on it."

He grinned bigger than I'd ever seen, and my legs went boneless. It was a miracle I didn't collapse or—

Someone on the other side of the room cleared their throat.

And they did it in a very loud, very fake way, making sure we knew it was only to get our attention.

We instinctively leapt away from each other, and my gaze reeled around, searching for the source of the sound, and as soon as I found him, everything in me went cold.

Well—not everything. Blood rushed hotly to my face.

Fuck.

Noah's father was tall and broad-shouldered. His gray hair was mostly dry already, and he wore a pair of jeans and a blue t-shirt that stretched across his belly. He was a big guy, and it made sense why Theresa would have a hard time helping him up, even without a bad shoulder.

A scowl painted his face, and my gaze dropped to the floor. Noah's dad was fucking intimidating, and him overhearing me tell his son I wanted to sit on his face wasn't just cringe.

It was horrifying.

"Dad." Noah straightened and pretended he didn't feel any awkwardness. "This is Charlotte." I sensed he was looking at me then, and found his expression was fixed. "Charlotte, this is Gabe Robinson."

My voice shook. "Hello."

The only acknowledgement I got from Gabe was a grunt, like I was unworthy of using full words. It held the room in tense silence and made me want to die. But Theresa appeared then, oblivious to it all, and strolled to the fridge. She opened the door and surveyed its contents.

"Noah," she said, "does your friend want to stay for dinner?"

His father laughed, only it wasn't warm like his son's could be, and he poured on the sarcasm. "I think they're a bit more than friends, Theresa."

I could feel the irritation rolling off Noah in waves, but he ignored his father's comment. "No, thanks, we already ate."

She closed the refrigerator, and it was then she noticed something was different in the kitchen. "What happened here?" Her focus went from the now-empty table to the bare counter beside the sink before zeroing in on me. "Did you *clean*?"

I nodded. "I hope you don't mind. I wanted to be useful."

She stared at me with disbelief and the discomfort grew inside me until I couldn't handle it anymore.

"Noah helped me," I added. "I'm sorry."

She blinked as she considered what to say next. Perhaps she was thinking up the perfect way to tell me what I'd done was rude but do it in a passive-aggressive manner like Southern women preferred.

Instead, she strolled over to a cabinet, opened it, and began to pull down some wine glasses. "All right. A drink, then." The bases of the glasses clinked against the stone as she placed them on the counter, and her tone walked the line of being teasing or serious. "I'm assuming your girlfriend is old enough to have a drink."

Noah gave his mother a plain look. "Yes, she's old enough to drink."

I pressed my lips together and steeled my expression so no one would know how excited I was when he didn't correct her. Maybe it was for his father's benefit, and it was just pretend for tonight, but I didn't mind in the slightest.

"Great." Theresa returned to the fridge and retrieved a

bottle of white wine from one of the shelves on the door. "I think we all need one after the evening we're having."

"I'm sorry," Noah announced, "but we can't stay."

She wasn't fazed. She unscrewed the top of the bottle and began pouring a glass, but it became clear it was only for her. "All right," she said. "Then you'll have to bring her by for dinner." She took a sip of her wine while her gaze slid to me. "I'd love to get to know this girl who's convinced my son to clean."

"Yeah, sure." He looked pained. "Maybe some other time."

She didn't act offended at his attempt to brush her off.

"You going to pour a glass for me?" Gabe asked his wife.

"You're not supposed to."

He groaned. "Oh, stop it with that. It's one glass."

She turned to her son and her expression screamed, *see what I have to deal with?*

Noah straightened. "I think we're going to head out."

"You sure you can't stay?" Theresa asked.

"No, thanks. As much fun as Charlotte and I have had, this wasn't part of the plan for tonight." He motioned to the doorway, asking me to start moving in that direction.

"Nice meeting you," I eked out before going.

"Oh, you too," his mother called back.

The goodbyes were quick, and we hurried down the front porch, and I didn't feel like I could relax until I was in the passenger seat of Noah's car, safely closed inside. It wasn't the same for him, though. Tension gripped his shoulders tightly as he started the engine.

"Are you okay?" I asked softly.

"Yeah." His answer came so quickly, it was a knee-jerk response, and he sighed. "It was fucking rough seeing my dad like that, all incapacitated. And you know what's even worse?

He was *pissed* I was there. He didn't know my mom had called and asked for help." His tone was bitter. "He was adamant he would have been able to get up on his own eventually, that he only 'needed another minute.' Never mind he'd been lying on the shower floor for twenty minutes already."

It wasn't my place, but I said it anyway because Gabe had been utterly silent when we'd left. "Did he thank you for your help?"

"Nope, he sure didn't." He set his hands on the steering wheel but didn't put the car in gear. Maybe he needed another moment to collect his thoughts.

"I'm sure it's hard," I said, "for you and them. You should all give each other some grace."

He turned to look at me, and I half expected him to tell me to be quiet or that I didn't know what I was talking about, but there was only surprise in his eyes. He wore the same expression he'd had in the kitchen when I'd asked for his help with the dishes.

"They were kind of prickly to you."

I pulled my mouth into a lopsided smile. "They were fine, and I'm giving them some grace too."

He finally put the car in reverse and began to back down the driveway. "Careful. That doesn't really sound like something a spoiled brat would say."

I shrugged and matched his playful tone. "Maybe I'm starting to outgrow that." I swallowed a breath. "I noticed you didn't correct your mom when she called me your girlfriend." I said it as a joke, even though I was completely serious. "I thought we were just friends."

He finished backing into the street, and as he put the car into drive, he glanced over to me. His, and his expression made my heart stumble and beat faster.

“Maybe,” he said, “we’ve outgrown that too.”

TWENTY-SEVEN

Noah

It didn't make any sense that I'd been sort of excited to introduce Charlotte to my parents, and the only thing that had given me pause was I knew how messy their house was going to be.

Not that it was a bad fucking idea to bring her along.

But it was too late now.

It was done, and honestly, I wasn't unhappy about how it had gone. Sure, my dad hearing her say she wanted to sit on my face was *less than ideal*, but at least the cat was out of the bag with my folks. They knew I was dating someone, and that someone was quite a bit younger than I was.

I was glad Charlotte and I had decided to put a label on it.

My girlfriend seemed happy about that too. She was practically radiating in the passenger seat of my car as I pulled into my garage. We didn't talk as we got out and made our way to the door to the house. I pushed it open for her, slapped a hand on the button to close the overhead door, and followed her inside.

I didn't bother turning on the lights. We stood in the small, dark hallway that led to my kitchen, toeing off our shoes, and as soon as that was done, I was on her. My mouth slammed into hers, and my hands seized her waist, and when she sighed into me, warm satisfaction spread through my chest.

It felt good having her here, in my place, in my hands.

But our evening had gone off the rails, and I'd promised to make it up to her, and I was going to make good on that right fucking now.

She let out a cute little yelp of surprise when I bent and swept her up into my arms. Her eyes were wide, and wild, lit with excitement as I marched toward my bedroom. I had no idea what expression I wore.

Maybe it was determination, because that was how I felt.

Once we made it through the doorway, I found the light switch and clicked it on. It hadn't been easy to do with her in my arms, but I managed, making the small table lamps on either side of the bed spring to life.

As I strode forward, she gazed up at me like I was all she could see.

When I reached the bed, I deposited her on top of it. I'd made it this morning, smoothing the gray satin comforter into place, hoping we were going to end up here. As soon as she hit the mattress, she began moving. She climbed up onto her knees and wrapped her arms around my shoulders, planting a kiss on my lips.

Charlotte had probably meant it to be a long, deep one, but I had other ideas.

"Can I ask you something?" I said while grasping the bottom of her shirt and urging it up.

She lifted her arms, and her pretty blonde hair splashed around her shoulders as I pulled her top off. She wore the same black bra from our first night together all those months ago.

"Oh, shit," I commented. "I think this one's my favorite."

"Is it?" She laughed as she clenched fistfuls of my shirt, dragging it upward. "What do you want to ask me?"

My pulse quickened, but I did my best not to show it. I focused on getting her out of her shorts next and kept my tone casual. "What's your stance on being tied up? Like, say I wanted to do that and," I put emphasis on it, "*play* with you."

Her expression shifted. This was how I expected her to look whenever she found out one of her videos had gone viral. Her smile was wide, but she pulled it back into mock seriousness. "I'd say my stance is very pro 'being tied up.'"

"Good." I'd been fairly confident she was going to give me a *yes*, but the confirmation was still really fucking nice to hear, and I was thrilled she trusted me enough to try it.

She stayed still, up on her knees on the edge of my bed, as I undid the zipper of her shorts and pushed them down over her hips. When she sat to the side to take them the rest of the way off, I strode to the nightstand and tugged open the top drawer.

Her gaze followed me as I did it, and she said nothing when I pulled out two pairs of leather cuffs, dropping them one-by-one onto the mattress beside her with quiet thuds.

But I heard her sharp intake of breath, and the atmosphere in the room began to thicken.

"Okay?" I asked.

Her gaze traced the thick, leather cuffs that were held closed by silver buckles and had a ring dangling from the center. Her focus lifted to me, a sexy smile tilted her lips, and she offered her wrists to me.

Well.

That was *way* hotter than I expected it to be.

I picked up one of the cuffs, holding it for her to slide her wrist through, then tightened the buckle. *One down, three to go.*

It didn't take long to get the rest done, and I liked how she waited silently and patiently for me to do it, as if she were trying so hard to be a good girl.

I motioned toward the pillows. "Lie down. Center of the bed."

My satin comforter rustled as she slid across it, pulling one of the pillows to the center so she could rest her head on it. While she got into position, I lifted the corner of the comforter, bent, and reached between the mattress and the box spring. I found what I was looking for immediately and pulled out the black strap I'd tucked there earlier today. There were four straps in the restraint system that I'd secured to my bed frame, and each had a sliding clip dangling from its end.

She made a soft sound of amusement. "Funny. I never noticed that whenever I was making this bed."

"It's new."

I clipped the strap onto the ring at her wrist, strolled to the foot of the bed, and hooked a finger in the ring on her ankle cuff. I gave it a jerk, pulling her leg toward me as I found the second strap and attached it.

Her gaze followed me as I walked around the end of the bed and repeated the action with her other ankle. I left her wrist for last, giving her a few more moments of freedom before clipping her in. And just for fun, I gave this strap an unnecessary tug, pretending to test its strength, before giving her satisfied look.

"I bought this restraint system for you," I said and began my journey back around the bed to my nightstand. "Along with this."

I reached into the open drawer and retrieved the vibrator, holding it up for her to see. It was a simple wand type, cordless and wrapped in black silicone. It was such a simple thing, and yet I found it sexy as hell.

"I finished charging it this morning," I added.

It was dropped to the mattress beside her, and although the squirm of delight she made was subtle, it gave me a ton of pleasure. I fucking loved how she looked with the black cuffs wrapped around her, trapped in my bed and at my mercy. The only thing that could possibly make this better would be if she'd had on that black choker she'd worn with her maid costume.

The one that had looked like a collar.

Maybe next time.

I took a beat, just letting her wait impatiently for me to do something.

Anything.

It was a way to build up her anticipation.

Finally, I dove into the drawer once again and retrieved a rolled-up towel. It was plain and white, and just big enough for what I needed.

Her chest rose and fell with hurried breath as I leaned over the side of the bed and began to slide the terrycloth beneath her lower body. This towel was a signal to her, and she knew what I planned to do, so if she didn't want that, all she had to do was say it.

But instead, she lifted her hips, making it easier for me to slip the white towel beneath her.

When it was in place, I striped out of my pants, down to my black boxer briefs, and snatched up the vibrator. Charlotte's expression was anxious and electric as I climbed on the bed between her legs. Her throat bobbed with a swallow. Was she excited? Did she want this even more than I did?

No. That couldn't be possible.

I wanted it too much.

A button was pushed on the handle, and the wand whirred to life. I grinned as I leaned over her, bracing myself on an arm, and dragged the buzzing toy up the inside of her thigh.

She laughed and tried to wriggle away because it obviously tickled, but I kept it in contact with her skin, dragging it up, and up, and *up* . . .

"Shit," she muttered under her breath.

The head of the vibrator was at the juncture of her legs, touching her clit through the lace of her black panties. It clearly felt good, but I studied her face as I rolled the tip of the humming toy around, searching for the spot where she wanted it the most.

Where it felt the best.

Her hips moved, grinding against it, and a smile peeled back my lips.

This girl—*my girlfriend*—was so goddamn sexy.

"Can you come like this?" I asked.

She looked at me like this was a ridiculous question. "Uh, yeah."

"Then do it," I ordered.

Everything up until this moment had been light and maybe a little playful. But my command flipped a switch, making the scene utterly serious.

Her lips parted and she sucked in a breath, telling me she felt the shift too. There was power swirling all around us, heating my blood and making my dick hard.

I pushed the vibrator against her, drawing quiet, sultry moans, but they escalated quickly, and I was fucking thrilled with how fast she complied with my demand. Her arms strained against the restraints, and her head tipped back, eyes slamming shut as she came.

The buzzing ceased when I turned off the vibrator and it was tossed away, falling on the floor with a deep thud. As she recovered, I splayed my hand over her beautiful body. It caressed the curves of her bra-clad breasts, slid over her taut stomach, down the length of her thigh, and then back up again.

She was still catching her breath when I straightened and sat back on my knees between her spread, bound legs. I curled my fingers around the crotch of her panties and pulled it aside, so I could stare at her. She was bare, a deep pink, and glistening.

"So fucking wet." My voice was low and rough. I swiped a finger through her arousal and then licked the pad of that finger, dragging it provocatively across my bottom lip. "Such a sweet, *helpless* little pussy."

Charlotte let out a panicked sound, like what I'd said had turned her on so much, it was alarming. And I fucking loved it, how attuned we were. Deep down, we were a lot alike.

"This is temporary," I warned.

I reached behind myself and unclipped one of her ankles, because I wanted her underwear out of my way. I grabbed the sides of her panties and tugged them down, all the way until she was able to pull her leg free. I left the scrap of lace hanging around the cuff where she remained bound, before setting my sights on her free ankle. She eagerly put it back where it had been so I could clip her to the strap.

She welcomed the restraint.

My pulse intensified as I looked at her.

The last few days, I'd come up with my plan, but now that it was here, I was second-guessing myself. Or maybe I was just being indecisive. There was so much I wanted to do, it was difficult to pick what to start with.

Stick to the plan.

I coursed my palm up her leg and pushed my index finger inside the wet velvet of her body. Her mouth dropped open, and she arched from the intrusion, so I put my other hand low on her stomach, easing her back down onto the bed.

One finger was joined by another, and I began to fuck her with them.

My tempo was languid. Almost painfully slow. It gave her time to adjust and for me to carefully watch her reactions as I tried to locate her G-spot. My thumb dipped down so it could rub circles on her clit, right above where my fingers were fucking her.

The moan she let out was so fucking sexy, I genuinely worried for a half-second I might come in my boxers. But when that didn't happen, I took a breath and focused on my task. It wasn't uncomfortable, sitting back on my heels, but I adjusted my 'stance' and widened my knees. I'd need a solid base to maintain the fast rhythm I'd need to bring her to orgasm.

Charlotte squirmed and writhed against the straps.

I gazed at her, spread-eagle and bound to my bed, and fuck me, I was so into it, I grew lightheaded. There was a need clawing at me, a craving to sink myself inside her mouth and order her to finish me off, but I ignored it.

Soon, but not yet.

I picked up the pace, moving my fingers faster. Deeper. Her pussy was drenched and hot as lava, and I spun tighter circles with the pad of my thumb on her clit. I felt confident I'd found her G-spot when she arched again, bowing off the mattress, and her shackled hands clenched into fists.

As she gasped for her breath, goosebumps pebbled across her skin.

She's ready.

At least, I hoped so. I jammed my fingers in and out of her, going as fast as I possibly could, and I moved like a blur. It was a speed I wouldn't be able to hold for long, and I'd be fucked if I'd ramped it up too soon.

"Oh, my God," she groaned, mindless with need.

It was murder on my arm and my back, and my breath went ragged from the exertion. *Get there*, a voice in my head chanted. My thumb was barely moving now, because all my focus was on the fingers I was driving into her.

It burst from me without warning. "Are you going to come for Daddy?"

Her cry was so loud, so sudden, it verged on a scream. She bucked, making the metal clasps of her cuffs jangle, and warmth spilled over my fingers. As I continued to pump at my furious pace, some of the rushing liquid flicked from my fingers, and it soaked the towel beneath her.

It was sexy as hell.

I slowed and savored the show she put on. Her entire body was quaking, and inside, her pussy clenched rhythmically on my drenched fingers. Her legs twitched and her arms strained against the straps, her hands clawing at the air. All the while, moans and gasps poured from her.

A dark, evil smile burned across my mouth.

She didn't see it, though, since her eyes were closed as she struggled through her bliss. I slipped down the bed, used my thumbs to peel her open, and lowered my lips to her pussy. My tongue fluttered, teasing the sensitive bud of her clit.

"Oh, fuck!" Charlotte flinched. She bucked again, trying to run from my indecent kiss, and whined, "Daddy, it's too much."

That word. It was a trigger in the best way possible.

I slapped the inside of her thigh, but not hard enough to cause any pain. I'd done it with just enough force to make sure she knew who was in charge right now.

"It's not too much," I said. "I know what you need. Maybe if you're good, later I'll let you sit on my beautiful face. Would you like that, baby girl?"

I didn't wait for her answer. My tongue was on her again, buried in her pussy, and my face was wet with her arousal. She let out little whimpers, like she wasn't sure if she liked what I was doing, but that she might also love it. The sound made blood rush loudly in my ears.

Every stroke of my tongue caused her to shudder.

"Fuck me," she blurted. "Oh, God, *please*."

Was she begging? My heart jerked to a halt.

I wanted this so much, but there was some reason I wasn't supposed to.

Right?

For the fucking life of me, I couldn't remember what it was. My mind was on fire, and all the doors to logic had been closed down to try to keep the flames contained.

She wanted it, and I was fucking *dying* for it.

Charlotte sensed my hesitation, and the whine in her voice was intoxicating. "Please. I *need* you inside me," she gulped a breath, "and you said you'd give me what I need."

Before I'd even approved the action, I was off the bed and reaching for my nightstand drawer. The condoms were near the back, and I grabbed one from the box so quickly,

I smashed the carboard. But I had what I needed. I tore the wrapper, and as I rolled the condom on, my goddamn hands shook.

Fuck, I needed her, just like she needed me.

When I climbed back up on the bed, my gaze swept along the length of her body. She was naked except for her black bra and the leather cuffs, tied down to my bed, and her expression screamed at me to hurry.

I crawled on my hands and knees until I was over her and then settled between her thighs. Her warm skin pressed to mine, and we were only a heartbeat away from sex. The desire for her was overpowering, overwhelming. I'd never been so disoriented in my goddamn life.

"Are you sure?" My voice was unsteady.

Her eyes were lidded and her expression desperate. *"Please."*

My heart raced out of control as I reached down between us, gripped my cock, and brushed the sheathed tip against her, searching for entrance. As soon as I found it, I claimed her lips at the same time I claimed her body.

Inch by slow inch, I sank into her, and the heat of our kiss rivaled the fire of her body. As I advanced, our moans mingled and were muted beneath our lips. The pleasure was white-hot, searing through my center and down my limbs.

I kept going until I was buried completely in her, and when that happened, our focus turned toward our kiss. It wasn't dirty, or meaningless, or simply for pleasure. This kiss was sensual. It brimmed with passion and some kind of emotion I didn't want to identify.

It was much safer to pretend it didn't exist.

Did she feel that same emotion? My chest was flattened

to hers, so I could tell her heart was beating as rapidly as mine. I eased my hips back, sliding almost all the way out of her, only to press forward once more—this time faster.

The sensation caused us both to tear our lips away and gasp for air.

"Oh, fuck," I murmured. "*Fuck*, Charlotte, you feel so good."

Charlotte, I'd said. Not *baby girl,* because that didn't seem right for this moment. I'd started this evening with the intention of it being a sexy scene, our first foray together into BDSM, but I'd lost control.

Everything had changed, shifted.

I reached for one of her wrists and ripped at the buckle, then undid the other wrist because I needed her to have her freedom, and I wanted her hands on me. The moment she was released, her fingers threaded through my hair.

Her mouth was soft and lush.

I drank up her moans as I established my tempo, and right away I knew I was in trouble. It felt way, *way* too good. I tried to slow down, but her hips rotated, urging me to go faster. One of her palms was on my ass, her fingers clenching, and the cold silver ring kissed my bare skin.

This sex wasn't like anything I'd had before. Did it even classify as sex? It felt like so much more.

Like our kiss, this act wasn't simply for pleasure. It wasn't meaningless.

This was about connection, and I could not get enough of it. Couldn't get enough of her.

Heat sizzled through my bloodstream. Everything was tingling with anticipation, begging for release, but I tried to push it down, to hold it back. Charlotte writhed beneath me, and her hands roamed over my back, my shoulders, my chest.

The faster I moved inside her, the shorter her kisses became, so she could pull in raspy breaths.

It felt like she was all around me. Maybe inside me like I was in her. I couldn't get a handle on these fucking feelings, and my heart stumbled wildly out of time. Pleasure was building at the base of my spine, growing too big and fast for me to stop it.

Even though I sensed it was coming, my orgasm still hit me without warning. The groan I gave was a combination of surprise, dismay, and physical satisfaction.

Shit, the orgasm was fucking *intense*.

It went on, and on, and my vision narrowed in, blurring. I sank as deep inside her as I could while delivering a scorching kiss. She moaned right along with me, perhaps enjoying the sensation of my climax. Or maybe she'd gotten secondhand pleasure watching me experience it.

My pulse was still roaring as the orgasm began to fade, and when the dust began to settle, awareness took hold.

Irritation sliced through me. "Fuck."

Charlotte tensed. "What's wrong?"

"I came before you did." I'd lasted, what? Less than ten minutes? I prided myself on my endurance, and making sure my partner was satisfied. This was embarrassing—but that wasn't even the worst of it.

I'd wanted this for so long, I couldn't believe it was already over.

She didn't look the least bit disappointed, though. Her laugh was light and warm. "Noah, you already gave me two orgasms. I don't even know if I have another one in me."

She reached up to cup my cheek, and her gaze wandered lovingly over my face as our breathing evened out. Her eyelids were starting to grow heavy with sleep, and I felt a similar exhaustion in my body.

"But," she added softly, "I'm willing to let you try anytime."

TWENTY-EIGHT

Charlotte

Off in the distance, a lawn mower rumbled to life, jarring me awake. I sighed loudly and flopped over in the bed, making my arm connect with Noah's bare chest.

"Hey, watch it," he teased.

"Sorry." I mashed my pillow under my head as I gazed at him. His focus returned to the iPad he'd been reading, some tech blog or stock market thing, but I knew I still had his attention. The lawnmower's engine grew louder, sounding like it was just beneath his window, and I groaned. "It's too early."

He chuckled. "It's after nine."

This time when I sighed, it was overly dramatic. "What? No." I pulled the covers up over my head and burrowed deeper into his bed. "That means I need to leave soon, and I don't want to. We haven't even had morning sex yet."

Noah pulled the covers down, exposing his confused expression. "What are you talking about? We had sex this morning."

I shook my head. "That doesn't count. The sun was barely up."

He laughed. "Oh, right. Of course."

I'd gone out drinking last night before coming over, so I'd had to get up early this morning to use the bathroom. After I'd finished and climbed back in Noah's bed, I'd decided to surprise him with a very early morning BJ. Naturally, it had led to sex, and he'd gotten me to come so hard, I'd fallen right back asleep afterward.

I'd had a bunch of cocktails last night because it had been Brianna's bachelorette party and we'd gone for the full cliché. Pink cowboy hats and boots for the bridesmaids, all white for the bride, and we hit the tourist bars downtown on Broadway.

There had only been a hundred other bachelorette parties out last night, but Brianna had said she'd felt special and had a blast and didn't mind that I was spending the night at my boyfriend's place rather than the Airbnb with the rest of the girls.

I worried she was lying and just being polite, so I triple-checked with Sasha to see that this was okay, and she confirmed it was. I was determined to be a better person than I'd been in the past. I wasn't going to be the kind of friend who vanished when they got in a new relationship . . .

Like I'd done to them when I was with Zach.

It softened the blow of not crashing with them when I promised Brianna she'd have my full attention at the wedding. I'd be attending it solo, after all.

I walked my fingers across Noah's naked chest, distracting him from whatever he was reading, and his tone was mock irritation. "Did you need something?"

I grinned. "Maybe some attention."

The iPad was chucked aside in a pretend huff. "Fine."

He jerked the covers out of his way and climbed on top of me so fast, I laughed. Then he nuzzled into the crook of my neck, kissing me there.

Damn. It was so nice sleeping in his bed and getting to wake up next to him. It had only happened a few times since we officially started dating. These last three weeks, we'd both been incredibly busy.

Plus, I could tell my parents I was going out and spending the night at a friend's house only so many times without them getting suspicious I was seeing someone. God, I hated that I had to lie to them. And I hated even more how Noah and I had to keep our relationship a secret from everyone but a few of my friends who'd promised to keep it under wraps.

As he kissed me, his short beard tickled my neck and distracted me. "I wish I could take you as my date to Brianna's wedding."

He paused his kisses. "Aren't your parents going to that?"

"They are." Because they'd known her since we'd become friends in the third grade. I was closer with Sasha these days, but for a long time, Brianna and I had been inseparable, and she would always be a bonus daughter to my mom.

Noah put his hands on the bed on either side of my head and rose onto extended arms, so I had a clear view of his disapproving look. "You know we can't."

"Of course I know," I grumbled. "I'm just whining, okay? It'd be nice if we didn't have to sneak around."

His expression softened. "Yeah, it would."

But he didn't say anything else, because we didn't talk about the future. He'd been resistant to us becoming more than friends, and now that we were, I sensed I needed to be patient about anything else.

I knew better than to press and ask him directly when we were going to tell my parents about us. And if I asked him where he saw this thing between us going, there was a chance I wouldn't like his answer.

I decided ignorance was bliss. We'd only been together a few weeks, and he'd probably argue that wasn't long enough to claim things were serious.

Why did it feel so serious, then?

I pushed the thought away, hooked a hand on the back of his neck, and pulled him down to me. "Forget I said anything."

His mouth against mine was a drug, making everything else drift away—

Until the lawnmower outside made another pass by the window and reality intruded back into my mind. There wasn't time for this kiss to lead into round two of morning sex. Noah had said it was after nine, and I needed to be seated at my laptop in my room, with hair and makeup camera-ready by ten forty-five.

This was because he'd booked me an Instagram Live interview with another influencer, one who had a huge following, at eleven. And after lunch, I had a Zoom call with a web designer to discuss my needs so they could provide a quote.

Noah was adamant I needed a website, because my little brand was really taking off.

Last week, *Hot Girl Cleans* had surpassed fifteen thousand subscribers on YouTube, and with monetization, I was earning money. Sure, sometimes it was less than ten dollars a day, but others it was more, and . . . everyone had to start somewhere, right?

"Okay, stop distracting me." I pretended to be annoyed. "I have to go."

"I'm distracting you?" He grinned and shook his head. "You're the one who asked for attention."

It took an enormous amount of self-control to climb out of his bed and get dressed. I had to make an even bigger effort to leave his house, because he didn't bother getting dressed before walking me to his front door. He was wearing only a pair of short, red boxer briefs as he kissed me goodbye, and he looked so damn good, it should have been criminal.

I hurried down his front path toward my car, but couldn't stop myself from glaring at the next-door neighbor and his loud lawnmower, like me being out of time was his fault and not my own. Really, the guy had done me a favor by waking me up.

With all the times I'd been over at Noah's, I'd only seen his neighbors on that side of his house twice. The man was a few years older than Noah, and I'd been told he was a surgeon, which explained why he rarely seemed to be home. The girl who lived with him was probably my age, so I had assumed she was his daughter.

Girlfriend, Noah had told me.

I'd been so fucking curious about them, but I hadn't seen them since. Their age gap was bigger than mine and Noah's, and yet they made it work.

I squinted against the bright morning sunlight to make out the man riding on the lawnmower that was steadily approaching. He wore a shirt with the sleeves cut off, a ragged baseball hat, and sunglasses. It made him look young, and sort of familiar, and—

"What the fuck?" I said.

Was that *Preston*?

We hadn't seen each other since he'd abandoned me on our date, so I half expected him not to recognize me, but as he drew closer, his shoulders snapped back. He jerked the machine to a stop, and the engine had barely finished shutting down when he spoke. "Charlotte?"

"What are you doing?" I demanded.

He dismounted and strode forward, looking at me with

the same disbelief I had about seeing him. His tone was unsure, like he'd thought it should be obvious. "I'm mowing the yard."

My gaze flitted to the house beside Noah's. "You live here?"

He nodded, and I held in the curse I wanted to make. What dumb fucking luck was this? Whatever face I was making, it must have said I wasn't happy about it, because he seemed eager to ease my anxiety.

"Not for much longer," he said. "I signed a lease on a new place last week." Even with his sunglasses on, I could tell by the tilt of his head he was looking up at Noah's house. "Are you visiting Noah for a Warbler thing?"

My brain struggled to come up with a plausible reason. "Uh . . . I'm his house cleaner."

His face contorted with skepticism. "You're cleaning his house at nine thirty on a Sunday?"

Fuck it, my mind said. *He owes you.*

I stepped closer and lowered my voice, even when there was no one else around to hear. "Listen, we're seeing each other, but we're, like, keeping it on the downlow." Troy Osbourne's release party had been more than a month ago and was a big success, so it stood to reason Warbler might hire Preston's planning company for other events. "I need you to do us a solid and not mention it to anyone at Warbler. Especially my dad."

His posture stiffened with surprise. Or maybe awareness?

There was the slightest tilt of his head in acknowledgment, before he abruptly turned and headed back toward his lawn. He lobbed it over his shoulder in a tone that was so casual, it nearly had me convinced he was clueless. "Mention what?"

I stood there in silence, watching him go, but when I

reached for my car's door handle, he abruptly stopped and reversed course.

"Wait, hold up." Preston marched back across the grass and tugged off his sunglasses, giving me a full look at his concerned expression. "I know I'm the last person you probably want it from, but can I give you some advice?"

When I was too stunned to say anything, that seemed to be answer enough for him.

"I have experience," he looked weirdly bashful, "with relationships being kept in the dark. A lot of experience, actually. I've been on both sides of a secret and let me tell you, it fucking sucks. Each time that secret got out, it blew up in everyone's face." There was a sadness in his eyes I couldn't look away from. "Just tell him. Don't wait for the right time, because it's *never* going to be the right time."

"I can't tell him." I scowled, and anger heated my body. I was mad because deep down, part of me worried he was right, but that was scary. It was easier to lash out, rather than deal with it. Plus, he didn't understand what was at stake. "You don't know my situation."

"You're right, I don't. But if you don't tell him and he finds out? Believe me. It fucks everything up and makes things a lot harder."

Did I make him feel like his advice was wasted? Because he lifted his hands in surrender.

"Okay." He began to walk backward toward the lawnmower. "I said my piece. Good luck, Charlotte."

His tone made it sound like he wanted to tack it on the end but barely held it back.

Good luck, because you're going to need it.

Preston's warning weighed heavy on me the next few days.

Every time I saw my father, I had that same terrible feeling in the pit of my stomach I'd had when I'd lied about my grades. Last time, I'd pretended the issue didn't exist, and I'd avoided thinking about it, but I didn't want to make that same mistake.

If my relationship with Noah had any chance of going somewhere, we were going to have to face this thing. Was it *really* that big of a deal we were dating? We were both adults, and I barely worked for Warbler.

I tried to bring it up with Noah when we'd been texting yesterday, but he'd been distracted with a work emergency, and I chickened out at the last second. I promised myself next time I saw him, we'd have to talk about it.

Face to face would be better, anyway.

And I missed that face—we were long overdue to see each other. He hadn't been home on Tuesday when I cleaned because he'd gone with his parents to his dad's doctor's appointment and it had, according to him, lasted forever.

Since we'd started sleeping together, my feelings for him had intensified, and now he seemed to dominate every moment of my thoughts, whether we were together or not.

Maybe once I was done cleaning Warbler, I'd see if he wanted some company and invite myself over to his place. I climbed the front steps of the office, carrying my cleaning caddy and filming equipment, and made my way through the door.

It was after six, so the office was closed, but I wasn't

surprised the place wasn't locked or that the alarm was off. I knew my father was still here because the light was on in his office and I'd seen his car was parked on the street out front, instead of the back parking lot.

I set my things down on the reception desk, headed to my dad's office, and knocked on the doorframe since his door was open.

"Hey," I said. "Were you waiting on me?"

I found him standing behind his desk and in the process of putting his laptop in his backpack, and when he saw me in his doorway, he smiled. "No, I had a last-minute thing to wrap up, but it's done now, and I'm heading home. Are you joining us for dinner?"

"Probably not. By the time I finish up here, it'll be after eight, so I might see what my friends are up to."

He finished zipping his bag closed and gave me a direct, knowing look. "Friends? Or *friend*?"

My pulse lurched forward. "What?"

"Your mother and I are wondering when you're going to tell us about him."

All the air drained from the room. "What?" I asked again. "Who are you talking about?"

"The boy you're seeing."

He looked so amused, so pleased with himself, while I felt like everything was falling apart inside me. I was in such a panic, it took me a long moment to process that he'd said *boy* and not *man*. My father had a habit of calling anyone younger than him *kid*, but there was no way he'd refer to Noah as a boy.

He wouldn't be standing there looking smug if he had any inkling of who my boyfriend was.

He mistook my fear for simple surprise and smiled warmly. "You think we haven't noticed how many nights you're going out, or how happy you've been recently?" He lifted his bag onto his shoulder. "When you came back home, things were different, and you weren't yourself. But they seem better now, and it's nice having *you* back."

I swallowed thickly.

What the fuck was I supposed to say to that? My gaze shifted away from my dad and to the bookshelf behind him that was decorated with awards I'd need to dust after he left.

My silence was the confirmation he needed.

"When do we get to meet him?" he asked.

My eyes went so wide they nearly fell out of my head. "Uh . . . I don't know. It's sort of new, and I'm not"—*ready*, my brain screamed—"sure that's a good idea right now."

Disappointment splashed on his face. "All right. He got a name?"

"Yes."

He tilted his head. "Are you going to tell it to me?"

"No," I said quickly, which was clearly an unsatisfactory answer, because he frowned. Shit, I needed to give him something. "Can we hold off on talking about him? Just for a little while. Like I said, it's new, and it might not even be anything."

Of all the lies I'd told so far, this one was the worst.

My father wasn't happy, but he must have sensed not to push and chose to respect this boundary. "Okay, Charlotte." He strode toward me in the doorway, and I moved to the side, giving him room to pass. "Don't forget to set the alarm when you're done."

Relief crashed over me. "You got it."

He only made it another step before a thought caused him to stop. "By the way, Noah was working late in the back office, so he might still be here." His tone was light. "Thought I'd give you a heads-up, so he doesn't accidentally startle you."

This time, when my pulse jumped, it was for an entirely different reason.

"Oh, okay." Excitement tightened my voice, so the pitch was higher than I wanted it to be.

But, thankfully, my dad didn't notice.

We said our goodbyes, he went out the front door, and my gaze landed on the equipment I'd brought in. The agenda for the evening had been to create content on deep cleaning a coffee maker, since there were two types here. The regular one with a pot and filters that made multiple cups at a time, and a fancy, newer one for individual servings that used pods.

Except now that I knew Noah might be here, my agenda was revised, and I practically skipped down the hall to the back office.

The space had once been the den of the house, so it was cozy and homey, even with the corporate-looking office furniture. My boyfriend was seated at the desk, and when he looked up to discover me in the doorway, a sexy smile split his lips.

"Hi," I breathed.

He shut the laptop in front of him and leaned back in his swivel chair, looking at me like he wanted to take it all in.

"Hi," he said finally. "Your dad still here?"

I pressed my lips together and shook my head. And then I catapulted forward into the room, rushed over to him, and crawled right into his lap.

Noah had zero issues with this. His arms were around me

and his mouth latched on to mine in a kiss that announced he had missed me as much as I'd missed him.

"Working late?" I asked when we finally came up for air.

He laughed, and it sounded sheepish. "Not really. I stayed because I wanted to see you."

God, I loved that and snuggled deeper into his arms. "I wanted to see you too."

"You did, huh?" He threaded a hand into my hair and peered at me with electric eyes, leaning in to kiss me again—

"We need to talk," I said.

The second my words registered, he went wooden, and his expression blanked.

"Fuck," I groaned. "I said that wrong. What I mean is, I have something I want to talk to you about."

He let out a breath like he'd narrowly dodged a bullet. "Oh." He chuckled, maybe needing it to release the tension in his body. "You know that phrase strikes fear in the heart of anyone who hears it."

"Sorry, I didn't mean to."

He showed me all was forgiven when he kissed me.

But his lush mouth was addictive and distracting, and when his tongue stroked against mine, the heat it caused was so intense, it burned away all thought. I gripped fistfuls of his shirt when he lifted me, rising onto his feet so suddenly that the chair beneath him rolled away.

My backside hit the desktop with a solid *thump* as he seated me on it, and our kiss deepened further. It was aggressive. Urgent. I wasn't the only one swept away by it, either.

Noah seemed just as consumed.

I tore my mouth away from his, just long enough to utter it. "We can talk later." I found a better option. "After."

"After." The repeated word from him was half question, half agreement.

I sat on the edge of the desk with my legs parted around his hips and had one hand on the back of his neck, and the other clenched on his ass. He ground his lower body against me, sending sparks skittering up my spine, and I went breathless in an instant.

His hand worked itself under the hem of my t-shirt, fingertips sliding over my bare stomach, moving up until he gripped one of my bra-covered breasts. I sighed into his mouth and squeezed his ass in encouragement.

"After what, baby girl?" His tone was sinful, pure seduction. "After you let me get you naked, bend you over this desk, and fuck you senseless?"

The room was hazy with lust. It felt like it had been weeks since we'd been together, and not days, and it was difficult to keep my mind coherent enough to answer.

But when I opened my mouth to speak, Noah's body solidified into cold stone.

We'd been too intoxicated with each other to hear the footsteps coming down the hall. It was why I flinched when my father's booming voice flooded the room.

"What the *fuck*?"

TWENTY-NINE

Charlotte

Up until this point in my life, if anyone had asked me if Ardy Owens was a violent man, my answer would have been a solid *no*. But the way my father barreled into the room now had me second-guessing everything.

I turned on the desk just in time to see him charging at Noah and me, with a face full of fury, and I gasped. I was too stunned to do anything, so when Noah pulled me down off the desk and to the side, I stumbled on my feet.

He'd flung me aside, out of my father's path, but in doing so, he'd given himself up. It made it easy for my father to latch his hands onto Noah's shirt and jerk him close, thrusting the men face to face.

Time slowed when my father reared back with his right arm, closed his fist, and readied a punch. I moved before my mind could approve it, putting a hand on each of their chests and wedging myself between the men.

"Daddy, stop!" I cried.

Everything went still.

The tension in the room was so great, nothing could move—not even my heart. My father still had a handful of Noah's shirt twisted in his fist, while his mouth was frozen open and his face was filled with disbelief. This was probably because I hadn't called my father *daddy* in at least a decade.

Noah stood stock-still, with his wide-eyed gaze fixed on

me. Did he . . . did he think I'd meant him when I'd used that word? It had worked to disrupt my father's anger, but it had thrown my boyfriend into chaos.

And the effect of the word was only momentary, because my father sprang back to life. He used his hold on Noah's shirt to give him an enormous shove, sending my boyfriend stumbling backward and crashing into the chair.

"You think you can come in here and put your hands on my little girl?" My father's face turned an ugly shade of reddish-purple, and the longer he yelled, the more his voice climbed with rage. "I give you a job and you say thanks, how? By sexually assaulting her?" He flung a sharp finger at the door. "Get the fuck out now. You're fired."

Oh, God. Oh, fuck.

"Wait, wait, no," I blurted. Adrenaline shot through my bloodstream, making me shake uncontrollably. "He wasn't assaulting me, we're—"

My father heard absolutely none of it. "Are you all right?" His focus swung to me so he could scour every inch of my body, searching for signs of injury. "Did he hurt you?"

Thoughts flew past me at a million miles an hour, and it was just as hard to grab one as it was to catch my breath. "I'm fine, Dad. Noah wasn't doing anything I didn't want him to."

"What?" His face contorted as he refused to accept what I was telling him. "No, Charlotte. He tried to take advantage of you."

I shook my head. "No, Dad, please listen to me. He wasn't doing that at all." It wasn't enough to convince him, so I had no other choice. I sucked in a deep breath. "Noah's my boyfriend."

As my father tried to grapple with that information, it

was like it shut down his brain. His posture was stiff, and his expression was unreadable. My gaze darted to Noah, who stood several feet away, but it might as well have been miles. He looked like he might throw up, or bolt, or maybe do one, followed immediately by the other.

"*Him*?" My father's voice was full of horror. "No."

I turned so I was facing my dad, and it came from me in a rush. "I'm sorry we kept it from you."

But his furious gaze went over my head and to the man behind me. "No," he repeated, only this time it contained enough force it pierced my heart. "Absolutely not. Whatever it is you think you two have, it's over. Done." His focus returned to me, and I shivered from his icy tone. "You will not see him again, you understand me?"

Everything had spun out of control, and I folded an arm over my stomach, trying to hold myself together. "But . . . but . . . " Hot tears sprang into my eyes, blurring my vision. "But I love him."

Breath was pulled into Noah's lungs in a sharp sweep.

Which was surprising to me since I couldn't seem to find any air at all. I sank my teeth into my bottom lip and risked a glance at him. I both did and didn't want to know what his reaction was to my sudden declaration.

He wasn't looking at me, and he wasn't looking at my father either.

Noah's guilty gaze was pinned to the floor in front of him, and my heart plummeted to my toes. He did nothing. Said nothing. It was like he thought if he stood still and was quiet enough, maybe we'd forget he was here.

It wasn't a shock he didn't feel as strongly about me as I did him, but his total lack of action or defense? *That* was pretty fucking surprising, not to mention hurtful. I felt abandoned.

On my own.

But I needed to deal with one problem at a time, and the issue with my father took priority.

I was no longer a stranger to seeing disappointment in my dad's eyes, but the expression he wore now was new. He peered at me like I was a spoiled child throwing a tantrum and he was fed up with it.

"You don't love him, Charlotte," he said plainly. "I know you think you do, but you're young and don't know any better." When I opened my mouth to argue, he lifted a hand to cut me off. "I've been here before with you telling me you love a man who's much too old for you. Don't bother telling me 'this time it's different.' I don't want to hear it."

Oh, my God. It wasn't fair to compare Noah to Zach in any way, but that was all my dad saw right now.

"When you came back, I had only one rule." Frustration spilled from my father. "And, goddamn it, you couldn't even follow that."

His disappointment was crushing, and I wanted to wilt beneath the weight of it. My feet ached to move, to run away and not have to deal with it. In a moment of weakness, my gaze flitted to the door.

"That's right, run away," Zach taunted in my head. *"It's what you're good at."*

I pulled my shoulders back and lifted my chin, standing my ground. "I know. I'm sorry."

Could he see how badly I meant it? How much lying and sneaking around had made me feel like shit? God, I wished I hadn't been so scared and had talked to Noah, tried to convince him that we needed to tell my parents. At least then my father wouldn't have found out in the worst possible way.

I pictured Preston, wearing a smug look as he reminded me that he'd tried to warn me.

"I am so tired of giving you chances, only for you to disappoint me time and time again." The weary expression on my father's face hardened. "You will end this, come home right now, and maybe—*maybe*—we can work through this." He glared at the other man, like it was all his fault. "But if you choose him over your family . . . " He sighed. "Then, Charlotte, I guess we're really done this time."

Suddenly, I was back in my college apartment, standing between Zach and my father. I'd screwed up then, and my father had offered me a lifeline, but I'd been too stubborn and embarrassed to accept it. Unwilling to face consequences. But I wasn't that same girl now, and—

Wait a minute. I blinked back the tears stinging my eyes.

I didn't need a lifeline, because I hadn't fucked up bad enough to require one. I'd lied, which was shitty, but I would apologize and make amends. Being with Noah wasn't a mistake. And this ultimatum?

It was stupid.

This didn't need to be an all or nothing scenario. Maybe I was a spoiled brat, because I didn't understand why I couldn't have both.

My father had said he didn't want to hear me say this time was different—but God. It fucking was.

"Why do I have to choose?" I demanded.

"You don't," Noah said from his far-off spot where invisible chains had him imprisoned. "I . . . can do it for you."

What the fuck? His expression was cryptic. Vacant. I

didn't understand—

Oh, shit.

It filled me with so much dread, my body ached with it. *No*, a voice in my head cried. Announcing I loved him had torn a rift between us, and with each passing second, the distance to him grew until it was vast and insurmountable.

"Wait," I pleaded.

My father didn't sense what was about to happen. Maybe he worried Noah was going to make some enticing offer and sway me to his side—or maybe he just wanted to twist the knife. "Think carefully about this. If you pick him, remember he's currently unemployed."

"We'll stop seeing each other." Noah said it like it was decided, a settled fact.

I'd seen it coming, but I gasped with shock anyway.

At the sound, he flinched. It was as if my pain was causing him pain, and his focus swung to me. God, his expression was fucking heartbreaking.

"I'm sorry." His voice was uneven. "But you and I both know this is the right call. I can't let you blow up your life over," he searched for the right word, "an infatuation."

I crossed the other arm over my stomach, trying not to double over. *Infatuation*? Was he fucking serious? I wasn't just wounded by his words—I was betrayed.

He knew I didn't sleep with someone until I cared deeply about them, and we'd been sleeping together for more than a month. Add on all the months leading up to that, all the times we'd talked, and kissed, and fooled around . . .

"How can you think this is just an infatuation?" A tremble worked its way up my legs, and my eyes widened in realization. "Oh, God. Is that how you see me? Just some foolish, lovesick little girl?"

My father disappeared from existence. It was only Noah and me, standing in this room with the great divide between us. His face was full of regret, and I hated it so much, I could barely look at him.

"I told you," he sounded so fucking small, "I don't have time for love."

"You don't mean that."

"I do."

And the scary thing was, he believed it.

But I was so tired of hearing that bullshit and my anger swelled until it became icy cold. "That's fine," I snapped. "I was fine with waiting for you, but you can't get mad at me for falling in love with you in the meantime."

Finally, his feet were no longer rooted to the ground, and he took a step forward. But it felt much too little, too late, and I backed away in response. He put a hand out to try to calm me, as if to say *steady*.

I found that . . . infuriating.

How dare he be calm when everything was falling apart? How dare he give up at the first sign of trouble, and not fight for what we had? The Noah I loved wasn't afraid, but I didn't recognize this man in front of me.

He wanted to run.

"I'm not mad," he said, "but, Charlotte, you can't wait for me." He leveled a gaze that made my heart stop. "Doing that would be a waste of time."

It was the final crack in the ground beneath us, forcing the earth apart so much, I could no longer see a way back to him. Tears streamed down my cheeks as my heart cleaved in two, and then shattered into a million pieces.

I wiped my face, angry I'd let him see the tears he didn't deserve. The ones I'd foolishly told him months ago I wouldn't have time for. He stared at me now like he'd evaluated our relationship with his cold shell of a stockbroker's heart and decided it was time to cut and run.

To mitigate our losses.

"This doesn't change anything," a voice said, and in my pain, it took a long moment to realize it was my father speaking. "Your employment here is over, and I don't want to see you again. You understand?"

Perhaps if my eyes hadn't been so blurry with tears, I would have seen in perfect detail just how shell-shocked Noah looked. He nodded, shuffled forward, and when he reached the doorway, he hesitated.

"I'm sorry," he whispered.

It was unclear who this apology was for. My father? Me?

My voice broke as I issued the order. "Just go."

He did as asked. He left me and the heart he'd broken completely, walking away like this was nothing more than a deal that had gone sour.

THIRTY

Noah

I stood in the emptiness of my kitchen, my hands resting on the island countertop, and wondered how the hell I'd gotten here. I didn't remember driving home, but my Mercedes was parked in the garage.

"What the fuck did you just do?" I asked myself.

I didn't have an answer, because my head was a total fucking mess.

I'd made mistakes before. Once, I'd misunderstood the terms of a deal and lost my client six figures on a single trade. My manager on the desk had helped me cover the loss, I'd worked hard to bounce back, and thankfully I'd been able to keep my job. I'd had terrible anxiety through that whole ordeal.

But it didn't compare to what I was experiencing now.

My stomach was queasy, my heart raced, and I couldn't focus on anything. Was this what a panic attack felt like? I sank to the floor, sitting with my back against one of the cabinets, and didn't care how weird it was.

At least the tile was clean. Charlotte had mopped it only a few days ago.

"Fuck." I pulled my knees up to my chest and rested my head in my hands.

I had the terrible suspicion the panic I felt right now wasn't over losing my job—it was all about her. And fuck if that didn't make me feel worse.

Her shattered expression haunted me.

I could claim I hadn't realized she'd fallen for me, but it was a goddamn lie. I ignored every sign. Told myself repeatedly her feelings were strong, but they hadn't grown enough to turn into love—because I needed that to be true.

If she fell in love, I'd have to end things, and I didn't fucking want to do that.

So, I selfishly pretended it hadn't happened until she came right out and said it, and I couldn't avoid it anymore. It had killed me to do it, even if breaking things off with her was for the best. Her relationship with her folks was tenuous and dating me made it worse.

I couldn't be the reason they cut her off.

Ending things with her was the noble thing to do.

Plus, any kind of future with Charlotte was hazy. I couldn't forecast what would happen, and the unpredictability scared me. There were so many things working against us, from our age gap to her disapproving parents, to my fear of commitment. The risk of failure was steep.

You're a fucking coward.

I couldn't even argue against it. All my years at Hale Banking and Holding, I'd prided myself on excelling under pressure. I made quick, smart decisions, knew when to take risks and how to keep my emotions under control.

But the moment Ardy caught me with my hand up Charlotte's shirt, it was as if my brain stopped working and fear took hold. And then when he'd fired me, I freaked the fuck out. The urge to run was so powerful, it was overwhelming, and I'd been so focused on not doing that, I'd stood there like an asshole, leaving her to deal with the whole shitshow on her own.

What did I do now? I'd never been fired before.

Until moving here, you never had a mortgage payment before either.

I had savings and could float for several months, but what then? I couldn't really afford to stay unemployed.

I pulled out my phone and looked at the clock on the lock screen. Even without the time change, it was far too late to call anyone in New York, and this was probably a good thing. Everything was too raw right now, and calling without a game plan was a bad idea. My previous manager would wonder the real reason I was sniffing around for a job opening, sense my desperation, and in the unlikely event he had room for me, I'd have no leverage for salary negotiations.

Everything would be better if I slept on it.

In the morning, I'd have more perspective on things. I'd confront what I'd done, decide the best way forward, and take action.

I stared at my phone in my hand and, without thought, found myself composing a text message to Charlotte.

Me: I fucked up. Can we talk?

I held my breath as I waited for the 'Delivered' beneath my speech bubble to change to 'Read.'

Usually, she was quick to respond, but the seconds ticked by and my dread grew. Maybe she was busy and hadn't seen the message, or maybe she was too distraught to look at her phone.

Or maybe she's blocked you.

I sat on the floor for an embarrassing amount of time before finally realizing a response wasn't coming.

She didn't owe me anything, and I didn't deserve

one, did I?

The plan had been to get some sleep, but it was hard to come by. Everywhere in the house, I saw reminders of her. There weren't any dirty clothes on my bedroom floor because they were all tucked away in the laundry basket in my closet. My bed was made because I'd started doing that every morning.

The new habit had come about because I always wanted to be prepared in case she came over. But I had quickly discovered I was making the bed more for myself than her. I liked coming home to a house that wasn't a mess, and I especially liked getting into a bed when it wasn't a rumpled pile of sheets.

Did she realize how much of an effect she had on me?

I barely slept that night, so it made sense I felt like shit in the morning. I used that, plus the fact that it was a weekend, as my excuse when I didn't make any headway on the job front.

I wallowed for an hour, and then guilt over hurting Charlotte stormed in, and that was louder than any other emotion I had. I was desperate to talk to someone, and it was fucking ironic that the person I'd grown closest to—the one person who knew me better than anyone these days—was the one person who wanted nothing to do with me.

> **Me:** Please, Charlotte. I'm so sorry. Can I call you?

This text message also went unread.

I waited hours before caving and called, only for it go straight to voicemail. I sat at my desk in my office, and the realization of how fucked I was slowly dawned on me. She hadn't just been my girlfriend; she'd been my best friend . . .

And I was terrified I might never see her again.

I wouldn't get a chance to apologize for hurting her or explain how badly I'd gotten scared and fucked up. That if I could do things over again, I would have done them so differently.

Shit, I would have stood beside her instead of running away.

My phone chimed with a text, jarring me from my thoughts.

> **Shannon:** Are you and Charlotte free next Friday? Patrick and I are going to Club Eros. Would love to see you there!

We hadn't played with them since the night on their boat. Shit, I hadn't thought about them much in the weeks since then. In fact, I hadn't thought about them at all.

I'd only wanted to be with Charlotte.

I stared at the text message for a long time and spent even longer trying to compose a reply.

> **Me:** We're not together anymore.

> **Shannon:** Oh no, sad to hear it.

The bubbles blinked as she typed out a new message.

> **Shannon:** Was it something we did? If so, I'm sorry.

> **Me:** No. It was something I did.

> **Shannon:** I hate that it didn't work out. Seemed like you two really liked each other.

I started to type out that we did but ended up deleting it before sending. I didn't want to open the door and make Shannon feel obligated to talk to me about feelings, nor did I want to explain what had happened with Charlotte.

Shannon: If you're still interested, you're welcome to join us at the club.

A frown twisted my face at the idea. I had enjoyed playing with Shannon, but now that I'd done it with Charlotte, I didn't want to go back to how things had been. It wasn't exciting or interesting without her, and—fuck.

Being with anyone else felt *wrong*.

Me: No thanks, but you guys have fun.

I didn't sleep much on Saturday night either. My appetite was gone, and my anxiety was at an all-time high. What was Charlotte doing right now? Was she over at her friend Sasha's place, drinking and cursing my name? She hadn't posted new content on any of her accounts, so maybe she was working on that.

Did she miss me even a fraction as much as I missed her?

It was mid-morning when I finally dragged myself into the kitchen and forced myself to make breakfast. I cooked up a plate's worth of scrambled eggs, carried that and my cup of coffee into my home office, and sat down at my computer.

I always took an hour on Sunday mornings to go over my trading wins and losses from the previous week. I'd spend time studying why those losses happened and then mark up my charts for the coming week. It was my typical routine, and I hoped sticking to it could help break me from this fog of depression.

I scrolled through the accounts, scribbling out numbers in a notebook as I went. Eventually, they'd go in a spreadsheet, but I preferred pen and paper first. I liked the tactile experience of recording the figures this way.

But it did have the potential to cause errors.

When I put the current market value for one of my

positions into the spreadsheet, I must have transposed a number, because there was no way the amount was right. I went back to the screen and account, double-checking the numbers—

"Holy shit."

I'd played a hunch and thought it might perform well, but this? It was ten times more than I expected. The rush of excitement was a hit from a drug, momentarily washing away my sadness. It wasn't the kind of money that was life-changing, but if I sold as soon as the markets opened tomorrow, it could net five figures.

I was riding the high, so when my front door swung open, my heart leapt. Was this Charlotte?

No.

My posture stiffened as my mom and dad walked in. They hadn't called or texted or been invited over, and irritation popped the balloon on my temporary good mood.

"Noah?" my mom called from the entryway, before looking to her left and spotting me at my desk. "Oh, there you are."

I'd warned them not to drop in on me, so I didn't stand to greet them or keep the coldness from my voice. "What are you doing here?"

She made it a few feet into my office before pulling to a stop and peering critically at my messy hair, worn t-shirt, and gym shorts. "Aren't you coming with us to Gabby's soccer game?"

"Fuck. That's today?" I rose from chair and started moving, my feet pounding across the hardwood toward my bedroom. "Give me ten minutes." I ignored my father's disapproving look as I blew by him. "There's coffee if you want some."

My oldest brother Paul and his family lived in Knoxville,

and my niece Gabby was on a highly competitive travel soccer team, so my parents didn't see them much during the season. When they found out her team was participating in a tournament downtown today, they'd jumped at the chance to watch and volun—told me I was coming along.

I'd asked for ten minutes to get ready but was able to get it done in nine and found my parents in the kitchen, pouring coffee into a mismatched pair of travel mugs from my time at HBHC.

"I guess your maid has the weekends off." My mom's tone was light and joking, because she had no idea I paid to have it cleaned, or who I'd been paying. I ground my teeth and said nothing—even when my parents' place had looked worse the night Charlotte and I had been there.

The skillet I'd used to make eggs was still on the stove, and dirty bowls and silverware were stacked in the sink. With everything that had happened, I'd reverted to my sloppy ways, which exacerbated my foul mood.

First thing you do when you get back from the tournament is clean this place up.

I needed to stay on top of it, before it got overwhelming.

"I've been busy," I mumbled. "You two ready?"

After my father and I did our typical back and forth about who was driving, I grabbed my keys and my phone, and we made our way to my garage. He was annoyed he'd lost, and I was aggravated with myself over the situation, so the car ride was awkwardly silent for the first few minutes.

My mother was the first to break. She leaned forward from her seat in the back so I'd hear her better. "How are things with Charlotte?

Immediately, I longed to have the awkward silence back.

"Uh . . . "

"When are you going to bring her by for dinner so we can get to know her?"

My hands tightened on the steering wheel. "We broke up."

My gaze was fixed on the traffic on the road, but I felt my parents' attention snap to me. My mother's tone was full of concern. "Why? What did you do?"

I shot her an annoyed look through the rearview mirror. "Why do you automatically assume I did something wrong?"

"Because I have three sons," she muttered under her breath. "Well, did you?"

"It's complicated," I said. "I don't want to talk about it."

My father, who sat in the passenger seat, let out a traitorous chuckle.

"Okay, fine," she said. "Then, how's work?"

Well, fuck.

I glanced at the navigation screen on my dashboard and the estimated arrival time. I could lie to them for the next thirty-four minutes, but what good did that really do me? I'd have to tell them eventually, and they'd be upset if they found out I withheld it.

My voice was flat and quiet. "I got let go."

"What?" My dad turned in his seat so he could face me. "Why?"

"I wasn't a good fit." This wasn't technically a lie, was it?

"That's it?" He was dubious.

"Oh, no," my mother said softly. "What are you going to do?"

"I don't know." That was the truth, and it caused my mom to make a face. "Don't worry about it," I added. "I'll figure something out."

"Oh, Noah." She said it the same way she'd say '*you poor thing.*' "You lost your job and your girlfriend in the same week?"

I muttered it without thought. "More like at the same time."

Oh, shit.

"What's that supposed to mean?" my father asked.

Every muscle of my upper body was tense, and I raked a hand through my hair as I struggled to come up with a way to backtrack. But my mind was a mess, and I was desperate to talk about it with someone, and . . . fuck it.

"Charlotte is Ardy's daughter," I announced.

My statement ate up all the air in the car, and I sat in tense, painful silence, waiting for the fallout.

My mother's question was quiet, and surprisingly free of judgment. "You're dating your boss's daughter?"

"Not anymore, it sounds like," my dad piped in.

"He didn't know, and when he found out, he fired me on the spot." I took a breath. "He didn't appreciate how we hid our relationship, and there's some history between Charlotte and her dad that makes her being with—" Shit, I had to correct myself. "*Made* her being with me hard for him to accept. Like I said, it's complicated."

"Oh." It was obvious my mom had no idea what to say. "But then, what happened with Charlotte?"

"When Ardy told her she couldn't see me anymore, she told him she loved me."

My dad's expression was pure confusion. "And then she dumped you?"

"No. I didn't know she loved me. She hadn't said that before, and," shame rolled through me, "I freaked out. I got scared."

"Scared of what?" My mom's tone changed, like she was asking a question that everyone already knew the answer to. "Aren't you in love with her?"

I was so uncomfortable, I twisted in my seat and threw one of my hands up. "I don't know."

"Really?" She had the audacity to scoff. "Well, I do."

"What are you talking about? You can't know that. You only met her for, like, two seconds."

Her laugh said I was being foolish. "More than enough time. Besides, it wasn't just the way you looked at her. It's how you've been since then. You think a mother can't tell when her son is happy?"

Frustration had me tightening my hand on the steering wheel once more. "I'm not going to argue that she makes me happy, but happiness is not the same as love."

. . . Right?

"Okay," she said, clearly just humoring me. "She makes you happy, loves you, and you *might* be in love with her. Noah, I have to be honest. These don't strike me as good reasons to break up."

I clung to the statement like a toddler refusing to give up the tattered scraps of what had once been their favorite blanket. "I don't have time to be in love right now."

"Now that you're unemployed," my dad said, "it sounds like you have lots of time."

He'd meant it as a joke, but all I saw was red. "Are you fucking serious right now?"

"Gabe, be nice," she scolded. "He's having a hard time, and if anyone can relate," her tone was so pointed it was almost accusatory, "it should be you."

Worry froze my father in place, and he seemed to sense

what was coming, but was powerless to stop it.

"You two are so alike," she said, "maybe he could learn from your mistake."

I glanced in the mirror and found her expression oddly smug. Meanwhile, my father looked like he wanted to crawl away with embarrassment.

"That was forty-two years ago, Theresa. Can you let it go?"

"Never." She laughed. "Go on and tell him."

No matter how much he didn't want to, she had the leverage, and my father sighed and scratched the side of his head. "Your mom and I had been dating for a while before we started talking about marriage. She wanted to know we were heading that way, but I wasn't . . . as sure at the time."

This tickled my mother so much, she let out a sharp, short laugh. It made it sound like he'd drastically downplayed the situation.

"Look, we were young," he said, "and she was my first serious girlfriend. I didn't want to rush into getting married. I wanted to be sure she was the one." His voice was small. "So I told her we should see other people."

She leaned forward between the seats so we could hear her better. "And what did I do?"

He looked at me like I should understand and take his side. "She said, fine, no problem, and called up my roommate that same day, asking him to take her out. Can you believe that?"

My mom's grin widened ear to ear. "And what did *you* do?"

"You mean after I threatened to kick his ass?" He begrudgingly admitted it. "I realized I was a goddamn idiot, and that you're the love of my life."

She sank back in her seat, crossed her arms over her

chest, and couldn't have looked more victorious if she'd tried. "I was never actually going to go out with him, you should know. You just needed a little nudge. Because sometimes people don't know what they have until it's gone."

"Your mother's right," he said. "I wasn't sure about my future until I saw one without her, and then I was damn sure she was my future." He tilted his head as he evaluated me. "You're not sure how you feel about this girl, and I understand that. But you sent her packing because you got scared, and you probably haven't thought about the fact that she's going to move on. You feel good about that?"

No, of course I didn't feel *good* about it.

I fucking hated it.

The idea of Charlotte with someone else turned my stomach and caused a cold sweat to break out on the back of my neck. This wasn't jealousy. My mind wasn't screaming that no one else could have her.

It was shouting at me about what a dumbass I'd been.

She couldn't be with anyone else—she belonged with me, and I belonged with her.

"Oh, fuck," I whispered.

"I told you," my mother said triumphantly.

I was in love with Charlotte.

Of course I would figure this out days after I'd fucked everything up with her. "What the hell do I do?"

My dad peered at me like the answer was obvious. "You tell her."

It wasn't that simple. "She won't talk to me."

"Oh, well, in that case, I guess you should just give up." His tone was plain. "I mean, you tried everything, right?"

That was . . . not helpful, but I stayed quiet because my

mind began to work the problem.

My father's teasing expression turned serious.

"I'll tell you what to do—it's the same thing I did." He turned in his seat so he could glance back at my mother, and he sounded more genuine than I'd ever heard him. "If you love this girl, you do whatever the hell it takes to get her back."

THIRTY-ONE

Charlotte

I sat at the breakfast bar in the kitchen, scrolling through Instagram, while my mother cooked dinner. She'd asked for my help, but it quickly became obvious she didn't really want it. Her goal had been to get me out of my room, and to try to force an interaction with my father.

But it didn't happen.

He was avoiding me just as much as I was him, and we hadn't spoken since the night Noah had broken up with me. If my dad was expecting another apology from me, well, he'd have to wait forever.

Because I'd apologized enough, and now I was fucking done.

My gaze lifted from the phone screen so I could glare at the gorgeous flower arrangement that sat as a centerpiece on the kitchen island. It was vibrant pink roses and white lilies, nestled in greenery and arranged in a tall, clear vase.

It was the first time a guy had ever sent me flowers. It had been delivered this afternoon, bearing a card that said it was from Noah, and that he was sorry and to please call him.

I'd been halfway to the garbage toter in the garage when my mom stopped me. "Throw out the card if you want," she had begged, "but these are too beautiful to go to waste."

I stared at the flowers, hating how pretty they were and that I couldn't like them on principle. Did he think this made up for what he'd done?

While she stirred the spaghetti boiling in a large pot on the stove, my mom tried to make small talk. I was polite, answering her questions, but I didn't engage at all in conversation.

"It doesn't seem like you need my help," I said. "Can I go back to my room until dinner?"

She asked it quietly. "So you can go back to moping?"

Irritation brewed inside me, but I kept it in check. "You know, I'm allowed to be upset. I had my heart broken."

"You're right." She stopped what she was doing, and her expression was pained, as if she were trapped between a rock and a hard place. "I'm sorry you're hurting. Your father is too."

That was rich, because he'd played no small part in it.

She set the wooden spoon down so she could give me her full attention. "Honey, you need to talk to him."

Frustration raised my gaze to the ceiling. "I'm not apologizing again. I already did it a bunch of times."

At this point, if anyone needed to apologize, it was him, but I didn't say that to her. After I'd spent the night crying over Noah, my tears had dried, and I'd made a plan for myself. I'd do as my parents asked and follow their rules, but I'd be completely disengaged.

I'd finally realized that while their safety net protected me, it also held me back. How could I live my own life if I wasn't independent from them? I'd watched my friends sometimes fail or struggle, and it had been fucking bewildering to me—

Because I'd *never* had to experience that.

Things always worked out for me because my parents were there, ready to catch my fall or solve any of my problems. Even with the whole Zach fiasco, part of me had known deep down they'd probably take me back.

But their purse strings went both ways. I couldn't take their help and then expect them to stay quiet about how I lived my life.

It was time to be a fucking adult and start doing things for myself.

"I'm not asking you to apologize." My mother's face softened. "I'm just asking you two to talk to each other. You used to be so close, and I hate this tension." She sounded like she was nearly beside herself. "You know your father and I love you so much, Charlotte. Your happiness is the only thing that matters to us."

I believed her, but I was too wounded to say anything. Yes, Noah had chosen to abandon me, but it was my father's ultimatum that had rushed him into making that decision. So, while I wasn't as mad at my father as I was at Noah, my dad wasn't blameless.

My mom must have thought I was unconvinced, because her eyes began to water with tears. "Please talk to him. For me."

I pushed away my emotions, trying to stay detached, and pulled in a breath to even myself out. "Okay."

She nodded and sniffled, sucking back her tears. When she picked up the spoon and returned to stirring the spaghetti, her shoulders didn't seem quite as heavy, like my agreement had lifted a weight off her.

I was glad she was relieved, but I didn't see the point of talking to my dad. He was upset and stubborn, and in the unlikely event he saw reason and said all was forgiven, that he was okay with me dating Noah—it didn't matter.

Noah didn't want me.

Being with me was a waste of time, he'd said, after all.

His words had crushed me to the point it'd been hard to leave Warbler and walk to my car without sobbing. I spent a long time sitting in the driver's seat of my Yaris, with tears rolling down my cheeks, trying to figure out how it had all gone so wrong.

He'd warned you this would happen, a shitty voice reminded me.

When the tears drained out of me, it made room for anger to take its place. I'd needed to do something, to take back some control. It was stupid and maybe immature, but I wanted to act like the careless way Noah had tossed me aside hadn't gotten to me.

It felt so fucking good to block his number and his socials, to pretend he didn't exist. I didn't want to see him again. To ever think about him again.

Too bad my mind and my heart wouldn't let me.

The following evening before dinner, I tracked my dad down in the living room. The TV was on, but, as usual, he wasn't paying any attention to it. His focus was on the tablet in his hands, reading his emails. When I approached and my shadow fell over him, he lifted his gaze and looked cornered.

"Do you have a minute?" I asked but didn't wait for a response. I plopped down on the couch beside him.

He put down his iPad and his expression was plain, announcing, *let's get this over with.*

"Mom asked me to talk to you." I crossed my arms over my chest, although I hadn't meant for it to look confrontational. I felt awkward and didn't know what to do with my hands. "I've got to admit, at first, I didn't want to. But now I think it's good because there's something I need to ask you."

He looked worried, like he had no idea what might come out of my mouth. "What is it?"

"You need to know my happiness these last few months wasn't just from being with Noah. Sure, he was a big part of it, but I also . . . I don't know." But I *did* know. "I feel like I've finally found my purpose."

"Your purpose." He repeated it almost like a question.

"Yeah. I started my cleaning channel as a side thing. It was just supposed to be fun, but it's grown, Dad. It's like a full-blown business now, and for the first time ever, it feels right. Like this is what I'm supposed to be doing."

His eyebrows pinched together. Maybe he was thinking he'd heard a version of this spiel before, when I'd asked to go to college, but couldn't he see how different this was? How different I was?

Before, I'd been coasting through life, and I'd known that college was the answer he'd wanted to hear. So I'd offered it up, hoping it would work out, even when I doubted it was what I really wanted.

"I'm sorry it took me so long to figure things out." I swallowed a breath so I could put everything I had into it. "And I really appreciate how patient you and Mom have been. I haven't done a good job of showing it, but I'm grateful for all the chances you've given me."

He was stunned and pleased to hear it, but unease moved through his expression. "Why do I feel like there's a 'but' coming?"

"Nope, no 'but.' I'm just saying thanks."

He peered at me, perhaps wondering what had happened

to his daughter and who this imposter was, before his cautious eyes seemed to sharpen. "What did you want to ask?"

"You need to give Noah his job back."

"Ah, there it is," he said. "Did he put you up to this?"

I shook my head. "No, we haven't talked since he ended things." I steeled my voice, keeping it controlled. "My relationship with him had nothing to do with his work, so don't punish him for being with me. I'm the one who lied."

"Charlotte," he started.

But I wasn't finished. "Neither of us wanted this, but then you volunteered me to work for him, and it was—"

"You're blaming me?"

"No." I made a face. "Well, maybe a little. What I'm trying to say is Noah really tried not to get involved with me. He warned me about how important his job is to him. He even said his identity is, like, tied up in his career, so I know right now he's lost. He's hurting."

Confusion splashed across my father's face. "That may be true, but he hurt *you,* too. So I'm not sure I understand why you care how he's feeling, or why you would want him to get his job back."

I gave a sad shrug. "Because I love him, even when he doesn't love me back. Plus, he's helped me so much with my business, I owe him this." I folded my fingers together and dropped my hands into my lap. "Also, Noah getting his job back wasn't the thing I wanted to ask you about."

"What?"

"What I want to ask is, why do you care that I was with him? Why was that so wrong?"

He stiffened. "You both work at Warbler, and that makes me uncomfortable."

I'd never realized before that my father was not good at lying. The way his gaze ran from mine confirmed my suspicion. This wasn't his real reason.

"That's a bit of a stretch, isn't it? I'm there twice a week after hours, and barely anyone knows I work there." I lifted my chin. "It doesn't matter. It's not going to be an issue soon anyway."

He frowned. "Why's that?"

"Because tomorrow I'm paying off the last of my debt."

He made a face, and I could see the thoughts in his eyes. He was scrambling to come up with another way to get me to stay. Not necessarily because he wanted to control me, but because he was convinced it was too soon. That I'd fail if I tried to do things on my own.

"You and I both know," I said, "you don't really need me cleaning Warbler. And certainly not twice a week."

He didn't want to admit it. "You do such a good job, though."

"Thanks. I mean that, too, because if you hadn't done this, I wouldn't have started my channel. But I need to know the real reason you said I had to end things with Noah."

We both knew the reason, but he didn't want to put it into words. He dragged it out so long, I worried he wasn't going to say anything.

But finally he let out a heavy breath. "He's too old for you."

"Ah, there it is." I couldn't help using the same phrase he'd given me. "I know it makes you uncomfortable, and I'm sorry for that, but I'm not your little girl anymore. I'll be twenty-four in a few weeks, and I'm too old for you to be telling me who I'm allowed to date."

"A guy like that," he hesitated, "he's not with you for love.

It'll run its course, and things will end exactly like they did with Zach."

My voice shook, because the comparison filled me with anger. "Noah is *nothing* like Zach."

"All right, fine." Worry creased his expression. "But he'll hurt you, Charlotte."

The laugh I gave was humorless. "Well, thank God you were there to protect me and stop that from happening." I took a moment to get hold of myself. "Look, I don't want to fight. Maybe it's true he wasn't ever going to fall in love with me, but I'll never know, because he didn't really get the chance." I shot him a hard look. "You had a hand in that."

He considered my statement for a long, tense moment. "I didn't handle it well, no, and I'm . . . sorry for that."

It was the best apology I could hope to get from him, and I nodded in acceptance. I shifted on the couch, turning so I was sideways and faced him completely. "Since you're so big on offering me deals, I have one for you."

Did he sense he wasn't going to like it? His expression was guarded. "What is it?"

"You give Noah his job back, and you and I can work through our issues together. I know there's still a lot I need to do to earn your trust back, and I promise to do it. And I'm going to work on not being so dependent on you and Mom—that one is regardless of what you decide." I said it more for my benefit than his. "I can't keep running to you whenever things don't go my way."

He stared at me with disbelief. "And if I don't rehire him?"

My pulse quickened and my lungs tightened, because I was giving him a version of the same one he'd given me. "Then, you're cut off emotionally. I'll obey your rules and do whatever you ask of me, but that's it."

He scowled, like the deal was too harsh or unfair, but I lifted a hand before he could say anything.

"It'd be inevitable," I said. "If I have to carry the guilt over Noah losing his job, it'll drive a wedge between us." I peered at my father with the hope he'd make the right decision, that we could repair the damage I'd done to our relationship together. "What do you say? Do we have a deal?"

THIRTY-TWO

Noah

It was strange to park my car on the street in front of the Warbler office, rather than in the lot in the back, but that was for employees, and I wasn't one of those anymore, was I?

There were other cars parked here, and I could tell right away what they were. There weren't enough photographers for it to be Ardy's client Stella, but there were enough for me to know there was someone big inside of Warbler right now.

I ignored the few paparazzi milling about and smoking cigarettes and made my way up the sidewalk. I climbed the porch steps, walked through the front entrance, and when the door hinges squealed, the receptionist glanced up at me. A shy smile warmed Irene's face. "Hi, Noah."

Had Ardy not told them what had happened, or was she just being polite?

"Hi," I said. "I'm a little early. I have an appointment with Ardy at ten."

"Send him in." Ardy's voice boomed through his open office door. "We're finishing up in here."

Irene waved me forward, and my anxiety ratcheted up another level. After I'd texted Ardy last night and asked for a meeting, I'd rehearsed what I wanted to say at least a dozen times, but now my mind went blank.

I stepped through the doorway and found the two chairs in front of Ardy's desk were occupied, but since the people had their backs to me, my gaze went straight to my former boss.

He didn't look at me, though. Ardy was wrapping up things with Erika and her client Troy Osbourne—which explained the photographers outside. His new album had dropped a little less than two months ago, and he was having a bit of a moment right now.

I lingered in the doorway, feeling horribly out of place while they discussed his upcoming appearance as the musical guest on *Saturday Night Live* and his tour that kicked off right after.

When everything was settled, Erika and Troy rose from their seats.

"You're going to be busy," Ardy commented. "You two going to have any time to plan that wedding?"

Erika chuckled. "Maybe we'll just elope."

Troy lifted an eyebrow, like that would never fly with him, before turning and noticing me in the doorway. "Hey, man."

We'd met twice before, and he seemed like a good guy. I liked how he was still humble, despite his recent fame. My gaze shifted over to Erika, who I hadn't seen in the office, or even in our neighborhood, since the proposal—but that wasn't surprising.

The bigger Troy got, the busier she, as his manager, became.

"Congrats on the engagement," I said.

"Thanks," they answered in unison.

Ardy waved them off and set his unreadable gaze on me. "Come on in, kid. Close the door and take a seat."

The first time he'd called me 'kid,' I'd thought it was strange, but today I found it oddly comforting. It was a hell of a lot better than him calling me an asshole, so I'd take this as a win.

I'd barely lowered into the seat when he spoke. "If this is to ask for your job back, Noah, let me save you the trouble."

"No, I'm not here for that. I wanted to meet with you because I have two things I need to do."

He hesitated, caught off guard. "What?"

"The first is, I want to apologize for keeping my relationship with Charlotte a secret from you. I know it was unprofessional. I promise I tried really hard not to get involved, and when we did . . . well, then I tried again not to fall for her. But it was all futile. It's probably as surprising to you as it is to me, but she's my best friend," I said it with my whole chest, "and I love her."

It was like I'd just told him I was from Mars.

He blinked at me, neither accepting nor rejecting what I'd said, unable to process. The tension in the room was so taut, it felt like the air between us was compressed, making it difficult to pull into my lungs. My body was on alert, though, prepared for him to spring into action at any moment and come at me.

Would he climb over the desk? Take a swing at me like he'd threatened to do the last time we'd been together?

He didn't move. Ardy sat in his chair, locking me under his intimidating gaze, and for half a second, I wondered if this was worse than getting punched in the face. His expression was cryptic, and his eyes were skeptical, evaluating me like he was searching for a lie.

But I was telling the goddamn truth, and I hoped he could see that.

"What's the other thing?" His tone gave nothing away.

I'd expected him to be mad and was totally unprepared

for this stoic version of him. Was this reaction . . . good? Did it mean he believed me? I chose to press on, like that matter was settled.

"Did Charlotte tell you she was paying me brokerage fees for the deals I negotiated for her?"

Again, he revealed nothing. "No."

"I didn't want them, but she insisted," I explained. "So anything I made off these deals, I looked at as 'play' money. 'Fun' money. I put it in a separate account and used it for high-risk trades. If I made any profit off it, the plan was to give it to her." The tension in my chest eased a degree, probably because I weirdly found comfort in playing the market. "Most of the investments lost money, but I had a hunch last week . . . and it paid off big."

He gave me a direct look. *Get to the point.*

"After I sold and took back my investment, there's still more than ten grand in that fund. I want to give it to her to invest in her business because as far as I'm concerned, it's her money."

He shook his head. "You earned that money."

"Mostly by luck, and I wouldn't have, without her hard work." I leaned forward in my chair. "It's amazing how fast she's grown her business. You must be so proud."

Finally, some emotion.

Was that embarrassment or guilt? It made me think he didn't know how well she'd been doing. Was he too busy to notice, or had she been keeping it from him? Maybe it had exploded so quickly, she wasn't sure it had staying power and didn't want to tell anyone until she was sure it wasn't a flash in the pan.

"I know this cash would be a big help," I said. "The web

design quote she got would eat a significant chunk of it, but she could use the rest for an advertising boost while she has all this momentum."

Ardy's expression shifted to one of suspicion. "You don't need my blessing to give her that money. What's the problem?"

"She won't take my calls or answer my emails." The flowers I'd sent hadn't worked either. "I need your help getting in touch with her."

His suspicion graduated to all-out distrust. "This is ploy."

"It's not."

Everything I had told him was true, but . . . he wasn't exactly wrong, either. I would have given her this money no matter what, regardless of my feelings, but if it also gave me a way in with her? A chance to apologize and plead my case?

Yeah, I wasn't mad about that.

He didn't buy what I was selling. "I don't like the idea of you dating my daughter. She's too young for you."

My heart sank, but there was nothing I could do about that right now. In the event I was able to win Charlotte back, I'd be starting in a hole with her dad—but that was a distant obstacle.

I needed to focus on the bigger one first.

"Fair enough," I said, "but that's not up to you."

"No, it isn't," he agreed.

His gaze drifted away, going to the keyboard on the desk in front of him, and he seemed deep in thought. When his focus finally returned to me, his demeanor had changed. He looked a hell of a lot more like the man he'd been back when he'd hired me.

"I said you didn't need to ask for your job back," he said, "because Charlotte already negotiated that for you."

I straightened, and my pulse kicked. "What?"

"She still loves you, even after all you said, but don't think that means getting her back is going to be easy. You broke my little girl's heart, and she can be stubborn like me. It means she probably won't forgive you."

I struggled to catch my breath, and my mind raced trying to wrap itself around this new information. "I only need a chance. Just give me five minutes with her."

There was movement, drawing his attention to his office window. Outside, the photographers rushed to throw their gear in their cars and follow the SUV that had just turned onto the street from the back parking lot. As it drove past, I got a flash of the newly engaged couple.

Erika was almost twenty years older than her fiancé, and Ardy had no issue supporting them. Was it wishful thinking maybe someday he could do the same for Charlotte and me?

He glanced at his phone screen, checking the time. "I believe she's home right now. You want me to text my wife and let her know you're coming over?"

The way he said it made it sound like a limited time offer, and I couldn't get up out of my seat fast enough.

THIRTY-THREE

Charlotte

The best mid-morning light in my house was in the kitchen, which worked out perfectly as the background during my Instagram Live. I put my ring light up on a tripod on the breakfast bar, and my microphone on the counter just out of frame.

I didn't realize until after I'd started the video that the flowers Noah had sent were still on the island behind me. It meant if he watched this video, he'd see I'd gotten them.

Whatever.

At least they looked good in the shot, and what were the chances he'd watch, anyway? The man wasn't into cleaning.

He wasn't into me either.

Engagement in the video was slow at first, but that was normal. I had a list of topics ready to talk about while waiting for the questions to start rolling in, plus I tried to return any of the greetings viewers sent me in the comments.

Most of the questions stayed within my brand. They wanted to know my preferred cleaning products on stone countertops, how to remove the sticky, baked-on mess on an air-fryer tray, or general tips on cleaning faster.

I didn't know the answer to every question, and I wasn't ready to call myself an expert. I was honest when I wasn't sure and explained the way I'd tackle the problem if I were facing it.

I wanted to get there someday. To be knowledgeable and always ready with the right answer, and I spent a lot of time doing my research. I was addicted to cleaning subreddits. I watched other influencers videos, not just for their cleaning process, but to see what worked style wise, what I responded to as a viewer.

In all my life, I'd never liked studying, but this was . . . sort of enjoyable. It was a full-time job that, so far, didn't feel like work.

I jotted down notes whenever a question came up I didn't know the answer to, mining the ideas for future videos.

Dryer vent cleaning, I scribbled in my notebook. *Apartment rental move-out.*

I'd only planned to talk for thirty minutes, but the comments were coming at me fast and furious, which was awesome, but I struggled to keep up. For time, I had to bypass the question asking which curling iron I'd used on my hair this morning.

The wannabe lifestyle influencer I'd been died a little at that.

I would have been happy to talk beauty stuff any other day, but I needed to stay on brand and get through all the cleaning questions.

When the front doorbell rang, my face froze with a smile, and I pretended I hadn't heard anything. My microphone was sensitive, but only at close range, so it probably hadn't picked it up.

I was sure my mom would deal with it, and I used this as my sign to wrap things up.

"Thank you so much for hanging out with me," I said brightly while staring at the screen of my phone. "This was a lot of fun, and I hope it—"

Breath halted in my lungs when a figure materialized in the background. The moment I recognized who it was, my heart bounced into overdrive, and I spun to face him. I forgot all about the camera, or the people who were watching, and gaped at him.

Noah took one look at my setup, saw the red record timer ticking away at the top of my phone's screen, and froze like a deer caught in headlights.

"Noah? What the hell?" I demanded.

A warning blared in my head, reminding me I was still live. I swiveled back around, plastered an enormous fake smile on, and like the doorbell, I pretended everything was fine. Nothing had just happened, and I definitely wasn't unraveling at the sight of him.

Comments flashed quickly by.

Who's that?

OMG, he's cute! Your bf?

Some were just emojis of heart eyed smiley faces.

Girl, your brother is hot AF.

My brain wasn't working properly, so I couldn't stop my knee-jerk response or the disgust in my voice. "He's *not* my brother." The statement hung for a beat too long. "He's . . . "

My ex? The man who ran away the second things got hard?

"He's my," I fumbled out, "business partner."

He remained frozen in the doorway as if every muscle in his stupid, hot body no longer worked, and he was trapped there forever.

My tone was sickly-sweet. "Say hi, Noah. Give the folks a wave."

Oh, so his body *did* work.

His expression was dazed as he lifted a hand and gave the worst attempt at a wave I'd ever seen. The comments kept scrolling by.

I would get nothing done if my coworkers looked like that.

Any job openings?

Is he single?

These people were entirely too horny at eleven o'clock in the morning.

It was hard to think with him so close and staring at me, but I stumbled through my sign off, ended the video, and whirled around to face him.

My hands balled into fists at my sides. "What the hell are you doing here?"

"I'm sorry. I didn't mean to barge in on your video." He lifted his hands in surrender. "Your mom let me in. She thought you were done filming."

It physically hurt seeing him again, and I tore my gaze away, studying the grout lines of the tile floor. What the fuck was he doing here? When he'd said I was wasting my time with him, I'd decided the least painful option was to make a clean break.

It felt extra cruel that he was here in my home, in my safe space.

"What do you want?" I tried to sound strong, but my voice was as raw as my emotions.

"We need to talk."

Out of the corner of my eye, I watched him take a step closer, and my dumb heart fluttered. "About?"

"Business." This word killed any excitement or hope I might have had. He took another tentative step. "Are you aware your 'business partner' has been trying to get in touch with you for days?"

He had enough common sense to look contrite when I lifted my chin and leveled a hard gaze at him. "Maybe I've been busy and didn't want to *waste* any more of your precious time."

He winced and glanced away, and his focus snagged on the beautiful flower arrangement he'd sent. How ironic. I'd worried he might notice them in the background of my video, never expecting in a hundred years he'd see them in person.

"I'm so sorry I said that. You need to know, I didn't mean—"

I spun away from him, unplugged my microphone, and turned off my ring light. "What business do we have to talk about?"

He hesitated, as if he wasn't sure he wanted to drop it but decided to push on. "The brokerage fees you gave me? I invested them, and one of the stocks did well enough I thought you needed to know."

I was working on collapsing my tripod, but my movements slowed. "You came over here to brag?"

"What? No."

He strode forward, closing nearly all the space between us, and hyperawareness lit up my traitorous body. It longed for him, and—God. I hated the sensation. I couldn't have him, and this was torturous.

"I told you I didn't need those fees," he said, "so I took it and invested it for you. If it made anything, my intent was always to give you that money." He massaged the back of his neck, unknowingly showing off the appealing muscles of his arm. "Even after I took my cut back, it's made a nice profit."

He peered at me with excitement in his eyes, like he was hoping I'd ask how much.

But I wasn't going to bite. "It's your money," I said flatly. "You earned it."

He gave a humorless laugh. "Yeah, that's exactly what your dad said when I told him."

Holy shit. He'd talked to my dad?

Noah rested his hands on his hips, and his tone was direct. "If you want to see it that way—fine. I would like to be an investor in your business, then."

"What?" My distrust spiked. "Why?"

His dark eyes peered at me with all the confidence of the Wall Street broker he'd been. "Because I want to see how far we can take this thing together."

Together.

The word sucked all the air from the room.

"This offer," he continued, "isn't contingent on anything, either. I have some things to say, and something to ask you, and if your answer is 'no,' I still want to invest." The faintest smile hinted at the corner of his lips. "I mean, we've both demonstrated how good we are at keeping our personal and professional lives separate, haven't we?"

A familiar sensation traveled across my skin like an electric charge. It was the same one I had whenever I unwrapped a present when I was nearly certain I knew what was inside.

Anxiousness tightened my vocal cords. "What's the question?"

"Hold on. We'll get to that." He dropped his hands to his sides, and his shoulders rolled back, giving him the posture of someone preparing to pitch an idea. "Charlotte, I am a mess without you."

Everything came to a halt. Had the Earth stopped turning? The word was barely a whisper from me. "What?"

"I don't mean my house," his voice was solid, full of conviction, "although I'm sure you'd say that's not great right now." He pushed the thought aside. "I mean that my life is a mess, because I'm in love with you, and I fucked it all up."

Whoa.

Blood roared through my ears, drowning out sound for a moment, and I couldn't catch my breath.

Did he just say he was in love with me?

I had to reach behind and put a hand on the counter to steady myself, because my legs were boneless. He must have sensed it, because he took the final step forward and put a hand on my hip to help keep me upright.

I peered into his eyes, desperately searching for the lie . . . but couldn't find one.

"I'm sorry for what I did." His voice was low and thick. "For the things I said. I need you to know I didn't mean any of it. It's not an excuse, but when your father caught us and fired me, I panicked. And when you said you loved me, I lost my shit." His expression was a mixture of embarrassment and remorse. "I got scared, and I," he emphasized the word, "ran."

I forced out a breath.

Well.

I knew a little bit about doing that, didn't I?

His hand rested on my waist, and beneath my shirt, my skin tingled from his touch.

The expression on his handsome face shifted, returning to the one of determination he'd been wearing. "All the time we were together, I was so worried about losing my job, I didn't realize that losing what we had was so much worse." His fingers gently squeezed, subtly drawing me in. "I miss you so fucking much. I miss my best friend."

My head spun, overwhelmed. "I'm your only friend."

I hadn't uttered it to be mean, it only came out because my brain wasn't working. He seemed to understand I was all out of sorts because the corner of his mouth tweaked.

"I have other friends," he said. "But even if that's true and you're my only friend, I'm okay with that. You're enough for me, Charlotte." He said it so softly, it was a whisper. "*More* than enough."

I hadn't a fucking clue what to say.

He'd stunned me utterly speechless, and my body went weightless. I was sure I'd float away if it weren't for his hand tethering me in place.

"I spoke to my old boss at HBHC," he said. "He told me there's a position available if I want it."

Oh, God. My heart thumped painfully in my chest, which was wild. This morning I'd wanted him cut out of my life, and now the threat of him leaving caused panic. "You're going back to New York?"

He looked relieved, glad to hear I didn't want that. "No. It's remote work. The hours and the pay aren't the best, but I'm planning on taking it."

"You don't have to. My dad said he'll give you your job back."

"He told me, and, shit, Charlotte. I really fucking appreciate you going to bat for me, especially when I didn't deserve it. But I think it's better if I don't go back to Warbler. I didn't realize how much I liked being a broker . . . until I wasn't one." His gaze slid over my face like he was studying each detail. "It'll be easier this way, me not being your father's employee." His head tilted. "Why'd you ask him to give me my job back?"

I bit my bottom lip, trying to stop tears from forming in my eyes. "I don't know," I lied. But he already knew the answer, so what was the point in pretending? "Because I love you."

"Yeah?" His other hand closed on my waist, so he was holding me. "I love you too."

He'd said it before, but I reacted like this was the first time, and a jolt ran through me from head to toe.

"How the hell did that happen?" I whispered. "I thought you didn't have time."

"I was wrong," he admitted. "Or maybe I didn't have time because I was waiting for the right person to come along."

I was nearly too afraid to ask it. "And you're sure it's me?"

His surprised laugh cut through the tension, and his hands slipped around to rest comfortably on the small of my back. "Yes, Charlotte, it's you."

There'd been a constant longing to be in his arms that I hadn't noticed. Not until now, when the ache for it was gone.

His mouth hovered over mine, threatening a kiss. "The question I need to ask is, can you give me another chance?"

All my life, I'd been given chance after chance, sometimes when I didn't even deserve them.

Giving us a second chance? That was easy.

The word burst from my lips. "Yes, of course—"

His mouth sealed over mine, and his kiss was full of so much love, the world began turning again.

EPILOGUE

Noah

After we'd finished desserts, Charlotte collected everyone's plates and carried them into the kitchen. My mom offered to help, but my girlfriend politely declined. She claimed it was because my mother had done the majority of the cooking, but I knew the real reason.

It'd be better if everyone stayed out of her way.

She already had her camera and lighting set up to film a timelapse of her cleaning up our Thanksgiving feast.

Hosting it at my house had made the most sense. My parents' place was too small because both my brothers and their families had come in for the holiday. There were twelve of us, but my oldest nephew was a teenager, and he'd eaten enough food for at least three people. My mom had been prepared, though, cooking larger portions and bringing an extra can of cranberry sauce that was solely for him.

I sat at the dining table I'd bought recently, catching up with my family while keeping one ear pointed toward the kitchen. Charlotte knew if she needed any help, all she had to do was ask and I'd be there. Otherwise I'd stay out of the shot. My brief appearance on her livestream had been more than enough for me.

Was she happy to have a break from my family right now? The introduction to everyone seemed to have gone well, but my younger nieces and nephews were loud and had zero boundaries, and honestly, so did the rest of my family. They were fascinated by my girlfriend, partly because I'd had so few in my life and brought even fewer 'home.'

But Charlotte didn't seem to mind. She thrived on attention, after all.

When I heard the dishwasher start, I stood. "Anyone need more wine?"

My mother held up her nearly empty glass. I nodded and strolled toward the kitchen, lingering in the doorway.

"Permission to enter?" I teased.

Charlotte chuckled. "Permission granted."

She stood by the island, wearing a pair of rubber gloves that went to her elbows because she didn't want to mess up her nails, and used a sponge to wipe down the countertop. Pans and cutting knives were stacked and drying on dishtowels beside her.

When she glanced up to see my approach, a bright smile warmed her face. Shit, even with those garish yellow gloves, she was so goddamn beautiful, it made me ache.

"Need any help?" I asked.

She nodded toward the pans. "You want to dry those?"

"Sure." Although I'd come a long way, this was still one of the few tasks she trusted me to be able to handle.

I got out a clean dishtowel and went to work.

"When do you think you'll have the video ready to upload?" I asked. "Squarespace wants approval before posting." Her sponsorships had grown considerably over the last month since she'd surpassed a hundred thousand subscribers.

"At least a few days because I need to record the voiceover, edit, and I might reshoot the stuff I did yesterday. I think I could do it better." She came to the sink, standing beside me as she rinsed the sponge and put it in the hanging holder she'd asked me to buy.

Charlotte wasn't my employee anymore. We'd done a great job compartmentalizing, but she was my girlfriend who didn't have the time for it, and she'd trained me well enough. It also helped that she was here a lot of the time, keeping me in check, and she continued to use my place for content.

I didn't mind cleaning. In fact, sometimes I sort of enjoyed it—although I'd never admit that to her. I liked the sense of accomplishment when it was done, the better organization, and the way it could lift my mood.

Why the fuck hadn't I lived like this before?

"Remind me," I said, "what time tomorrow?" Because we were doing Thanksgiving with her side of the family at her parents' house.

"My mom said three, so that means dinner won't be ready until at least four." She'd been amused with herself, but it vanished, becoming totally serious. "But be there at three. Because she gets mad if anyone points out she's running behind."

"Got it." I wiped away the water droplets clinging to the inside of the roasting pan. "Are you nervous about tomorrow?"

She hesitated and her voice dipped low. "About going to the club?"

Heat spread through me at her meaning. After dinner tomorrow, we had plans to go to Club Eros.

Since we'd fallen in love, we hadn't played with anyone else. These last two months, we'd just been enjoying our time together. We'd discussed if we wanted to play with others, but we'd see how we felt about it when we got there and only do it if we were both interested.

There was a strong possibility we'd be satisfied just watching this first time. No matter what, I was confident the evening would be a lot of fun, not to mention, hot.

"No," I said, "I meant the part where I'm meeting your family."

"Oh." She considered it as she rinsed the sink. "No, I think they'll love you."

"Even your dad?" I said it as a joke, but I was serious. I'd only seen Ardy twice since our meeting where I'd asked for his help, and both times had been awkward as fuck. But she assured me he'd come around.

"Yeah, even my dad." She had a thought. "But, maybe, bring some bourbon. He likes the expensive kind."

I chuckled. "Of course he does."

Footsteps shuffled across the tile, and we both turned to look.

Tyson was only a few years older than I was, and he had classic middle child syndrome. The guy loved flying under the radar. He pulled open the fridge, grabbed the tin of pumpkin pie and a tub of Cool Whip.

"Dude," I said. "We just ate dessert."

He shrugged. "I got sent in here to see what you're doing. Mom wants to know the status on the wine."

I stared at him as he pulled down a plate from a cabinet and dug through my silverware drawer for a fork, spoon, and knife. "She ask you to get her some pie too?"

"Nope, pie's for me." He cut himself a slice and used the knife to transfer it to the plate, sending pie crust crumbs skittering across the counter. The tub of Cool Whip was opened, and the spoon scooped out a dollop and plunked it down on the slice of pie. "I figured I'd get some as long as I'm in here."

I felt Charlotte's intent gaze watching him as he stood at the island, holding his plate while eating and making a mess where she'd just cleaned. But she said nothing, maintaining a perfect smile. It made me think of the GIF where the dog was sitting at the table, saying everything was fine while the house around him was on fire.

"Are you two," Tyson said with a mouthful of food, "about ready to start game night?"

I forced the irritation from my voice. "Yeah, we'll be done in a minute."

He scraped the plate with the fork, getting every last bit of the pie, before setting the plate down. He pulled the spoon out of the Cool Whip, tapped it on the side of the tub . . . and set the dirty spoon on the counter like a goddamn savage.

He did the same with the knife he'd used to cut the pie, carelessly smudging pie filling across the stone.

My brother didn't hear her sharp intake of breath or notice how her shoulders tensed.

"Really, Ty?" I sighed.

"What?" He capped the tub and pulled the plastic wrap back in place on the pie, before putting them away in the fridge.

"Come on," I groaned, moving swiftly to the island so I could stack his dirty utensils on the plate.

Tyson watched me with wonderment. "Bro. When did you become such a clean freak?"

His question was rhetorical. Or maybe it wasn't, but I ignored it. Charlotte moved beside me, grabbed the plate, and swept the crumbs onto it with the sponge.

"Thanks," he said to her.

She flashed him a smile. "Well, thanks for not making me

sit at the kids' table."

He feigned seriousness. "We had a lengthy discussion about it, and I was the deciding vote for you to join us." He jerked his thumb toward me. "Can you believe this guy was against it?"

She chuckled at his bullshit that he probably thought was charming, but I found annoying. His gaze shifted to me, giving me a look that said, *I like her*.

My irritation with him vanished. *Me too.*

When he turned to leave—

"Aren't you forgetting something?" I opened the fridge and handed him the bottle of wine.

Once he was gone, I returned to the sink and my stack of drying dishes, while she handwashed the pieces Tyson had just used.

"Game night?" she asked quietly.

"It's a tradition, and I need to apologize in advance. My family is so competitive, they can be kind of obnoxious."

She laughed. "Should I apologize in advance for beating all their asses?"

"Definitely. They'd love that."

We fell into comfortable silence for a moment before she pulled off one of her rubber gloves. She'd done it so she could unlock her phone and turn on the camera.

"Picture," she asked, holding it high up and at an angle.

I leaned in and stared at the screen, seeing her wearing the rubber glove and me with the dishtowel cast over my shoulder. We stood together with bright, happy smiles, and it might have looked staged, but those grins on our faces?

They couldn't have been more fucking real.

I'd never thought I would want something like this, but

shit, she'd changed me so much. And I'd done the same to her, hadn't I? Not just with her flourishing business, either. We'd grown into better, more complete people with each other.

Everything else? It was just a bonus.

Because we were all each other needed.

* * *

Need a little more
Charlotte and Noah in your life?

(Plus Clay, Travis & Lilith!)

Subscribe to Nikki's mailing list
and you'll get instant access to
an **exclusive bonus scene** from
THE BROKER called THE LESSON!

Scan the code to sign-up now

MORE FROM NIKKI

NASHVILLE NEIGHBORHOOD SERIES

The Doctor

The Pool Boy

The Architect

The Frat Boy

The Good Girl

The Broker

THE BLINDFOLD CLUB SERIES

Three Simple Rules

Three Hard Lessons

Three Little Mistakes

Three Dirty Secrets

Three Sweet Nothings

Three Guilty Pleasures

FILTHY RICH AMERICANS SERIES

The Initiation | The Obsession | The Deception

The Redemption

The Temptation

THE SORDID SERIES

Sordid

Torrid

SPORTS ROMANCE

The Rivalry

THANK YOU

Thank you to my husband Nick for his endless support, his great ideas, and his understanding that my writing process always results in stressful deadlines. As always, this book would not have been possible without him.

Thank you to my friend Aubrey Bondurant for her encouragement. She was always there to listen to me vent and ready to talk things out when I was struggling with a scene. I couldn't have asked for a better partner to be alongside me in the trenches!

Thank you to my editor Lori Whitwam, who had to deal with constant rewrites and drafts that were Frankenstein-ed together. You went above and beyond on this one, and I'm so very grateful.

ABOUT NIKKI

USA Today bestselling author Nikki Sloane landed in graphic design after her careers as a waitress, a screenwriter, and a ballroom dance instructor fell through. Now she writes full-time and lives in Nashville with her husband, two sons, and a pair of super destructive cats.

She is a four-time Romance Writers of America RITA® & Vivian® Finalist, a Passionate Plume & HOLT Medallion winner, a Goodreads Choice Awards semifinalist, and couldn't be any happier that people enjoy reading her sexy words.

www.NikkiSloane.com